THE SHADOWCUTTER

By Harriet Smart

THE SHADOWCUTTER

by

Harriet Smart

Published by Anthemion

© Harriet Smart 2015

Seventh Edition

ISBN 978-1-907873-56-0

Made with Jutoh

Chapter One

Stanegate, July 1840

"Mr Bryce is going to open his fencing room in Northminster," said Major Vernon as they climbed the stairs. "There will be more business there for him. And he is going to give the men cutlass training."

"I had better lay in a stock of sutures, then," said Felix, not entirely confident that the men of the Northminster Constabulary could be trained in the finer points of swordsmanship without a certain amount of damage.

It was not yet seven in the morning and Felix could not help yawning. It was typical of Major Vernon to insist on rising even earlier on holiday than he usually did. That morning, he had goaded Felix into accompanying him to his fencing lesson, hoping to persuade him to take it up. Feeling languid from the heat, Felix was not inclined.

The fencing master, Bryce, came out to greet them with an enthusiasm which matched that of Major Vernon. He was a Scotsman and not young – he had snow-white hair and a leathery complexion, but he had a sprightly air about him, as if he never grew tired. He was, as Major Vernon said as he presented him to Felix, a very fine advertisement for his art.

While the Major changed into his kit, Mr Bryce took the opportunity to look Felix over.

"You are right, sir, the gentleman does have the physique for it," he said to Major Vernon. "And you never took lessons, Mr Carswell?"

"I took one or two when I was first in Edinburgh," said

Felix, "but it got in the way of my work. And I was extremely clumsy."

"But the scar?"

"A piece of glass and a madwoman."

"Then perhaps you do need to learn to defend yourself," said Bryce.

"Steady, Mr Bryce," said Major Vernon, buttoning up his chamois leather jacket. "I want you to persuade him, not drive him away."

"There is nothing the young ladies like better than a man who can handle a sword," Bryce went on. "And it will help you with your dancing, sir, make you nimble and light on your feet." Bryce executed a waltz step or two to demonstrate and then finished with a bow.

"I don't have any plans to go dancing," said Felix, wandering over to the open window in hope of finding a little air. That Major Vernon could think of exerting himself in a leather coat in this temperature astonished him. He did not much like hot weather, and the air in Stanegate struck him as enervating. He had come from Northminster the day before, hoping for some relief from the heat and stench of the city. Stanegate did not smell so foul, but there was no refreshment in the air.

"I can't persuade you, sir? I am at your disposal," said Bryce. "There is another gentleman here who is anxious to practise the epée, Major Vernon, and I told him I was expecting an accomplished opponent."

"I would hardly say that," Major Vernon said, picking up his gloves.

"He's a Spanish gentleman from the West Indies, would you believe, sir? From some island, I can't remember the name, Santa something or other – I'm not sure what he said. We do get all manner of people these days, in Stanegate."

"Heavens," said Major Vernon. "I suspect he will slaughter me."

"He's a young man," said Bryce, "and he does have a certain style about him, but I think you will be more than a match for him. Shall we?" He opened the double doors and ushered them through into a thirty-foot room of lofty proportions. It was large enough to have held a score of swordsmen, all parrying and thrusting. As it was, Bryce had only one pupil, who stood at the far end fencing an invisible opponent.

He stopped as they approached and bowed elaborately.

"Would you care for a bout, sir?" he said, addressing the Major slowly and carefully. He had a thick Spanish accent. "I can see by your bearing that you are a true devotee of the sword."

Major Vernon returned the bow but with much less flamboyance.

"At one time, perhaps, but you will have to forgive me if you find me a little rusty, Mr...?"

"Oh, a hundred apologies, forgive me, sir. Allow me to present myself. I am Don Xavier Perez Martinez." He made another elaborate bow.

"Giles Vernon at your service," said Major Vernon. "I will fight you, of course, sir, but you may be disappointed with the sport. Whatever Mr Bryce may have told you –"

"Ah, yes, I understand – you Englishmen are masters of the feint," Martinez said.

"This will be no feint, I assure you!" said Major Vernon. "Epée?"

"Epée," concurred Martinez.

Felix went and sat down on one of the benches by the wall. While the men fixed on their masks and took up the weapons, he tried to recall the names of the islands of the West Indies that were Spanish colonies, and failed entirely. His mother had attempted to cram a little geography into him as a child, but clearly without much success.

Major Vernon and Don Xavier took up their positions

and after saluting each other with flourishes of the sword, began their first bout.

Felix knew little of the complexities of what he was witnessing, but it struck him at once that Don Xavier was not holding back. He went straight on the attack, with notable aggression, as if he meant real harm. For all the Major was doing his best to defend his position, he was clearly very soon under pressure. In a matter of moments, Don Xavier had knocked the sword from the Major's hand. It went clattering to the floor, skittering across the boards noisily.

Major Vernon threw up his hands, clearly startled by this very speedy defeat.

"I told you I was not a good enough opponent," he said, reaching to retrieve his sword. "You are most accomplished! Congratulations! Again?"

Don Xavier did not reply. Felix noticed his chest rising and falling as he recovered his breath. It seemed he was quite winded by his victory, and then he began to cough in a fashion that alarmed Felix at once. It was a severe bronchial spasm which caused him to turn away, bending double as he did so, entirely overcome by it. His sword went crashing to the floor and he buckled at the knees.

Felix leapt from the bench and threw himself down beside him, scrabbling to get the fencing mask clear of his face and hold him into a position so that he would not choke. A mixture of sputum and blood was frothing from his mouth, and his whole frame was shaking from the violence of his coughing. Felix's handkerchief was soon clogged with the expectorations: a mass of greyish white globules, streaked with blood and stinking ominously of fresh plaster.

Major Vernon, who had crouched down to help support him, offered his own handkerchief, leaving Felix staring down at the evidence. He reached for Martinez's wrist and took his pulse. It was racing. The signs were not good: chronic phthisis, if he was not mistaken.

"Where is he staying?" Major Vernon asked the fencing master.

"At The White Horse, I think."

"Do you have towels and water?" said Felix, wishing he had his medical bag with him.

"Of course, right away," Bryce said, hurrying off.

The coughing subsided and Don Xavier stared at Felix, with glassy, sunken eyes, his forehead damp with fever. He opened his mouth as if to speak.

"No, quiet for now, if you please, sir," said Felix. "I am a surgeon – I will do all I can for you, and then we will find your own attendant."

Don Xavier shook his head, as if it were the most painful and exhausting thing in the world.

"I... I...." he rasped and then gave up, his head sinking back against Major Vernon.

"All in good time," Felix said, but wondered how much time he had.

~

The White Horse was not one of the most expensive or fashionable hotels in Stanegate. It lay in the oldest part of the town, hard up against the graveyard of the parish church. The grudging landlady showed them up to his room, which was inconveniently on the third floor.

"Shouldn't you have taken him to the infirmary?" she said, as they got him onto his bed.

Felix did not trouble himself to answer her. Martinez was gasping for breath and needed his full attention. The stairs had been a desperate struggle for him, although he had Carswell and Major Vernon supporting him. They had been obliged to carry him up the last flight. He had, of course, considered

5

taking the man to the infirmary, but summer was always a dangerous time in a public hospital, especially in a town full of visiting invalids. The chance of catching a passing fever would be considerable. With Martinez's already weakened constitution, it would be akin to negligence to have taken him there.

But the room at The White Horse was, in its way, equally unpromising: a long, narrow slot, with a dormer window at one end. A miserable room at the best of times, and not at all suitable for an invalid.

"When did he arrive?" Major Vernon asked the landlady. Martinez appeared to have only half unpacked. His travelling trunk lay open at the end of the room but he had taken the trouble to set up on the table by the bed a black crucifix with a white ivory figure of Christ, a string of rosary beads and an image of the Virgin Mary.

"Day before last," she said.

"No servant with him?" Major Vernon said.

"No, sir. We don't usually take that sort here."

"And he didn't call for a doctor?" said Felix.

"Not that I know of. I shouldn't have let him have the room if I'd known he was in this state. And he's a papist," Felix heard the landlady mutter when Major Vernon sent her for water, brandy and more pillows.

"Well, I am sorry for that, Don Xavier," Major Vernon said, when she had gone. "A very poor specimen of our national hospitality."

Martinez made a gesture that suggested he was not offended. He was beyond being offended, Felix supposed, the poor fellow.

"Come, sir, let's get you more comfortable," Felix said, and together with the Major got him out of his clothes. He was wretched with sweat, and the closeness of the room did not help. As he sponged him down, attempting to reduce the fever, Felix wondered what had possessed him to go fencing

6

that morning. His symptoms were of such a nature and severity that they would have presented themselves before, and with disabling consequences. He would know exactly what was wrong with him.

Major Vernon had found a fresh shirt for him, and they sat him upright to remove the old one. As the old shirt was taken off, Felix noticed that his back was covered with a horrific lattice-work of scars, many clearly old, but there was also a nasty crop of fresh and extremely livid weals, which needed urgent cleaning and attention. It looked for all the world as if he had been regularly flogged. He glanced at Major Vernon, frustrated that there could be no discussion nor any questioning of their patient at that moment. Martinez was too weak for it.

Fortunately Bryce, who had been sent to retrieve Felix's medical bag, arrived shortly afterwards.

"There's a woman who lives next door to me who has a good reputation as a nurse," Bryce said. "Shall I fetch her for you, Mr Carswell?"

"Yes, good idea," said Felix, taking his bag and searching in it for a suitable dressing for the weals.

As he did so, he noticed Major Vernon opening the drawer of the table on which the crucifix had been set up, and frowning at what he saw.

"What?"

"Later," Vernon murmured, sliding the drawer closed again.

Felix dressed the wounds, and was glad to observe Martinez's breathing became a little more regular, although it could not be described as comfortable, and he was still perspiring heavily. He took a few soundings with his stethoscope and what he heard only confirmed his earlier intuitions.

Martinez took a little brandy and water, into which Felix had mixed a grain of opium. It was best to sedate him and let his body rest before the next inevitable, bloody coughing fit.

When Martinez had slipped into unconsciousness, Felix opened the drawer and saw a fearsome-looking whip made of a dozen knotted cords.

"Self-inflicted, I suspect," Vernon said.

"You may be right, given the pattern of scarring," Felix said. "But why? What would possess you to do that when..."

"Might this have something to do with it?" Major Vernon said, lifting a long white tunic-like woollen garment out of the trunk. "I think this is a monk's habit."

"Good grief," Felix said, coming over and looking into the trunk for himself.

"A wandering friar, perhaps," said Major Vernon, hanging the tunic on one of the hooks on the wall, "who fences like an officer."

"And in the last stages of consumption," said Felix.

"Is it that bad?"

Felix nodded. "There's no doubt. When I sounded his chest —"

"He's a long way from home to be in such a condition. What about his mother church? Why aren't they taking care of him? And why is he here, of all places?" He went over and looked down at the now sleeping man. "Poor soul. Well, we shall have to do what we can for him. I'm sorry, it's not much of a holiday for you."

Felix did not like to say that he did not really regard his visit as a holiday. He had come out of duty as much as anything; although he was pleased to see Major Vernon, the pleasure was coloured with a certain amount of discomfort.

It had been his idea that they go there in the first place, and he now regretted the suggestion. He should have sent them further away, to the seaside, beyond visiting distance. He had only thrown out the idea in the mildest terms, that it might be beneficial at some point or other, now that Mrs Vernon was so much recovered that a course of waters at some spa town might do her good. He had not expected to be taken seriously, for he could scarcely imagine that Major Vernon would ever willingly take leave from the Constabulary.

But the notion had fallen on surprisingly fertile ground. Major Vernon had seized on it and, being a man who liked to put things into action with great zeal, it had soon become a settled project. He was due some leave, he had said, and it would do him as much good as Mrs Vernon to have a holiday. What did Carswell think of the waters at Stanegate? It was close enough to Northminster, a mere hour and a quarter by the new railway, to make it possible for him to get away without undue worry. If there was a problem, he could get back easily. Furthermore it would give him a chance to put Superintendent Rollins in charge – he could be made Acting Assistant Chief Constable.

"I want to see what he makes of the job – this will be an ideal chance for him."

"Be careful, or you will lose him to another force if you let him learn all your arts," Felix had said.

"That is entirely possible," Major Vernon had said with a shrug. "A man as talented as Rollins, who has made so much of himself from so little, deserves all the opportunities we can give him. But he is very loyal, and his family are all here. It is a risk I will take."

So a house had been taken, and all was organised. Felix had had to admit to considerable relief when Major and Mrs Vernon had left for the wholesome dissipations of Stanegate and its spas. Out of sight, he hoped to God, would be out of mind. But the Major had extracted a promise from him that he must visit, and he could not in all conscience avoid that. Mrs Vernon was still his patient, after all. Poor, mysterious Martinez, as he wheezed in his uneasy slumber on his wretched bed, could not know how helpful he was being. He was sparing Felix the tortures of breakfast with Mrs Vernon.

"Should you not go, sir?" Felix said. "I have all in hand

here. Mrs Vernon will be wondering where you are."

The Major consulted his watch.

"Yes, I am late. She will be anxious, and we are supposed to be driving up to the Bower Well – it's a pretty spot, although I think the water there is the worst tasting of them all. But there is a sort of loggia with a wonderful view over the country. Laura wanted you to see it – she thought you might wish to go sketching with her again. It is certainly a wonderful day for it."

"I might manage to get up there later," Felix said, his conscience queasy now. Mrs Vernon would feel it keenly to have such a plan spoiled, and it would not do to upset her fragile equilibrium. If he were careful, and as Major Vernon would be with them, any potential awkwardness might be contained. Avoidance never much solved anything, he reflected. "If Mr Bryce's neighbour is as good a nurse as he says."

"I will make a few enquiries on my way back," said Major Vernon. "There is a Roman Catholic chapel tucked away somewhere here. If I can find one of their clerics, they may be able to help him."

Chapter Two

"You'll come with us?" Giles asked Sukey Connolly, meeting her in the passageway.

"Are you sure, sir?"

"It's a glorious day – you've been indoors too long. You look pale."

"I do?" she said. "I don't think so."

"Come and drink the foul waters with us," he said. "Then you will have something to write to your sister about."

He glanced into the drawing room. Laura was standing in front of the glass, making minute adjustments to her hat – a broad straw leghorn, with long lilac ribbons. It was good to see her taking such trouble with her appearance. "And you are always of use to my wife," he added as he went into the room. "Is that the new hat?" he ventured. "Very handsome."

"A wide-awake," said Laura. "Like Mr Carswell's."

"So it is," he said.

"Mr Carswell's is not so pretty, ma'am," said Sukey, from the doorway. "Which shawl would you like?"

"Where is Mr Carswell?" asked Laura.

"We stumbled across a mystery," said Giles. "A rather tragic one. A poor Spanish gentleman with consumption. Mr Carswell is with him now."

"So he is not coming to the Bower Well?"

"He will try to if he can," said Giles. "Sukey, do you know where the Roman Catholic chapel is? There is one here, I think?"

"I don't know. I haven't been to Mass here," she said. "I suppose I should have."

"You came to church with us."

"That doesn't count, sir," she said. "Well, you know what I mean." She went up to Laura with the shawls she was carrying. "Which of these, Mrs Vernon? The blue is best with that dress, I would say, but it is very warm; perhaps just your lace?"

It was on the tip of his tongue to ask her why she had not gone, for he was curious about this deviation from her usual habits. But he did not. He felt he might sound like a domineering master, anxious to make sure she did as she should, and he had no wish for her to think of him like that. He owed her too much, for one thing.

The drive to the Bower Well passed without incident. Laura was quiet, but not uncomfortably so. It was another of those many changes in her. It still astonished him that they had come so far. Over the last few months she had emerged from her profound withdrawal, like some shy animal coming out from its lair.

Day by day her confidence had grown, in large part due to Carswell's diligence with her. At first it had been a matter of getting her to eat properly and play simple games. Carswell had arrived one day with a box of coloured building blocks and had begun to build a tower of red bricks. She had sat watching him for some time, and then at last she had begun to sort the blocks, and built a blue tower next to his red one.

Carswell would not claim much credit for it. He had said he had read dozens of papers suggesting that puerperal insanity in many cases resolved itself, like a morning mist rising from the sea, but Giles could not quite believe that. He had seen the careful tutoring that had gone on – first from Carswell, and then from Sukey who had learnt quickly what he was about.

He had been there when Carswell explained it to her, and his words had stuck with him: "The patterns of our minds – our thoughts – run on accustomed courses, and it is all too easy to fall onto bad roads, which clog our boots with mud and where there are villains lurking at the corners to ambush us. Mrs Vernon had a shocking experience with the birth of her son – the pain and stress threw her mind from its sensible courses into the wilderness, and worse, when the boy died, it only increased her disorientation. We must teach her how not to get lost again."

They walked up and down the terrace a few times, and then went to collect their mandatory half-pints of sulphurous water from the well. It was as disgusting as ever, even on a warm day when a drink might have been welcome, and Giles threw most of his away – discreetly, he thought, but Sukey noticed and smiled at it. Laura dutifully drank hers down, the first time she had managed to do so.

"Mr Carswell will be pleased with me when I tell him," she said. "In fact, I would like another cup," she said, holding out her tin cup.

"Of course," said Giles, and went to fetch another for her.

This time he had to wait a few minutes to fill the cup, as a large family party had arrived at the well head: all very elegantly turned out, but somewhat alien to the place, and chattering loudly in a foreign tongue.

"What language is that?" Giles murmured as he returned to Laura and Sukey. "Spanish?"

"I think so," Sukey said. "I wonder if they are anything to do with your consumptive Spanish gentleman."

"I was thinking that myself. Should I go and speak to them?"

He did not have the chance, for Laura had begun to walk away.

"I don't like all these people," Laura said.

"Let's go and find a quiet spot in the shade," said Giles, offering her his arm. "That tree is waiting for us, I should say. And the prospect from there will make a very nice sketch."

She did not take his arm, but she did not disagree with the

suggestion, which pleased him. Together they walked to the shade of the tree, with Sukey a few steps behind them.

"We will be able to see Mr Carswell coming from here," she said.

"He may not come," Giles said.

"Of course he will," said Laura.

"Where shall I put this up?" he said, holding up her sketching stool.

She scanned the view again and chose her spot, and Giles set up the stool. He settled on the ground beside it, waiting for her to sit down, and took a book from his pocket.

"Another chapter of Nicholas Nickleby?" he said, watching as she hesitated. "While you draw?"

"We ought to wait for Mr Carswell," she said. "So he doesn't miss any." Giles had begun reading it last night after dinner.

"He has already read it, I think," said Giles. He patted the stool, but still she stood there, gazing out, as if she expected him to appear in the distance at any moment.

Giles felt uneasy. He wanted her happily occupied with her pencil. He did not like this state of hers – it was like the uncomfortable period of heavy air pressure that presages a great storm.

He wished he had said nothing about Carswell joining them. It had been thoughtless on his part. He had thought it would please her, rather than set her on edge with this excitement. It had been the same all the previous day when he was expected from Northminster, and he had not liked it then. She was too hungry for his presence.

"Perhaps you should get on with your sketch, Mrs Vernon," Sukey said. "So that you will have something to show Mr Carswell when he gets here." Laura turned and looked at her, with that long cool stare that Giles never knew what to do with. But Sukey, unabashed, said, "And another chapter will soon pass the time."

Another long moment passed and she sat down. Giles held out her bag of sketching equipment but her eyes were still fixed on the landscape before her. He put down the bag and decided that he would start to read, and hope she would find the story distracting enough to stop her thinking about Carswell.

But as he did, he felt Mr Dickens' latest would have to be a very superior novel to do that. Laura had made Carswell the hero of her own narrative. That was now plain to see. Ever since they had come to Stanegate she had been pining for him, like a forlorn spaniel. It was entirely understandable that it would happen – he had heard of such cases when a doctor became a kind of saint to a grateful patient. Carswell had transformed her existence. How could she not make an idol of him?

Giles was sure Carswell himself was as aware of the problem as he was, but he had not yet had a chance to discuss it with him. It would have to be broached sooner or later.

In the meantime, there was Nicholas Nickleby.

He had barely read a few pages when they were interrupted. His man Holt was striding up the hill towards them. He had obviously come in some haste, for he had broken into a sweat. He held out a letter to Giles.

"For you, sir," he said.

"Where is Mr Carswell, Holt?" said Laura, who had jumped up at the sight of him.

"No idea, ma'am," he said, mopping his face with a handkerchief. "This is from Lord Rothborough, sir. He's sent a carriage for you. Urgent business."

Giles opened the letter.

Dear Major Vernon,
An unfortunate situation has developed upon which I would welcome your professional opinion, if it might be managed. I would be profoundly grateful if you might return with the bearer of this message.

"It seems I have to go to work," said Giles, getting up. "We had better go home."

"Sukey and I will stay here," said Laura. "If Mr Carswell comes all this way and does not find us, then —"

"Then he will not be broken-hearted," Giles said.

"It will be rude if we do not wait for him," she said.

"He will probably have gone back to the house first," said Giles. "And it is rather warm for you to sit too long out here. I think we should all go home."

"You may, of course," she said, sitting down again. "I will stay here with Sukey."

"I think the master is right, ma'am," said Sukey. "It is very warm. And Mr Carswell probably will not come now."

"Don't tell me what to do!" Laura said. The remark was thrown at Sukey, but Giles felt it was directed at him as much as anything.

"I cannot leave you two here alone. I have to go to work," Giles said. "We are going home. Holt, go and find our carriage, will you?"

Holt departed.

"Lord Rothborough would not send for me unless something terrible had happened," Giles said. "You must understand that, Laura. I can't leave you here."

"Why not?" Laura said.

"Because —" he began.

"I will not be alone," she cut in. "Sukey will be here, and that ought to be enough for you."

"Yes, but it is not so long since —"

"I am perfectly well now," Laura said. "And anyway, Mr Carswell will be here soon enough. I am sure of it."

"I would rather you went home," Giles said. "For my peace of mind, since I have to go to Holbroke."

"You would rather I were safely locked up," she said.

"That is it."

"I can't leave you here without protection."

"You would lock me up again, if you could. I know you would much prefer that."

Of all the places to have a scene, this was not the one. Giles bit his tongue. It was always better not to respond.

"Ah, look, ma'am," said Sukey. "Here is Mr Carswell!"

Saved again by Carswell, thought Giles. It was becoming a debt that would be difficult to settle.

~

Just as he was about to start for Holbroke, Major Vernon showed Felix the letter from Lord Rothborough.

"Can you shed any light on that?" he said.

"All I know is that they are all at Holbroke," Felix said. "I don't envy you."

"He wouldn't call on me without some good reason," Major Vernon said. "How was Martinez?"

"More comfortable. The nurse is a competent creature, but she was forthright about her charges. Nurses are expensive here, it seems."

"I had better give you some money," said Major Vernon, reaching into his pocket. "Shillings or guineas?"

"Shillings," said Felix, "mercifully. Ten will cover it all."

"Here's twenty," said Vernon. "See if you cannot get that landlady into being more useful with it."

He took the money and saw the carriage off, and then went back into the house.

As he climbed the stairs, Mrs Vernon was playing the piano in the upstairs drawing room, practising scales diligently, but then breaking into a slow melancholy melody, full of yearning. He had encouraged her to take up the piano again as a way of giving her some serious occupation and focusing her passions. Sometimes it felt that the focus was too intense, as a magnifying glass left in sunlight was in danger of starting a fire.

He hesitated at the drawing room door, wondering if he should go in, or continue upstairs to his room.

"Will you be wanting luncheon, sir?" It was Sukey Connolly, coming upstairs with a tray. "I have something for Mrs Vernon here."

"What did she have for breakfast?"

"Only a piece of toast. I did try." She shrugged. It was an old struggle.

"Then I will eat with her, yes. She will eat properly then." He was famished himself and wanted nothing more than a pint or two of dark Edinburgh beer and a greasy pie, the fodder of his student days, and to eat it in the casual anonymity of a smoky howff. "Tell her I will be down in a minute," he said, starting upstairs. The music followed him, inexorably, almost as if she meant him to hear every plangent note.

He closed the door on it, and pulled off his coat, waistcoat, cravat and shirt. He sponged himself down with cool water, trying to cool his own anxiety.

As he dried himself, he could not avoid looking at the little posy of flowers in a water glass that decorated the washstand. They were obviously her handiwork, gathered from the flower garden behind the house. Usually this would have meant nothing more than the action of a thoughtful hostess seeing to the comfort of a guest. It was exactly the sort of normal behaviour that they had been working to encourage in her, but when he had seen the flowers there last night, he had been sure that they had been chosen and placed with careful significance. He knew women sometimes used flowers to make declarations of their feelings and that every flower and leaf had a meaning to those who knew their language. He did not, and he was glad of it. Their presence alone was enough to disturb him.

When he had come up the hill towards the Bower Well and she had caught sight of him, she had seemed to surge with joy, as though he were the only thing capable of giving her any pleasure. Then in the carriage back to the house, as he sat opposite her and the Major, he had been acutely aware of her gazing at him. Had Major Vernon guessed that she had developed feelings? For a man as observant as the Major, it seemed likely. How could he have not seen the looks she gave him and interpreted them for what they were? Felix wished that they might discuss it. He had been thinking last night that the topic must be broached, sooner rather than later, but this business at Holbroke had carried the Major and the opportunity for that conversation abruptly away. The Major trusted him implicitly, he knew, and he would have walked a hundred leagues in his bare feet rather than betray him.

He put on a clean shirt, retied his cravat, and forced himself back into the formality of his waistcoat and coat. Despite the heat, it would not do to send such a signal of being at ease with her. He had to be cool and remote, every inch the professional man.

Yet as he descended the stairs, she broke into a melody of such gorgeous intensity and played with such obvious finesse and feeling, he had to catch his breath. He paused on the bottom step, wondering if he had better visit Martinez, rather than go in and be alone with her.

Sukey came out of the drawing room.

"Sukey, don't go just yet," he said. "Mrs Vernon may want you. Come and sit with us."

"I'll just fetch my sewing," she said, slipping past him.

He went in as quietly as he could, attempting not to disturb Mrs Vernon. But she heard him, and stopped at once.

"No, don't," he said, seeing her rise from the piano. "Please, not on my account. I was enjoying it."

"You were?" she said, smiling, and he realised that was the wrong thing to say. "I have been working hard at it, just as you suggested."

He took care not to respond to that. Instead he pulled out a chair for her at the round table that was used for meals, and waited there for her to join him. It was only good manners to do so, yet he wondered if it might be better to act the boor with her and take the seat for himself, and begin eating as if she were not even there.

"Shall we have some lunch?" he said.

She nodded and came and sat down, but used the excuse of his standing there to slip past him, like a cat circling his legs. Her skirts brushed against him, and as she sat, she twisted her head and looked up at him, with a look that was so terrifyingly full of gratitude that he was tempted to walk straight out of the room.

But he had a duty to make her eat and the power to accomplish it, for as he offered her the plate of ham and the bread and butter, and the radishes, she took her portion, anxious to please him. She ate too, not just pushing the food about the plate, as was so often the case. In fact she consumed a full slice of ham, three radishes and two pieces of bread and butter, which was quite astonishing.

"This spa water makes one hungry," he said, taking some more ham for himself. "Even if it does taste so foul." He had grabbed a cup from the Bower Well to quench his thirst after he had walked up the hill.

"I did have two cups," she said. "Just as you told me."

"Then you must go and take it again tomorrow," he said.

"Yes, I would like that," she said. She looked down at her empty plate, surprised by it. "Have I not done well?"

"Very well."

"It is only because you are here," she said. "It is not the water, it is because —"

The door opened and Sukey came in, with her work-basket.

"Yes, what is it?" said Mrs Vernon, looking round at her

with some hostility. "I did not ring for you, Sukey."

"Mr Carswell asked me to come in, ma'am," said Sukey.

"Why?" Mrs Vernon said, staring across the table at him, as if he had betrayed her horribly.

"Because I have to go out now and see a patient," Felix said, throwing down his napkin and getting up. "And –"

"Am I not your patient?" she said, also rising from the table.

"Yes, but Mr Martinez is in a terrible condition and needs me."

"And I don't?" she said, with a slight sob.

"I shall be back as soon as I can," he said. "Do some more piano practice. You are getting on so well with it."

"You do not care one iota, do you?" she said. "Not one!"

And she ran out of the room, pushing past Sukey, the door banging behind her.

"Oh, God!" Felix could not help exclaiming. He stared helplessly at Sukey.

"Two steps forward, one back," she said. "You said that yourself."

"But this, this is –"

"You woke her up from the dead," Sukey said. "She's bound to be grateful."

He nodded.

"I had better go and see Martinez," he said.

"Of course. She will be all right. I'll get her busy with something else. Don't you worry about it."

"I will try."

It was not the first time that her good counsel and infinite common sense had prevailed upon him. Mrs Vernon would never have recovered to such a degree had not Sukey enacted and improved all his ideas for her treatment. She was a most sensible, practical, intelligent woman, worth her weight in gold, and as Major Vernon had once pointed out, possibly wasted on domestic life.

"We are lucky we do not live in a world where women can take our posts, for we should be in for stiff competition with the likes of Mrs Connolly. She could command a regiment with ease, or direct a ministry."

To Felix it was a mystery that she had not been snapped up by a man as soon as was proper after the death of Mr Connolly. It was true she had no tangible assets beyond good looks – for she was handsome, with dark red hair that was liable to escape from time to time from under her cap – and her remarkable intelligence. She seemed content to work for the Major and Mrs Vernon, but Felix wondered how long it would be before some prosperous bachelor in Northminster lured her away with the prospect of her own establishment. When it happened, it would be a great loss.

Chapter Three

One could be aware of the facts about a man and all his possessions, Giles reflected as he drove to Holbroke in the Marquess of Rothborough's travelling carriage, but until one saw it for oneself, it was not knowledge.

He had heard much of the great prospects of Holbroke and its park. He had seen engravings and been told the extent of it, but he was not prepared for the sheer scale of the place. It was like crossing the border into a different realm. Even before they passed into the park itself, they drove through several extremely orderly villages, where the hand of a great owner was much in evidence. The roads were excellent. The cottages were well-maintained and picturesque, with latticed windows, neat shutters and painted garden fences. A benign tyranny was clearly in operation, which sat strangely with some of Lord Rothborough's more laissez-faire pronouncements.

The entrance to the park itself was marked by a great arch and tunnel, formed from two substantial, symmetrical buildings of golden stone. The gilded gates swung open at the sight of the carriage – of course they would, because it was Lord Rothborough's personal travelling carriage. Yet Giles felt he ought to be stopped and asked for some form of identification, as if at a foreign border.

The carriage sped through, drawn by a pair of the most elegant greys he had ever seen, a pair of horses that would make any man jealous. He had recently been thinking of setting up a carriage for Laura and he knew he would never be able to afford such fine horses.

Once through the gates, the famous prospect of the house could be seen, vast even in the distance. On this brilliant summer day, it glittered like a fairytale palace. Giles, the younger son of a respectable but by no means expansively landed Northumbrian gentleman, could not help feel a long moment of envy at the sight of so many acres formed into parkland alone. It was impossible not to wonder what it might feel to be the master of such a domain. What sort of life would he have made for himself if he had had such good fortune, he wondered. Would he have done good, or would too much ease have destroyed him? That Lord Rothborough was so active and energetic beyond the boundaries of his fabulous realm said a great deal about his character. Giles felt he might never have left the place if it were his. At the same time, Carswell's own uncomfortable predicament as Rothborough's natural son came home to him in a way it had not done before.

"Are we not going straight up to the house, sir?" Holt remarked, swivelling around on the tip-up seat to see where they were headed, as the carriage had made a sharp turn to the right.

"Apparently not," said Giles. They were heading into a woodland drive, and the road had begun to wind.

"And there I was hoping for a pint in the servants' hall," said Holt. "I imagine the beer here will be a decent brew."

"You'll get port with the house steward, with any luck," said Giles.

"Maybe," said Holt. "But I'd rather have a glass of beer on a day like this, and I dare say you would too, sir."

"Yes," said Giles. "But that will have to wait."

The carriage left the woods and suddenly they were driving around a large pond, heavy with white lilies, towards a fanciful-looking building on the far side. It had broad hints of the rustic about it, with a portico whose columns were painted tree trunks. On the portico stood Lord Rothborough with a young woman who Giles guessed must be one of the Marquess' daughters. She was dressed in a riding habit made of sand-coloured linen and he instantly wished he might carry such an outfit back to Laura, as well as the pretty grey mare with a side-saddle on it that stood tethered nearby. A horse might absorb some of her attention. She had always loved to ride, and if they went riding together then perhaps she might find it easier to bear his company again.

"My dear Major Vernon," said Rothborough, approaching the carriage to greet him, "I cannot thank you enough for coming so quickly. I am sorry that my note was rather cryptic. The fact is – well, all will be clear enough soon. Charlotte, may I present Major Vernon?" he said, turning to the young woman. "This is my eldest daughter Lady Charlotte Harald, Vernon. She has a half-share in this unfortunate business, I am afraid to say."

"Lady Charlotte," Giles said, bowing to her. "An honour."

"I am glad to know you too, sir. My father is always speaking of the great Major Vernon. It is excellent to put a face to the name."

"So, this business –" Giles said.

"This way," said Lord Rothborough, going to the double doors of the rustic pavilion. They went into a charming hall, the walls of which were painted with garlands and goddesses and the ceiling with sky and birds. But there was no time to admire the artistry. Lord Rothborough had opened the doors to the adjoining room, which proved to be an elaborately tiled dairy, with marble benches all around the walls and in the centre, a great marble table, upon which lay the corpse of a woman, her head decorously covered by a large white handkerchief.

A perfect place for ladies to play at dairymaids and equally perfect to house a dead body, Giles thought as he went over to the body. He lifted the handkerchief. The woman's face was swollen and her features bore considerable signs of violence. She would have been young and handsome in life. He glanced down at her clothes – plain, respectable working clothes and altogether unremarkable.

"You did not find her here, like this?" he said.

"No, no, she was floating in the grotto pool," said Lady Charlotte from the doorway. "I thought they should bring her in here. It is closer than the house, and cool. It seemed best to get her out of the heat, once we had taken her from the water."

"An excellent suggestion, yes?" said Rothborough, with some pride.

"Yes, very," Giles said, wishing Carswell were there. "I am sorry – where precisely was she? In the lily pond outside?"

"No, another pool. It is a little way from here, but not far," said Rothborough. "Shall we show you?"

"Yes, that would be helpful. Do you know who she is?"

"I think she is Lady Warde's maid," said Lady Charlotte.

"Lady Warde is one of my wife's guests," said Lord Rothborough.

"But we are not sure it is her maid," said Lady Charlotte.

"We will know for certain when we get back to the house," said Lord Rothborough. "She is not one of our people, though."

Giles arranged the handkerchief back over her face.

"This way," said Lord Rothborough.

Giles considered how he might send for Carswell without offending the ladies, given Carswell's awkward position within the family. Lady Charlotte would understand the need for this and explain it to Lady Rothborough. She certainly seemed intelligent enough.

They passed through a gateway that was either a ruin or pretending to be a ruin, into a gloomy shrubbery. Here, the winding paths had been laid between high hedges of yew that had been allowed to grow into the most fantastic and grotesque shapes.

"What is this place, if you don't mind me asking?" Giles said.

"We call them the Pleasure Gardens," said Lady Charlotte.

"It was built by my grandfather," Lord Rothborough said, "to amuse his young wife and keep her from wanting to go back to London, which he detested. We have the grotto, the pool, the Italian maze, the rambles, the tea house and the dairy. Oh, and there was a large aviary out here at one time. I have to confess, you are not seeing it all at its best. To be honest, I cannot decide what to do with it. We keep the lawns cut and the hedges in check, the buildings in repair, but nature has had her way rather readily. I think some more serious renovation is required. But what?"

"You shall not spoil it, Papa," said Lady Charlotte. "My sisters and I will not forgive you. We used to love coming here when we were young. I hope to bring my own children here."

"Then you must help me draw up a plan, Charlotte."

"With pleasure. One can only hope that this unfortunate business does not cast a shadow over the place," she said, with a sigh. "Poor woman."

"Do the servants usually take walks here?" Giles asked.

"That is what is odd," she said. "It is not part of the Park, which is more or less public, but rather it is reserved for our family. Our indoor people do not come here for their recreation. Half of them think it is haunted anyway."

"Oh, that old story," said Lord Rothborough. "A great piece of nonsense."

"But they do believe it, Papa, and my sisters did for years."

"But you never did," said Lord Rothborough, with a smile.

"Of course not," she said. "I think it was made up to keep the servants out of the place."

"Here we are," said Lord Rothborough. "The grotto and St Gertrude's pool."

They had emerged through another pretend ruin, this

time with the suggestion of an old abbey about it, into a deep basin surrounded by high rocky cliffs, heavy with vegetation. In front there was the pool, a mass of dark green water. It looked forbidding even on such a bright day.

At one point the cliffs fissured to form the entrance to what Giles supposed must be the grotto itself. A perilous-looking bridge, without rails, arched high over the water where it flowed into the grotto. A narrow path edged the pool giving access to the grotto itself, and at first glance it looked as if it had been made deliberately narrow in order to increase the thrill of the approach, perhaps to give visitors the sensation that they were in a scene from one of Mrs Radcliffe's novels. An elaborate, expensive conceit, Giles thought, and then wondered if simulated decay combined with real decay had made the place dangerous. Even though the weather had been dry, the shade cast by the overhanging trees and the large quantities of moss might have made the path slippery, even at the best of times.

"Has anyone ever fallen from that path before?" Giles asked Rothborough. "Or the bridge?"

"Not to my knowledge. You girls never used the path or the bridge, I am sure," Rothborough said.

"No," said Lady Charlotte. "Very sensibly you forbade it. We had a little boat to get into the grotto."

"How deep is the water?" Giles said.

"At least twenty feet in the middle," Rothborough said. "But it goes down by steps. It was quarried out to form the cliff."

A stupid young lady in silly heels, anxious for a thrill, might lose her footing and tumble and drown, but a servant in her mid-twenties, wearing sensible flat boots (he had noted them) – would she be likely to risk the path? Would she have any interest in exploring a grotto? What had she been doing there? That was the puzzle.

"Perhaps you could tell me how it was you found her, my

lord?"

"We left the horses with the groom, at the tea house, and then went on foot. As I said, I am deliberating what to do with it all, and it seemed a good opportunity to look it all over. We went exactly the route we have just walked with you, and there she was."

"Face down in the water," said Lady Charlotte.

"At the edge or in the middle?"

"At the edge, in those rushes there, by the little jetty."

"What time was this?" Giles said.

"A little after ten," said Lady Charlotte. "I know because I had just asked my father the time, just as we came through the Italian maze."

"And that was all you found?"

"Yes."

"I sent the groom to get some of the gardeners so we could get her from the water," said Lord Rothborough. "And then we put her in the dairy, as Charlotte suggested."

"I suppose it is most likely an accident," said Lady Charlotte. "At least I hope so. But it all seemed so strange. Papa and I were agreed on that at once. It was odd that she should even be here."

"And so I thought I had better send for you," said Lord Rothborough.

Giles took out his notebook.

"Certainly it's a case for the coroner. That is Mr Haines at Market Craven, I think? And we need a doctor," he said. "And strictly speaking this is not my business to investigate. We ought to tell Sir Arthur Felpsham and he should send some of his men."

"Ah yes, Sir Arthur and his merry men," said Rothborough. "That is precisely why I did send for you, Vernon, knowing you were in Stanegate. I do not have much faith in the County Constabulary and their Chief Constable. You might set them to find a poacher, if you were desperate, but I would not trust them with a matter like this, that may or may not be delicate. I scarcely need to tell you this – you must know it for yourself. The force in this locality cannot be said to be remotely effective. I did my best, but my neighbours and fellow Justices are such a nest of Tories that I could not prevail upon them to attach sufficient importance to it. They do not seem to see which way the wind is blowing – Market Craven has three manufactories now, and another being built. The people are flooding in. The place is a disgrace, but will they consider expanding the force? And Stanegate – well, you will have observed for yourself how busy that is. With people of fashion too who will want to feel safe. But still old Sir Arthur keeps his place, with his dozy underlings!"

"That may be," said Giles, "but I think it would be better if he were involved. I don't wish to make an enemy of him. I cannot afford to do so, I am afraid."

"You are right," said Rothborough. "But we will be making a rod for our backs. Have you met Sir Arthur?"

"No."

"Prepare yourself to be annoyed. Still, he will have to retire before too long, and this time, I will get a man in who knows what needs to be done. Someone like you, Major Vernon. In fact, the job would be there for the asking. It might suit you better than Northminster – being a countryman."

Giles tried to think of a suitably bland response to this; fortunately Lady Charlotte came to his rescue.

"Major Vernon?" she interjected. "Do you need me any longer? I think I ought to get back to the house. My mother will be wanting me, and I wonder if I ought to speak to Lady Warde."

"I think I had better do that, if you don't mind, Lady Charlotte," Giles said. "But if you were with me, it might be useful."

"Of course. May I go, then?"

"Yes, ma'am. And thank you – you have been extremely

helpful."

She nodded in acknowledgement and walked away, the long skirt of her habit elegantly tossed over her arm.

"There aren't many girls who would have dealt with this with such a cool head," Lord Rothborough said, with some pride. "My other girls – they don't have her composure."

"Women can be as sensible as we are, if we only allow them to be so," Giles said.

"My sentiment entirely," Lord Rothborough said.

"I want to just look over the scene a little more closely, just to satisfy myself on a few points. Have you a reliable man to keep the dairy guarded? Otherwise, I have my man Holt here –"

"Two of the gardeners can keep watch on her," said Rothborough. "They can tidy up that creeper on the trellis at the same time – it's in a shocking state. I can't believe that Macgillray hasn't set them on it."

"And about the doctor – is there a man about here who has any experience in these matters?" Giles said.

"No, unfortunately," said Lord Rothborough, scratching his temple.

"I did not like to mention it in front of Lady Charlotte, but Mr Carswell joined us in Stanegate yesterday. I would welcome his opinion. To be frank, I am not sure we can establish the truth of it without an experienced eye. He has told me himself that drownings are often misleading."

"It would seem expedient to get him over here, then," said Lord Rothborough. "It is not the best moment, of course, but that poor creature and justice must take priority. And if we are discreet, no one will have to know."

"He would not need to be here for long," said Giles. "A morning at most. And he has a new patient in Stanegate whom he cannot neglect. A gentleman from one of the former Spanish colonies – Santa Magdalena – who is dying of consumption in rather miserable circumstances, apparently quite alone. But what is odd is that there seems to be quite a Spanish presence in the town at the moment. When we went to take our water at the Bower Well this morning, there were a dozen of them. It was most exotic and unexpected."

"Ah, yes – that will be the former Chancellor of Santa Magdalena, and his suite," said Lord Rothborough. "I had heard they were here, along with the President's widow, taking the waters. Fabulously wealthy, I believe. They have taken over a whole floor at The Queen's Hotel. I was intending to go and call on him. The talk is that he is only biding his time in Europe before he goes back and takes back the crown, so to speak. The island is important for us – there is a quite significant merchant colony there, Scots mostly, trading out of Glasgow, and we need to keep them safe. These people should not be ignored, even if they are out of power at the moment. But they are a little hard to keep track of, these erstwhile Spanish colonials. They are always squabbling among themselves now they have thrown off the shackles of Spain. It is all coup and counter-coup. What did you say your man's name was?"

"Don Xavier Martinez. But he may have a clerical title as well."

"Martinez? That's the name of the late President – General Martinez. He fought with Bolivar, and then went home and pushed the Spanish out of Santa Magdalena, well, some fifteen years ago now. He ruled the place like a prince until last year, when someone put a bullet through his head."

"Then our poor man may be some connection – which makes his neglect all the more inexplicable, unless it is some kind of family quarrel."

"Those are wretchedly common. So you saw them all this morning taking the waters?" Giles nodded. "The *on dit* is that former Chancellor Ramirez has been travelling about Europe trying to raise support for a counter-coup. It is the widow Martinez I should like to see. She has the reputation of being a shrewd tactician who had the people in the palm of hand. The opinion is that the rebels made a serious mistake when they did not shoot her!"

Chapter Four

Lord Rothborough left him to his examination of the site. Giles wanted to see if there was any evidence of where she had entered the water, so he made a careful circuit of the pool, edging along the sloping path of the far side with care. As he approached the little bridge, the flagstones forming the path turned into dark but dry mud. He got down on his hands and knees to look for recent footprints. There were marks in the mud but he could not be sure if he was seeing footprints. He would have to look at her boots.

To enter the grotto cave it was necessary to cross that rickety, rail-less bridge. In wet weather, due to the steep arch, this would have been a risky undertaking. Today, in the dry, warm air, the sound of his feet on the wooden planks echoed in the sounding chamber of the basin around him.

The interior of the grotto was surprising – but he was sure that this was the desired effect. It was all part of the theatrical trickery of the place. He had expected darkness, but it was in fact illuminated from above. Irregular fissures forming roof lights had been glazed with stained glass, creating eerie but effective pools of coloured light on a white floor made from fragments of shells pressed into cement. Presiding over all, from a rocky niche, was the milky marble statue of a woman in a long robe. She had her eyes raised towards Heaven and a cross pressed to her bosom. Presumably this was St Gertrude.

Despite her saintly presence, Giles wondered if the cave was not an attractive place for a tryst. It was sheltered from the elements, private and scarcely visited – in short, excellent if one did not wish to be interrupted. No one would know of such a spot by chance. As a visitor to the house, had the dead woman heard about it from one of the resident staff? Perhaps she had gone there to meet one of them. Lord Rothborough and Lady Charlotte might think that the servants did not go into the Pleasure Gardens, but masters usually knew little about the private lives and desires of their employees. The fact it was a forbidden place would only make it more alluring, especially to those in search of privacy and intimacy. Men and women of that class were forced to take opportunities where they could find them. Was this how the business had begun? If that was the case, then what had gone wrong? How had she ended up in the pool, dead, and not safely back at the great house?

He searched around for evidence, but found nothing. There were no obvious traces of her presence.

He emerged again and carefully crossed over the rickety bridge, stopping for a moment at its slightly perilous summit. From there it was a drop of at least ten feet down into the water.

Had she meant to kill herself? Had she thrown herself into the deep, dark waters in a fit of despair when her lover had failed to come? That sounded all together too much like a novel. The heat was clouding his mind. He made his way back to the dairy.

Holt was in heavy conversation with the coachman, but jumped to attention at the sight of him.

"Let's find you that pint of beer in the servants' hall," Giles said, getting into the carriage. Holt got in after him and sat as before, on the tip-up seat. "But not more than that. I need you to keep your eyes and ears open."

~

Lady Charlotte was waiting for him in the great marble entrance hall at Holbroke.

"I hope you don't mind, Major Vernon," she said. "But I have been to talk to our housekeeper, Mrs Hope. She has not seen Eliza Jones – for that is her name – since after dinner last night. Well, the upper servants' dinner, that is. They eat at five in the steward's room. But I have not spoken to Lady Warde yet, just as you requested. She must have seen her, because she went upstairs with the other maids when the dressing bell was rung at seven."

"We shall have to talk to all the lady's maids," said Giles.

"We?"

He had said it out of force of habit, but it struck him that she might be a useful assistant, and there was something about the way she had hurried across the hall to meet him that suggested she was eager to assist him.

"If you can spare the time. I would not wish to impose."

"It would be no imposition. It would be..." – she hesitated a moment, choosing the right word – "interesting to assist you, Major Vernon. You are staying tonight, I think? I have had them make a room ready for you."

"Thank you, it would be a pleasure."

"My mother and sisters are in the drawing room. As is Lady Warde."

"I think I ought to make myself presentable first."

She nodded and signalled to the liveried man who had opened the door to him.

"Henry, show Major Vernon to the Wellington room." She turned back to Giles. "If you have any messages, give them to Henry. He will see you have everything you need. And he will look after your man."

As they followed the footman up a great gilded staircase and then along a broad passageway, Holt said, in a quiet voice, "Did she say Wellington, sir?"

"Yes."

"Do you suppose it is where he sleeps when he comes here, sir? I suppose he does come here, sometimes?"

"He may do," said Giles.

"Lord preserve us," murmured Holt, as Henry opened the door and showed them into a room with an impressive canopied bed in the centre of it, hung with watered blue silk. On the writing table in the window was a bust of the Duke himself.

"Does he –?" Holt ventured to ask Henry, who was drawing up the blinds. "His Grace the Duke, I mean?"

"Oh yes," said Henry. "He comes once a year, for four nights." Holt looked for a moment as though he might fall on his knees, like a peasant entering a particularly celebrated and holy pilgrimage chapel. "I'll just get you some hot water, sir. If you'll come this way, Mr –?"

"Holt," Holt managed to say.

Henry and Holt departed, leaving Giles with the Duke of Wellington's bust and a view of the peerless parklands of Holbroke.

~

Giles found the Marchioness of Rothborough sitting in her drawing room on a low chair, occupied with a piece of plain sewing. Three fashionably dressed young women sat with her, one of them Lady Charlotte. They were all busy with their needles. Patches of grey flannel and white calico lay spread over their brightly coloured skirts.

A handsome young clergyman, tall and commanding in his figure, was walking up and down the room, reading aloud with great earnestness from what sounded like an evangelical sermon.

If this was how she was expected to spend her days, it

was no wonder Lady Charlotte was eager to assist him, Giles thought.

"For the truth is evident, that whoever does not freely allow the Lord Jesus to enter into his heart, then –" The clergyman broke off, catching sight of Giles. At the same time, Lady Charlotte leapt up, throwing her work down onto the floor and coming over to greet him.

The Marchioness looked quizzically at Lady Charlotte, who made the introductions.

"You are a friend of my husband?" Lady Rothborough said, putting out her hand. He took it and bowed over it.

"I have the honour of his acquaintance," he said.

"Major Vernon is a policeman," said Lady Charlotte. "He has come to help us with some rather unpleasant business."

Lady Rothborough frowned.

"You are from Northminster, I think," she said.

"Yes, ma'am."

She frowned again.

"I do not like Northminster," she said.

"These are my sisters, Major Vernon," said Lady Charlotte. "Augusta and Maria." Giles noted that these young women did not resemble Mr Carswell quite as much as their elder sister.

"I wonder if I might speak to Lady Warde?" Giles said.

"Lady Warde?" said Lady Rothborough. "Yes, of course, but –" She glanced about her.

"She is not here, Mama," said Lady Augusta.

"How strange, she is usually about the place. What do you want with her, sir?"

"It is for police business," said Lady Charlotte said, with something of a flourish.

"I'm afraid so," Giles felt obliged to add. "I regret the disturbance, Lady Rothborough."

"I will go and find her," said Lady Charlotte. "She must be in her room."

"You may send one of the servants," said Lady Rothborough. "You have not finished your portion of sewing yet, Charlotte."

"Yes, of course, Mama," said Lady Charlotte. "But first I must take Major Vernon to my father. This way, if you please, Major."

"You will come back directly," said Lady Rothborough. "Police business can certainly not be your business."

"Of course, of course," said Lady Charlotte, with a wave of her hand, her manner displaying some of the breezy insouciance of her father. Giles had to repress a smile.

"You may begin again, if you please, Mr Syme," said Lady Rothborough, and the clergyman began to read his sermon again even before they had left the room.

"I must apologise for that," Lady Charlotte said as they reached the other side of the drawing room door. "My mother is utterly in the thrall of that terrible man – since he has got her ear, it is as if every day is the Sabbath here. You must have your excuses ready, Major Vernon, or you will be dragged off to Bible study." Giles, rather astonished, did not quite know how to respond. "And now I have shocked you," she said, quietly.

"In my experience," Giles said, "clergymen are men like any others, equally fallible or virtuous."

"I thought you would see it. Papa is incandescent with fury about him. We are working to get him out of here, but it does not seem easy to dislodge him. Perhaps you might help us with that as well?"

"How might I do that?"

"You are supposed to have the knack of finding out everyone's secrets. That is what my father said. I am sure the detestable Syme has some secrets that would discredit him."

"And are you not worried I will find out your secrets, Lady Charlotte?"

"No, not the slightest. I think it might be quite

interesting."

She gave him a smile which he knew he was supposed to find devastating. It might have been, in other circumstances – if he had been ten years younger, and not married. He wondered if he should tell her to keep her weapons for those worth wounding.

"Most people do not like to hear the truth about themselves," he said. "I never do. It is never pleasant. My wife, only this morning, pointed out something about myself that I did not want to acknowledge and I am still feeling sore from it."

"Ah yes, Mrs Vernon," said Lady Charlotte. "I do hope we shall see her here soon. You will write and tell her that she must come, Major Vernon?"

"Yes," he said. "Of course."

They found Lord Rothborough in a room that opened off the great library, and which Giles could not help but envy. As a private office it had everything to recommend it, a mixture of elegance and efficiency. One of the walls was lined with neat cupboards and shelves, so that everything was to hand and in perfect order, while two great windows showed a magnificent prospect over the park. The sashes were pushed open, admitting a gentle breeze which stirred the muslin glass cloths and made the room an agreeable temperature for concentration. Lord Rothborough sat at his desk, working at his papers, but at once abandoned his study to greet them as they came in, as if Giles were a person of vast importance.

"Here he is, Papa," said Lady Charlotte. "I shall go and find Lady Warde. I will bring her into the library for you, Major Vernon."

"Is she being useful?" Lord Rothborough asked when she had gone.

"Extremely."

"I have written to Sir Arthur," said Lord Rothborough. "My man is about to ride over with the letter. You might wish to add something."

"I have a letter ready for him here," said Giles, taking it from his coat. He had written it at the writing table in his room, under the blank gaze of the hero of Waterloo. "And these others. I was not sure of the coroner's correct address."

"Woodward, will you see that this is correct?" said Rothborough, signalling to his secretary, who had his own desk in the corner. "And send one of the footmen with these."

"About Mr Carswell?" Giles asked, when the secretary had left.

"He will be with you tomorrow morning. I have arranged it. You have seen my wife?"

"Yes."

"Was Syme there?"

"The clergyman? Yes. Lady Charlotte did mention –"

"She is extracting a terrible revenge on me," said Lord Rothborough, throwing up his hands. "On us all. I had rather she had turned to Rome. That would be comprehensible – and a few Jesuits at the dinner table, I could bear that, just about – but this! She might as well be a Dissenter!"

"Lady Charlotte suggested I might investigate Syme to see if he had any weak spots."

"Ha, did she? Well, that is an excellent plan, but probably not entirely to your taste, Major. And you are going to be occupied, I fear, with this business. The more I think about it, the more strange it seems that she was there at all."

Lady Charlotte came in again.

"I have Lady Warde for you in the library," she said.

~

The lady belonging to the dead maid sat in her widow's weeds in the grandeur of the great library, looking, Giles reflected, a trifle out of place. Her clothing had an old-fashioned air, as did her manner as she sat there, rigidly upright, her hands folded neatly in her lap. She was in middle age, as far as he could judge, but looked older than she was, as if the cares of her existence had put years on her face and dulled her brown hair.

He presented himself to her and said, "Lady Warde, I hope you don't mind my summoning you like this, but I have a few questions for you."

"Not at all. Lady Charlotte came knocking at my door and asked if I was indisposed – such a great kindness of her to come and fetch me and not send a servant, but Lady Charlotte has always been consideration itself, like all the Rothborough ladies, of course!"

"Of course," said Giles. "I understand you have a maid with you, Lady Warde?"

"Yes, yes, Eliza Jones."

"And when did you last see her?"

"Last night. She helped me dress for dinner. But another girl came to help me at bedtime – a nice girl, like all the servants here. She told me that Eliza was ill – she sometimes gets these wretched headaches, and I thought, poor girl, I will not disturb her. It is often best to sleep off a headache, I find, and I think that is the case with my Jones. Why do you ask, sir? Is everything all right?"

"We think Eliza may have met with an accident," said Lady Charlotte, sitting down beside her.

"Oh, surely not," said Lady Warde.

"She has not been seen since last night," said Giles, "and this morning, the body of a young woman in a pool was discovered. Lady Charlotte recognised her as your maid."

"Oh my," said Lady Warde. "Dear Lady Charlotte, is this true? How can it be true?"

"I am so sorry, Lady Warde," said Lady Charlotte, taking Lady Warde's hand in both hers. "She has drowned."

"But how?"

"We do not know exactly," said Giles. "But I am afraid I will need you to identify her formally." Lady Warde stared at him blankly, her mouth opening as if she meant to speak. But she was unable to find the words. "Please take a moment to compose yourself, ma'am. I do understand this is distressing for you."

"Yes, indeed, Lady Warde," said Lady Charlotte. "Would you like a glass of water? Or some brandy?"

"You are sure it is her?"

"It seems likely," said Giles. "That is why we need you to identify her. There is a chance that it may not be her at all."

"It can't be. Why on earth – what would she be doing drowned? How?"

"As I say, ma'am, we don't yet know."

"I do not think it can be Eliza," said Lady Warde. "I do not understand how it could be. She is not a girl for running off, always so reliable and dependable. I simply do not understand!"

~

Later that day, Giles and Lady Charlotte took Lady Warde down to the Pleasure Gardens in the carriage and into the Chinese Dairy. The housekeeper, Mrs Hope, was also there and they both identified the woman as Eliza Jones.

Lady Warde's reaction was one of genuine horror and sorrow. She fainted and had to be carried out and revived in the adjoining room. Fortunately Mrs Hope had brought her smelling salts. When she had recovered a little, Giles pressed on with his questions.

"How long had she been in your service?"

"Since she was a girl – I took her on when she was about seventeen. About ten years ago now, I suppose."

"And she has never given you any trouble?"

"None at all. She was hard-working, loyal, honest, devoted," she said, swallowing her sobs. "A perfect servant. It is too terrible – that she should end her life so wretchedly!"

"How did you come to employ her?"

"I can't really remember. I was staying somewhere and she was looking for a place, and I had no maid at that time, so I took her on, and she has been with me ever since."

"Does she have any family that you know of?"

"No, none, I think. She was quite alone in the world. That is what is so awful. I think she was an orphan."

"No brothers or sisters?"

Lady Warde shook her head. "Not that I knew of."

"Any followers?"

"Certainly not," she said. "She would not allow that. She was devoted to me. I never knew what I did to deserve such a paragon, sir, and now she has been taken from me!"

She could no longer control her distress.

"Thank you, Lady Warde, that will be all for the present. Perhaps, Mrs Hope, you would escort Lady Warde back to the house?"

"Yes, sir."

"I shall want to interview all the staff when I get back," said Giles. "I would appreciate it, Mrs Hope, if they did not know at once why."

"As you like, sir."

The carriage was brought round and Mrs Hope and Lady Warde got in. Giles expected Lady Charlotte to climb in with them, but she did not.

"Will you not go back in the carriage?" he said.

"I thought I would walk back. I need exercise and now the heat has eased off a little –"

"Perhaps you can show me the way back, then?" he said. "I have a few questions for you, as it happens."

"Of course," she said.

They set off together, and after a little way, Giles said, "What I wish to know is this – who exactly is Lady Warde?"

"Who is she?" said Lady Charlotte. "That *is* a good question. She is a person... well, a person of a type one often finds in large houses such as ours. She is a permanent guest. A poor widow of good family who goes from house to house and is useful to her hostess. About whom one knows nothing, really. How odd it is, now I think of it."

"She has been here a while?"

"She came with us from Sussex – from my mother's house there."

"And she was with you in London before? For the Season?"

"No, not in London. I think she was at Lady Sutton's before, in Dorset."

"How long were you in Sussex?"

"Six weeks – we always go there in the middle of May until the end of June. Then we have a month here – no longer, because my mother does not care much for it. And then my father goes to Scotland and we go back to Sussex. Except I am hoping to go to Scotland this year."

"So she has been with you since mid-May? Almost two months?"

"Yes, and that is common enough. She generally stays two to three months with us, and then goes on elsewhere. She is well connected. And she is no trouble. She will wind wool and soothe sick children, turn pages and chaperone young people. She can be counted upon. My mother is fond of her for that reason."

"And you?"

"I am ashamed to say I do not know her well enough to have any sort of opinion, and I have never taken the trouble to know her. She is someone I overlook in general. She is so dull and wordy. I suppose I ought to like her. I certainly ought to have tried to like her. I have pitied her – but that is no defence.

But I feel for her now. A loyal servant must mean a great deal to a woman like her who is always in someone else's house." She shrugged. "Yes, you have my secrets out of me, now Major Vernon. You see what little attention I pay to those around me, what a shallow creature I am!"

"No, I think what you say is acute. Did you not find it strange how little she knew about Eliza?"

"Yes and no."

"I am sure you know a great deal more about your maid, Lady Charlotte."

She considered for a moment.

"Yes, I suppose I do."

"And how long has she been with you?"

"Two years."

"And what do you know about her?"

"She is one of seven. Her father is Welsh, her mother is from Devon. Her father used to be butler to Lord St Germain and her mother makes beautiful lace but would not teach Jane because it would ruin her eyes. Oh, and she does not much like dogs, but thinks a black cat the most perfect creature in the world. She has three brothers at sea – one is en route to Valpariso, and we are awaiting a letter. He is to get his master's ticket, with luck!"

"All that in two years. You see my point. Whereas Lady Warde –"

"She was shocked. Surely that is enough for you?"

"Ten years – and she cannot remember where she comes from and who her people are? But then people can be indifferent to those who work for them, I suppose. If Lady Warde is wordy, as you say, she may have never stopped to listen." Lady Charlotte laughed. "Or she is being deliberately bland. Never speak ill of the dead? We must give her a little time to recover and then she may say something more useful. In the meantime, there are the other servants. And of course, when the surgeon has seen her –"

"You have sent for Mr Carswell, I take it?" said Lady Charlotte.

"I am afraid I have," Giles said, rather surprised she should raise the subject.

"There is no need to apologise on my account," she said. "To tell you the truth, I am curious about Mr Carswell."

"It must be difficult for you," Giles said.

"Yes, but perhaps not as difficult as it is for him," she said. "I may have the disadvantage of being female but I have the advantage of legitimacy. What sort of man is he?"

"Clever, good at his work, warm-hearted. Somewhat impulsive and passionate, but that is really to his credit. There is something rather fine about him, to tell you the truth. I owe him a great debt. He has done wonders with my wife who was very ill."

"I should like to know him," she said. "But my mother would never forgive me."

"He will be here tomorrow – you had better take care to be busy with something else."

"I shall. It is only idle curiosity, after all – I think."

"I think it might be more than that," he could not help saying. "A sister or a brother – well, it's a precious thing, whatever the circumstances. We cannot pretend that these bonds of blood do not mean something."

"I am so glad to hear you say that!" she exclaimed. "This subject – it is one I have so wanted to speak of to someone – to anybody – I cannot talk to my father, he would be too mortified, but I know he wants to speak of it. It really is quite impossible. Thank you, Major Vernon, for being so frank."

"Perhaps we should head into the shade of those chestnuts? It's rather warm out here in the sun," he said after a moment.

"Yes, yes, what a good idea. Do you like these plantings?"

"They're very fine."

"My grandfather's work – he inherited when he was in his

minority and he set about planting trees, almost at once."

And for the rest of the walk, Mr Carswell was not touched on again.

Chapter Five

A summons to Holbroke from Lord Rothborough would normally have been a matter for a scowl and some reluctance on Felix's part. But the letter made it clear that it was Major Vernon who required his presence and that the matter in hand was significant, so he had no difficulty getting up that morning at six. He crept downstairs and found Sukey Connolly waiting for him. She had made him tea and toast, which he consumed standing up in the dining room.

"If there is any problem with Mrs Vernon –" he began.

"There won't be," she said. "I will keep her busy."

"And explain to her why I have gone?"

"You don't owe her any explanation," said Sukey.

"Yes, but it would be civil, I think," he said.

"But perhaps not in her best interest – nor yours," Sukey said.

"Perhaps," he said, embarrassed and yet grateful how clearly she had read the situation.

Lord Rothborough had arranged for a horse for him, with a groom to escort him, and although he was no great horseman, it was certainly pleasant to ride out from Stanegate on a fine morning, knowing that he had something specific to accomplish. There was a strange comfort in the prospect of a dead body.

Felix found Major Vernon in attendance on the body in an octagonal room, tiled with picturesque and extremely idealised scenes of peasant life through the seasons. He had only been to Holbroke twice, but he had heard of the Pleasure Gardens and their fantastical nature.

"What is this place?" he said.

"An ornamental dairy," said Major Vernon. "But today it is our morgue," he added, drawing back the sheet to reveal the corpse of a woman lying on a large marble table. "This is Miss Eliza Jones, servant to Lady Warde, one of Lady Rothborough's guests. She was found floating in the grotto pool near here by Lord Rothborough and his eldest daughter yesterday at about half past ten in the morning. She was taken from the water about eleven, and she's been here ever since."

"Last seen alive?"

"The night before last, just before dinner, which is served at eight here. That is the last sighting of her I have been able to establish so far, but I haven't questioned everyone yet. One of the groundsmen or gardeners may have seen her after that."

"Bodies in water are always something of a puzzle."

"I remembered you had said that," Major Vernon said. "Which is why I sent for you."

"I am glad you did. This is –" He squatted down peering at her head, which had a mass of contusions. "Quite interesting."

"What do you think caused them?"

"I can't say at once," said Felix peering at the wounds. "This pool – are there rocks in it? A corpse can get quite battered in the water, and the face here has certainly taken a pounding, but you would expect that because the body will have been face down in the water. A corpse in water always is."

"There are rocks about the edges, I think," said Major Vernon. "We will go and look in a minute."

"But, you know," Felix went on, "this one here is really quite deep, and there is a considerable amount of blood matted in her braid, and the fact it is on the back of her head rather than the face – it makes me wonder..." Gently he slipped his hand under her head and lifted it so he could look better. It was not easy to see clearly even then, for her hair was dark, dense and sticky with blood. He squinted again, catching sight of something white embedded in the wound. "Now, what is that there? I need a pair of tweezers. Here, sir, could you put your hand under there, and hold her in place while I get some?"

The Major obliged and Felix went scurrying to his bag.

"There we have it," he said, after a moment's more work. He held it up to the light and examined it. "It looks like a piece of shell to me."

"The grotto cave is full of crushed shells," said Major Vernon. "And perhaps some of her blood is there. I shall have to take another look. Could she have cracked her head open like this against a rough stone wall or the floor?"

"Yes, possibly," said Felix. "You can put her down now, sir."

"So perhaps she slipped backwards and cracked her head?" Major Vernon said. "Then, dizzy from that, she staggered and fell into the water and drowned? There are plenty of treacherous spots if you have already injured yourself."

"Do folk often fall backwards against a wall?" said Felix.

"They might – if they were intoxicated."

"Or you might fall if you were pushed by someone," Felix said.

"That assumes there was someone else there."

"Well, maybe there was. Perhaps it was a tryst."

"That crossed my mind. Why else would she be all the way out here? The servants are not supposed to go into the Pleasure Gardens."

Felix looked down at the body, rehearsing the possible scenarios in his mind.

"So did she die before or after she entered the water?" he said. "Was she drowned, and if not, what killed her? Why was she in the water, and if she was alive when she entered the water, why did she not survive?" he said. "Those are the questions. And it won't be easy to answer any of them until I have done the post-mortem and we have more information about the circumstances of her being here."

Major Vernon nodded, and then said, "Assuming you are allowed to conduct the post-mortem. Haines, the coroner here, may have his pet physician. And you may not be popular, being somewhat connected with this house."

"What?" said Felix. "Oh, for the Lord's sake!"

"I gather that Haines and Sir Arthur – the county Chief Constable – are implacable Tories."

"Lord Rothborough told you that, no doubt. And I am not connected with this house!"

"In their eyes you are. It is as well to be aware of these matters. If we are to make a case for you, we need to know where their allegiances lie. In the meantime, I suggest you make as thorough a survey as you can without taking a knife to her. And then we will go and examine the scene again."

Felix nodded and pulled off his coat.

"Could you perhaps take notes for me, sir?" he said. "That will speed up the process. And I think we do need to be speedy if this gets snatched away from us by local stupidities. But first we need to get her undressed."

Together they removed her layers of clothing, which revealed nothing very particular until he had got her stays off and ripped open her shift to find a characteristic swelling of the abdomen.

"Is that –?" began the Major.

"Possibly," Felix said, rolling up his sleeves. "I can find out soon enough."

He began an internal examination. His fingertips had just made contact with what was unmistakably a foetus of four to five months' growth, when the door flew open. He glanced up, his mind still making sense of the implications of what he had just felt, and saw an elegant young woman dressed in a riding habit standing in the doorway. She took in the scene before her and her gloved hand flew to cover her mouth. She then turned and fled.

"Lady Charlotte..." Major Vernon said and went rushing after her.

With his index finger, Felix discovered what was the top of the child's head and found himself shaking with pity and rage for this poor unborn creature and its horrible fate. Or at least he told himself it was for the child, for at the same time his heart was set adrift on a vast and boiling ocean of feelings.

With all the effort he could muster, he collected himself, gently taking his hand from the dead woman's womb, and then, with great care, covered her again.

A moment later Major Vernon returned, closing the door behind him.

"Is she all right?" asked Felix.

"Yes," said the Major.

Felix went towards the door.

"Are you sure that is wise?" said Major Vernon.

"I don't know," Felix said and opened the door.

He saw she was standing in the room on the other side of the hall, but in the doorway, as if she were hesitating on the threshold.

In this fanciful, pleasure-driven place that their common ancestor had built, where painted birds cavorted above them, they stood in their doorways. It was as if a physical force was pulling them together, yet they both advanced but half a step each.

"My lady —" he began, and she at the same moment said, "Sir —" and then she made a gesture to say that he was to speak first. But his mouth was dry. He found he could only offer up his filthy, shirt-sleeved arms and hands in a gesture of apologetic supplication. He would have embraced her if he could. It was what his muscles and his heart were straining to do. She was a stranger, and yet not at all a stranger.

He stood there, looking at her, scouring every detail of her face, regretting he had never laid eyes on her before, feeling the loss of never having seen her as a child, never having had her as a companion in youthful adventures.

At length she spoke.

"I am sorry. I did not mean to come. I ought to have stopped myself, but –" and she threw up her own hands just as he had done.

He nodded. She was like himself: impulsive, driven and confused.

"I am glad you did," he said, and took a step towards her. "I am glad to see you at last."

"You should get back to your work," she said. "Major Vernon..." Felix glanced behind him. Major Vernon was discreetly observing them. "We will have time enough in the future, but she has no time left."

He nodded, and turned and went back in, closing the door behind him.

Major Vernon reached for his notebook.

"She's right," Felix said.

"So?" said Major Vernon glancing at the body.

"She's with child," he said.

"How many months?"

"Four to five, but that's an approximation."

"That adds to the puzzle. Suicide?"

"God forbid!" he exclaimed. Clinical detachment had deserted him. He could only see the tragedy. He swallowed and said, carefully, "Unlikely. That head injury. That is the key to this."

"Then we must go and look at the site when you are done here."

~

When he had finished his examination, Felix went with the

Major to the scene of the discovery of the body. As they left the dairy, there was no sign of Lady Charlotte, which both relieved and disappointed him.

"This way," said Major Vernon, leading him through a fantastical garden of statues and billowing dark yew hedges, until they emerged to face a mass of water, overshadowed by a cliff that dripped with ferns and which was fissured to create the entrance to a cave.

"And you have to go over that bridge to get into the grotto?" he said.

"Yes," said Major Vernon. "And that is where I saw the crushed shells."

"Quite the spot for a tryst," Felix said.

"Exactly," said Major Vernon. "But there are any number of points at which she could have stumbled into the water."

"Or she could have been pushed," said Felix.

"Or held down under the water in the shallows. Drowned by the father of the child."

"Is that what you are thinking?"

"Come and look at this cave. But mind your step as you go."

Felix followed him round the narrow path and across the rattling bridge over the water.

"This is not my idea of a garden," he remarked as they went into the cave.

"No, nor mine," said Major Vernon. "But it is well done, you must concede."

"We are lucky to have those lights in the ceiling," said Felix.

"And I have some candles," said Major Vernon, producing two from his pocket, along with a box of lucifers. He handed one to Felix and struck a lucifer to light it. "Now, what are we looking for? Blood?"

"Blood," Felix said, and together they began to examine the walls of the cave.

"Mr Carswell," called the Major, "is this not...?"

Felix took his hand lens from his trouser pocket and went to look at what the Major had discovered. A patch of dark, dried matter was staining the rubble wall, at about the height of the victim's head.

"Yes, possibly blood," said Felix, handing his candle to the Major. He needed his hands free to get a knife and take a sample to examine under the microscope. "And do we have spatters?" he went on, glancing to the right and left of the stain. "Yes, we do. Look, sir, there – that might be consistent with the back of the head cracking against the rock with some force."

"Not a fall, then," said Major. "Someone, in a quarrel, accidentally pushing her back, so that she collided with the wall, or more deliberately taking her by the shoulders and smashing her head. Which is quite a different matter. What we can establish is that, with reasonable certainty, she was not alone. She could not have sustained such an injury alone."

"No," said Felix. "There is too much force involved. I need to make a record of those spatter patterns and get this sample."

"There is shell in the mortar here," Major Vernon remarked. "Just like the white shell you found. You'd better get a sample of that too."

Felix nodded and set to work.

Chapter Six

After Felix had recorded as much of the evidence in the cave as he could, they retraced their steps through the Italian maze to the dairy. He wanted to look again at the head injury in the light of what they had seen, but as they passed under the faux-Gothic arch, they were met by the sight of a covered stretcher being loaded into a hearse.

"What the –?" he said, turning to Major Vernon.

"That will be on Mr Haine's – the coroner's – instructions. How regrettably efficient of them."

"I haven't even begun!" Felix said. He would have sprinted over to stop them, but Major Vernon laid his hand on his arm.

"Let's go and present our credentials civilly – that will help your cause. If I'm not mistaken, that is Mr Haines and Sir Arthur in the barouche."

Felix nodded. Major Vernon had a way of getting what he wanted in the most unpromising circumstances – it was best to trust to his judgement on such occasions.

"It's a shame we look so dusty," Major Vernon said with a smile, putting his coat back on. They had been working in their shirtsleeves in the cave. "Holt will be ashamed of me." Felix hauled his own coat on and they set out to tackle the two gentlemen in the barouche.

"Major Vernon," said one of them, a gentleman with iron-coloured hair and the ruddy complexion of a countryman. "Thank you for your communications. It was fortunate that you were to hand in the first instance. I did not know that you were a guest at Holbrook."

"I am not, sir. I am staying at Stanegate," Major Vernon

said.

"This is Mr Haines, the coroner," Sir Arthur said.

Major Vernon made a respectful bow to the coroner, who looked to Felix like the sort of man who would quibble with his cook for putting too much butter on the bread.

"And this is?" Sir Arthur went on, with a gesture towards Felix. There was something in his voice that suggested he had guessed who he was, and Felix felt piqued by it.

"Forgive me, yes, of course; Sir Arthur, Mr Haines – may I present Mr Carswell. My colleague at Northminster."

"Ah yes, your surgeon," said Haines, in a raspy voice that one could grate cheese on. "A Scotsman, yes?"

"Yes, sir, indeed he is."

Felix made his bow and grinned like an idiot, but held his tongue, not trusting himself to speak.

"Don't you have some connection to Lord Rothborough?" said Sir Arthur.

"My father has charge of a parish on Lord Rothborough's Scottish estate," Felix said, with care.

"That isn't what I had heard," said Haines, with such insolence that Felix was tempted to snatch the whip from the coachman and strike him with it.

"About this business, if we may?" Major Vernon said, indicating the hearse.

"An accident, one must suppose," Sir Arthur said.

"Drowning is, in the main," said Mr Haines.

Felix could hold his tongue no longer.

"The circumstances and the condition of the corpse suggest otherwise. As the first medical man to see her, I would strongly recommend that the inquest be adjourned until a full post-mortem can be performed. Time is of the essence."

"And you would like the job and the fee, I dare say?" Sir Arthur said.

"I do not care a whit for the fee," said Felix. "I am only interested in getting to the truth."

"I suppose you need not care," said Haines. "After all, you have the rents from Ardenthwaite. A nice gift that is for the son of a poor Scots clergyman, I should say. That is the case, isn't it, young man, that you have title to the place? No doubt, you'll be putting up for Parliament soon enough. This doctoring of yours is just a pastime. But don't you think that we will let you have the seat for the say-so. Your 'connection' may think he can buy the votes of the Ardenthwaite tenants, but good Sir Robert will be out of his tomb and haunting them if they try and vote for a godless Whig, I can tell you that for a fact!" He punched a bony finger towards Felix.

"Mr Haines, if we might deal with the matter in hand," Major Vernon said. "The inquest?"

"Tomorrow at ten, at The Golden Lion in Market Craven," said Haines.

"We will be there, of course," said Major Vernon. "As will Lord Rothborough."

"That won't be necessary," said Sir Arthur. "One of my men will give a report and that will be sufficient for a verdict of accidental death, which is the most likely case here. The only other sensible possibility is that she was a mad woman who drowned herself. Better we record accidental death, Mr Haines, and let the poor creature have a decent burial."

"And let her murderer think he can get away with it?" Felix burst out. "For if this isn't murder, then –"

"The circumstances are ambiguous," said Major Vernon. "This young woman may have been brutally attacked – that needs to be established, and if it is, then surely it is in the public interest that we discover who might be responsible?"

"We, Major Vernon?" said Sir Arthur. "I do not think this is your responsibility. This is not Northminster!"

"Forgive me – that was force of habit. However, may I at least offer my services as a neighbour? Mr Carswell and I have already begun to gather some useful evidence. Let me at least brief the officer you have put in charge of the investigation.

That can do no harm, surely?"

"I really cannot see the need for it, unless you wish to set all my men on chasing about the district looking for phantoms? This is not Northminster, Major Vernon, my establishment does not run to such luxuries as yours. A silly woman, a servant, a nobody, has drowned herself. The kindest thing we can do is let it be recorded as an accident so she may be buried before she rots."

Felix glanced at Major Vernon, wondering how he would proceed.

There was a long pause.

Major Vernon scratched his temple and then said, rather quietly, but with a certain steel in his tone: "If your conscience is easy with that, sir, then so be it. But my conscience cannot be easy. This woman has had her life stolen from her in a brutal manner and there is nothing to say that other women in the district may not suffer the same fate. Imagine if you found your daughter in such a condition, gentlemen, and then think how you ought to act!"

"It is not for you to tell me how to act, sir!" said Sir Arthur. "This is not your business! You have already trespassed. You ought to have declined Lord Rothborough's summons to come here in the first place – let your precious conscience think on that, rather than stand there telling me how to run my affairs. Drive on, Peter. We have wasted enough time here."

The barouche pulled off, with the hearse, drawn by a miserable pony, going on behind at a much less smart pace. Major Vernon took off his hat to acknowledge its departure.

"Poor creature," he said. "We shall get to the bottom of this, by hook or by crook, we shall. I need to get back up to the house and you need to get back to Stanegate."

"I'm not riding back in this heat," Felix said. "At least not without something to eat and drink first. There is a tolerable inn in the village at the gates."

"The Peacock, I think it is called," said Major Vernon. "I'll come with you. I need to think a little tactically before I throw myself back into the gilded delights of Holbroke."

"You see what I mean about it then, sir?" said Felix.

"Heavens, yes. At dinner last night we had a dessert that was the ruins of Palmyra in sponge cake. I would have preferred the steward's room with Holt. Speaking of whom –"

There, in the shade of a handsome Spanish chestnut, where their horses were tethered, Holt had made himself comfortable. He was stretched out on the grass, reading.

As they approached he hauled himself up to attention.

"What are you reading, Holt?" said Major Vernon.

"Nicholas Nickleby," said Holt. "It's the grandest thing. Far better than The Pickwick Papers, in my opinion, sir."

"Don't tell me the story," said Major Vernon. "I've only just begun it."

"No, sir, of course not. Shouldn't dream of spoiling it for you."

~

The Peacock was a comfortable, unpretentious and respectable establishment, cool and pleasant on a hot summer's day. The front door opened directly onto the parlour, and there Felix found James Bodley, Lord Rothborough's man, sitting eating bread and cheese with a woman who looked like the landlady. On seeing him, they stopped eating and stood up.

"Mr Bodley," he said, slightly surprised at this show of respect.

"Master Felix," Bodley said with a nod. "His Lordship did mention you would be hereabouts today. And you must be Major Vernon, sir?" The Major nodded.

The woman came over to inspect Felix.

"Goodness me!" she said. "I haven't seen you, sir, since you were a tiny thing. That summer before you went up to Scotland it was. And look at you now! And the image of his Lordship! My, my!"

"This is Mrs Taylor," said Bodley, "my sister. She and her husband keep the house here."

"I used to work up at the big house," put in Mrs Taylor. "Now, what is it you gentleman wish? I've a lovely cold fowl pie if you're hungry. It's a favourite of his Lordship's."

"That sounds excellent," said Major Vernon. "And if we might have a jug of beer and some water to wash in?"

"Certainly, sir," she said. "The private parlour is just this way. It is where Lord Rothborough always sits when he is so kind as to visit us. It has a nice view of the garden."

"Thank you," said Major Vernon. "My servant Holt is outside with our horses – perhaps you could see he gets what he needs as well?"

"I'll send the boy," said Mrs Taylor.

"And if we might borrow Mr Bodley for a few minutes," said Major Vernon. "Your master may have told you why we are here, Mr Bodley."

"That poor dead woman, yes," Bodley said.

"I have a few questions for you."

"This way, if you please," said Mrs Taylor, and she led them from the tap room, across a flagged passageway and into a neatly furnished room with a large map of the Holbroke Estate hanging on the wall, which at once absorbed Major Vernon's attention.

"So, sir, what was it you wanted to ask me?" asked Bodley.

"Forgive me," said Major Vernon, turning from the map. "A map is always a great aid in such cases as this." He took out his notebook. "I gather from Lady Charlotte that Lady Warde and her maid have been staying with the family since the beginning of June. First at Lady Rothborough's house in

Sussex, and then here."

"Yes, sir, that is about it."

"Now, I know you are often away with your master, but I imagine you have had a chance to see quite a lot of Miss Jones, at dinner with the other servants, and so on?"

"Yes, a fair bit, I suppose," said Bodley.

"What was your impression of her?"

Bodley thought for a moment.

"Well, sir, that's an interesting question. As lady's maids go, I should say she was not the usual type. Of course, she was not in the first rank, sir, if you get my meaning, not like her Ladyship's maid, Miss Le Roche, and a person like Miss Le Roche is a clever, elegant woman, and interesting to talk to. Most of the other lady's maids are in her pattern – a lady likes a servant who is cheerful and full of news but always knows her place. It's a delicate position to hold, and it takes a particular type of person, and usually they are grand company for us downstairs. But Miss Jones was reserved. Quiet and kept herself to herself. But given her employer is a lady in reduced circumstances and not young, I suppose it seemed right enough. She wasn't really one of us, if I can say that."

"Do you know if she had any particular friendships? Or a suitor?"

"No," he said shaking his head. "They all sit together, the lady's maids, and do their sewing, in Mrs Hope's sitting room – she's the housekeeper, and it's quite a sight – for they are as pretty as they come, and a lively bunch, and I sometimes stop there to get a cup of tea, and perhaps to ask them to do a bit of mending for me, for there are some jobs only a woman's hands can do, and – well, she'd be there, but she wouldn't be in the heart of it. I never saw her exchanging confidences with any of them, or giving one of the men the eye, if you know what I mean."

Major Vernon nodded.

"And the night she vanished – two nights ago, she was at

dinner with you as usual, in the steward's room?"

"Yes, sir, she was."

"And do you remember anything particular about that night?"

"Well, now I think of it, yes," he said. "She excused herself. Left early. Said she had a headache and couldn't eat. That was it. And that was the last I saw of her."

"And she would have known that the Pleasure Gardens were out of bounds?"

"Of course," Bodley said. "She's stayed here enough times."

"And is that rule always observed?" Major Vernon said. "By the younger staff, for example?"

"I should say so," said Bodley. "I should hope so, at least. But young people nowadays, they can be flighty."

"But that isn't how you would see Miss Jones?"

"No, no, but women are weak creatures, and easily persuaded. Now there's one or two of the lads, new to the house, who perhaps don't always realise what lucky souls they are to be here, and might be inclined to abuse their good fortune now and then. I could imagine – well, we've a new third footman, a Londoner, who I have my doubts about. He's a splendid looking fellow, of course, but I wouldn't be surprised if he wasn't a dangerous sort. Something about him I don't like at all. Jack Edwardes is his name, sir – you might want to talk to him. He was winking at the housemaids all through prayers this morning. Jack by name, Jack by nature, I fear."

Mrs Taylor came in with a tray of food and beer, along with a maid who brought water and towels.

"Thank you, Mr Bodley, that was helpful," said Major Vernon. "If you think of anything else about Miss Jones, please do tell me."

"Of course, sir. Glad to be of help. I take it that – well, from what his Lordship said to me this morning, that you're here because she's been done away with, poor soul? Is that so, Master Felix?"

"It's not clear what happened yet," said Felix.

"Let us pray it was just an accident," said Mrs Taylor, as she laid the table. "Imagine that poor woman's family, what torments they will suffer if it was not. Her poor mother! I could not bear it if something like that happened to my Annie. She's away in service, you see, sir – she's lady's maid to young Lady Heathfield, down in Lincolnshire. Imagine getting that letter. It does not bear thinking about."

When Bodley and Mrs Taylor had gone, Felix and Major Vernon, having washed the dirt and dust of their morning's work from them, sat down to a meal of cold chicken pie, bread, blue cheese, and a bowl of strawberries, accompanied by a jug of ale.

"How long has Mr Bodley been Lord Rothborough's man, do you suppose?" Major Vernon said.

"Oh, at least twenty-five years," said Felix, draining his glass. "He is an immemorial fixture."

"A footman who winks at housemaids is not necessarily a murderer," Major Vernon remarked. "Though he might be inclined to organise a tryst in a forbidden grotto." He got up from the table and began again to study the detailed map of the estate. "I walked back from the Pleasure Gardens yesterday afternoon. It was a leisurely stroll and it took over half an hour. Now she was last seen by her mistress helping her dress for dinner after seven, and then we can assume she left the house, perhaps to meet someone. But who? Jack the footman wouldn't be able to get away, because he'd be wanted in the dining room to serve dinner."

"So perhaps it wasn't someone from the household that she was intending to meet?" Felix said, coming up and joining him at the map.

"Exactly," said Major Vernon. "It could be anyone, couldn't it? Coming from anywhere. And long gone now, if he has any sense."

"He?"

"In the first instance, I think we could make that small assumption. The father of the child springs to mind."

"You mean she meets him, tells him she's with child and he decides to deal with it, so to speak?"

"It wouldn't be the first time that a man has evaded his responsibilities in such a fashion. And it's an ideal place to carry out such a brutal, pragmatic act, wouldn't you say? She could have screamed all she liked in that cave and no one would have heard anything. And there's the pool there to dispose of the body, creating confusion about the manner of her death."

"That might do as a working hypothesis," said Felix.

"It will have to do," said Giles. "It is all we have at present, thanks to Sir Arthur and Mr Haines!" He shook his head. "We can only hope that common sense and decency will prevail with them tomorrow."

"Yes," said Felix. "But I don't feel very optimistic, given what Haines said about Ardenthwaite. Why on earth does he think I would want to run for Parliament? How dare he make such assumptions about me? What kind of people are these? I think Lord Rothborough has dropped me into a viper's nest. I ought to have known better than to let him –"

"But you said yourself it was a fine house when you saw it."

"Yes, it is," said Felix. "Too fine. Too big. Too significant, it seems."

"You should take ownership. Let your neighbours see who you really are. Perhaps, if it might help, you might like to entertain Mrs Vernon and me there one afternoon? It would make an easy excursion from Stanegate, especially with the weather like this. She likes old houses and it would do you good to practise playing host."

"You're as bad as he is."

"It's not a sentence of transportation," Major Vernon said.

"I know, I know," said Felix. On several occasions they had discussed Ardenthwaite, the property that Lord Rothborough had acquired for him, and the Major's sensible arguments had generally prevailed with him. But after that humiliation from Mr Haines, a mere country coroner, he felt the foundations of his being cut from under him, like a keen axe going through the slender, fragile trunk of a sapling. How could a bastard whore-son ever lay honest claim to a place like Ardenthwaite? It would be presumptuous folly.

And at the same time, an odd fancy sprung up in him, in which he sat in one of those fine old rooms and talked at length with his sister, who might, from time to time, ride over to see him there – no, that was a pernicious fantasy, and he dismissed it carefully, distracting himself by consulting his watch.

"I need to get back. Martinez was quite frail last night when I left him. He isn't a monk, by the by, but a Dominican friar, it seems. I got that much out of him. Found him on his knees. Took all my efforts to get him to rest in bed."

"Some of his countrymen seem to be at Stanegate. They were at the Bower Well," said Major Vernon. "According to Lord Rothborough, they are a sort of government in exile, forced out by a coup. He may have a connection to them."

"Why on earth would they go to Stanegate?"

"Maybe it is more fashionable than we supposed," said Major Vernon. "Certainly the millinery shops are expensive enough. Yes, you had better get back. I have a note for Mrs Vernon here," he said, taking it from his coat pocket. "There was nothing for me from her, I take it?"

"No, sir, I'm sorry."

"There was no reason why she should write," Major Vernon said. "Tell her I will be back as soon as I can. Certainly tomorrow. I am going to interview the household, but I think I will have to cast the net a little wider, soon enough."

Chapter Seven

Lady Charlotte was again waiting to meet him in the great marble entrance hall.

"Mr Carswell, has he –?"

"Gone back to Stanegate, yes," said Giles.

"Ah, good," said Lady Charlotte, although she did not sound happy. "By which I mean, that is for the best."

Giles nodded, sensing her confusion. It seemed best to offer her a distraction.

"Are you still willing to help me, Lady Charlotte?"

"With great pleasure."

"I want to talk to all the lady's maids – Miss Jones' circle, so to speak, although from what Mr Bodley has told me, I am not sure she was 'of' their circle, if you understand me."

"Oh yes, perfectly."

"Now, I have asked for the steward's room to be put at my disposal. I was just on my way there."

"Do you know the way?"

"I was going to get one of the footmen – Henry, I think it is?"

"I can show you."

A large swinging door, upholstered in buff-coloured baize, led to a hallway. Here, a stairwell contained a brass cage suspended by an elaborate mechanism of hooks and pulleys.

"You turn the handle here, and it goes up and down. To fetch the food from the kitchens," Lady Charlotte said. "We used to get Bodley to give us rides in it when we were little, but Mr Grainger, the house steward, would get cross with us."

"Remarkable," said Giles, admiring the mechanism.

"Oh, we have perfected all the arrangements – or rather

my father has. It is a mania with him, after eating so many cold dinners in his friends' houses. One never has cold food here at Holbroke, unless of course it is intended to be so! The trolleys come out of the cage and go straight into the serving room here."

She opened the door to a room that would not have disgraced itself as a kitchen in an ordinary gentleman's house. "And beyond that is the dining room and our breakfast room is just to the side there. It is so convenient and efficient. I don't think I shall ever find a house to match it. Perhaps that is why I am a spinster yet!"

"You could always improve your future husband's house, I suppose."

"He will have to be tolerant," said Lady Charlotte. "And very rich. Quite a rare combination." She began to go down the stairs. "And this is the tunnel and the railway."

"Goodness. More of a crypt than a tunnel, I would say," said Giles.

The steps led into an underground chamber, poorly lit by a few scanty skylights and oil lanterns hanging on hooks. There was a central aisle, with tracks laid in the floor, like those Giles had seen at mines or factories, but instead of the carts there were trolleys set up to carry the dinner trays back and forth, pushed along by a kitchen boy, Giles supposed. To the side, broad archways led to darker areas which were full of lumber. It was efficient, but gloomy.

"Holbroke is full of surprises," he could not help remarking, thinking of the elaborate fancies of the Pleasure Gardens.

"We are the eighth wonder of the world," said Lady Charlotte, rather proudly, as they started off down the central aisle. It was most unjust that the house and all its glories could not pass to her on Lord Rothborough's death, he thought, when she was clearly so fond of it. An entail was an entail, but he could not help thinking that a fairer system ought to prevail. If a young Princess could ascend the throne and become Queen of England, then why should Lady Charlotte not be a Marchioness of Rothborough in her own right?

~

"You have all the women waiting for me, Mrs Hope?" Giles asked the housekeeper.

"Yes, sir."

"Before I begin on that, perhaps you might give me your impressions of Miss Jones?"

"I tell you, it's a shock. She is not the sort you would imagine meeting her end like that – what was she doing there? I cannot think how she could be mixed up in anything that needed the police looking into it. She was so quiet. And she's stayed here quite a few times, and I've never really got to know her. She was not a talker. Some people come and you learn their whole life story in a matter of minutes, but Miss Jones, no. Very odd, now I think about it."

"And the last you saw of her was at the upper servants' dinner that night?"

"Yes, sir. She excused herself before dessert, that's all I remember."

"I should also like to see where Miss Jones was sleeping."

"Of course, sir. That's back in the main house, up in the South Pavilion."

"I shall see that Major Vernon finds it," said Lady Charlotte. "In the meantime, perhaps we might have some tea brought in, and Miss La Roche, if she is ready?"

"Yes, of course, my lady," said Mrs Hope.

The four maids employed by Lady Rothborough and her three daughters were friendly, eager to help, and often quite talkative. They came in one by one, all in turn distressed by the

71

loss of Miss Jones, but none of them able to claim any intimacy with her. Some of them were ashamed by their lack of knowledge, as if they had failed to bring her fully into the circle.

Only one of them, Lady Charlotte's maid, Jane, bold like her mistress, dared to venture a criticism.

"Sometimes I found her a little sly. As if she had secrets she didn't want to share with us, that she was somehow special."

"What gave you that idea?" Giles asked.

"There was a woman in my last place, she thought she was better than all of us because her father was the bastard son of an attorney. So she kept herself to herself, as if we could never be good enough for her. There was something about Miss Jones that made me think of her. It was just a feeling, but I did feel it. You would try your best with her, and it would never be more than a few words, and it wasn't shyness, because there was a way she had of looking at you, as if she were trying to size you up. Does this sound silly, my lady?"

"No, not at all," said Lady Charlotte. She glanced at Giles.

"I think we need to look at her room," he said.

"Oh, I can show you, sir," said Jane. "She sleeps next to me and Agnes."

When Lady Charlotte's maid had gone, and they were alone, Giles said, "This woman is a *tabula rasa*. It takes a great deal of self control to be that self-contained, wouldn't you say?"

"Yes. Unless she was slightly deaf and couldn't hear what people were saying."

"An excellent observation," said Giles. "Let's see what you make of her room."

"You still want me to help you?"

"If I don't get you into trouble," he said. "A second pair of eyes and a different point of view is always useful."

"Then of course," said Lady Charlotte.

Jane took them back through the tunnel, and then upstairs by the back stairs to the South Pavilion where most of the female guests and the Rothborough daughters lodged. The maids, it appeared, found their accommodation nearby in smaller bedrooms, subdivided for the purpose. Eliza Jones had been put in a long slot of a room, its window divided by a partition wall, on the other side of which lay Jane and Agnes' room. The walls were papered with a faded pattern of oak leaves and suggested that this might once have been a grand room, but the plain and modern furniture told another story. A deal table and chair, a jug and bowl, a narrow bedstead and the woman's own box were the limit of it. On the wall a few hooks held her clothes. There was a Bible on the bed. Giles examined the flyleaf, hoping for a revealing inscription. There was nothing. He shook it over the bed, but nothing fluttered out.

"Let's have a look at her box," he said.

"Won't it be locked?" said Lady Charlotte. She tried the lid without success.

"There are ways around that," said Giles, taking his keys from his pocket. He had added the skeleton key to his own bundle of keys, thinking it was safest in his care. "This is a lock-picker's friend," he said, showing her the key. "I confiscated it from a rogue."

"What a useful item," said Lady Charlotte. "I should not like to see that in less responsible hands, though."

"No," he said, gently easing it into the lock and agitating it a little until he felt the lock yield. "There we are!"

As would have been expected, the box contained clothing and folded linen. There was also a sewing box and one or two unremarkable books.

"What do you think of her clothes? Anything out of the ordinary?" Giles asked, as Lady Charlotte looked through them.

"No, nothing. Very plain, but suitable. Not her mistress'

cast-offs – but I have never seen Lady Warde wear anything but her weeds."

"Stop a moment – may I see that one?" Giles said, catching sight of something that intrigued him. Lady Charlotte handed him the dull blue flannel petticoat with some surprise. He examined it, and his suspicions were confirmed. "Well, my goodness. Look at this." And he showed her the deep pocket formed by the hem of the petticoat, fixed at intervals by a button to stop it opening. "Can you guess what that is for?"

"It's very large, for an ordinary pocket."

"Quite! You could hide anything you liked in there, couldn't you?" he said. "That's why they are popular with the light-fingered sorority – what we have here is a thief's petticoat."

"No!" exclaimed Lady Charlotte. "Surely not?"

"Miss Jones clearly had specialist knowledge of the trade. I've seen these before. I have seen a silver teapot stashed in one of these. Some of the better shops in Northminster could not understand how things were disappearing. Turned out that a woman called Lucy Peele, apparently a respectable middle-class woman, was coming in and looking at trifles. She would then stash something away when the shopman's back was turned. Obviously, that's a ruse that takes some practice to perfect. I wonder how Miss Jones learned about such things."

"Are you implying she might have had a criminal past?"

"Or a criminal present," Giles said. "Staying in so many grand houses, running in and out of rooms which are full of tempting bibelots. A silver spoon from the morning breakfast tray here, a snuff box there..."

"That is a rather disturbing thought."

"It is just a possibility. But given that she was so self-effacing and that no one knows anything about her – well, that is a known criminal strategy, among successful criminals, that is. They learn to be practically invisible. This is the first interesting thing we have found about her, wouldn't you say,

Lady Charlotte?"

She did not answer for a moment.

"But to steal, from the very people who had been so kind to her mistress?" she said. "It seems inconceivable."

"If Lady Warde is effectively an object of charity," Giles said, "which you implied to me the other day, then I doubt she pays her maid very well. If at all. Eliza may have got into bad habits somewhere and was using them to supplement a rather paltry income. Thinking of her old age, perhaps? Or possibly the more immediate future?" he added, thinking of the dead woman's swollen belly. "I know it may be hard for you to imagine, when your people are so well looked after during their employment and in their old age."

"No, I see your point," she said. "How sad it is, to think of her doing that."

"If she did," said Giles. "After all, there is no sign of anything here that should not be here. But then she may have stashed it elsewhere, or possibly she has already sold it on."

"But how would one do that?" said Lady Charlotte.

"It's the same sort of knowledge that comes with the petticoat," Giles said. "There are people who make a trade of buying stolen goods – but you need to know who they are and where they might be found." He glanced around the room. "I think we need to talk to Lady Warde again," he said. "We need a precise record of their exact movements over the last year. I hope she is one of those ladies who keeps a detailed memorandum book!"

Lady Charlotte picked up a black silk dress and shook out the creases from it.

"I think this would do for her burial," she said. As she straightened the sleeve, something fell from the deep cuffs onto the white counterpane: a dark brown mess of dried leaves. "What is that?" she said. Giles stepped forward and examined it. "Is that tea?"

"Tea," she affirmed. She pinched up a little between her

fingers and sniffed it. "Most definitely."

Chapter Eight

"And this is *Dido and Aeneas*, by Rubens," said Lady Charlotte.

They were standing in the Picture Gallery, a room of magnificent proportions hung with a series of Old Masters. They had been walking through the great reception rooms in search of Lady Warde, but she could not be found, and Lady Charlotte had fallen into the role of hostess, pointing out the treasures of the house to him.

"I think it is my favourite," she said. "The colours, the draperies, the landscape, it is all so beautifully done."

It struck him as an unusual choice for a young woman, indeed a brave one, but the men were handsome and the women had a fleshy beauty and elegance, in their sensual déshabillé.

"It is very well done," he said, enjoying the tenderness of the sleeping couple in their bower. It was a vision of harmonious love as well as nature perfectly realised. "The dogs at the bottom there – they are beautifully painted, the fur in particular."

He bent down to see what painter's trick had caused such a life-like effect.

The door opened behind them and he glanced over his shoulder to see Mr Syme coming in.

"Ah, here you are, Lady Charlotte," he said. "Lady Rothborough has sent me to find you."

"You have found me now," she said. "What of it?"

Syme did not reply but came up and stood next to them as they looked at the Rubens.

"This may be considered by some to be great art," Syme said after a moment. "But surely, in this day, we must consider the effect of such work on public morals? This is, in effect, a celebration of sin." His tone was mild and reasonable. Such people always were, Giles thought; that was the danger of them. In that fashion they were able to say things that were outrageous. "Very degrading. I am sure you agree with me, Major Vernon."

"I am not sure I do," Giles said. "It is a beautiful piece, and nothing so beautiful can be really dangerous."

Syme frowned.

"That painting was created not to instruct, but to arouse. It is not a suitable object for young people to look at. I fear for the morals of the servants who polish these floors."

"But they don't know the subject of it," Lady Charlotte said. "They only see a pair of sweethearts, asleep in each others arms. An old married couple, perhaps?" She shot Giles a mischievous glance.

"I think they see a great deal more than that," said Mr Syme.

"Look how well that dog is painted," Giles said. "This is a celebration of God's creation, surely?"

"That scarcely excuses the rest of it," said Mr Syme. "I would prefer that it were not so prominently on display."

"Perhaps you would like to rearrange the furniture in my mother's drawing room as well, Mr Syme?" said Lady Charlotte, and walked off down the gallery. "Now, you must look at Master Rembrandt – a self portrait, Major Vernon. And you too, Mr Syme. Not even you could object to it! It will do us all good."

The Rembrandt was indeed powerful: a sobering, honest portrait of a man in early old age, who knew his sins and had learnt to live with the burden of them.

Giles tore his gaze from it – for it had a sober, compulsive quality to it – and observed his companions as they studied the painting: Lady Charlotte, in all the glow and lustre of her youth, and Syme who was not much older; their faces, smooth, well-made and quite untouched by time. Giles wondered what Rembrandt's brush would have made of them, or for that matter of his own face. How would it feel to be the subject of that merciless gaze?

Syme broke the silence.

"This terrible business with Lady Warde's maid – how are your enquiries progressing?"

"Slowly but steadily," said Giles. "As is usually the case with these things."

"I understand from Lord Rothborough that you are making quite a career of this sort of work."

"Unfortunately, yes. Although I would prefer it if people did not break the Fifth Commandment."

"My father says you have a genius for it," said Lady Charlotte.

"That is too extravagant," said Giles.

"And that you ought to think about using your talents on a wider stage," she went on.

"I think not," said Giles.

"I think so," said Lady Charlotte. "What a deterrent to murderers you would be, Major Vernon, if they knew of your existence and your powers. Why, they would stay their hands!"

"There are plenty of far better reasons for murderers to stay their hands," said Giles. "The noose, for one, but that does not seem to stop them, does it?"

"The only real deterrent," Syme said, "is a vision of the Lord's redeeming power, and the absolute fear of Hell itself."

"A man will murder because he must murder, I think," Giles said. "It is a sort of compulsion. That is what is so interesting about it."

"Interesting?" Syme said. "Sir, I cannot believe you find it interesting. Deplorable, yes, but –"

"It is like any problem in human affairs," said Giles. "Our curiosity must be aroused to get the problem solved. Medical men seek out the cause of disease in order to prevent it and they are moved not just by a wish to put an end to that particular branch of human suffering but because the problem is there. It exists to be cracked, like a nut."

"One might say crime is a disease of sorts, then?" said Lady Charlotte.

"Yes, certainly," Giles said. "And murder is a particular disease, with symptoms and causes to be investigated, in order to get at the truth of it. Why one man will murder, and another not."

"And what of their souls?" said Syme.

"That is your business, Mr Syme," said Giles. Syme nodded sagely in a manner that did not suit his youth.

"I have read of several cases," he said, "of men – hardened, wicked, violent men – who have realised, on the eve of their hanging, at the last moment, that with utter submission to the love of God, they can be saved from the torments of Hell. As a result they have opened their hearts entirely to God and they have faced death with equanimity and peace. A sort of cure, you might say, Major Vernon? A miracle, indeed, that He shows Himself to them with such clarity!"

Giles hoped that Syme would soon learn not to sermonise at every opportunity. He could quite understand how he had managed to irritate Lord Rothborough.

"Perhaps you could tell me, this, Mr Syme," said Lady Charlotte. "Can a man who has lived a good life all his life, and done good to his neighbours and never broken a commandment, who has not been moved in the spirit in such a fashion, who cannot feel it in his heart, will he have a place in Heaven? A Jew, perhaps, or a Roman Catholic?"

"It is doubtful, Lady Charlotte," said Syme.

Lady Charlotte looked as though she were about to say something fierce in response to this, but she turned away, silently.

Syme was about to say something more, when to Giles' relief the double doors at the end opened and Lord

Rothborough came in, attended by a stranger and a pair of the liveried footmen.

"Set yourself up in here, Edgar," Lord Rothborough was saying to the stranger. "If the light suits."

"The light suits perfectly, my lord," said Edgar, looking around him. "And what a setting!"

"You will be working in our hall of the great Masters. I hope that doesn't put you off your stride!"

"Oh, I think not, my lord!" said Edgar.

"Charlotte, my dear, this is Mr John Edgar, the shadowcutter. Edgar, my eldest daughter, Lady Charlotte, Major Vernon, and Mr Syme."

Edgar, a slight, demure, dandy of a man in a wine-red velvet coat, made an elaborate bow. There was a distinct flavour of the stage about him. He had lace ruffles on his shirt cuffs and carefully curled and pomaded hair; on his fingers were rings set with stones of such size it was obvious that they were paste. But they glittered impressively, none the less, as he flourished his hand in his bow.

"You found him, Papa!" exclaimed Lady Charlotte, clapping her hands. "Maria will be so pleased."

"It is a surprise for her," said Lord Rothborough. "A late birthday present. Edgar here was meant to come earlier but he was too busy – on his wedding journey, no less!"

"That is an excuse we must forgive," said Lady Charlotte. "All good wishes, Mr Edgar, and to Mrs Edgar!"

"She will be honoured, my lady, very honoured," Edgar said with another bow.

Lady Rothborough now entered with Lady Maria and Lady Augusta. On seeing the stranger in the velvet coat, Lady Maria squeaked with delight and kissed her father. It was the best surprise she had ever had, she declared. When Edgar offered to demonstrate his skills by first cutting pictures of her two little spaniels, her enthusiasm grew boundless.

All in all, it was an impressive performance. In less than a minute he had cut a lively outline on black paper of the first little dog, and he had done the second while the young lady was still exclaiming over the first.

"Who next?" said Lord Rothborough. "A human subject this time, I think?"

"What interesting faces you all have, ladies and gentlemen!" said Edgar, looking them over. "Oh, I am going to enjoy myself, my lord. Such beauty and distinction! What a great privilege." He stalked up to Giles. "The military gentleman – well, you, sir, are a fine example of your type, if you will permit me to say. A more handsome profile I have not seen in many a year."

"I can see why you are successful, Mr Edgar," Giles said. "You have realised the great truth that all officers cannot resist a compliment about their looks. We are all deluded peacocks."

"I think, Mr Syme, that you should sit first," said Lady Charlotte. "If you don't consider it improper to have your likeness taken."

"How could it be improper?" Lady Maria said. "Yes, Mr Syme, do sit."

"Of course, Lady Maria, anything to oblige you."

So Syme was led off and made to pose for Edgar.

"Lady Rothborough, I wonder, do you know where Lady Warde is?" Giles asked, sitting down beside the Marchioness.

"Poor creature – she really is not well," said Lady Rothborough. "I think she feels the loss of her maid deeply."

Mourning someone she seemed to know nothing about, Giles thought. Perhaps in the way one feels the loss of a beloved animal. After all, how well did any of them know their servants? Was he wrong to judge her for knowing so little? That she felt the loss strongly meant that she had affection for the girl. At the same time, he wondered when it would be possible to question her properly again. He did not particularly want to be idling here, watching young ladies exclaim over silhouettes, when there was a murderer to be identified.

Edgar had finished his portrait of Syme and Lady Augusta was examining it.

"Oh, Mr Syme, that is a distinguished likeness. You must send it to your mother and sister, they will be pleased with that," Lady Augusta said. "How clever you are, Mr Edgar!"

"I wondered if I might instead present it to you, my lady, as a keepsake, and as a token of my great gratitude for all your kindness?" Syme said.

Giles thought he saw Lady Augusta blush. Was there something going on there?

"Oh, thank you," Lady Augusta said. "Thank you. I shall put it in my keepsake book."

"I understand you will be with us for a few more days, Major Vernon," Lady Rothborough said to Giles, "because of this business."

"It is very good of you and Lord Rothborough to entertain me in these circumstances."

"You have left your wife behind at Stanegate?"

"Yes, she is taking the waters."

"Would she like to join us?" said Lady Rothborough. "You would prefer her to be here, I am sure."

Giles did not have a chance to answer as Lady Maria now interrupted to beg her mother to come and sit for the miracle-worker. Mr Syme was insistent too, and Lady Rothborough agreed.

Giles was glad not to be obliged to give his answer at once. For a start, he did not know what Laura would make of such an invitation. She was not, in his opinion, entirely ready for general society. Although there was only a family party at Holbroke, with the addition of Mr Syme and Lady Warde, the grandeur and formality of it all might prove difficult for her to negotiate safely. She was like a nervous horse, not quite ready for the road. It would probably be better if she did not come.

However, he sensed she might resent it terribly to discover he had declined such an invitation without consulting her. They were now beyond the stage when he, necessarily, made all the decisions about such things. She had her own mind and opinions that needed expression. But whether she was as yet capable of making the right decisions was another matter entirely. He had managed it badly at the Bower Well that morning in saying she must come home with him. She had lashed out at him for being high-handed. It was too much to expect she would always concur and obey. She would be more likely to insist on being allowed to go and then, if thwarted, throw herself into one of those dreadful passages of melancholic withdrawal, which had in the beginning presaged the whole terrible decline of her spirits.

Could such a visit be managed as an experiment? Perhaps Lady Charlotte would make a friend of her? But that would be unfair on Lady Charlotte, who was burdened enough with the business of being a useful young woman. Laura might not like her and she might not like Laura. In her present state, Laura was often difficult to like. When she chose to let the sun of her nature shine on her companions it was dazzling and delightful, but the weather was often bad, despite the huge progress she had made. Mr Carswell was the recipient of the best of it, and there lay another problem.

"I hate to interrupt," said Lady Charlotte, "when you are so lost in thought."

She was smiling at him in such a way that he knew he should send for Laura at once, to remind her he was married. Lady Charlotte was too bewitching a thing, too dangerous. Why had her mother not filled the house with marriageable young bucks to distract her and her sisters? What on earth was she doing playing at piety with the odious Syme instead of looking to the future happiness of her daughters?

"I'm afraid I must go and write some letters," he said.

"Can I not persuade you to sit – or perhaps that should be stand – for Edgar?" she said. He shook his head.

"I must go, forgive me."

She assented with a gracious nod.

His leaving the room did not pass unnoticed. As he was making his way down the great gallery, he heard Lord Rothborough calling out to him.

"Vernon, if I might have a word?"

"Of course, my lord."

"Forgive me – I meant to speak to you earlier, but the silhouette man got in my path. He is a pleasant amusement, don't you think? I am going to have him stay and take all the servants' likenesses. A clever fellow, indeed! But I digress. Might I ask how your enquiry is going?"

"Steadily enough. We did, however, have an interesting meeting with Sir Arthur and Mr Haines this morning – it seems I am not welcome here, and as for Mr Carswell, Mr Haines was quite vehement."

"I am not surprised. He's a presumptuous bumpkin. He tried to buy Ardenthwaite, tried to outbid me for it in fact! My apologies, I should have warned you he is difficult. So, the inquest?"

"Is liable to be a farce. The body has already been removed. There is scant hope that Mr Carswell will be allowed to perform a post-mortem. The evidence is pointing at manslaughter, at the very least, but it may fall on deaf ears. I will attempt to present my case, of course, but I wonder if it might be better if they were left to investigate after their own fashion and I went back to –"

"That is nonsense, Vernon, and you know it. Justice will not be served if you abandon this business now. And I don't suppose your conscience would allow you to do that anyway."

"Naturally I would like to take the matter to the end. And I will do all I can, of course, but it may be difficult."

"It strikes me," said Lord Rothborough, "that is the only thing we can do, in the circumstances. Now if this was some lesser matter, I would say, yes, step back, let them do it, watch them flounder and fail, then do the job yourself and show how much better equipped you are for the task. If one was pragmatic, that would be a course open to one. And it would achieve a great end – which is to demonstrate that the county force is in desperate need of reform, or perhaps ought to be absorbed into the superior urban force. However, this is the wilful murder of a young woman, and time is of the essence. We cannot afford to let others fail."

"Do you think that desirable, ultimately?" Giles said, taking in the implications of his speech. "That the Northminster force take over the county force?"

"Yes, very much so, and I think you do too."

"It isn't something I had much considered, to tell you the truth."

"Have you not?" said Lord Rothborough, as if surprised. "You certainly ought to. Put it on your agenda, Major Vernon! And consider yourself for the post of its future chief. This is not a time for false modesty. Action is required."

Giles went up to his room, and with the Duke on the writing table, he sat and tried to write his notes and his letters. But his mind felt clouded.

He no longer felt like the great organiser, burning with reforming, administrative zeal, concerned with public order and the creation of a new institution. His mind had begun to travel down different paths. He had discovered the fascinating puzzles made by human wickedness. He was beginning to learn the strange and secret language of the deviant and the criminal, and to imagine, by extrapolation, who these people were, why they acted as they did.

Why had an unknown person smashed that poor girl's head against the walls of the cave? He could picture the crime in his mind, with devastating clarity, but there were still a thousand unanswered questions to which he longed to find the answers. It was not just a matter of justice and doing the best for a dead woman. It was more than that. It gave him a shameful but visceral thrill to know that he had it in his power to break the apparently unbreakable code. Nothing, he realised, had ever filled him with such satisfaction as the pursuit of murderers.

He sat back in his chair, a little astonished at the conclusion to which he had come. To have found, at the age of forty, what he had been put on Earth to do. He was not to be a soldier, nor an administrator, but this strange beast: a man who hunted murderers.

Chapter Nine

Felix was relieved to find Martinez's condition had not significantly degraded since his visit the previous evening. He had been much cheered by a long visit from Mr Bryce, who was still at his bedside when Felix arrived.

"Managed to persuade him that rest was the best thing for him, though it was a struggle," Bryce said, speaking to Felix alone on the landing before he left. "He is full of notions, and doesn't seem to see what a state he is in. I suppose for a young man it's hard to accept that this might be..." he shrugged. "Poor gent!"

"If he is careful, he might prolong his life," Felix said. "But it is a gamble, even in the best circumstances, and these are not. If he were at home and with his family around him, the prognosis might be slightly more cheerful."

"He shall have to make do with us," said Bryce, "and Major Vernon."

"Just us," said Felix. "Major Vernon has been called away on business."

"That is a pity," he said. "I had better get home. I shall come back this evening. Mrs Bryce has been making baked custard for him. Give him a bit of strength, maybe?"

"A good idea," said Felix.

When Bryce had gone, Felix sent the nurse away and made a thorough examination of Martinez.

"I am glad you are managing to rest better. Is there anything else you need to make you more comfortable?"

Martinez managed a wan smile and shook his head.

"I am more than comfortable."

Perhaps because he is used to the austerities of a friar's

cell, Felix thought.

"It is a pity there is no pretty view from this window," said Felix. "Might you think of moving lodgings? It would do you good."

"I have pretty views in my head," Martinez said. "When I close my eyes, I see the gardens of my mother's house. That will do for me. And this place is secret, which is..."

"Secret?"

"I need to be away from prying eyes, from those people who –" He sighed. "You are wondering why I am here, I am sure?"

"Yes, but you must not speak if it tires you," Felix said, noting the struggle in his tone.

"I want to speak of it. I must, since it is clear to me that my time is limited. God and his angels are calling me – that is true, is it not?"

"Your condition is grave, but with care, anything is possible. Such cases, when the individual has the determination to go on, often defy expectations."

"But they still die?"

"Yes, I regret so," Felix said.

"Do not trouble yourself, dear sir, for this is a truth I have known a long time. I have carried this burden of my infirmity and its meaning with me for some time. This is why I am here, to see to something important before it is too late. And it is growing late for me, which is why I must speak."

His voice was a faint whisper now, and Felix leaned forward to hear him better. As he did, Martinez took his hand and pulled it against his chest. He stared at Felix with his glassy, sunken eyes, and said, "I pray to sweet Jesus, God the Father and the Holy Spirit that all my sins will be forgiven me! That I will be spared the eternal torments of hell-fire."

Felix felt that these statements implied that some sort of confession was ahead and that it was not for him to hear it. He was not a priest; he could offer no consoling words, no benediction nor absolution.

"I have done many foolish things, many wicked things and I will pay my dues for them in purgatory. But then, I do believe, one day, I shall be admitted to the sight of the angels and of Our Lord. But for now, I must contemplate my last worldly actions, and I cannot die until justice is done. There is a great wrong to be righted. I would have acted long ago had not my timidity and this wretched body of mine prevented it. For a long time the matter was not clear, and when it was made known to me I scarcely believed it, but it is the truth and it must at all costs be made known."

His voice was fading fast, and his breathing was exhibiting a dangerous rattle. Felix was worried that if he spoke any more he would bring on a spasm.

"Don't speak any more," he said. "Find a little more strength before you go on."

Felix made him rest back on the pillows for a while, and sat there, but it was no good. His breathing grew agitated and soon he was in the grip of a violent spasm. The basin was stained with blood and the man was in clear torment which Felix could do nothing to relieve. It only had to be endured.

When finally he was free of the spasm, his mouth began to form words.

"It must wait, sir, it must wait," Felix insisted.

Martinez, who really had no choice, acquiesced, and allowed himself to be directed. Felix wiped him down with a wet rag, for he was sticky with fever, and he fell into a languid, exhausted state which might soon lead to sleep. Felix mixed up a little brandy and opium in a wine glass and was about to give him a spoonful or two to speed the process, when Martinez pushed his hand away.

"Dona Blanca," he said, in the faintest whisper. "Dona Blanca. Tell her that..." Then he began coughing again, and this time so violently that there was no controlling it.

Within moments it was clear enough this was more than

spasm. He was in the grip of a life-threatening cardiac attack, of such intensity that his already weakened frame had no power to resist it. In less than a minute he was insensible in Felix's arms – he had reached out to support and assist him, but it was in vain. He checked frantically for any signs of life, but the pulse was gone, the heartbeat too.

His shirt soaked through with the man's blood, Felix laid him back on the bed, and checked again for life signs. The man was dead. There was no doubt about it.

He staggered up from the bed and looked down at the wretched body on the bed, his nightshirt soiled, his face stained with blood and vomit.

No prayers, no priest – for such a man it was surely a horrible death, to go unshriven to the grave. Felix cleaned his face again, closed his eyes, straightened his limbs and then pulled the sheet over him. He felt sick and miserable. He had failed to help him. It was a wretched end.

He took the rosary beads and cross from the table by the bed and laid them on Martinez's chest, feeling woefully ignorant of the correct forms in such a case.

He went to the window and opened it as wide as he could, thinking of an old story about allowing the souls of the dead to escape. Outside, the late afternoon air was no cooler than the stuffy air of the room and there was no breeze to carry Martinez's soul anywhere. The man was trapped there forever, in a body that no longer worked, in a dirty attic, with his great secret only half-told to someone who was not capable of understanding it. He looked back and expected to see him standing there in his nightshirt, a new-made ghost, whispering at him for ever more: "Dona Blanca. Dona Blanca..."

~

He did not get back to the Vernons' lodgings for another two hours. Fortunately Mr Bryce returned promptly, as he had promised, with the egg custard. Being a local man, he was able to direct Felix to a reputable undertaker and found a woman to lay out Martinez's body. The sullen landlady became slightly less sullen, and allowed a small private dining parlour on the ground floor to be used for the body to rest until the burial. Felix and Bryce carried Martinez down between them, so that he could be laid out. The woman who had come to do the job was a homely-looking, tender creature, younger than the women who usually practised that trade. She explained she had taken over from her mother who was too old for it now. Felix felt some relief in leaving him with her – her kindness was palpable.

He walked back smoking a cheroot, which he reluctantly threw away before he went into the house. Mrs Vernon shared her husband's prejudice against them.

Sukey Connolly came upstairs from the basement at the sound of the door.

"How is Mrs Vernon?"

"Resting. We went for a long walk and this heat tired her out. What happened to you?" she said, taking in his disordered appearance.

"My Spaniard died."

"Oh, heavens," she said, and crossed herself. "Are you all right?"

He nodded. There was a part of him that would have thrown his arms about Sukey and wept on her shoulder. There was something about her, so straightforward and ridiculously wise, that he was tempted. "I must get clean."

"I'll get you some water."

"Thank you," he said, heading towards the stairs.

"Go up quietly," she said. "You don't want to disturb her."

It was a good point. The stairs were constructed badly

and it was all too easy to hear anyone going up or down them. So he went as quietly as he could and into his little room which lay on the half-landing between the first and second storey. The Vernons' rooms were on the next flight up. He closed his door gently and sat down on the bed to take off his riding boots. As he did so, he noticed another posy of flowers had been put in the room, this time in a small jug on the mantel. They were pale pink wild roses, already drooping miserably in their confinement, dying a slow death. From Mrs Vernon, he supposed, with a sigh. He would ask Sukey to take them away when she came in with the fresh water.

There was already some water in the jug on the washstand, at least enough to begin with, and so he began to strip off his clothes.

"Not yet, Sukey, I'm not decent!" he said, now quite naked, but the door continued to open. He turned and saw that Mrs Vernon, dressed only in her shift, was standing with her back against the door. She had slipped in like a cat.

He grabbed the shirt which he had just thrown to the ground and held it against him, in all its bloody magnificence. It was the only thing covering him.

"Oh my God, are you hurt?" she said, seeing the blood. "What happened?" She took a step towards him, and he retreated, protecting his nakedness with the shirt.

"N... nothing..." he stuttered. He felt as if every inch of his skin had turned crimson.

"What happened?" she said again, apparently immune to the fact he stood there naked. It was the blood on his shirt that transfixed her. "You've been away so long. Please tell me you are not hurt."

"No," he said, and tried to shoo her towards the door with one hand. But she stood there and then began to look him over. It might have only been for a second or two, but it felt like a burning, eternity of mortification and confusion, to have her look at him like that, so innocent and yearning, and yet at the same time so dangerous. And as she looked, he could not help but notice her bare feet and legs, her tumbling, crinkled gold hair and the line of her form beneath her thin shift. Since she had begun to eat again, she had become less alarmingly angular, and there was healthy colour in her cheeks again.

He felt the desire in her long gaze and it disturbed him, not least because he felt the compliment in it, and he felt, despite everything, the natural response to it. She was a beautiful, vulnerable creature and she admired him. It was hard for a man to deal with that decently.

He wanted his dressing gown but it was hanging on the hook on the door behind her, and the room was too narrow for him to reach for it without tangling with her. So he continued to stand with his blood-stained shirt as his only defence against indecency.

"I really think you should leave, now!" he said. He was aware that his voice sounded hoarse and shrill with anxiety.

"Oh, don't be angry with me! Please!" she said, taking another tiny step towards him. "Oh, why do I always make you angry these days? I so wanted to see you. I was worried. You have been away so long, I thought you were cross with me, because of what I said today. You aren't still angry, are you? I didn't mean what I said."

"No, I'm not angry," he said carefully. "But –"

She pressed her fingers to her lips and threw her head back smiling, as if she were offering up a prayer of thanks.

"Did you see the roses?" she said. "We found them on our walk. I thought you would like them."

"They don't cut well," said Felix. "They are better left on the branch."

"Oh! You *are* angry with me," she said.

"Go back to your room, ma'am," he said. "Go back upstairs and rest. I beg you!"

"Why are you always so harsh with me now? Why can't I

94

do anything right? I used to please you."

"You still do," he said, and then knew he should not have said that. "What I mean is, that I am pleased with your progress. What I want or feel is not what you should be concerned with. You should be looking to please yourself. Other people's approbation is…" He broke off, feeling how ridiculous it was trying to get such a point across as he stood there, still holding that wretched dirty shirt against him. "Please, will you just go?"

She twisted up her lip. She looked as if she were about to break down and cry just as she had done the previous day.

"I see how it is," she said. "It is always the same. There is no kindness in anyone. There is nothing."

She reached out for the flowers, and pulled them dripping from the jug, holding them against her as if they were precious. "And you, sir, are the worst of them all!"

Then to Felix's profound relief she stormed out of the room, leaving the door wide open. But his relief was only momentary because Sukey was coming upstairs with his water, and would have seen her flight. He dashed to slam the door shut to hide himself. He scrabbled into his dressing gown, and opened the door.

"Go and see to Mrs Vernon," he said. "She's…" He faltered. He had no words for her state.

Sukey nodded, handed him the jug, and said, "You might think about drawing the bolt when you are dressing."

He finished washing, and dressed himself again. He went cautiously out onto the landing, and stood there, wondering if he should go up to her, wondering if there was any good he could do, but after a few moments, Sukey came out of Mrs Vernon's room, and carefully closed the door behind her.

He moved towards the stairs, and gave her a questioning glance. He was relieved when she shook her head. Thank God she was there and able to deal with her, he thought, as they went downstairs together.

They went into the dining room, still in silence.

Felix pushed up the sash and reached for his cheroot case. He had just put one to his lips when Sukey said, with a gesture towards the open box, "Might I? My husband used to smoke them, so I..." She gave a slight shrug that implied she was embarrassed to ask but needy all the same. He understood perfectly.

"Of course," he said, and offered her the case. She took one and sniffed it with evident appreciation. He struck a lucifer and bent to light it for her, then watched her take the same obvious pleasure in that first glorious mouthful of smoke. He lit his own and they stood for some moments in silence, smoking by the open window.

"She cried herself out," she said, at length. "That's something."

"What are we to do?" he said. He had no difficulty being so honest with her.

"What do I know?" she said.

"As much as I do."

"Pray it will pass?" she said. "Maybe when the weather breaks."

"There isn't much sign of that," said Felix, leaning against the window embrasure, attempting to catch what cool breeze there might be coming from the common opposite.

"It will break, soon enough," said Sukey, coming to the window and standing beside him. "Maybe in the small hours. I can feel it coming."

"Wishful thinking," Felix said.

"Maybe," she said. "I hope so – just to prove you wrong."

Their eyes met for a moment through the cheroot smoke and they both smiled.

"It would be pleasant," Felix said, "if we might be somewhere else at this moment, don't you think? If just for an hour or two, we could put away all this, and be entirely careless... You have been hard at work for too long. I don't know how you stand it."

"Because I'm needed. That is something. But you're right. I would like to be away."

"Over the hills and far away?" he said.

"For a while. For a rest, yes," she said.

"I know the spot – just about a mile from my parents' house – an easy mile, mind, that would do the trick. A waterfall in a shady forest. The Birks of Pitfeldry. We could sit and be cool and quiet. Or bathe in the pools," he could not resist adding. The vision of Sukey, her skirts kilted up and stockings removed, wading into the milky waters of the foaming burn was a powerful one.

"You think you can charm me with your Scottish waterfalls?" she said, with a smile that suggested she knew exactly what he was thinking. "It would be grand to be able to compare, certainly," she continued. "And I am sure you would make a good guide, Mr Carswell."

"I would take the greatest pleasure in proving to you the superiority of my Perthshire scenery," he said.

"And I will probably say 'it's very fine' but it is not my country, which is the finest."

"We may have to agree to differ," he said.

"I think so. Oh, we have a visitor," she said, as a carriage came rolling down the street towards them.

"It's from Holbroke," he said, recognising the livery of the coachman.

The carriage drew up and Major Vernon climbed out.

"Quick," he said, and snatched the cheroot from Sukey's hand. "If he sees you smoking that –"

"Or you," she said. Hastily he stubbed them both out and tossed them into the empty grate.

"We both look guilty," he said. She nodded, waving away the smoke, just as the front door was opening.

"Welcome home, sir," Sukey said, going straight out to

the hall. She dropped a curtsey, the perfect servant once more. "Can I fetch you anything? Mrs Vernon is upstairs resting."

"No thank you, Sukey. I'll just go straight up." He looked from one to the other, with his searching gaze. "Is everything all right?"

"Martinez is dead," said Felix.

Major Vernon exhaled. "Poor fellow. Was he alone?"

"No, I was there. I lost him."

Major Vernon nodded.

"Those Spaniards are putting up at The Queen's, I understand. You should call on them."

"I'll go and do that now," said Felix. "You should go up to Mrs Vernon."

"Yes, I need to speak to her. We are leaving for Holbroke as soon as possible."

"We?" Felix said.

"Lady Rothborough has asked her to join the party," said Major Vernon. "And you must come too, Sukey."

"Of course, sir."

Major Vernon went upstairs, and Sukey went back to the dining room grate and picked up their half-smoked cheroots. "I'll take these down to the kitchen," she said. "Perhaps going there will be good for Mrs Vernon."

"I don't know," Felix said. "I find the place a torture. I can't imagine any pleasure in it."

"It'll do her good not to be treated like an invalid," Sukey said. "Don't you think?"

"I don't think my opinion about anything is worth sixpence," said Felix, "to be frank."

Sukey paused at the door and said, "Don't be so hard on yourself. You did all you could for the poor man."

"But I still lost him."

"He was a consumptive; what could you have done?"

"But it was so wretched."

"He had you, that was something," she said. "Well, more

98

than something."

He saw her bite her lip, as if she regretted saying so much, and it moved him to reach out and lay his hand on her arm.

Then in a moment, he stepped a little closer and brushed his lips across her forehead. She did not move or make a sound of protest. He kissed her again, this time on the lips, and she laid her hand on his cheek, before gently moving away. However, she did not leave the room at once, but looked straight at him, breathing hard.

"You should go and see those people," she said.

He nodded, and then as he went by her into the hall, he saw her smile, and his heart leapt.

Chapter Ten

Laura was lying on the bed, wrapped in the embroidered shawl Giles had recently given her. He was pleased to see his gift in use. She had received it with the barest minimum of gratitude and he had been seriously discouraged for a day or two, feeling nothing he did would make any impression upon her, before he had sternly told himself that he should not expect miracles.

It was midnight blue silk, with peonies embroidered on it, and in the subdued light of the room the soft lustre of it looked well against the pale skin of her hands and arms. She did not lie facing the door but diagonally across the bed, her hair loosened and flowing across the counterpane. The shawl and her flimsy chemise were twisted around her, showing the dip of her hips and the curve of her bottom. He remembered a time, early in their marriage, when he had returned home to that stuffy, primitive little house they had shared in a dusty Ontario township, and found her sleeping, in just such a pose. Then he had roused her with kisses and they had made love, and ignored the rest of the world.

She stirred, having become aware of his presence. She rolled over to face him. She did not smile in greeting nor did she stretch out her hand to him, but he hardly expected that. Yet she looked at him with wide eyes and without hostility, which pleased him, and he wondered if she, like him, remembered that delightful afternoon and evening.

"May I?" he asked, indicating the spare corner of the bed, so that he might perch there. She did not seem to mind when he did, so he took her silence as consent. "Did you pick those today?" he said, noticing a posy of wild roses in the water glass by the bed. They were wilting somewhat and some of their petals had fallen onto the floor.

"Yes. And you will tell me I was wrong to," she said rolling onto her back and staring up at the ceiling.

"No. Why?"

"Because to pick them is to murder them."

"Hardly. Who says so?"

"Mr Carswell. He was cruel to me," she said, turning round again, so that she faced away from him. "I think he hates me."

"Oh, I do not think so." He wondered if he should pull her gently back to face him. He settled for resting his hand lightly on her shoulder.

"Why do I ruin everything?" she said. "Why does everything I touch spoil? Perhaps you should put me away again where I can't do any damage. Why did I have to pick those roses? They would still be alive if I had not –" As she spoke, she pulled herself into a tight, tense, ball.

"They never last long, even on the branch," he said, kneading her shoulder a little with his fingers, hoping it might soothe her. "And I will never put you away again. Upon my honour."

At that she suddenly leapt up and, half on her knees, faced him, her hands now on his shoulders.

"Perhaps you should!" she exclaimed. "Given what a horrible, wicked person I am! Wouldn't you rather be rid of me? I am such a trouble to you, such a terrible nuisance."

Then, to his astonishment, she flung herself against him, her face pressed to his chest, sobbing.

"No, no," he said. "You are not a trouble to me. It is your illness that causes the difficulty – and we are chasing that away now, a little more each day, and each day you are improving."

He wrapped his arms about her, almost giddy with the pleasure that she had chosen him to comfort her. He kissed the top of her head and she inched closer to him, and tightened her grip, as if to remove every tiny chink of space that might separate them. She was crying violently still, and he felt his shirt soaked through with her tears, and felt his own tears on his cheeks.

After a while, the storm of her misery subsided a little and she lay with her head in his lap. As he combed her tangled hair with his fingertips, her breathing became steady and regular again.

"Lord and Lady Rothborough are anxious for you to go back with me to Holbroke tonight. Do you think you might oblige them?" he asked at length, when he had composed his own thoughts and feelings.

As he had expected, the question caused her to sit up. She pushed back her hair and gazed at him.

"Truly?"

"Truly."

"You did not say no on my behalf?"

"No. It is for you to decide. Of course, I would rather –"

"That I stayed here?"

"I was going to say 'came with me.'"

"Oh," she said. "Are you sure?" He nodded. "But what if –"

"It is for you to decide," he said, again. There was no knowing what might happen, but he felt it was an experiment that needed to be attempted. "If you could manage it, then you would feel the worth of all you have accomplished."

"But –"

"It is grand, but it is also extremely pleasant. Lord Rothborough will treat you like a duchess, and his daughters will be friends to you, I'm sure."

She got up from the bed and walked over to the dressing table, standing before the glass looking at herself, dressed in only her shift, with her hair cascading down her back, her eyes red with tears. She frowned.

"I don't look like a duchess," she said.

"Who is to say what a duchess looks like in her

bedroom?" said Giles getting up from the bed and wrapping the shawl around her. "There." She spent some moments arranging it to her liking. "You will be fine enough for all of them."

"And you will not be angry with me if I disgrace you?" she said, turning back to him.

He took her hand and kissed it.

"No," he said. "And you will not." She pulled back her hand and looked down at her fingers where he had kissed them, rather as if she expected to see a mark. "Trust me, please. And trust yourself. And if you do not care for it, if it frightens you, you can come straight back here. And you will not be alone. I will be there, and Sukey."

"But not Mr Carswell," she said, sitting down on the edge of the bed.

"No, you know he cannot go there."

She nodded and twisted the fringe of her shawl in her fingers.

"I will try," she said after a long silence. "I will."

Chapter Eleven

Felix found his way to The Queen's Hotel like a drunken man. He had kissed Sukey and she had not rejected him. She had kissed him back and smiled, and dear Lord, it felt like no other kiss.

All those months, seeing her every other day, working with her, and suddenly this extraordinary clarity of feeling about her: not a creature to be petted, or a goddess to be worshipped, but a partner. That was the conclusion that stopped him in his tracks, the impossible conclusion – that he had at last met his wife and she was entirely perfect, and at the same time, it could not be done. His parents, Major Vernon and Mr and Mrs O'Brien – let alone Lord Rothborough – not one of them would give their blessing. It was as hopeless as it was miraculous.

He had now reached The Queen's Hotel, which rose up above the extensive formal gardens which fronted it, the epitome of glittering, fashionable modernity. In the gardens, elegantly clad guests were taking the after-dinner air, strolling along verdant avenues lit with Chinese lanterns. In a bower somewhere a German band was pumping away, playing the waltz of the moment.

He passed by all this, and entered into an impressive hall, and stood for a moment, wondering how to proceed. He wished that Major Vernon was with him – he would know exactly how to get him taken to the right person at once, without anyone doubting his authority or legitimacy. He managed to catch the attention of a waiter, who was supercilious enough to be a flunky at Holbroke.

"I need to speak to someone from the party from Santa

Magdalena," he said. "I have news of a countryman of theirs. I am a surgeon." He took out his card. "It's urgent," he added.

The waiter looked at the card as if he were presenting false credentials.

"The party you mention – well, sir, how do I put it? They don't take kindly to unsolicited interruptions. There are instructions in place. The management, you see, have told us –" He gave a shrug.

"This is an important matter," said Felix. "Take me up to them at once, if you please!"

"I am not sure I can do that, sir," said the waiter. "Not without..." He gave a discreet cough.

He might as well have put out his palm for the coin, Felix thought, digging in his pocket. He found a few pennies and a half-crown; he felt sure that the pennies would not do it, so he surrendered the half-crown. The waiter smiled and made an obsequious bow.

"This way if you please, sir. They will still be at dinner," said the waiter, as they climbed up a gilded staircase. "They eat late, but I will see what I can do."

Just at that moment, another waiter came down the passageway.

"Jim, this gent here wants to see one of your gents. He's a doctor. Something about a countryman of theirs."

"I'll get that secretary fellow," he said.

"It's about Don Xavier Martinez – tell him that," said Felix.

Felix wondered if another half-crown would be necessary, and indeed if he had one.

Fortunately, the servant did not seem to expect it and went off, armed only with Felix's card, in the direction he had come from.

"There's quite a few of them, then?" Felix asked.

"Oh yes," said the waiter. "Twenty-five of them, including their servants. They've taken the whole floor here for the rest of the month and they live like princes. We've not seen the like of it before. You wait here, sir, and Jim'll see to it."

So Felix idled for some more minutes in the passageway, growing nervous and impatient by turns, until Jim returned.

"This way, please. Don Luiz himself would you like to see you. He's the master. Pricked up his ears at the mention of that name, I can tell you."

Felix followed Jim into a reception room of some kind – a gloomy and unbearably stuffy apartment, which curiously had the hushed atmosphere of a private chapel. Above the mantelpiece, illuminated by a row of burning votive candles, hung a huge portrait of a man in elaborate military dress, his scarlet tunic heavy with gold lace. The painting itself had been draped with swags of foliage and black ribbons, while in the corner stood a great silken flag, presumably in the national colours of the Republic of Santa Magdalena.

Left alone, Felix studied the portrait and noticed that there was in the man's face a distinct resemblance to his dead patient.

A tall, powerfully built gentleman dressed in immaculate evening clothes now came into the room. He was holding Felix's card.

"Mr Carswell?" he said in a thick accent. "I believe you have some news for me, of Don Xavier Lopez Martinez?"

"Yes, I am sorry to say I do."

"Sorry? Why?"

"I'm afraid he died this morning. At The White Horse."

"That is here, in Stanegate?"

Felix nodded.

"How extraordinary. We did not know he was here. We thought... Would you excuse me, a moment. The shock is quite –"

"Yes, of course, sir. I am sorry to bring you such news."

The gentleman sat down.

"You see," he said after a moment, gesturing towards the portrait crowned with laurels. "That was his brother, the late President of our country."

"I am sorry," Felix said again.

"I should present myself," said the gentleman. "I am Don Luiz Ramirez. I was a close confederate of the late Director, his second in command, and his cousin. Don Xavier was my cousin." He rubbed his face. "How did it happen?"

"He was in the tertiary stages of consumption. I only began treating him two days ago. I met him by chance. We did our best for him, but his condition was so advanced, there was little that could be done. I tried to find him a priest, but there was no time."

Don Luiz gave a great sigh.

"This is terrible news, terrible..." he began, and then shook his head, overcome by emotion.

Now a woman entered the room. It was hard not to stare at her. She was stupendously dressed in a low-cut blue satin dress that looked like a ball gown. There were sapphires glistening at her neck and ears.

She looked at Don Luiz and said something to him in Spanish.

He got up at once and went to her, and, taking her hands, spoke to her in rapid, quiet Spanish. She looked shocked as he spoke, glancing at Felix, and then she crossed herself.

"Excuse me, sir, if you will, we must..." Don Luiz said, escorting the woman towards the door.

"Yes, yes, of course."

And he was left alone again. He sat down and wondered what he ought to do next.

Then, as if he were watching a play, the door on the other side of the room opened, and another woman came in, this time dressed in widow's black.

He got to his feet.

"Can I help you, sir?" she said, in English, but with a soft

Irish accent, that made him think of Sukey.

"I came to call on Don Luiz," Felix said, stumbling on the pronunciation. He pointed at the door Don Luiz left by. "He went out with another lady."

She came a little closer to him, and looked at him curiously.

"Do we know each other, sir?" she said.

"I don't believe we do, ma'am," he said, although there was something oddly familiar about her.

"You say you have to come to see Don Luiz?"

"Yes, about a patient of mine, Don Xavier Martinez."

"Don Xavier is my brother-in-law."

Felix said, "Perhaps you should sit down, ma'am. I am afraid I have bad news."

He indicated the sofa where he had been sitting. She sat down obediently, but staring at him all the time, wide-eyed.

He sat down beside her and said, "I regret to tell you he died this morning."

"Oh dear Lord," she said, and covered her face with her hands. "I didn't even know he was here. What was he doing here?"

"I don't know, ma'am."

She looked at him again with that strange, piercing gaze. Her hands were knotted together, the knuckles white as if she were clutching them together to find some strength.

"He was your patient?" Her voice was quiet now.

"Yes, I am a surgeon. My name is Carswell, Felix Carswell."

"Felix Carswell," she repeated. "Indeed."

She was staring at him now. He looked away, disconcerted.

"Ma'am?" he said.

Suddenly she reached out and touched his cheek, only for a fraction of a moment, and even then so that he barely felt it. But it astonished him that she should do this. She, for her part, horrified at her own audacity, had pressed her hand against her mouth. She jumped up from the sofa and fled the room, banging the door behind her.

He touched the spot her finger had touched. He felt a little nauseous and faint, and he tugged at his cravat, longing for air. The room was unpleasantly warm. He went to the window and pulled back the heavy damask curtains and then drew up the blind, before forcing open the sash. As he did, a little breath of air came into the room, just enough to set the candle flames dancing. He turned from the window and saw that the door the lady had left by was now ajar, and that she was standing behind it, looking through the gap at him.

"Is there anything I can do for you, ma'am?" he asked.

She came out of the room slowly.

"You must excuse me," she said. "I have had a great shock."

"Yes, your brother-in-law –"

"Not just that," she said, going to the portrait and looking up. She was breathing hard, attempting to steady herself.

"Your late husband, ma'am?" he hazarded.

"Yes," she said, still looking up at the picture. He half expected her to fall on her knees before it.

"So you are Mrs Martinez, ma'am?" he asked.

She turned and said, "Yes, I am. But on the island I am known as Dona Blanca. That is the custom there."

"Then he spoke of you," Felix said. "Don Xavier, I mean, at the end –"

"Oh," she said. "Oh, no..."

She turned back to the portrait and he could see she was mastering her tears.

"I am so sorry," Felix said.

"How strange fate is," she said, still gazing up at her dead husband. "How strange."

"His body is at The White Horse, near the parish church," he said.

109

"Is that where he died?"

"Yes, I'm afraid so. It was rather wretched. I tried to get him to move, but events overtook us, so to speak. I wish he had told me earlier that I could find you here so that he might..."

"I think," she said, "he was taking the trouble not to be found."

"But why?" he could not help saying, and then tempered his enquiry, "if it is not presumptuous to ask."

She looked as if she were about to say something else when the door to the right opened, and Don Luiz came out again.

"Oh, you are here," he said. "You have heard, then?"
She nodded.

"Does Clara know?" she asked.

"Yes, I have told her. She is praying for him."

"Then I will join her," said Dona Blanca. She moved towards the door and then stopped, looking back at Felix. "Thank you for finding us," she said. "We owe you a great debt, I am sure."

Chapter Twelve

They reached Holbroke just after the family had finished dinner, and since it was such a close evening, the ladies had quit the drawing room and were sitting out on the great portico, in order to catch the breezes. Many lanterns had been lit, creating a soft, golden light in which the Marchioness and her daughters, all dressed in gauzy summer silks, made an impressive sight, as they came down the steps to greet them. Lady Warde, in black, struck a dull note, and Giles noticed how she shrank back as the others came forward, her face as pale as the skirts of Lady Charlotte's white dress. He wondered what more information about Eliza Jones might be got out of her. Her blandness was as conspicuous and intriguing as that affected by her servant. He longed to seize the moment, draw her to one side and question her properly.

But this was not the time. Laura was glancing fearfully at him, her eyes begging for reassurance, as Lord Rothborough came forward to hand her out of the carriage. It was possible that the striking resemblance to Mr Carswell unnerved her. He squeezed her hand, and hoped that his nod and smile were enough to calm her for now. It was not the easiest entrance for her.

"Mrs Vernon! A great pleasure to know you at last," Lord Rothborough said, taking her hand and helping her from the carriage. "My, you are quite the Diana," Rothborough went on, observing how she was taller than him. "And what could be more appropriate, for the wife of our huntsman here? Vernon, good evening again. I am glad you are back so speedily. There has been – but that can wait. Come and meet my wife and daughters, Mrs Vernon."

He offered his arm and took her up the steps to present her to them all. Even though her dress was not at all expensive or elaborate, Laura's natural beauty and elegant bearing made it appear so. She looked quite the equal of the Rothborough girls. Her long, lithe body and her graceful movements, the things that had made him first notice her, now struck him anew, and powerfully. He hastened up the steps to join them, feeling proud of her courage as she shook hands and smiled and managed to make small talk.

Laura was soon sitting in the place of honour by Lady Rothborough, while Giles found himself with the ladies Maria and Charlotte.

"Papa is right. Mrs Vernon is a Diana," Lady Maria. "She would be wonderful in a tableau, don't you think? It has been so long since we had an evening of tableaux."

"Mr Syme has told Mama it is a sin," said Lady Charlotte rather sharply.

"I cannot see the harm in it at all," said Lady Maria. "Papa does not, and Mama loves it."

"Where is Mr Syme?" said Giles.

"He didn't come to dinner. He had a headache," said Lady Maria. "Major Vernon, would Mrs Vernon like to appear in some tableaux, do you think? Does she like that sort of thing? In fact, would you?" she said, giving him an appraising glance.

"I should think Major Vernon has far better things to do," said Lady Charlotte.

"I like a little theatrical nonsense as much as the next man," said Giles. "And I am sure Laura would be delighted. She likes dressing up."

"Oh excellent! I will try and persuade Mama. Since Mr Syme is not here to pour cold water, we stand a chance. It is a favourite thing with her – well, it always was until he put the idea into her head that it was sinful. Which it cannot be, surely?"

"No, I don't think so," said Giles.

Lady Maria went to make her petition and Giles was alone with Lady Charlotte.

"Your wife is very beautiful," she said.

It felt like a criticism rather than a compliment, as if he had suddenly acquired a beautiful wife in order to hurt her feelings. He wondered what fantastical notions had been running through her head.

"I shall need your help tomorrow," he said. "I need to talk properly with Lady Warde."

"Would you not prefer me to look after Mrs Vernon?"

"I think Mrs Vernon will have all the attention she needs," said Giles, noticing how Lady Maria was talking animatedly at her.

"She is like a child playing with a new doll," said Lady Charlotte, then sighed. "Oh, that was cruel of me, I know. It was jealousy. Maria is so easy with people, so warm-hearted, so good."

"And you think you are not?"

"I know I am not."

"You have been listening to Mr Syme too much."

"He may have a point."

"Do not judge yourself by his standards."

"And what other standards am I to abide by, if not those of a clergyman?"

"By those that you discover for yourself."

"What do you mean?"

"One must apply one's intelligence and work out what is the right thing to do. It is not easy, of course –"

"It is impossible!" she said. "Well, it might not be for you, but for a foolish young woman like me, who is all at sea. Ever since Papa and I found poor Eliza, it is as if my house of cards has collapsed. Mr Syme says that I am resisting the call of my Saviour, and that I need to acknowledge Him and be saved or I will never find peace again. Perhaps he is right."

"It is too simple. There are plenty of clergymen who would disagree strongly with that view, Lady Charlotte. My brother-in-law, Canon Fforde, for example."

"Perhaps," she said. "He is so relentless with it. He would not stop talking at me this afternoon. No wonder I cannot think straight. I think he gave himself a headache with his sermonising." She laughed, which relieved him.

"You must take care not to let him do that again," Giles said.

"I know," she said. "It was unwise. He caught me at a moment of weakness. After you left —"

Fortunately the conversation could go no further. Lady Maria had come bounding back to tell them she was showing Mrs Vernon up to their rooms.

"You are in the Indian chintz rooms now, Major Vernon," she said. "But I think Papa wants to speak to you first. Come, Chartie, let us go and make sure Mrs Vernon is comfortable."

"Yes, of course. Excuse me," said Lady Charlotte and went with her sister.

Soon only Giles and Lord Rothborough remained on the portico.

"You cannot imagine how glad I am that you decided to come back to us tonight, Vernon," said Lord Rothborough. "The strangest thing has happened, and I think you are the only man I know who might get to the bottom of it. Not only do we have a murder to deal with, but this afternoon I discovered that some extremely valuable jewellery has gone missing."

Giles took a moment to digest this information, and reached for his notebook and pencil.

"How distressing," he said. "How did you discover this?"

"Every year I have a jeweller come from Northminster to check everything over – Hammersly, you probably know the fellow?" Giles nodded. "He looks for loose stones and so forth, to see if anything needs cleaning or restringing, that sort of thing. He is expected tomorrow. So what usually happens is that Woodward, my secretary, gathers up all the various pieces – some are kept in a locked cabinet in my wife's dressing room – the pieces she wears frequently; others are in the care of my daughters, while the bulk are kept in the strong room, off the plate room, in their own cabinet."

"So do you know exactly what is missing and from where?"

"Yes – the Rothborough parure."

"That is a set of matching jewels?"

"That's right – in this case a tiara, two bracelets, earrings and a stomacher, I think it is called, worn on the bodice. Diamonds, rubies and pearls. My wife doesn't care for it – she has family pieces of her own that she prefers – so it does not often see the light of day, and is kept in the strong room. Which is the greatest mystery. How could it have been done?"

~

By the time Giles found his way up to the Indian chintz room, he found that Laura was asleep in the great bed. Sukey was still there, hanging up clothes in the adjoining dressing room.

"I am almost done, sir," she said.

"Are they looking after you?" he asked.

"Very well, thank you. I am just along the passageway, next to Lady Rothborough's maid. It's quite grand, all in all."

"That's good," said Giles. "I have a job for you, if this isn't enough. As well as this poor girl being murdered, a quantity of jewellery has vanished from its cabinet in the strong room, presumably stolen. Now, the household don't know about this yet – only Lord Rothborough and Mr Woodward, his secretary – and I'd like it to stay that way." She nodded. "But I want you to tell me if you see anything downstairs that makes you think someone is keeping secrets, or is up to anything unusual. I think Mrs Hope the housekeeper has a sewing circle for the lady's maids?"

"Yes, she said I was to come and join them," Sukey said. "Do you think it was someone in the house?"

"Possibly," said Giles. "Is that a fresh pot of tea?"

"It's camomile," she said. "And it's not been sitting there long. Mrs Vernon had her usual cup and went straight to sleep."

"How did she seem?"

"Happy," said Sukey.

"Truly?"

"Lady Maria was very kind to her," said Sukey. "So would you like a cup of this, Major Vernon?"

"Yes, thank you. Now, where am I to sleep?" he said, glancing back into the large bedroom from the dressing room doorway. There was no bed there. "Is there another dressing room?"

"I don't think so, sir. I think they thought —" she broke off, embarrassed. Sukey knew well enough that Giles and Laura did not share a bed. "Well, you know. Holt has put your things in here."

She busied herself with the tea.

"You had better get to bed, Sukey," he said. "You look tired."

"Yes, I am a bit," she said, and closed the trunk. "This can wait." She went to the door and stopped. "I hope you don't mind me asking this, Major – about Mr Carswell?"

"What about him?"

"Is it true that he's Lord Rothborough's natural son?"

"Yes. I suppose you noticed the likeness?" She nodded. "Why do you ask?"

"Just for that reason. It is striking," she said, quickly. "Good night, sir," she added and left, closing the door quietly

116

behind her with her habitual care.

Giles finished his tea, which was tepid but pleasantly refreshing, and got into his nightshirt, which he found laid out for him on a chair. He went through to the bedroom and climbed up into the great canopied bed, and for the first time in many years lay down beside his wife.

Laura stirred and woke a little. She rolled onto her side to face him.

"I hope you don't mind," he said.

"No," she said.

She turned and pressed herself against him, letting him put his arms about her. He felt her relax in his arms.

He felt ashamed then of all his own moments of weakness: of his betrayals, mental and real. She had not been unfaithful as he had. He wished he might confess it all to her, but that would be for his benefit, not hers. She had suffered enough without having to know of his cruelty.

Chapter Thirteen

Felix returned to the house in Stanegate and found that the Vernons and Sukey had already left for Holbroke. He ate a melancholy supper of cold-boiled mutton, runner beans and stewed apricots, too sharp to be pleasant. It was served to him by the resident housekeeper, Mrs Bolland, who was put out by the sudden departure. Having brought the tray in, she stood asking him questions in a surly manner that he could not readily answer. He wished Sukey were there. She would have dealt with it and got the irritating old hen out of the room.

"So you will be here tomorrow night, sir?" Mrs Bolland pressed on. "For your dinner? I need to know."

"I don't know," Felix said. "It depends on when a man is buried. I shall let you know as soon as I can. Is there any more wine?" She had given him a solitary glassful.

"Major Vernon didn't say anything about your having his wine," said Mrs Bolland.

"I don't think you need to worry about that," said Felix. "Bring up the rest of the bottle."

"Whatever you like, sir!" said Mrs Bolland, irritably.

Alone, he lit a cheroot and pushed the apricots about the bowl, wishing again Sukey were there and not just to bring domestic peace and comfort. He wanted to feel her close to him. That kiss had been a tantalising prelude – not to something sordid and transitory but to something so profound that it frightened him as much as it gave him joy. Just to have had her sitting there with him, smoking a cheroot, would have been enough. To kiss her again would be an extraordinary privilege.

In his mind's eye, he pictured her calmly negotiating the

strange oceans of Holbroke, her neat dark-skirted figure walking the crimson carpets. She would take the whole thing easily in her stride; that was one of the glories of her – he had noticed a hundred times her calm competence in the face of whatever life chose to throw at her. Yet for all that, he wanted to ride through the night and fetch her away from there. The thought of those powdered flunkies who had such a high opinion of themselves leering at her, as pretty women servants were always leered at, disturbed him not a little, and he had no idea to what unpleasant licentiousness she might be exposed in the servants' hall.

Was she thinking of him, he wondered – thinking of that kiss, and the half-smoked cheroots and that afternoon's conversation? Would she even have time to consider what had happened, as she climbed into her strange new bed? Was she, like him, feeling exhausted and lonely and yet too stirred up to sleep?

When he went to his own bed, after a few more glasses of the claret that Mrs Bolland deigned to give him, he lay tossing and turning. The events of the day clung to him, keeping him from sleep with their painful potency – not just the taste of Sukey's sweet lips, but Don Xavier's miserable death and Dona Blanca's peculiar manner and puzzling words: "He was taking the trouble not to be found."

~

Felix had arranged to meet Don Luiz at The White Horse the next morning to settle the matter of Don Xavier's burial and hand over his possessions. He had the key to his room in his pocket, and he was seized with a desire to look over his things in a more thorough fashion. Dona Blanca's words and manner had piqued his curiosity.

The landlady took the opportunity to ask his opinion about a rash on her son's arm – an entirely trivial matter which took up rather more time than Felix would have liked. He went upstairs and began his nervous search, hoping he had enough time before Don Luiz appeared.

There were footsteps on the stairs and he heard the voice of the landlady saying, "This way ma'am. The door on the left."

"Thank you," the distinctive voice of Dona Blanca replied.

Felix went to the door, wondering if she had had the same idea in coming here. He opened it and saw her on the landing, dressed in fresh mourning and heavily veiled. She saw him, and approached him, putting up her veil. At the same time, her scent came wafting towards him, as if fanned by the action of raising her veil: a powerful mixture of violets and carnations that made him slightly dizzy. As she slipped past him into the room, it surrounded him, and he was astonished at the strange memories it provoked in him. An image of a pile of pink silk cushions on the floor and a toy horse on wheels flashed into his mind, the latter a toy from his childhood which was no doubt still in the press in Pitfeldry. Why on earth should he think of that now, he wondered.

"Mr Carswell, I am glad to see you again," she said, looking about the miserable room. "Your kindness to him will not be forgotten by his family."

She went to the bedside table where the little image of the Virgin and Child remained, and took it up and examined it.

"It is a shame he could not be with his people at the end," Felix said. She nodded and carefully put the picture down again.

"There was a family squabble, if you like," she said, after a moment. "He had difficult feelings, quite inappropriate for a man who had renounced the world. But it is the case sometimes that the world will not allow us to renounce it. He was young and prayers cannot stop a young man from – well, you cannot always dam a stream."

"I've always thought celibacy for the clergy was a foolish thing. It makes sinners out of good men."

"A man who is called to be a priest is not like others," she said. "He must try to live up to that calling. Many do succeed."

"Many fail. Like your brother-in-law," Felix said. "He had scars all over his back from flogging himself. Self-mortification, I understand it is called." She nodded. "For a man in his state of health to do that to himself –"

Dona Blanca turned away.

"Poor Xavier," she said. "Oh the poor, poor boy. It is all so wretched."

There was a silence as she mastered her tears.

"It is all my fault," she said, turning back to Felix. "That is clear enough. I didn't encourage him, you must understand that, but he would be encouraged. Perhaps you are right and celibacy is not a good thing. He might have been married and happy instead of forming such a desperate, wild, unnatural attachment –" She broke down utterly then. "Oh dear God, forgive me!"

Felix felt his cheeks burning with embarrassment. Did she mean that Xavier had been in love with her, and if so, why the devil did she think him a fit person to whom to confess?

"I shall leave you for a moment, ma'am," he said, going towards the door.

"No!" she exclaimed. "Please, please don't go!" Then to Felix's horror she threw herself on her knees in front of him and clasped his legs. Then, worse still, she bent her head so she was on the verge of kissing his boots, and would most likely have done so, had Felix not sunk down at once to attempt to stop her prostrating herself in this astonishing manner.

"Ma'am, ma'am, I beg you, please –"

There was a struggle, an undignified, unpleasant tangling

of limbs. She was a writhing briar bush of miserable emotion, and Felix was able to do little to calm her. In the end, he let her hold him, her arms clamped about him, her damp cheek pressed against his chest. He felt a little like a rock in an ocean being battered by forces beyond his comprehension – to be in such a situation with a stranger, who was not a patient, was decidedly unnerving.

Yet at the same time he was acutely aware of that perfume, so distinctive and unforgettable. It awoke something from the distant recesses of his mind. He found he knew the notes of it in the same way he knew the old French songs his first nurse had sung to him. Again he saw the pink cushions and the floor on which they were scattered – a floor of polished wooden diamonds set in squares that smelled of something sweet and waxy, mingling with that same odour he now smelled, and it shocked him, making him stiffen.

She sensed this and it brought her from her fit. She detached herself, and sat in a pool of her black skirts, her hands in her lap, staring at him with widened, reddened eyes, with such intense scrutiny that he had to look away. Yet there in his mind, it remained, that room: the wood smoke from the fire, violets and carnations, floor polish, and a painted squirrel on the wainscot. *Ecureuil...* A woman's voice, soft and Irish-accented: "Squirrel. Yes. Your little squirrel."

He looked back at her, his heart pounding. He studied her face for too long. The conclusion he came to defied all reason and he would not have it.

He scrambled clumsily to his feet, and turned his back on her, intending to leave the room at once. But on getting to his feet something had caught his eye, something wedged between the bed frame and the wall, either by accident or by design.

Now he stooped to fetch it out, relieved to have such a tangible distraction. It was a narrow, flat document case, the sort used by couriers, made in soft, dark red leather, with a coat of arms and a monogram containing an X and an M. It was safe to assume it had belonged to Don Xavier.

He opened it. It contained a packet of letters in Spanish, so far as he could judge.

"What is it you have there?" he heard her say.

"I think this must have belonged to your brother-in-law. He seems to have hidden it."

"Oh," she said.

He turned, hearing her rise. He offered his hand to help her to her feet. She refused it, steadying herself on the bedstead instead.

"May I see that?" she said, swallowing her tears.

He held it out to her. She drew out the pile of letters and began to scan the first one.

"Wedged down there?" she said.

"Seemingly," he said. "Deliberately, perhaps?"

She bit her lip, reading a little more. Her concentration on the documents was intense and contrived to banish her hysteria.

"It is important," she said after a moment, "that these do not fall into the wrong hands." She slid the documents back into the case and fastened the buckle. "May I ask a favour of you?"

"Yes?"

"Keep this somewhere safe. Very safe. Do not show them to anyone without telling me first. I know that is a great imposition and God knows, I ought not to impose on you!"

Yet she thrust the case at him and he was obliged to take it.

There was the sound of footsteps on the stairs.

"Put it away in your coat," she said. "Do not mention this to anyone!"

A moment later, the door opened and Don Luiz appeared.

Chapter Fourteen

In a great house the size of Holbroke, it was easy to mislay things and people.

Giles wondered if there was a simple solution to the missing parure – that it had not been stolen, but merely lost. Perhaps it was in the strong room at the London House, or at Lady Rothborough's house in Sussex where they had spent June. Although it was an extremely valuable item, it was only one among many treasures.

These thoughts occurred to him as he was breakfasting with Laura and the three young ladies the following morning. They were sitting in a delightful room decorated with Chinese wallpaper, and the breakfast itself was delicious enough to pique even Laura's dilatory appetite. She looked comfortable, and he had allowed his mind to wander onto the problem of the parure as he drank his coffee and ate the excellent toast.

"We shall go for a drive and set up our easels," said Lady Maria. "Yes, Mrs Vernon?"

"Giles..." Laura murmured, and glanced at him with a wary look. "Should I?"

"Oh, certainly," he said. "Yes, of course you must go. But may I suggest that Sukey go with you? Lady Maria, might there be space in the carriage for Mrs Connolly, my wife's maid? Mrs Vernon has been ill, and it would ease both our minds if she were there."

"Ill, oh dear – Mrs Vernon, I had no idea," said Lady Maria. "But of course, that is why you were at Stanegate, taking the waters. You are a convalescent."

"What was wrong with you, if it is not indelicate to ask?" said Lady Augusta.

"Gusta —" said Charlotte.

"No, no, I don't mind," said Laura. "I really don't. You see, Lady Augusta, it is hard to talk of. Nobody ever talks of these things, at least not people like us. I... I... I was cloudy in my mind," Laura went on. "I lost my little boy and after that —" Giles reached for her hand under the cover of the tablecloth, astonished by her bravery. "It is quite common. Mr Carswell says it happens more than any of us know. It really is nothing to be ashamed of."

"Mr Carswell?" said Lady Augusta in a whisper.

"Mr Carswell has helped me to get better. If it had not been for him, I should be lost still."

"Oh," said Lady Maria. "Oh, my goodness."

"You should be proud of him," Laura went on. "I can see him in your faces. I should be proud to have such a man as my brother."

There was silence. Lady Augusta was looking most offended, and shot a fierce glance at Giles as if she expected him to apologise on Laura's behalf, but Giles could see nothing to apologise for. Laura was right to be so plain-spoken. She had seized a sword of truth and run across the battlefield with it. He squeezed her hand again and she squeezed it back, with some intensity. He knew what this show of courage was costing her, and he felt humbled by it, and at the same time, proud of her.

It was Lady Charlotte who broke the silence.

"I have had the pleasure of meeting Mr Carswell, Mrs Vernon, and I am glad to hear that he was such help to you. It seems to me that we need more men of talent in the world, whatever the circumstances of their birth."

"You have met him, Chartie?" said Lady Maria. "When?"

"Two days ago. He came to help Major Vernon."

"Mama will be —" Lady Augusta began and then broke off. "Oh Charlotte, how could you?"

"It was an accident," Charlotte said. "Well, not entirely. I knew he would be here and I wanted to see him. I have wanted to see him ever since I heard he existed, to be frank."

"So what is he like?" Lady Maria said.

"Maria!" exclaimed Augusta. "Mama would not like you to even –"

"Oh come now, Gusta, are you not curious? I am, just like Chartie. I would love to know him! Papa loves him so dearly. It is so, so – oh, I cannot put into words, but I feel it, just as you do, Chartie. I know that it *is* important, even though we are not supposed to talk about it! Well, I should like to talk about it!"

"When it breaks Mama's heart even to think about him? Nothing that Papa has done could be crueller to her than his misguided –"

"It is not misguided," said Lady Charlotte. "He is acting as a father should! How could he do otherwise than love him, just as he loves us all so dearly? He is the best of fathers!"

"But not the best of husbands," said Lady Augusta. "How would you care to be treated that way by your husband, Charlotte?" She turned to Laura. "I am glad to hear you are better, Mrs Vernon, but I am afraid I cannot be a party to general paeans of praise concerning Mr Carswell. I have my mother's feelings to think of. If you will excuse me." With which she got up from the table.

Giles stood up, but Laura held fast to his hand. When the door shut behind Lady Augusta, she burst out: "Oh, I am sorry, I did not mean... I should not have, should I? I knew I would do something..." She stared up at him, fear in her eyes. "What have I done?"

Giles sat down again and kissed her hand.

"You have acknowledged a debt that we needed to acknowledge," he said quietly.

"I am so sorry," Laura began again, looking at Charlotte and Maria. "When you have all been so kind. What will Lady Rothborough say? What will Lady Augusta tell her?"

"With luck, nothing," said Lady Charlotte. "I will have a word with her. But first, I think, some more coffee."

"I feel most strange," said Lady Maria.

"You are feeling the abrasive effect of the truth," said Lady Charlotte. "Will you have another cup of something, Mrs Vernon? Major?"

"I wish you had taken me with you," Lady Maria said. "I wish I had seen him for myself. Does he really look like Papa?"

"I had better go and speak to Gusta," said Lady Charlotte, having swiftly drunk her cup of black coffee.

"Careful you do not find her weeping in the arms of Syme," said Lady Maria, as Charlotte rose from her chair.

"What?" exclaimed Charlotte, sitting down again.

"Tell her that if she says one word about this to Mama, I will tell Mama that I saw Mr Syme kissing her."

"You saw them?"

"Oh yes," said Maria with a slightly wicked smile. "How she can bear to be kissed by him, I can't imagine, but she did seem to be quite enjoying it."

"Did they see you?"

"No," said Maria.

"I knew he was a wretch!" Charlotte said. "The insolent, presumptuous wretch! Well, we shall not have to look hard to find something to discredit him with now, Major Vernon!"

~

Laura having been happily carried off by Maria to look at piano duets, Giles turned his attention to business. He looked through his notebook and decided that he needed to talk to Lady Warde again.

He found his quarry sitting alone in a sunny corner in one

of the great reception rooms. On seeing him enter the room, she had avoided meeting his eye and had at once left her place and made swiftly for the door.

Her determination to be rid of him obliged him to give chase. He followed her through a seemingly endless enfilade of dimly lit reception rooms, the holland blinds down against the sun, until he found her progress stalled by a locked door.

She stood there, trying the handle with some agitation, her back to him.

"Lady Warde, it really is important that I speak to you."

"Evidently, or you would not have pursued me. I understood, sir, that you were a gentleman." She addressed these words to the door, in a tiny, breathless voice. It was curious behaviour, to say the least – somewhat reminiscent of a common criminal taking flight at the sound of the constable's rattle. Yet Giles knew that people were scared of the police, simply because they were the police, as if their secrets were more visible to them, whether they had broken the law or not. "It is shocking that I am to be hounded in such a manner, when –"

"I will not keep you long, I promise, ma'am," said Giles, in the calmest, sweetest, most humble tone he could manage.

"I should hope not," she said, permitting herself to turn a little towards him. "What can I possibly tell you, sir? I have already told you everything."

"Perhaps we should sit for a moment, Lady Warde?" he said. "And if you feel equal to it, you might tell me again about Eliza Jones."

He gestured towards a chair, but she did not take his cue.

"Why again?" she said.

"Because previously you had just heard some shocking news. In such cases one's thoughts can be disordered. Sometimes there will be omissions. Therefore, I would like to talk to you again."

"I do not know what I can add," she said, "but if you

insist, I must oblige, sir, although I should rather not speak of this at all."

How prickly she was, he thought, standing so firmly on her threadbare dignity.

"Justice demands that you should," he said, pulling out a chair for her and placing it. "That you must see."

She consented to sit, but there was something about the manner in which she did it that suggested she was not going to give up her secrets easily.

He hoped he would not offend the rules of housekeeping at Holbroke by taking up the blind a little, but he needed to read her features as well as hear her words. She flinched a little as the light struck her, and he noticed her hand clasped around the locket she wore on a long ribbon about her neck. He struggled for a moment to remember if she had been wearing it the other day. For a woman who did not wear any other jewellery than her wedding ring, it was notable.

She was certainly an interesting case: a woman who had made a career of being useful, earning her place at a succession of noble tables by means of a life of trivial servitude. No paid domestic would consent to such a life. Her birth and her marriage had conspired to earn her this strange existence, of endless visits to those who ought to have been equals but who were in truth her superiors. Rank without money was meaningless. All it afforded Lady Warde was crumbs and crusts, and what sort of life for her was that? It would require the disposition of a saint, and was Lady Warde a saint? It was an important question, all in all, given how strangely she had just behaved towards him.

"I will get to the point, Lady Warde," he said, opening his notebook, "since you wish to get this done with as quickly as possible. You will excuse me if my tone is a little direct."

She made no sign that she would.

"When did you last pay Eliza Jones?"

"Of what interest can that be to you?"

"I am trying to find out as much about her as I can."

"Surely that will not find her murderer?"

"The more I learn about a victim, the more I find I know about their killer. The one reflects another. There are always connections between them."

"Always? When a footpad sets upon a stranger walking home and slits their throat? How are they connected?"

"To return to my question —"

"Not until you have answered mine."

"Very well — the stranger may have been observed by the footpad for some hours previously. Perhaps he saw him selling his horse and putting a fat purse into his pocket. Or he observed the good cut of his coat and saw the glint of his seal fob. A hunter always observes its prey, even if it is only for a few moments. There is strategy in even the most opportunistic crime — indeed, one might say that opportunism is a form of strategy in itself. Does that answer your question?"

"I do not know," she said. "I still find yours offensive."

"I regret that you do, but it must remain on the table, so to speak. It would be useful to know. How much did you pay her? Does that make it easier?"

"Six pounds a year," she said. "And gifts, of course. As one does. We must always help those less fortunate than ourselves."

"So at such a wage, you would feel that she had nothing to complain about?"

"No, nothing at all, given how pleasant her life was. Her duties were light. Necessarily I do not have an extensive wardrobe. Compared with the work that Lady Rothborough's maid does, I think she was fortunate in her post."

Giles wondered how much Lady Rothborough's maid got paid — a visit to the steward's room and the account books would be in order.

"You said she came from an orphanage."

"Yes."

"It was charitable of you to take the risk of taking on an untrained girl as your personal attendant."

"I trained her myself – which was not difficult, because, as I have said before, my needs are simple. I did not need her to be skilled. Just a strong, sensible girl to mend my things, run errands, pack my box and help with my hair, and so forth. I did not wish for an expensive French girl with airs and problems."

"I see. Perhaps you could have done without a maid entirely, given the expense?"

"It did occur to me, but a clergyman friend told me about this poor girl. He asked if I might help find her a post through my connections, and in the end I took her on myself."

"And she came to you when?"

"About ten years ago. She was fifteen, I think."

"And you cannot recall anything more about her family background? Please try, Lady Warde, it may be important."

"I am afraid I know nothing about it."

"That is a pity," he said. He turned a page of his notebook. "Now about the last few days, before she was discovered – can you recall anything in her manner or behaviour that struck you as odd?"

He watched her hand again fold around the locket.

"Perhaps," she said. "I cannot be certain but I think, well, there is a gentleman in this house who would be more worthy of your attention, Major Vernon, than I. I think – I do not know for certain – but it struck me that Mr Syme and Eliza – one does not like to throw accusations around lightly, which is why I did not say anything at first, but now I consider it necessary."

"Mr Syme? That is interesting. Thank your for candour, Lady Warde."

"I do hope it is not true, of course," she said. "But I observed them talking once or twice when we were at Limpersleigh and it unsettled me. It was not quite right."

"How long were you at Limpersleigh?"

"From the end of the Season. From the end of May."

"And Mr Syme was there all that time?"

"Oh yes," she said, and gave a little sigh. "Oh dear, I do hope I have not said something slanderous."

The note of regret struck him as entirely false.

"Is that the first time you met Mr Syme? At the end of May?"

"No, no, he was at Richmond too. Lady Rothborough doesn't care to use Rothborough House during the Season but always stays at Richmond. He was there when I arrived in April from the Landishams."

"He was with you then for the whole of the season?"

"Yes."

"You only observed them talking, Lady Warde, nothing more than that?" Giles asked, thinking of Lady Maria's confident assertion that Syme had been kissing Lady Augusta. "I take it she was a pretty girl?"

"A pretty girl," she said. "And I fear he notices such things more than he ought. It was not just talking. It had an air of flirtation about it. I am not such an innocent that I do not know that when I see it."

"I shall certainly speak to Mr Syme," said Giles, closing his notebook and getting up from his chair. "Thank you very much, ma'am, for your time." He was not entirely surely he had got everything he needed from her, but her accusation was at least something he could begin to explore.

She rose also, still with her hand on the locket.

"Yes, a pretty girl," she repeated, almost absently.

"She did not confide in you, ma'am, even by hints?" he said.

"What do you mean, hints?" she said.

"The doctor who examined her body discovered she was with child."

"Oh..." She swayed for a moment and steadied herself on

132

the chair. "A child – no… two souls, not one… Dear Lord in Heaven!" She laid her other hand on Giles' arm, seemingly affected. "Your doctor is sure? That there was a child?"

"Yes, I am afraid so."

Her fingers gripped at his arm for a moment.

"Speak to Syme. That is what you must do!"

And then she fled the room. This time Giles permitted her to escape.

Chapter Fifteen

A woman murdered by the father of an unwanted child – that was an old and miserable tale, but was that the case here?

Syme was in the great library, surrounded by all the worldly knowledge that the Rothborough family had acquired over the centuries. Giles wondered how many of the books Syme would have gladly tossed on a bonfire to improve the general chances of mankind's salvation. Sitting there, his work spread out in front of him, he appeared lean-faced, committed, utterly in earnest and without discernible faults.

"Greek, I see, Mr Syme."

"Yes."

"Never my strongest subject," Giles remarked, wandering over to one of the bookcases and examining the titles of the books. "In a library such as this, I feel rather aware of the holes in my education."

"Greek would be an excellent place for you to start with that, sir," Syme said. "Any Christian who can, ought to try and read the Gospels in their original tongue. The word of the Lord is clearest here," he went on, tapping the open text in front of him.

"It will have to wait until my retirement," said Giles. "I have more urgent studies, such as the study of human nature."

"The study of the Gospel is one of our first duties. I hope you do not neglect that, sir."

Presumptuous whelp, thought Giles, taking his office so seriously.

"I have been given some information about you, Mr Syme, which may be pure slander. I have come here to give you the opportunity to refute it, as I am sure you will be able to do."

He pulled up a chair to Syme's work table and sat down.

"What sort of information?"

"A most unpleasant assertion. That you had an improper relationship with Miss Eliza Jones."

Giles studied his expression a moment to see how he took the news. Syme did not meet his eyes, but busied himself carefully, placing an embroidered marker in his Greek text and closing it. Giles wondered which female admirer had worked that for him. He continued: "Perhaps you might tell me how someone might have conceived such an idea? You were seen together and somehow my witness formed the impression that you and she were intimate."

"Your witness? Who is this witness?"

"I would rather not say."

"I think I should be told. If it is a question of my word of against theirs."

"You deny it, then?"

"Yes, yes, of course! It is a slander."

"So what did my witness see? You were seen together."

"This is the gossip of servants," said Syme. "Malicious, ignorant gossip. I am surprised to find that you give such stories even a moment's credit."

"I am giving you the opportunity to refute this slander, Mr Syme," Giles said. "I do not entirely credit it myself: what a person thinks that they have seen is sometimes a misinterpretation. However, a young woman has met her death in truly desperate circumstances, and I must sift through every piece of information I am given about her, in order to find what really happened. The fact that someone says that you and she had some sort of relationship, that you were seen in compromising circumstances – well, I must pursue that."

There was a silence. Syme picked up his pencil and turned it in his fingers.

"How old are you, Mr Syme?"

"Twenty seven."

"You ought to be married by now."

"I am hoping that I may be in the not too distant future."

"I think I can guess the name of the lady you have in mind."

Syme bit his lip and went on twisting the pencil. Giles reached out and took the pencil from him.

"An allegation such as the one I have heard against you, would make that alliance an impossibility, I think," Giles said, pointing the pencil at Syme. "You ought not to let it go unrefuted. You should gather your weapons and defend yourself against it."

"I deny it. Is that not enough for you?" said Syme.

"That is not sufficient. You must tell me how you think such a slander arose. What was seen was seen. Now, was she in distress of some kind? Did you offer some pastoral guidance? Young women who are vulnerable and troubled often cross the boundaries of respectful behaviour when they seek help."

Syme now closed his eyes and seemed to be offering up prayers.

"She was certainly troubled," he said, after a moment.

"In what respect?"

"She was altogether curious. For a person of her station, at times she had the manner of someone quite different. It was as if she were the daughter of a gentleman, but given that she was also a common thief –"

"You know that for a fact?"

"I caught her with several valuable little boxes. She took them from a side table at Lady Rothborough's house in Richmond. I saw her do it. I made her put them back, of course."

"You did not think of mentioning it to Lady Warde or Lady Rothborough?"

"No, since the boxes were put back, and she promised

me she would never do it again. It had been a single moment of folly. Or so she told me. I am not so sure now, given what happened afterwards –"

He covered his face with his hand, writhing with mortification.

"Which was?" Giles said gently. "This will feel better for the telling, Mr Syme. And you have a God who is loving and forgiving."

Syme took his hands from his face and stared across at Giles.

"Yes, sir, indeed! How right you are to remind me! And thanks be that He has called you to witness His infinite mercy."

"What happened, Mr Syme?"

"She... she..." He got up from his chair and began to pace about. "She was worried that I would betray her, although I had given her my word. She wished to make sure I kept it, and so she – oh, it was impossible! How was I to resist such an onslaught?"

"She offered herself to you?"

"Yes. Yes. And I failed. I failed myself and my God. I sinned, and on more than one occasion. She had me in her serpent's arms. I could not escape her. I was lost when I was with her!"

Then he fell to his knees and began to weep. It was a most unedifying sight and Giles wondered if it was not something of a performance.

"Come, Syme, control yourself," said Giles, going and standing over him. "Do not try to cloud the issue with hysteria."

"What do you mean, sir?" said Syme, gazing up at him with watery, wheedling eyes. Even the Holbroke spaniels would not have attempted such a trick.

"How are you different from other ordinary young men? You paint yourself too white and Miss Jones too black. Get up!"

Giles wondered for a moment if he ought to haul the wretch to his feet, but fortunately Syme began to master himself a little and dragged his long frame upright.

"Given that this seems a great burden to you, Mr Syme," Giles said, while the young man blew his nose, "I wonder why you did not approach me about it earlier. It can't have weighed so heavily. Perhaps you were distracted by another young person."

There was a long silence.

"Lady Aug – will she – ?" Syme began, with a gulp.

"Oh, I think so – unfortunately for you. I can't imagine that she won't find out what you have been up to. You are a material witness in this case, Mr Syme. Don't think that I can keep this quiet. Lord Rothborough will want a full report of my progress. The information you have given me is not something that can be concealed, even though it will not do your reputation much good."

"I am ruined," Syme said, throwing up his hands.

"You were reaching for an apple very high on the branch, while helping yourself to the windfalls at the same time," said Giles. "A game with high stakes. You might have avoided disaster, had you not let your prick be your master!"

"Sir!" exclaimed Syme.

"A pregnant girl has been murdered. That is what you should be concerned about. Not your reputation."

"Pregnant?" said Syme.

"Yes, an innocent unborn, four months at most, the surgeon said. And I wonder who the father might be?" Syme looked a little pained by this information, to do him credit. Giles went on: "Is that really such a surprise to you, Mr Syme?"

"There might," he said after a moment, "have been others. Given her disposition."

"That would be convenient for you. And at the same

time, most men, having made that sort of connection with a woman, are liable to find themselves angry at such behaviour. Even if we don't think we value a thing highly, when someone else makes a play for it, we are apt to see how much it means to us. Perhaps her infidelity has been eating away at you, Mr Syme, causing you some distress?"

He took a chair and forced Syme to sit down. He did not take much forcing. He collapsed upon it, his head again in his hands.

"Tell me when you last saw Eliza. When and where?"

"I... I simply don't... well, it may have been that day, that Tuesday that she –"

"The Tuesday she went missing?" said Giles, keeping his tone quiet and confidential. Syme's manner was promising – his voice scorched dry by his emotion. It would perhaps only be a matter of leading him along the right road and all would be revealed. A few more suggestive questions and he might break. Giles sat down beside him. "The Tuesday she went to meet someone in the Pleasure Gardens, yes?"

"That Tuesday, yes."

"When did you see her?" Syme gave a great sigh. "When?"

"That night," Syme said. "Only briefly. I was in the gardens – after dinner."

"Whereabout in the gardens?"

"The parterre – I had not gone far from the house. I had only gone out for a breath of air. I saw her – and she saw me. That was all."

"You did not speak?"

"No, no of course not. I was not alone, you see," he added.

"I do see. Then tell me who you were with on the parterre after dinner?"

"I would rather not say."

"By which I can infer that it was Lady Augusta?"

139

Syme nodded.

"Did Lady Augusta see Miss Jones?"

"No, no, I do not think she did. She was facing the other way. Miss Jones passed behind her."

"And saw you there with another woman? Perhaps in a compromising attitude?" Giles said.

"I may have had my arms about her. Only to comfort her, naturally – she was distressed."

"About what?"

"Some feminine trifle. A quarrel with one of her sisters, I think."

"Are you sure that was why you had your arms about her? This sounds rather like a tryst to me, Syme. Had you prearranged this meeting with Lady Augusta, or was she just taking the air after dinner? Did you meet by chance or design?"

"Does it matter, Major Vernon?" said Syme. "I cannot see how it matters."

"Every little detail matters in a case like this," Giles said. "What Miss Jones saw and the fact she saw you with another woman matters extremely. In fact, I think you should show me the exact spot where this took place, Mr Syme," said Giles. "Let us go out onto the parterre."

"Must we?" said Syme. "Can you not take my word for it?"

"A practical demonstration will make it all perfectly clear," Giles said.

It was a little past eleven when they went out onto the great south terrace, and the sun was already blazing down on Lord Rothborough's famous parterre. Here, a platoon of gardeners had created an ornate carpet of beds, planted with contrasting coloured flowers, and maintained meticulously. A couple of men were working on it even as Giles and Syme stood blinking and hatless in the scorching sunlight. They were carefully replacing any plants that had passed their prime, weeding and dead-heading. It was a fantastic and rather ridiculous labour – the effect, although impressive, could not be considered particularly beautiful. Giles hoped the men took some pleasure in it, especially on such a fierce day.

But there was something to be said for being caught hatless in the blazing light of high summer at noon. Syme was clearly suffering, and Giles wondered if, as the conversation proceeded, he would weaken and admit to the truth.

"Perhaps you could show me where you were when you saw Miss Jones?" he said.

It was now forming in his mind that, having been seen by Eliza Jones entangled in the arms of another woman, Syme now had even more motive for murdering her. This accident would have given her a powerful weapon against him. She could have easily brought his ambitions crashing down with a word to the right party. If she wanted him to do his duty by her and her unborn child, then she had plenty to keep him to her word, and perhaps that had made Syme anxious to the point of murderous distraction. It was a theory worth pursuing.

Syme walked towards one of the two corners of the parterre that were farthest from the house. The parterre was edged by low walls, each corner of which formed to make a convenient seat, and Syme sat down rather wearily on the bench and mopped his forehead with his handkerchief.

"And Lady Augusta was standing where, approximately?"

Syme made a gesture towards the ground in front of him.

"So you were looking back towards the house when you saw her?"

"Yes. She was in the lee of the wall, coming along there," Syme said, pointing.

It was certainly a prudent route for someone discreetly leaving the house to take. The ground was covered with mossy turf, which could be walked on soundlessly, and the wall provided some cover. A slight woman in a dark dress could be mistaken for a shadow if she took care not to be noticed.

"And which way did she go after she had passed by?"

"I don't know. I didn't look. I didn't wish to draw any attention to the fact we had been seen, so I simply –"

"Went on with what you were doing," Giles said. "I see. And for how long did you remain here?"

"I don't know. Not long. Naturally, Lady Augusta could not remain long. She left and I –" He broke off.

"Yes?"

"I sat here and contemplated my conduct," Syme said. "I prayed to be delivered from temptation."

"And were you?" Giles said. "Or did you go after her?"

"I… may have."

Giles sat down beside him.

"It would have been understandable if you did. You would want to explain to her, I think?"

Syme covered his hands with his face, and made a sort of nod. Feeling that something significant might soon be said, Giles pressed on gently. "So you sought her out?"

Syme took his hands from his face and gave a great sigh, and then in an instant, his demeanour changed entirely, in response to something he had caught sight of. Giles glanced behind him, and saw to his annoyance that Lady Augusta and Lady Rothborough were making a stately progress towards them. They were accompanied by one of the household's tallest footmen, who carried a great fringed parasol to shelter them from the sun, giving the whole ensemble a rather oriental effect.

Syme was on his feet already and heading towards them, his steps springy with relief at having escaped further questions. Indeed for a moment it looked as if he meant to hide behind the wide skirts of his noble patroness.

Giles got up and contemplated how he should go on, watching as Syme bowed and scraped to the ladies. He imagined quite another scenario, involving Syme and Eliza

Jones. Had Syme found her in the cave because he had known that was where she was going? Had there, in fact, been a pre-arranged tryst there between them which, because of Lady Augusta, then turned into a dangerous and aggressive quarrel? A torrent of angry, bitter words exchanged which then degenerated into violence? Perhaps she attacked him, causing him to lose his temper and retaliate. That, Giles knew, would be the way to get him to admit it: to suggest that he was provoked; to put all the blame on the woman; to insinuate that he might get away with manslaughter and escape the gallows.

He had established enough to make Syme a notable suspect, but not quite enough to arrest him at once, however tempting that might be.

"I do think we should go back into the house," Lady Rothborough said. "It is *trop fatigant* out here. It is unhealthy."

"Might I offer you my arm, my lady?" Syme said, and Lady Rothborough assented.

Giles was left to walk back to the house with Lady Augusta, who did not look like she would accept his arm if he offered it. Although her face was shaded by a deep bonnet brim, a glance was enough to reveal she was not at all at her ease. Giles wondered if she had come out to rescue her lover from him. The timing of their appearance was altogether too convenient.

"Lady Augusta," he said, slowing his step so that they fell far behind the others, "if I might have your attention. There are a few things we must discuss."

She stopped and nodded, but he saw her bite her lip.

"We will talk inside, of course, but I am glad you understand we must talk."

She nodded again, as if she did not trust her voice. She raised her hand and nervously adjusted her bonnet ribbon, which did not need adjusting.

They came into the pillared undercroft, which was hardly the place for this conversation, although it was delightfully

143

cool. Lady Rothborough stopped at the threshold to the great staircase hall, and turned, expecting Lady Augusta to come back to her side.

"Now, sir?" Lady Augusta said to Giles in a whisper.

"Yes, I would prefer it," Giles said.

It was imperative that he spoke to her before Syme could get to her and coach her in her answers. "Perhaps you could make some excuse to your mother now? Else I will be obliged to ask her to be present at the interview."

She darted forward, clearly galvanised by this threat. She was not ready to expose herself to her mother. She said something to her mother, which had the desired effect, and she went upstairs, accompanied by Syme.

"I said I would show you the chapel," she said.

"That is as good a place for this conversation as any," Giles said.

Chapter Sixteen

"You didn't say anything about visitors, Mr Carswell," said Mrs Bolland.

"Visitors?"

"Aye. With luggage." She gestured towards the box and travelling bag that were sitting in the hall. Felix recognised both these items by their shabby antiquity, and their appearance there was alarming. "Looking like they are planning on staying."

"Are they –?" He gestured upstairs towards the drawing room.

"Aye, sir. I gave them tea, as well," she added, as if she had given them her entire worldly goods.

"Thank you," he managed to say, as he pushed past her and strode up the narrow stairs, taking two steps at a time, his hat still on his head.

He walked into the drawing room, and immediately stumbled over the large shepherd's crook which was lying in his path. This wretched item was, as ever, in entirely the wrong place. Felix had spent most of his childhood falling over it.

He exclaimed loudly at it, and only just managed to restrain himself from using a coarse expression and kicking it across the room.

However, the sight that met his eyes – a woman in a black dress stretched out on the couch in the far corner, under the window – was enough to silence him. For a long and terrible moment he thought he was looking at the corpse of his mother, so still and white did she seem, with her head fallen back on the cushion, her cap gone awry.

He rushed over and knelt down beside her. He grabbed

her hand, anxious to feel her pulse – mercifully it was in evidence, but at the same time, her emaciated appearance could only excite his alarm. She had always been slight and delicate in her build, but now she struck him as dangerously wasted, and her greyish white pallor frightened him. Her hand was cold too, as if the heat of the day had no effect upon her. He began to rub her hand between his.

"Oh Felix, there you are," she said, stirring into life. Her eyes scarcely opened though, and her smile seemed an effort. "Was I asleep?" she went on in a dry whisper. "How strange. I did not mean to..."

He could not speak for a moment.

Behind him, there was a creaking in the easy chair, and he glanced over to see his father waking.

"But the journey was tiring, I suppose," she said.

A host of questions crowded his mind and it was not the moment for asking them.

"Here he is, James!" she said, and reached out and stroked Felix's cheek with her cold, bony knuckle.

"How long have you been in this state?" he said, unable to restrain himself.

"What do you mean?" she said.

"You're not well. You look so –" He let go of her hand and sprung round to come face to face with his father. "Why did you let her come all this way in this condition?" he burst out. "It's obvious that she is gravely ill. What on earth were you thinking?"

"That's no way to greet your father," he heard his mother say. "And I'm not ill, truly I am not."

To his horror she began to attempt to get up from the couch, when it was plain she scarcely had the strength to do so. She fell into his arms.

"I am only tired from the journey," she said, protesting still, as he helped her back onto the couch. "I am quite well, Felix. Just a little hungry and thirsty. There was tea, was there not? I think a cup of tea would set me straight."

His father made a discreet gesture, out of her eyeshot, that Felix was not to say another word on the subject. A fiction was clearly being kept up.

"Where is Molly?" Felix asked. Molly was a devoted servant and he would have been comforted to see her.

"Oh, she is not here. No, Molly would not have liked it. And I needed someone to feed my chickens and look after dear Tam." Tam was her beloved grey cat.

"The tea has gone cold," Mr Carswell said. "I will go and get Mrs Bolland to get some more. And you can rest upstairs, Mother. Major and Mrs Vernon are not here at present." He refrained from saying that they were at Holbroke. "So there are beds to spare. You will be more comfortable." Then he hoped he might make a proper examination of her – if he were allowed to. "And brandy and hot water, I think." Three glasses of brandy, he thought, for he felt he needed one as much as any of them.

He left them and went downstairs to give his instructions to the ever-grudging Mrs Bolland. In the end she was pacified by his handing over some money to cover the extra expenses of housekeeping. He ascertained that there was a jug of chicken broth made by Sukey for Mrs Vernon, sitting on an ice block in the larder, and she promised to send the girl out for fresh butter and rolls.

"That lady is your mother, sir?" she said.

"Yes," said Felix. "What of it?"

"It seems right odd, gentry folk arriving just like that." Her curiosity was clearly roused. "Smells of something, well –" She gave a little shrug.

What on earth was she thinking, he wondered. Did his parents, with their weathered and shabby appearance arriving unannounced and apparently throwing themselves upon his mercy, look to her like the actors in some sordid scandal?

"You are not paid to speculate on such things," he said,

rather sharply. "Do as I ask, and quickly, please!"

~

In the end he carried her up the stairs – she was no great burden – and laid her on Laura Vernon's bed. The room was, of course, in immaculate order, left so by Sukey.

"You've grown very strong, Felix," Mrs Carswell said. "You never could have lifted me so easily before."

"My work must be doing me good, then," he said, making an attempt to smile.

"Yes, you look well. Very fine. I like your coat," she added, touching the cloth of his sleeve. He was wearing a linen summer coat, the colour of a milky cup of tea, that Mr Loake had made for him.

"You look like a man of fashion," said Mr Carswell. It was quite a relief to hear him resume his usual tone. "I hope this Major Vernon of yours has not led you into vanity, Felix."

"Hardly," said Felix.

"This house seems vain enough," said Mr Carswell, touching the elaborate fringe on the bed curtains.

"He did not furnish it," said Felix. "He took it for the summer so his wife could take the waters. He has the plainest taste."

"I shall take the waters," said Mrs Carswell.

"They are extremely unpleasant," said Felix. "I couldn't recommend it. But Su–" he was forced to correct himself – "Mrs Connolly makes an excellent chicken broth. That would be a better idea."

"Mrs Connolly, that is Major Vernon's housekeeper?" said Mr Carswell.

"Yes, of course she is," said Mrs Carswell. "You have often mentioned her in your letters. She sounds a great treasure."

"She is," Felix said, and wished to God that she *were* there. She would have managed this situation perfectly. She would have known how to offer kindly and discreetly all the assistance his mother needed, and done it with such sweetness that it would have seemed like the greatest of pleasure for her to do it. She had nothing of servitude about her.

And he longed for her to be there, for his own sake, just to watch her going about her tasks. It would have calmed him, steadied his jangling nerves. As it was, he was struggling.

Mrs Bolland came in with the fresh tea and the brandy and hot water, and Felix was relieved that his mother took her glassful without much protest.

"We thought we would find rooms somewhere," his father said, having drunk his own brandy.

"You had better stay here," said Felix.

"We have brought our own sheets, of course," said Mrs Carswell, the brandy bringing a little welcome colour back to her complexion. "They are in the box. One never knows about the sheets in lodgings."

"I'll go and bring up the box," Felix said, draining his glass.

His father followed him downstairs.

"What is wrong with her?" said Felix, when they were in the lee of the stairs, and out of earshot.

"Her heart. Murray said..."

"Professor Murray?" said Felix. "You took her to Murray in Edinburgh?"

"Yes, that was the man you set great store by, I think?"

"Indeed," said Felix, though he wished they had not consulted him. Any diagnosis he made was liable to be extremely accurate, and suddenly Felix wanted as much room for error as possible. "And?"

Mr Carswell took a great breath: "He said –" But it was clearly too painful to repeat. Instead he laid his hands on

Felix's shoulders, gripped them, and said, "She thought – we thought – that you might be able to do something. And if not, then –"

"What did Murray say?" Felix said, again, but his father would not answer. Instead he began to climb upstairs with the bag. "Papa, you must tell me."

"He wrote it out for me," said Mr Carswell. "You may look at it later."

Murray might be wrong, Felix thought as he heaved the box upstairs. Even the greatest physicians made mistakes at times. There was always room for a second opinion, though he wondered how objective it was possible to be when the patient was an intimate. There was a detachment needed to make a really precise diagnosis, and he knew he could never achieve that when it came to her.

Mrs Bolland reappeared with the broth and the bread, and they proceeded to arrange themselves to make an odd sort of picnic luncheon in Mrs Vernon's bedroom. The old customs could not be disregarded and his father said a long and sincere grace over the unbroken bread, and Felix, who in times past might have been annoyed by this, was oddly moved. The quiet family circle of the three of them, unexpectedly reconstituted after such an interval, held its old comforting power, despite the quicksands of uncertainty.

Chapter Seventeen

A young lady who had entered into a foolish romantic entanglement deserved to be treated delicately, no matter how silly she had been. Lady Augusta was going to suffer enough when the truth came out: from a broken heart and from considerable loss of face, and the latter, Giles suspected, would mean more to her than the former. For a women to allow herself to be trifled with by a social inferior was a sin not easily forgotten.

They entered the chapel, which was as sumptuously arranged as the rest of the house and had the appearance of a theatre rather than a place of worship, with a velvet-hung gallery, entered from above, where the family might pray in comfort. The household, however, sat on benches in the main body of the chapel below. Some of these were furnished with squab cushions, presumably for the upper servants, but apart from that, comfort was in short supply.

Giles chose a lowly bench in the shadow of the gallery and Lady Augusta sat down beside him.

"I cannot lie to you here, can I?" she said, in a tiny voice.

"Were you thinking of doing so?" he said.

"He —" She broke off, and stared at the cross above the communion table. "Oh dear, oh dear..."

"Let us go back a step or two," said Giles, feeling her heaviness of heart as if it were his own. The poor creature, for all her advantages, had been pulled into a net. "That will make it easier. And remember, this is the right thing to do. To act for justice, no matter how painful, is always right."

"Yes, yes," she said, straightening. "Thank you."

"I want to talk to you about last Tuesday night," he said,

opening his notebook. "What happened after dinner, to be precise."

"Tuesday last. That is the day Eliza Jones went missing."

"Yes, and I think you may have seen her that night."

"Yes, I did."

"And where was this, Lady Augusta?"

"In the garden, after dinner. I was in the little pavilion at the far corner, and I saw her pass by the edge of the parterre."

"And?"

"I don't know what you mean."

"You don't know what time this was?"

"No. I was there after dinner, that is all I can say."

"And why were you there?"

"Because, because... I think you know why, sir."

"I need to hear your account of it, I'm afraid."

"Very well. I went to talk with Mr Syme."

"And how long did you talk with him for? Were you there half an hour, perhaps, or longer?"

"I am not sure. We had a great deal to discuss."

"And what happened when you saw Miss Jones? Did you simply see her pass by or did she see you?"

There was a long silence, and Augusta said, "She saw us."

"How do you know this?" Giles said.

"Because she spoke to him. And in such a fashion. I think she had been drinking. She was very wild. It was quite shocking."

"What did she say, precisely?"

"I cannot repeat it. It was indelicate."

"Can you give me the gist of it, then?"

Lady Augusta hesitated for a moment. "She reproached him, in strong language."

"And how did Mr Syme take this?"

"Of course, he told her to hold her tongue and tried to get her to go away, but she would not. So he went out of the pavilion and took her to one side, and said something, and that silenced her and she went on her way."

"And how did Mr Syme explain all this to you?"

"He said she was a poor sad creature who had lost her wits, who had conceived a passion for him – which of course he had done nothing to encourage."

"And you believed that?"

"Yes," she said, after a moment. "Of course I did. He had just asked me to share his lot with him, and I would never agree to marry a man I could not trust entirely."

"So he spoke to her and returned to you?" said Giles.

"Yes."

"And you are certain about that?"

"Yes."

"And how long did you remain there?"

"Another hour, perhaps. Until it got dark."

"You did not think you would be missed from the drawing room, then?"

"No, I had said I was going to bed."

"When in fact you had a tryst with a lover?"

"With a man I intend to marry, Major Vernon," she said, with a touch of defiance.

"Still?" he said.

She covered her face with her hands.

"You said you would tell me the truth," he went on. "I am not sure this is it in its entirety, Lady Augusta. A man who asks you to lie for him is not worthy of your affection, let alone your hand."

Slowly she got up and walked up to the communion rail and stood staring again at the cross, her hand pressed to her breast. Giles could see that there were tears streaming down her face.

"I am sorry to have to press you like this, but you know in your heart that it is for the best."

She nodded.

"You see, I don't think you would have stayed with him

after Eliza Jones came and said those shocking things to Mr Syme. You would have taken flight, leaving him there with her. You had already lied to your parents about your whereabouts, for his sake, and your conscience was burning like fire already, I should imagine."

"Yes, yes," she said, reaching for the rail to steady herself. She turned slightly towards him. "How did you know?"

"I know you are a good daughter. Anything he has made you do is an aberration. Her distress will have roused your suspicions, I think."

"She was so unhappy," she said. "And to think he might have caused that – yes, I was frightened and confused and so uncomfortable, so I ran back to the house when he went to speak to her. You are a magician, Major Vernon, you can see into my head!"

"So your earlier story?"

"He told me to say that was what happened, should I be asked." She now fell to her knees and covered her face. "Oh dear Lord! And since then I have told myself a hundred thousand times that he could not do such a thing to a poor creature, but now –"

Giles left her there to her prayers and self-reproaches. He came out of the chapel to find Sukey waiting in the undercroft.

"I saw you out in the garden, sir," she said. "I hope you don't mind. I wanted a word. In private."

"Is it Mrs Vernon –?" he began.

"Oh, no, she's quite well – she and Lady Maria are practising piano duets together. They decided it was too hot to go out, mercifully. No, it is about this business with the jewels. You did say they went from a cabinet in the strong room?"

"Yes?"

She nodded, thought for a moment and said, "Then I think I have worked out how it might have been done – if you'll let me try and explain."

"I am all ears," Giles said.

"This morning, I was going down to the servants' quarters and I wanted something from the housekeeper – some more camomile tea for Mrs Vernon – so I was waiting outside her room." She broke off. "Perhaps I should show you – it would be easier to explain if we are there."

So they went together down the tunnel and into the complicated tangle of rooms and passageways that kept the great house running so comfortably.

Sukey stopped at a bend in the corridor.

"Now, if you stand here, you can see everything coming and going along that passageway."

"And that is the housekeeper's room there?"

She nodded. "Almost at the centre of everything. And it is quite busy along here at that time in the morning, because they are taking the plate out of there to clean it. Four of the footmen went into that room several times with it and came out again without closing the door behind them, let alone locking it. It struck me, that if you had a mind to it, and you knew what you were doing, it would be easy to slip in when the door was open and do what you had to, and all the time the men would be standing gossiping over there, taking their ease – just like they did this morning." She gave a slight shrug. "But perhaps I'm just being daft?"

"No, not at all," Giles said, rather impressed with her analysis of the possibilities.

"And then I thought, if you had the right tools, then it would be easy."

"Yes, quite." He found he was slightly shocked. "Tell me, how do you know about such things?"

"My late husband – he and his friends were great ones for the craic. They would sit by the fire, drinking and talking of everything, politics, poetry, crime – everything under the sun. I was in the corner, listening. It was an education of sorts."

"I am sorry you were exposed to that," Giles said, rather disturbed at what she might have heard. O'Brien had said that

Sukey's husband had been a wastrel, who fancied himself a writer, but had preferred the bottle and bad company. "They should have stopped their tongues, out of consideration to you."

"I don't think they even noticed I was there. And there was nowhere else for me to sit, and I was not an object of any interest to them. Besides, I am glad I heard it – all of it. Ignorance is as corrupting for a woman as coarse talk. Stupidity is a dangerous condition. Isn't that what you tell your men?"

"I can't argue with that," he said with a sigh. What she had endured was not pleasant to contemplate. "And I have to say I am glad of your knowledge and observations. As a hypothesis that is plausible. One might make a broad assumption that Eliza Jones is our jewel thief."

"Perhaps it was for her lover," Sukey said. "A woman will take stupid risks for a man she loves, and stealing a set of jewels like that is taking risks."

"She was with child. I wonder if she was trying to secure her future."

"Oh poor soul," said Sukey. "Yes, that makes sense. But then how is she to sell stuff like that?"

"To a fence or to someone who knows a fence."

Giles thought for a moment. Syme was most unlikely to have that kind of connection, and he had mentioned other men.

"I thought half an hour ago that I might have identified the father," he went on, "but you are making me wonder if there isn't something more complicated going on here. If she had the right contacts then she might have stolen to order. That is often what happens with serious thefts. Someone asks for it to be obtained. She would have to know it was there in the first place, as well."

"That would be common knowledge, surely, Major, amongst the maids, among all the servants, for that matter? If

156

Miss La Roche goes down there regularly to fetch things for Lady Rothborough, then anyone standing where I was would know that was where the jewels were kept. She would see Miss La Roche going in and out with the jewel cases. If Miss Jones was staying here with her mistress all those times before, then..." Sukey shrugged. "She might even have seen them. Perhaps she asked to see them. I could imagine that. Maybe on another visit. You did say she had stayed here before?"

Giles nodded. "We must talk to Miss La Roche again. What you say makes perfect sense."

"And did you not say that her Ladyship does not like the parure, that she never wears it?"

"So it might have been stolen months ago, and no one would be any wiser, because no one has asked for it – until yesterday."

"But if Miss Jones were still alive," Giles said, "would we suspect her? Is the fact she has been murdered making us construct a false connection? Perhaps she is just an innocent victim."

"I would say that people get murdered for a reason," said Sukey after a moment.

"There is something in that," he said. "Now did you say you were down there this morning to ask for tea from the housekeeper?"

"Yes, camomile."

"Where did that tea come from?"

"A tin in the dry stores room. I went in with Mrs Hope. It's just off her sitting room."

"Yes, of course it is!" said Giles. "And was the door to the store locked?"

"No. Why?"

"We found tea, dried tea, in Miss Jones' cuffs. I was wondering where it might have come from. How would you come to have tea in the cuff of your sleeve? May I?" He caught Sukey's hand, and looked at her cuff. Like Eliza Jones' it was deep and the end was folded back. "Excuse me," he said, dropping her hand. "I need to try an experiment. Will you help me with it? It is rather a wild thought, but there might be something in it."

A few minutes later they were with Mrs Hope in the large, well-appointed dry store room that, as Sukey had pointed out, adjoined her sitting room. It resembled a fashionable grocer's store, with every edible commodity imaginable having a specific container, from tiny cannisters of expensive, exotic spices to great wooden barrels of flour and meal. However, it was the large japanned tea chests that interested Giles.

He took a folded piece of paper from his pocket. It contained the tea leaves he had found in the cuff of Miss Jones' sleeve.

"Now, Mrs Hope, what sort of tea is that?"

She put on her glasses and examined it.

"That's a black Indian."

"And which chest is that in?"

"This big one here, sir."

"May I see inside it?"

She pulled out the chest and opened it.

"When was this refilled?" he asked, observing it was almost full.

"Oh, about a fortnight ago, just before the family got back. I can give you the exact date – it is in my ledger."

"You supervised the filling?"

"Yes, sir, of course. Bard the grocer from Stanegate supplied it. I like to see exactly what goes in there. You can never be sure with these people. Why, sir?"

"If you will just indulge me a moment," Giles said, taking off his coat and handing it to Sukey. He then rolled up his shirt sleeve, plunged his hand deep into the chest, and began to rummage around. Mrs Hope and Sukey looked at him as if he were a madman, which he felt himself to be for some long moments, until his fingers suddenly came across something hard. He seized it and pulled out his hand, causing a small explosion of tea leaves over the floor. In his hand he held a simple drawstring bag, made of linen ticking. It jangled and clattered as he set it down on the table.

"That isn't... is it?" Sukey said, in an excited whisper.

"I think it might be," he said, taking his coat back from her. "Please do the honours."

Sukey opened the bag and reached in tentatively. She came out with a glittering crown, thick with diamonds, rubies and pearls.

"Oh my!" exclaimed Mrs Hope. "It's the Rothborough tiara. What on earth was it doing there?"

"With luck, we have the whole parure," said Giles, looking into the bag. It contained a dazzling jumble of jewels.

Sukey stood gazing at the object in her hands, quite transfixed by its extraordinary lustre. Then, as if it were about to burn her, she quickly set it down on the table.

"What is that all worth, do you think?" she said, watching as Giles reached into the bag and came out with a matching bracelet.

Mrs Hope could not resist the lure of the tiara and was turning it in her hands.

"It's so heavy!" she said. "No wonder her Ladyship doesn't care to wear it. It would give you a terrible headache. But on the right head, it would look very fetching. Lady Charlotte, for example –" She sighed and put it down on the table.

"We had better go and see Lord Rothborough," Giles said putting the tiara and bracelet back into the bag. "Come Sukey, you did most of the work of finding them. You can give his jewels back to him," he said, giving her the bag.

~

They found Lord Rothborough with Charlotte and Augusta in his private study. It was clear that a scene that was far from pleasant had been taking place. Augusta was obviously in some distress, and the moment Giles came in she made for the door.

"Augusta –" Rothborough said, but she ran past Giles.

"This is perhaps not the best moment," Giles said.

"I hope you have good news for me, Major," Lord Rothborough, with a great sigh. "I have been hearing some sorry tales just now."

"We have recovered the jewels, but that is probably poor consolation in the circumstances," Giles said.

He gestured to Sukey who presented the bag to Lord Rothborough with a curtsey. He stared at it with some astonishment.

"In here?"

"In a tea chest," said Giles, "in the dry goods larder."

"How extraordinary," said Rothborough, opening the bag and laying out the pieces on his desk. "There is a bracelet missing – but otherwise, this is the complete set. Here, Charlotte, this was your grandmother's favourite piece. It was got from Russia, I believe." And he handed Lady Charlotte the tiara. "Put it on," he said. "I have often thought you should wear it."

Rather self-consciously, to her credit, Lady Charlotte obeyed her father and crowned herself.

"Magnificent," said her father. "Thank you, Major Vernon."

"It was Mrs Connolly who solved the greater part of the puzzle," Giles said.

"Be careful he does not make you a constable, Mrs Connolly," said Lord Rothborough.

"Now, that is a good idea," said Giles. "I have often thought that women constables would be of great service in certain situations."

"Oh, I should not care for such a cut in my wages," said

160

Sukey, with a smile.

"Too sensible by half," said Lord Rothborough.

Giles studied the display of jewels.

"Does the other bracelet resemble this one?"

"Yes, they are a pair," said Lord Rothborough.

"I wonder where that might have got to. We should search Miss Jones' room again. But she was perhaps too clever for that. Of course, the bracelet may have gone on ahead, so to speak, as an advance sample."

"Perhaps to the man who killed her," Sukey said.

"Perhaps," said Giles. "And Syme may help me with that, when I have put him a little longer on a mental rack. He may give me some clue as to who this other man might be."

"I am glad to hear that!" said Rothborough. "And I am glad you are here to deal with him, for I am not sure I could be responsible for my actions if the wretch were to cross my path. He has used Augusta abominably! I have a mind to have Bodley lock him in his room. He will be grateful for it – a stout door will protect him from me, the insolent beggar."

"From what Augusta said," Charlotte said, "it seems he may have killed Miss Jones."

"I am not sure of that," Giles said. "But he is certainly a strong suspect at present. I trust that with a little pressure, he may tell us a great deal more."

"You mean he will confess?" she said.

"He may exonerate himself or hang himself. We shall see."

Chapter Eighteen

Syme was in his room. He had sent for his luggage and was packing, or rather he was throwing things into his box in a fashion suggestive of panic.

"Do not imagine you will be allowed to leave in these circumstances," Giles said, closing the door behind him and leaning against it. "You and I have only just begun talking."

Syme put down the bundle of folded linen he was holding and said, "Whatever Lady Augusta has said to you –"

"I am to disregard?"

"She may be confused about what occurred. Women are liable to misinterpret things, especially when they are swayed by their feelings."

"Lady Augusta struck me as anything but confused," Giles said. "Sit down, Mr Syme, will you?" He took his notebook from his pocket and consulted it. "Now, you claim that you only saw Miss Jones pass by the pavilion where you had your tryst with Lady Augusta."

"Yes, yes, that is all," he said, sitting down in the armchair.

"Yet you told Lady Augusta to spin quite a different tale should I ask about this. She claims that you asked her to say that you went and spoke to Miss Jones, but only for a moment." Syme studied his fingers and made no move to answer. "Is she mistaken about that?"

"She may have recalled it wrongly."

"Or you forgot what you told her to tell me?" Giles said. "That is the trouble with lying, one is liable to make mistakes."

"I think she was mistaken," he said.

"That's interesting," said Giles. "So now I have three

versions of what happened." Syme glanced at him nervously. "Your initial account, the version of events that you asked Lady Augusta to recount and, finally, another one entirely, which she eventually admitted to me, in a state of some distress."

"If she was in distress then you must doubt the veracity of it," Syme said after a moment.

"You are a fine lover," said Giles. "Very gallant. This third story is rather inconvenient for you, so I will excuse you. Lady Augusta told me that after Eliza Jones appeared and abused you, she was so shocked at what she saw and heard, that she at once ran back to the house."

"She may have done," Syme said.

"Leaving you alone with Eliza Jones, yes?"

"Yes," said Syme after a pause, not meeting Giles' eye.

"And how did it go on from there? What did Eliza say to you? Lady Augusta said she was angry with you."

"She was."

"Why?"

"Because I had resisted her. She did not care for that. She was so... depraved. She was determined to compromise me. She was determined to drag me down with her. When she saw me with – well, her vile temper got the better of her, and of course, she had no compunction about making a scene! Her language was beyond belief. It shocked me, for generally she had this air of gentility about her, almost as if she were a lady, but that night..." Syme shook his head.

"How long did this outburst last?"

"I can't really say. I was attempting to calm her, of course, because I was afraid it would attract attention, but I did not seem to get through to her."

"You did not lose your own temper?" Syme glanced away. "It must have been provoking. Most men would struggle to keep their tempers in such circumstances."

"I may have raised my voice."

And smashed her head against the cave wall? Giles wondered.

"And this all took place where?"

"By the little pavilion. Just as I showed you earlier."

"And why was she there?"

"I suppose she had come to find me."

"Had you met her there previously?"

"We may have done," Syme said after a moment.

"When?"

"Two days previously."

"And what happened then?"

There was a long silence.

"We went into the woods."

"For what purpose?" Giles said, already guessing the answer.

There was another long silence. Syme got up from his chair and turned away before he found the courage to speak.

"She demanded it from me. She insisted. She was like an animal. I had no choice! And after that, that was when I said 'no more!'"

"Where in the woods?"

"Does it matter?" Syme said.

"Yes, very much," said Giles. "Sit down again, please." Syme obeyed. "Where?"

"We went to the Pleasure Gardens."

"Whereabouts?"

"There is a little rustic shelter, in that part where all the yews are cut in strange shapes."

"So three nights before Miss Jones is discovered drowned in the pool in the Pleasure Gardens you were having congress with her in the rustic hut not twenty five yards away. Yes?"

"Yes," Syme said.

"And how did you know about this convenient rustic hut?"

"We... we had been there before."

"I see. And did you go there again? Well, sir? On the night in question, before she died?"

Syme looked up at him, with a pitiful expression.

"Yes. We did," he said. Then he got up, strode over to the bedside and took up his Bible. "But I swear to you, sir," he said, clutching the book to his chest, "on the Holy Bible, that she was alive when we parted. I did not murder her. I may have wanted to, Lord forgive me, but I did not!"

"Tell me how it was that you left her, then," Giles said.

"She was sitting on the bench. She was laughing at me. She said I was a dirty fellow and that she should ask me for a sovereign for her trouble in future."

"That would be provoking," Giles said mildly. "Given her earlier conduct towards you."

"I was not provoked!" said Syme.

"You would have felt quite justified in striking her for that," Giles went on. "If there was an accident of some description, Mr Syme, tell me now. I will do all I can to help you if that is what happened. Her behaviour was certainly shocking enough to make any man lose control, if only for a moment. But sometimes it only takes a moment for disaster to strike."

"I did not lose control," said Syme. "You are misunderstanding me, sir. I am not your murderer. I have sworn to you that I am not! I told her the time and left her there, living!"

"You told her the time?" said Giles.

"Yes, she asked me what time it was, just before I went."

This little detail struck Giles as most intriguing. "And what time was it?"

"A little before eleven. Ten to. And then I left. I swear to you, sir!"

"I believe you," said Giles.

"You do?" said Syme.

"Yes," said Giles, various other interesting ideas forming

in his mind.

"Oh merciful Lord!" Syme clasped his hands together and closed his eyes for a moment. Then, he opened them again.

"Will I be able to leave?" he said.

"I shall need to take a written statement before then," said Giles. "A full and honest account of your relations with this woman, yes?"

"Yes, yes, of course." He was a little delirious. "Oh thank you, Lord!"

"He might have spared you from the gallows, Mr Syme," Giles could not resist saying as he went to the door. "But He may not save you from Lord Rothborough."

~

"I've just heard a bit of talk, sir," Holt said coming into Giles' room with a pair of freshly cleaned boots, "that might be of use to us. There is a dog fight on tonight at The Three Horseshoes in Byrescough – apparently always attracts a good crowd, and is reckoned to be a regular thieves' kitchen. I was thinking, if you didn't need me, sir, I could go and see what the talk is, if anyone is talking – who might be buying, that sort of thing."

"A sound plan," said Giles, reaching for the map of the district he had borrowed from Lord Rothborough's library. "What was the name of the place again?"

"Byrescough – just beyond Low Arden. At the crossroads."

"Show me," Giles said, unrolling the map on the writing table in front of him. Holt pointed out the village. "A promising spot," he said, measuring the distances with his finger. "Five miles south of Market Craven and a dozen north of Stanegate – just about close enough for the swell mob of

166

either town to come for an evening's entertainment."

"Full moon and fine weather too," said Holt. "It'll be quite a draw."

"Then we'll seize the opportunity."

"We, sir?" said Holt.

"I'll come with you."

"Begging your pardon, sir, for the liberty, but I don't think that would be wise. In such company, you'd be, well —"

"I don't intend to go as myself," Giles said. "I'll go incognito, as will you, Holt. I will rough myself up and you can be my master. We'll invent some story."

Holt did not look at all convinced by this plan.

"You look too much the gentleman, sir, you wouldn't fool a babe. Especially if you open your mouth."

"I know it doesn't seem likely, but I have a little experience of this. In Upper Canada I eavesdropped on a nest of rebels in the guise of a simpleton from Morpeth. That fellow might do the trick tonight."

"If you say so, sir," said Holt. "But I had better do the talking."

"Aye, right you are, master," said Giles, in the broad Northumbrian accent that he had learnt from his nurse. "And I'll swear off the hard stuff."

Holt absorbed the impression for a moment and then, said, with a sly smile, "And you'll speak when you're spoken to."

"Aye, master."

"You'd better not do that too long, sir," Holt said, "or I'll get used to it and forget my place."

"For the purposes of getting good intelligence, the more convincing we are, the better. Do what you must, Holt. Now, we must find some suitable rig-outs. Lady Charlotte may be able to help us with that."

Given the family's fondness for dressing up and theatricals, Lady Charlotte was indeed able to help. She took them to the dressing room next to the theatre room. It contained trunks full of old clothes and accoutrements, gathered over the years, and Lady Rothborough and Lady Maria were already there, sorting through the treasure for that evening's entertainment.

"Just in time, Major Vernon," said Lady Rothborough. "Mrs Vernon is trying on her costume."

As if on cue, Laura, attended by Sukey, came out from behind a screen, dressed in a high-waisted, old-fashioned, silver and white muslin gown of the sort Giles remembered women wearing in his childhood. She stood barefoot in the centre of the room, the silver spangles flashing in the sunlight, while Lady Maria draped an amber gauze scarf about her. The dress was short on her long frame, increasing the impression of a classical tunic, and she wore a quiver containing real arrows, which added to her authority. Yet her expression was one of shy excitement as she scanned the room, anxious to see what they all thought.

He did not know what to say, but went and took her hand, squeezed it and then raised it to his lips. If they had been alone he would have taken her in his arms and kissed her.

How had this transformation occurred? How had they been so fortunate after so much misfortune? She had been so lost and now here she was, recovered, as beautiful as ever. For there was now in her something more – the core of her was stronger, more lustrous and more admirable because of what she had endured. Experience had made a woman of her. She had been tried by the direst of afflictions and yet she stood here now, a dazzling, barefoot goddess, the object of every eye in the room.

"Your crown, Mrs Vernon," said Lady Maria. "Your crown!"

Giles felt no further touch could improve her, but Lady Maria was intent on a coronation. The crown of brass and paste was styled like a classical diadem and Lady Maria was at pains to arrange it 'just so.' This involved some undignified stooping on Laura's part, she being so tall and Lady Maria so small, but it made them all smile, and to see Laura smile in such an unforced way was another delight for him.

Lady Rothborough said, "We must look out your costume, Major Vernon – and something for your man, I think. He is a splendid looking fellow. What is your name?" she said to Holt.

"Edward Holt, my lady," said Holt and made a courtly bow. Giles wondered if he would soon lose Holt to the comfort and splendour of the Rothborough household. A lively, good-looking and intelligent servant like Holt would always be on the look-out for a more comfortable situation.

"I believe we have some armour that would fit you well, Holt," said Lady Rothborough.

"Oh yes, and the plumed helmet!" exclaimed Lady Maria.

"This will be very splendid," said Lady Rothborough, clapping her hands. "We have never before had a couple who will look so well as Dido and Aeneas."

"When are we doing the paintings, Mama?" Lady Charlotte asked.

"Tonight, after dinner."

"Then I must apologise, Lady Rothborough," Giles said. "Holt and I will not be able to participate. We have business tonight. I'm sorry."

"Tomorrow, then!" said Lady Rothborough. "We will defer our pleasures for a good effect. Holt, when you have finished your duties for your master, go and speak to Mr Bodley, my husband's man, about the armour. He will get you tricked out."

"That'd be a great honour, my lady," said Holt.

"Now, I think it is time for us all to retire, ladies," said Lady Rothborough. "This heat – the Spanish with their siestas are really so sensible! And Mrs Vernon, I think you look rather pale." She stepped forward and with a gracious gesture, proceeded to wrap Laura in her own shawl.

They all left, except for Lady Charlotte who was sorting through the trunks of costumes.

"A filthy old coat for me," said Giles, taking off his coat, "and something flashy for Mr Holt. Although that armour might come in handy where we are going."

"Will this do?" said Charlotte, producing a much patched and stained fustian redingote. "This is our usual beggar's mantle. It might just fit." She handed it to Holt, who took it with disdain and helped Giles into it.

"It does have a rather distinctive odour, I'm afraid," said Lady Charlotte.

"Rather you than me, sir," said Holt, stepping back as Giles settled into the coat.

"A beggar canna be a chooser," said Giles, turning up the collar and burying his hands into the pockets, so that he was stooping. "My old faither's coat does me well enough, my lady."

"Is there no end to your talents, Major Vernon?" said Lady Charlotte. "Even your wife will not know you."

"That is the plan," said Giles.

He remembered with a smile that night in Upper Canada. After having spent the evening in a low tavern pretending to be a common farm servant from Morpeth, he had appeared in their bedroom still in his disguise, and proceeded to stay in character, wooing Laura, as if she were a dairymaid and his sweetheart.

She had been delighted. They had only been married a month, and their eagerness for one another was entirely undimmed. It had been a passionate charade. He had promised ribbons in return for allowing him liberties and she had played up to her part, demanding a new bonnet for a full conquest. They had slept until noon the next day, earning Giles a dressing-down from the Colonel for missing parade duty, but he was soon forgiven when it became clear he had identified a nest of rebels as a result of his escapade.

Would Laura be as amused this time, he wondered, if he again appeared in disguise? Could those pleasant ghosts be raised and allow them again to be man and wife as they once had been? He would have to be made of stone not to feel moved to action, having just seen her so gloriously decked out in that spangled muslin dress, with her hair down. When Lady Rothborough had wrapped her shawl about her, it had been like the clouds obscuring the full moon.

Chapter Nineteen

Luck was with them. The night was clear and warm, and the full moon a great gold lantern to guide them on their way. There would be a good crowd on such a night, and there was the sense of holiday in the air as they made their way from the East Lodge of the park at Ardenthwaite.

Lord Rothborough, to whom Giles had been obliged to outline their plan, had suggested this strategy, knowing the district well. He advised them to leave their horses in the care of the farrier in Ardenthwaite village.

"Jem Harris – an excellent man, and a good friend of mine," Lord Rothborough said.

Mr Harris was as obliging as Lord Rothborough said he would be. Giles described their intended exploit in terms of enforcing the recent Act of Parliament against animal cruelty, rather than searching for a fence. A breeder of fine Water Spaniels himself, the farrier was no friend to those who organised dog fights.

"I'll take you to within sight of the place myself, sir, but I can't trust myself to go in with you. I would do more harm than good," he said. "I should get myself into a scrap."

His caution was to be regretted. His trade had made a heroic figure of Jem Harris – he was decidedly brawny, and would have been a useful ally in a fight as well as a noble figure in one of Lady Rothborough's tableaux. But Giles could not help but admire his good sense. "Anything to put an end to those dirty ruffians," Mr Harris went on. "I could tell you some tales about what goes on, and I am glad to see the law taking an interest in it at last. The constables here, well –" He shrugged.

In this he echoed his noble friend. Lord Rothborough had been pleased to hear of Giles proposing to gather intelligence at an illegal dog fight. He had sponsored the Bill himself, and made a fair few speeches on the subject in the House. "It is an embarrassment that such a barbaric custom persists in my own country. It is another of the great failings of the wretched Sir Arthur – he does not like the legislation and as a result his lacklustre constables do nothing to enforce it. But this will be a great weapon for our cause, Major Vernon, if you are a witness to such an event. A full report from an impeccable source – arrests will have to follow."

"You may be sure of that," Giles had said.

"There are no dog fights in your domain, I suspect, Major Vernon. You would not tolerate such a thing."

"That's true," Giles said. "But I think it has been driven elsewhere. That is the problem with criminal activity. It is like water. If you block the flow in one place, it will find an outlet elsewhere."

"And that is a fine argument for universal, uniform systems of law enforcement, is it not? Not our present, antiquated, piecemeal system. Still, inch by inch, we do progress, do we not?" Lord Rothborough concluded.

"I hope so," said Giles.

"All strength to your arm. And perhaps we may recover that bracelet!"

~

True to his word, Jem Harris led them across the field roads to the outskirts of the hamlet of Byrescough, which was not really worth the name of hamlet. It consisted of a few dirty-looking cottages, a scrappy area of common which no local landowner had considered worth enclosing, and The Three Horseshoes, which squatted toad-like in the corner of the crossroads, its ancient walls bulging and sagging under a badly tiled roof. It was the sort of establishment that only the most desperate traveller would visit.

The crowds were there, as Giles had predicted. There was a group standing in the road drinking and smoking, as if the inn were already packed to the rafters.

"I hope you've got something to protect yourself with, gentlemen," said Harris.

"Oh, aye," said Holt, tapping his coat. "We have."

"Only to be used in extremis, Holt," Giles murmured, "remember."

"Good luck to you," said Harris. "I'll be off now and leave you to your business."

Giles and Holt made their way to the inn, with Holt assuming the jaunty stride of a professional ne'er-do-well who had done well for himself after all, his splendid silk hat flashing. There were plenty of other stovepipes in evidence – some perched on the heads of young men in fancy waistcoats. From their stance and manners, Giles recognised them as officers out on a spree. Other silk hats were sported by more solid, middle-aged characters, who might have been wool merchants, solicitors or manufactory owners. They were mixing comfortably with prosperous farmers in their low-crowned billy-cock hats and creating a rare and interesting mingling of town and country. All in all, there were many men that one would not have expected to find at an event that had so recently been declared by Parliament to be illegal. However, old habits died hard. What had been an acceptable entertainment in Giles' own youth was now rightly outlawed. It had had its day and had no place in a modern, civilised country. Yet it often took time for custom to catch up with legislation.

Giles bent his shoulders and followed his master for the evening into the thick of the crowd. They made their way into the tap room with some difficulty, past a bevy of ribboned women who were sitting on the long benches in the hall, eyeing up potential customers. One of them caught hold of Holt's coat tail and was determined to pull him into her smiling, silky web.

"Later, darling," said Holt. "Save yourself for me."

The tap room was vast, but the crowd was equal to it. Giles scanned the room, looking for likely characters. He saw some faces he recognised from the shadier districts of Northminster, and realised he would need to be careful, despite his disguise.

They had decided that Holt was to make enquiries for trinkets to pacify his missus after a quarrel. Something pretty and unusual, and as special as could be got. Holt bought himself a glass of brandy and water, graciously allowed his hapless servant a small mug of beer, and then set to work making suitable sporting small talk with likely coves.

Within a few moments Giles felt his instincts concerning Holt to be vindicated. His impersonation was faultless – his manner calculated nicely to place him squarely as a man of honour in the shadow fraternities. It struck Giles as so convincing that Holt might easily have made this life for himself, instead of that of a loyal soldier and then obedient domestic. Would he not prefer at heart to be his own master than always someone's servant?

Sermons and society had always exhorted everyone that it was right and meet to stay in one's allotted place, from birth until death, yet in this world, this strange new-old world, where wool barons and gentry sprigs rubbed shoulders in a dirty old public house, ruled by a dubious, self-appointed meritocracy of criminal types, Giles wondered if those sacred hierarchies would last much longer. This demanding, railway-powered, nineteenth-century world that could make an ancient custom like dog-fighting into something cruel and illegal, could surely also make a nonsense of all the old rules. Watching Holt at work, a man of talent, enterprise and intelligence, made him speculate.

"Lunn's dogs – well, I shall have to see 'em first, but I take your tip, sir, that I do. And with thanks!" Holt raised his glass.

It was then that Giles, who was leaning against a flaking plaster wall while his master sat in a huddle nearby, noticed John Edgar sitting in the far corner. He was with a couple of girls and had left off his velvet coat and frills, and was dressed plainly in a brown coat. He appeared to be simply enjoying a drink and the company of the two girls, and there was no reason that he should be there for any other reason than the fight. He, like Holt, had presumably heard the talk about it in the servants' hall at Holbroke.

Yet Giles continued to watch him, and was glad that he did, for a few minutes later another man joined them, and sat down in the shadows, as if he did not wish to be seen. But it could only have been a coincidence, for one of the girls now joined him in the shadows. Still, there was something about him that Giles recognised, but he could not at once place him. He moved a little in order that he might see better, but the girl was now sitting on the stranger's lap, her arms about his neck, effectively masking his face with her large brimmed-bonnet. All Giles could see was his white hand placed on her back, with a jewelled ring catching what light there was.

Holt left his conversation and was heading towards the bar. Giles joined him. They were alone and it was safe to speak.

"Edgar, the shadowcutter, is there. Do you think he would know you?"

Holt took his time and then glanced over.

"Probably not."

"That man with him –"

"It's one of those foreigners," Holt said. "The Spaniards, from Stanegate."

Giles looked again. Holt was right. The man was one of the noisy party at the Bower Well who had disturbed Laura, and possibly one of the exiled government of Santa Magdalena. What was he doing talking to John Edgar? How did they know each other? Had Edgar come and cut his paper portraits for the Santa Magdaleneans in their opulent chambers at The Queen's Hotel? It was certainly interesting, but it was not immediately relevant to the business in hand.

"Anyone I should go and talk to?" said Holt.

"You might try that fellow there – by the window. With the checked waistcoat and the red neckerchief. If I'm not mistaken, that's Jim Saddleworth, who has form for housebreaking. By rights he should be on his way to Tasmania. I shall get him sooner or later. For now, he might be a good source."

Holt did not have a chance. A pair of double doors at the far end opened and the crowd began to stream through into the dog pit beyond, formed from a partially roofed courtyard with rickety viewing galleries and raked seating below. It was an elaborate, if crudely made, structure, with the lower rails stained with blood from previous combats. The dogs could be heard howling and barking offstage, a truly chilling sound.

Holt and Giles managed to jostle in with the rest of them, but Giles found himself shoved violently backwards by an intemperate little man in a green coat who complained loudly about "great tall buggers getting in the way of their betters!" Finding himself against the back wall, he asked the young man next to him, in his best Northumbrian manner, "Who the hell does he think he is?" The young man had the build of a navvy and sported the characteristic printed neckerchief that often marked them out.

"Oh, that's Hutton, a gangman from over Lancrigg way. He's sore 'cos he bought a bad horse and wants to win back his tin."

"You work for him?"

The young man shook his head. "Not my line, and I wouldn't if I could. Filthy temper and doesn't pay on time. Looking for work?"

Giles shook his head.

"Lunn's dogs are supposed to be the business," Giles said.

"I wouldn't say that," said the young man. "I wouldn't put my money on them."

"I haven't any money to put on anything," Giles said. "I just like to know what's what."

"You're not from these parts, are you?" said the young man, looking at him curiously.

"Just passing through," Giles said. "Man, this is a fair crowd. You could find anyone here."

"You're right there," said the young man. "Anyone and everything."

"What if I were looking for a particular sort of fellow," Giles said, after a moment. "The sort of fellow who might know what to do with some property I might have happened to come by."

"Oh, I see," said the young man with a laugh. "You would be passing through if that's your line."

"Know anyone?"

"Sorry," said the young man. "Not my line." Giles was glad to hear it.

"No harm in asking," Giles said.

"No harm," said the young man, smiling still. "Tell you something, though, now I think of it – do you see that man over at the front there? That fair, burly fellow with the flash waistcoat?"

He was pointing at the man Giles had earlier identified as one of the Santa Magdaleneans.

"I see him," Giles said.

"I heard a funny story about him. That he was handing out gold pieces – real gold pieces – that he bought a set of pistols off a friend of a friend of mine with gold pieces. I don't reckon it's true, but it's a good story."

"Where did your friend of a friend get the pistols?" Giles asked.

"Got them off some old widow for a farthing and sold them on for gold pieces – the crafty bugger. But I don't believe it. The lad was always a boaster."

The conversation got no further. The first pair of dogs were released into the ring and the noisy blood-lust of the crowd was unconstrained. Death was in the air and Giles was glad that he could see nothing of it.

Chapter Twenty

They returned to Holbroke at two in the morning, and as Giles entered the bedroom, the moonlight was seeping into the room through the gaps in the curtain, crossing the room with white beams. He went to the window and opened the curtains a little wider, flooding the room with pale light. Laura stirred awake and saw him standing there, still in his disreputable old riding coat. She sat up and wrapped her arms about her.

"It's me," he said, worried he might have frightened her. He had left the house in his ordinary riding clothes. "I told you I was going adventuring, just like I did in Canada. Do you remember that night?"

She nodded.

He went and sat on the bed.

"All of it?" he said, reaching out and stroking her bare arm. As he leant towards her she wrinkled up her nose, and covered her mouth. It was clear the smell of his disguise was a little too pungent.

"I'll go and give myself a scrub," he said, reverting to his accent. "I'll no be a minute, lass."

He went to the dressing room and cast aside the offending garments with some pleasure. They were not agreeable to wear on such a warm night. He poured some water into the bowl on the washstand and sponged himself clean before reaching for one of the large, luxurious towels that were provided with all the typical prodigality of Holbroke.

He turned as he dried himself and saw Laura standing in the doorway. Her nightgown was slipping from her shoulders, showing the curve of her breasts. Her pale hair was gleaming in the unearthly light. The same beauty he had seen earlier, dressed in fancy dress, now showed itself in a more intimate, seductive light.

He went to her and kissed her, gently pushing the nightgown further from her shoulders, relishing the feel of her warm skin beneath his fingers.

"Do you think we can be like that again?" she said. "As we were then?"

"I very much hope so," he said, burying his face into her loosened hair and drawing her closer to him.

"But what if I –?"

"We will go gently," he said. "There is no need to rush. We have all the time in the world."

"Do we?"

"Yes," he said, and kissed her again. She pressed herself against him, clamping her arms about him in a fierce, frightened way, as if she meant to squeeze reassurance from him. She was breathing fast.

"I want to be your wife again," she said. "I want to be a good wife, but I don't feel I can be good. There is so much inside me that is – confusing."

"And with time that will lessen, I am sure," he said and smoothed her hair. "Shall we –?" He gestured towards the bedroom.

They got into bed together and she surprised him with an onslaught of kisses and touches, all signals that she wanted him fully. She seemed eager to lose herself in a storm of passion, and lay there, her nightdress thrown up, waiting for him.

He found himself hesitating. It was not that he was unaroused – that he certainly was, and it was in many ways everything he had hoped for, to find himself in this place at last with her – and yet, he was not entirely ready to act the husband.

"Giles?" she said, stretching out her hands to him.

Her half-naked form struck him as over-slender and

181

fragile. It was as if her illness had returned her to a girlish, virginal state.

He felt he might break her if he were too rough and there was the danger of her conceiving a child to consider. She was not sufficiently recovered for that. He decided then that he would forgo his own pleasure for her own. He had said they would take matters gently, and now he would prove it. So he touched and stroked her and kissed her until she gave out the soft cries of satisfaction that had always given him so much pleasure to hear.

He was woken by the sound of urgent rapping on the door. He did not recall having fallen asleep, only that she had fallen asleep in his arms in a state of deep contentment.

"Major Vernon, sir?" It was Holt.

"What is it?" said Giles, not at all wishing to disentangle himself. Now Laura stirred.

"It's urgent, sir," said Holt.

"I hope so," said Giles, getting out of bed and going to the door. "Yes, what is it?"

"They've found a body in the gardens."

~

"It's Edgar," said Lord Rothborough, striding across the lawn to meet him, the tails of his silk dressing gown flapping behind him. "One of Macgillray's boys found him. Nothing has been touched, but I had them cover him up. It's most unpleasant."

There, at the base of a statue of Flora scattering stone flowers, lay a body-shaped mound, covered in sacking.

Giles crouched down, removed the sacking and frowned.

It was indeed the shadowcutter, lying in a pool of his own blood, his head smashed up. He covered him up again and went back to Lord Rothborough.

"I need Mr Carswell," he said. "Can it be done?"

"It will have to be," said Rothborough.

Chapter Twenty-one

"That is certainly an interesting contusion," said Felix.

Now that Edgar's body had been transferred to the game larder where the light was better, he was able to see the full extent of the head wound. "Considerable force. Someone managed to do a lot of damage. Some of it may even be post-mortem. As with the bruising on the lower limbs, here – I cannot say for certain yet."

"So a violent confrontation, leading to unconsciousness, and then the assailant continuing the attack?" said Major Vernon.

"Making sure the job was done," said Felix.

"What about blood? There is going to be blood on the assailant, I should think."

"Yes, undoubtedly. Face, hands, clothing."

"Any thoughts on a weapon?"

"It could be a club – or something resembling a club – something spherical on a shaft, perhaps, but look at this – these lacerations at the edge of the wound. It is hard to picture what might have caused that."

"Indeed," said Major Vernon.

Felix took his glass, and began to look more closely into the head wound. Seeing a foreign body, he reached for his tweezers and extracted it.

"Now what is that?" he said.

"May I?" said Major Vernon, indicating the glass. Felix handed it to him. "It looks like a bit of ormolu – that fancy metal gilt stuff you find on clocks and desks, and so forth."

"Of course," said Felix. "And this place is slathered in it."

"That's a useful observation, then. Perhaps it is some sort

of ornament, a statuette or some such."

"An odd choice of weapon."

"Certainly," said Giles. "But murder is usually odd, even when it seems straightforward."

"Which this is not."

"No. And we must ask ourselves, how is this related to Eliza Jones?"

"I am surprised you say that," said Felix, turning his attention to the pattern of bruising. "You have warned me previously about making false associations between events."

"Yes, but the questions must be asked, if only to discard them. I don't know of any link between them – yet."

"But you think there might be? She was dead before he got here. How can there be?"

"There may be nothing. But at this point we cannot say. We know next to nothing about this man. We may uncover an interesting connection or a mere coincidence."

"I hope for the sake of Lord Rothborough and the ladies, it is the former. I can't think it is pleasant to find one's home overrun with random violence. They will want a reason for all this. Insofar as there is ever reason in these things."

"We shall do our best to find one. Why else do you think I sent for you? I should be fairly in the dark without you. Although Lady Charlotte and Mrs Connolly have been very able assistants, they don't quite have your expertise."

"Mrs Connolly?" Felix said.

"She has been invaluable. She unravelled a great mystery. She is quite a fund of brilliance – and she confirms my feeling that Eliza Jones was responsible for the theft of the jewels."

"And you think her murder is connected with that?"

"It's possible, but it is difficult to be any more precise than that. She must have had a fence – and Syme says there was another man. I can't help but conflate the two, although that may be erroneous. But she was a thief, and she may have been tempted to take a greater risk for a greater reward: money and a husband. Starting a family enterprise, perhaps with a lover, as Mrs Connolly suggests, who might be the father of her child."

"So we need to find the fence," said Felix.

"Yes," said Major Vernon, frowning at the corpse. "Not an easy task. And the interesting thing is that I saw this fellow last night, squiring a pair of sylphs at a dog fight. He was talking to one of the gentlemen from Santa Magdalena. I couldn't tell if was merely accidental or there was a purpose to their being there together. Whatever it is, it intrigues me."

"What did the gentleman look like?"

"Broad-shouldered and fair-haired. Very striking fellow, but discreetly dressed. I saw him the other day at the Bower Well, which was why I recognised him. There he had very much the air of the pater familias; less so last night. Have you got a name for me?"

"It sounds like Don Luiz Ramirez. He doesn't look as I imagine a Spaniard to look. Fair hair and burly. But we only buried Don Xavier yesterday afternoon and he was all piety and grief then. Would he go to a dog fight that evening? Perhaps you were mistaken."

"Perhaps."

"But then again," said Felix, thinking of Dona Blanca thrusting the document case into his hands and swearing him to silence, "who knows what those people are about. Something strange is going on there, certainly."

"I shall go and talk to him about Mr Edgar. It is an avenue to be looked at. But first we must question the household here. I have already started Holt on the menservants. I shall go and see what he has uncovered."

He left Felix to continue his investigations. He had not begun to make much progress before there was a knock at the door. Felix opened it a crack, looked out and smiled, not at all annoyed to be interrupted.

Sukey was standing in the passageway, looking neat and

crisp in a print dress, as fresh as a newly picked rose.

"I'm looking for Major Vernon," she said.

He came out of the room and shut the door behind him.

"He's already gone."

He wanted to say, *"I'd hoped you might have been looking for me."*

"You have the poor fellow in there?"

"Yes. He's in quite a state."

"Poor man," she said.

He nodded. He could not think what to say. He wanted to pull her into his arms and kiss her, but standing there in his shirt sleeves, covered in blood and dust, it was not possible. Instead they were reduced to awkward silence. He had once been so easy in her presence, as if they had been strolling across a broad, sunlit plain, but now it was as if they were on a precarious mountain path. Every step had to be carefully considered – a single misstep might lead to disaster. A word out of place and all could be ruined. *If it is not already ruined*, he thought. *If only I had not kissed her, if only I had left it where it was. I have spoiled everything between us.*

"Did he say where he was going?"

"Major Vernon? The servants' hall, I think."

"I'll go and have a look," she said, and without another word she departed back down the passageway, as if she were glad indeed to get away. What had he done? He was about to shout out "Sukey!" but the sight of Lord Rothborough turning the corner silenced him. Sukey stopped, made a low curtsey and carried on her way.

Felix had the feeling that attempting to capture her was like the childhood game of catching a dandelion seed and making a wish. It was hard enough to catch one, and if you did, the wish never came true. Was that to be the case with Sukey?

"A smart creature, that," said Lord Rothborough. "Major Vernon seems very taken with her – which does not surprise me in the least."

"What do you mean by that?" said Felix.

"Nothing," said Lord Rothborough. "You look tired, my boy."

"I am. I did not sleep last night. I have unexpected guests."

"What?"

"My parents are here – well, they are at Stanegate. My mother is in a state and I do not know what to do about it."

"She's ill? Oh, dear Lord."

"Yes. I was in two minds about coming here, to tell you the truth; although she claims there is nothing wrong with her, it is evident –" He broke off. "They should not have travelled! What on earth possessed them to do it?"

Lord Rothborough laid his hand on Felix's shoulder and said, "Send them to Ardenthwaite. You will be able to supervise her better from there, and the air is much healthier than at Stanegate. You will need to be close at hand while we sort out this wretched business. Where could be better? It is perfectly habitable, and the housekeeper there can easily take on a few more servants. I will arrange it all."

"But – but my father will not – I think, you know as well as I that he –"

"If Mrs Carswell is ill then he will be glad to fall in with what is best for her. Besides, Ardenthwaite will be far more to his taste. There is a fine library there to keep him occupied. He will be persuaded. I will persuade him."

Felix had no doubt that he would. Neither could he disagree that it was a sound plan, even though it had implications that he disliked. He had been keeping Ardenthwaite at arm's length. He had gone over the old house a couple of times now, in the company of Lord Rothborough, who had been making various small improvements, but had managed to remain detached from the place. But Lord Rothborough was right. It would suit his parents very well and

188

it was an easy ride to Holbroke. He had met the housekeeper and she was a great deal more kind and willing than that impossible Bolland creature.

"So?" said Lord Rothborough.

"I suppose so," said Felix. "It is as good a plan as any."

"I will see to it. In the meantime, I think you will have plenty to keep you from worrying too much about Mrs Carswell. Any progress?"

"A little. Major Vernon is talking to the menservants. How is Lady Rothborough, sir?" he said, remembering himself. "And your daughters – they must be distressed by all this."

"Somewhat. But Charlotte is like you, Felix, made of steely stuff, and she has taken charge of the others. It is a marvel when one realises that one's children are now old enough to share such burdens!"

"I ought to check on Mrs Vernon," said Felix. "She is still somewhat fragile. If that might be managed without my giving any offence to Lady Rothborough."

"I dare say it might," said Lord Rothborough. "Perhaps later. I believe she is with Maria at the moment. She is a charming woman, I must say. And to have brought her from such a grievous condition – well, Felix, you may count that as a great feather in your cap."

"It was not all my doing. Mrs Connolly and Major Vernon, and Mrs Vernon herself – they have all worked very hard."

"Yes, but you were the guiding hand, the chef d'affaires. You must not hold back your contribution from the world. It may unlock the door to great advances in your profession. You will publish, I trust?"

"In time, perhaps, if her condition does not deteriorate again. We are not out of the woods yet, by any means. And then, of course, Major and Mrs Vernon might not like me to make a great noise about it."

189

"Major Vernon is a friend to reform," said Lord Rothborough. "I cannot see that he would object if it were done discreetly. It would be of great interest to many people, not just the medical profession. For example, I know Lord Stambury has been looking at some of these questions. He wrote to me only the other day on the subject of the County Asylums Bill –"

"I must get back to work," Felix said bluntly, turning away.

"Yes, yes, I suppose you must," said Lord Rothborough. "But Stambury – you must meet him, sooner or later, Felix, he could be useful to you. He likes his shooting, you know. We could have him here in the autumn, and you could let him have a few days with his guns at Ardenthwaite – that would be a pleasant treat for a sportsman."

~

Giles found Holt sitting in the office belonging to Mr Grainger, the house steward, quite as if it were his own. He was interviewing one of the pages, a pale-faced boy of sixteen, who sat nervously fiddling with the buttons on his waistcoat. He jumped to attention when Giles came in.

"Just in time, sir," said Holt, getting up. "Jacob here has something interesting for us. Tell the gentleman what you just told me – about the book."

"But Mr Holt –" Jacob began, in some alarm.

"Come on, now lad," said Holt.

"I didn't make a bet, Mr Holt, I'm just saying," Jacob said. "And they'll kill me if they find out that I told you."

"We will make sure they don't," said Giles, taking Holt's place. "Sit down again, won't you? Are we talking about a betting book?"

Jacob nodded.

"Walter – that's the first footman, my lady's footman, he has this book, and you can make a wager with him, or if you want to make a wager with someone else, he puts it in the book. I've never made a wager, sir, I swear it. I know it's a sin to gamble, but the others do."

"The others being?"

Jacob thought for a moment.

"Most of the lads, and even old Tom the clock man does it. Some of the women too. There was a right daft bet last week about Mrs Hope's Sunday bonnet – whether she'd have green or blue ribbons on it. I guessed blue and I almost wish I had put tuppence on it, because I'd have made myself something, 'cos I was right, like, but I know it's a sin, and Mr Bodley and Mr Grainger, they would have given me a right thumping if they'd found out I'd done it."

"I see," said Giles. "So why did you mention the book to Mr Holt just now?"

"He asked me when I last saw Mr Edgar. I told him I saw him with Walter and he was taking bets for the dog fight and putting them in his book. Walter wanted to go, but he couldn't, but I know Mr Edgar was going, 'cos I heard him say so."

"Where?"

"I have to sweep the servants' hall, and they were sitting there, having a smoke and talking about which dogs they reckoned would win. And Jimmy Watson, from out the stables, he was there too, and he said he wanted five shillings on Lunn's dogs. And he gave the money to Walter, and he put it in the book. And I thought – five shillings: where did he get that from? That was the last time I saw Mr Edgar. I went to my bed after that."

"That's useful," said Giles. "Thank you, Jacob. You can go back to your work now."

"Are you going to talk to Walter about this now, sir?"

"Yes," Giles said.

"He'll kill me if he finds out it were me that blabbed. That book, it's supposed to be a secret."

"Don't worry, I shan't tell," said Giles. "Mr Holt, will you go and get Walter for me?"

Walter was a magnificent specimen, no doubt picked for his fine physique as much as his character. He was dressed in his full chocolate and gold livery with a powdered wig, his tricorn hat tucked under his arm. He carried himself with great pride, and had all the hauteur of a privileged position, taking on as much reflected lustre as he could from his noble employers. Being Lady Rothborough's personal manservant was clearly something he relished.

"I can't be long," he said. "Her Ladyship has ordered the carriage."

"In the circumstances, her Ladyship may have to wait, or take another footman, Mr Walter," said Giles, getting up. "Sit down, will you?"

"As you like, sir. How may I help you, sir?" he said, deferential, but a touch insolent.

Giles studied him. It was easy to imagine one of those large white-gloved hands cracking poor Jacob about the head, but such rough treatment of underlings was unfortunately commonplace. It did not make him a murderer.

"I want to talk to you about Mr Edgar," said Giles. "I am sure that does not surprise you, given the circumstances."

"Of course not, sir," said Walter. "Very unfortunate."

"I understand you were seen sitting in the servants' hall with him last night, smoking and talking. Around ten o'clock at night."

"That is possible," said Walter. "I don't remember."

"You were seen talking together. Well, rather more than talking. Doing business, I understand."

"I'm not sure what you mean, sir."

"I think you are a sporting man," said Giles, "and that

you run a betting book."

"A betting book?" said Walter as if he had been insulted. "I should not dare, sir, not in a house like this, where her Ladyship particularly hates gambling."

"Enough flannel, Mr Walter. You will get yourself into far more trouble for lying about it in these circumstances. Would you rather lose your place or go to the gallows?"

"What do you mean by that, sir?"

"You were seen taking bets for the dog fight at Byrescough last night."

"I did no such thing," said Walter.

"I was at Byrescough," Giles went on, leaning on his chair back. "Lunn's dogs, yes, fine animals, and on tip-top form, but then that Irishman Coulter came in with a pair of brindle terriers and took everyone by surprise." Walter frowned. "There was a lot of money lost last night. Some people thought that Lunn was a certain thing, but it turned out he wasn't. Now I've been told Jimmy Watson put money on Lunn. Did you?"

"What if I did?" Walter said after a moment.

"How much did you lose, Mr Walter? I know it's painful to revisit these details, but I am afraid you will have to tell me. You know what I think? You made a wager with John Edgar, on your own behalf, with all the money you had gathered from the others, and some of your own, for good measure, on Lunn's invincible dogs. Edgar talked it up, told you he could get the best odds on a sure-fire thing. Irresistible, yes? You'd have been a fool not to give it a punt."

Walter made an uncomfortable grunt and looked away.

"How much money did you lose last night?" Giles said again.

"He bloody conned me – he knew about those Irish dogs."

"And how do you know about the Irish dogs?"

"He told me."

193

"When was this?"

"About two this morning. I met him on my way back from – well, I'd gone down to the laundry, to see my girl."

"Where did you see him?"

"In the clock yard, that's the big yard out the back. We'd arranged it, you see."

"So you were standing there, waiting for your certain winnings, and he told you that he'd lost the lot, Mr Walter? Is that the substance of it?"

"Pretty much," Walter said after a long pause.

"And then what happened?"

"Nothing, sir, I went to my bed."

"Nothing?"

Another long silence.

"I wouldn't have taken such news so meekly," Giles said. "After all, we are talking about quite a sum of money." Walter shifted uneasily.

"We may have had a few words," he said carefully, and glanced away.

"The full truth, Mr Walter," Giles said softly. "It will not be so hard."

"It's not what you think, sir!" Walter said, jumping up. "I didn't do away with him. We had words, and I didn't hold back, and I may have cracked one on him, but I didn't... I didn't... kill him! He was alive when I left him. He walked away, cursing me, that's how it was, I will swear on the Bible that is how it happened! You have to believe me, sir!"

Giles was formulating his answer, not entirely taking this statement at face value. He decided he would ask Carswell to examine him for signs of a fight. Edgar might have been small and slight in comparison but he would have fought off his attacker. There might be bruises and scratches in evidence. He pulled up the green blind and flooded the room with light, making Walter stagger back, blinking. He saw what the dull light of the room had concealed – Walter's handsome face

194

bore signs not of a fight, but of skilful painting. Was it vanity that had led him to the cosmetic box or a desire to conceal a battered face?

The door opened without a warning knock, and Lord Rothborough came in.

"Sir Arthur has arrived," he said. "I never expected him to be so prompt. I hope it is not too inconvenient for you? Lady Rothborough is delaying him with small talk, but that cannot be managed indefinitely."

"I will come at once," said Giles. "Walter, you will stay here and take your paint off. We are not finished."

"My paint, sir, what do you mean?" said Walter.

"Good God!" said Lord Rothborough looking at him. "Walter, what the devil have you got that stuff on for?"

"That is a question we will leave with him, my lord," said Giles. "Mr Carswell will come and speak to you presently, Walter. And if you think you have anything to add to what you have just told me, you must tell Mr Holt or Mr Carswell, and we will talk again."

"I swear to you, sir," said Walter, with a touch desperation in his voice. "And to you, my lord, on my mother's grave –"

"Save your breath, Mr Walter. We will get a full written statement from you in good time."

"Walter?" said Rothborough as they left the room. "Surely not. Walter has been a good servant. He's been with us for years."

"He was in a fight with Edgar, at two in the morning. Whether that is all remains to be seen. I wonder what scars are hiding under all that paint."

"That is a little out of character, certainly," said Lord Rothborough.

They met Carswell coming along the passageway in his shirt sleeves, looking most annoyed.

"Major Vernon, two constables have barged in and

commandeered my cadaver!" he exclaimed. "This is Sir Arthur at work, I take it, sir?" he said to Lord Rothborough.

"Yes, unfortunately," said Rothborough.

"You had an hour's work," said Giles. "That is better than nothing. You have that sample?" Carswell nodded. "Will you go to the steward's room and examine the man there, Mr Carswell? I am looking for signs of a recent fight."

Chapter Twenty-two

"Tell me, Lord Rothborough," asked Giles as they went upstairs to speak to Sir Arthur, "how did you come to hear about Edgar?"

"It was all Maria's doing – she was at my sister's house in Berkshire, at some neighbour's party. He was the entertainment. After she had seen him, she never stopped talking about it. So I asked my sister to enquire of the neighbour. She gave me his address."

"Which was?"

"Swalecliffe, of all places. He had a little shop there when he was not travelling about. Presumably his wife keeps it. The new wife – oh dear, I had forgotten about her."

"I think I shall go and see her," said Giles. "Edgar was at the dog fight last night, with a couple of whores in tow, and talking to Don Luiz Ramirez. I want to find out a little more about our shadowcutter before we clap poor Walter in irons for his murder. And if I go to Swalecliffe, Sir Arthur will be able to get on in his own way here, for the time being, and all will be peace."

"A good plan," said Rothborough. "He won't make much progress, I don't suppose."

They found Sir Arthur waiting in the library outside Lord Rothborough's study. With the air of a man who had prepared his words, he at once launched into a speech full of justifications and precedents, only to be swiftly disarmed by Lord Rothborough, who said, "Yes, of course, Sir Arthur, of course. It cannot be otherwise. It is your business and Major Vernon is entirely in agreement with me. Major Vernon is going away, I understand, yes?"

"Yes, I am," Giles said.

This took the wind quite out of Sir Arthur's sails and would have sufficed, had not Carswell then joined them.

He looked as if he had put his head under a pump to cool his temper – he was wet-haired and scarlet-faced. He had at least put his crumpled linen coat back on, but it did little to help his dishevelled appearance.

"And what is he doing here?" Sir Arthur said to Lord Rothborough.

"Mr Carswell came over from Ardenthwaite," said Lord Rothborough. "I thought it best, the moment the body was found, to get the nearest medical man in the neighbourhood to look at it."

"The nearest medical man!" said Sir Arthur. "Your own man, you mean, sir, your b... b..."

"It was simply a matter of convenience," Lord Rothborough went on. "I do not mean to belittle Dr Conway's expertise, of course not."

Sir Arthur did not look very convinced.

"The body will go to Dr Conway's house at Dallingham," said Sir Arthur. "He has agreed to undertake a full post-mortem."

"It will do no good for your men to haul it off in this heat," Carswell said. "Given the extreme weather, you ought to bring a medical examiner to the body, rather than take it elsewhere – and as soon as is practical, before any more useful evidence is lost."

"I do not care for your tone," said Sir Arthur.

"As the only qualified man within ten miles of the cadaver, I think you should take note of my suggestion. This one can't be written off as a suicide!" he added.

"You are offensive, sir."

"Whether you are offended or not scarcely matters," Carswell went on. "I am only trying to help you, sir, in a matter of justice, which rather takes precedence over petty matters of local politics."

"Mr Carswell, please!" said Lord Rothborough. "It is all settled. Dr Conway is to be instructed. It is quite out of your hands, though I dare say Dr Conway would be extremely grateful to have your preliminary notes. Two heads are always better than one, after all. Yes, Major Vernon?"

"Yes, certainly."

"And I believe Major Vernon has some other work for you that will take you away from here this very day," Lord Rothborough went on breezily. "Now, Sir Arthur, let me see you to your carriage."

When they were alone, Carswell asked, "What business is that?"

"We are going to Swalecliffe to talk to Edgar's widow," Giles said. "How did you get on with Walter?"

"He had certainly been in an altercation. He has some bruising and an impressive amount of scratching to his face, as if someone went for him with their nails. And I didn't get a chance to check Edgar's nails. Those dolts wouldn't let me in!"

"Men don't usually scratch in a fight," said Giles. "I wonder if his sweetheart was the one who spoiled his face for gambling away their savings. He told me he came from her bed to meet with Edgar. Perhaps he went back and confessed?"

"And she let him have it?" Carswell said.

"A visit to the laundry next, I think," said Giles. "And at the same time we can see if they have been given any suspicious shirts to launder."

~

The visit to the laundry confirmed Giles' suspicions and revealed soon enough the cause of Walter's battered face. His sweetheart, a strapping young woman called Janet, was happy to confirm she had given him a battering for his recklessness. The wedding, she declared, was now off if he was going to be such a fool with money. Further enquiries revealed no blood-stained garments had been tossed into the great baskets of soiled linen that arrived each morning from the house.

"It's a pity we cannot direct a search of the house," Giles said to Carswell as they walked back together. "But our hands are tied. We shall go to Swalecliffe and see what we can discover there."

"Must we go today?" Carswell asked. "I have this devilish business with my parents – I have let Lord Rothborough take them to Ardenthwaite, but I feel I should see them in person."

"We shall make a slight detour to Ardenthwaite, then," Giles said, as they went inside. "But the important thing is that we leave here as soon as possible. It is all rather irritating, but needs must. I shall have to explain to Mrs Vernon, but I think she will understand. Coming here, for all this perturbation, seems to have done her good. Lady Maria has been so kind to her."

They came up the stairs to the sound of some energetic piano music – Scottish airs, arranged in a modern style that sounded complex but not unpleasant. A half-opened door revealed Laura and Lady Maria seated together at the piano.

"Listen to that!" he murmured to Carswell.

He could not resist the opportunity to take some rest and savour the sight of Laura in her blue and white striped muslin, absorbed in her music, playing the lower part with enormous competence. If Lady Maria had the showy upper portions, Laura was the steadying hand in terms of rhythm and harmony. She played better, he thought, than she had ever done before. It had been Carswell's idea that she take up her music again – he had made it a priority that regular practice be part of her daily regime. It had certainly paid off; it had given her a place to channel her passions.

They reached the grand climax of the piece and finished with a tremendous flourish.

"None of us could manage the bottom part until you came," Lady Maria said. "Too many octave spreads."

"I suppose I just have large hands," Laura said quietly, looking down at her spread fingers.

"You have beautiful hands, Mrs Vernon," Lady Maria said, taking her hand. "I wish I had your hands."

Laura flushed becomingly and smiled. Giles wanted to dash in and snatch her hand back from Maria. He wanted to steal her away for a quiet, inconsequential talk in one of the cool corners of the great house. He longed for a slow, idle, intimate conversation that might lead again to the pleasures they had rediscovered last night. He had no wish to get on with business at all. In that moment, he could have tossed the whole case into Sir Arthur's ample lap and not cared any more about it.

Lady Maria caught sight of him in the doorway.

"Oh, and Major Vernon heard it all!" she exclaimed, jumping up from the piano and flinging open the door. As she did so, she revealed Mr Carswell, who had been at his heels. He stepped back at once, as if searching for a shadow in which to hide himself.

Lady Maria was having none of this. One glance was enough to make the situation clear to her and she advanced towards him, a look of wonder on her face.

"Oh, is this... my goodness, sir?" She looked to Giles for affirmation of her instincts. "Is this Mr Carswell?"

"Yes, I am afraid so," Carswell said. "I should not be here. I will be gone in a –"

"No, no, do not go! And do not apologise," Lady Maria said, and with great aplomb, grabbed his hand in both hers and stood gazing at him, with utter delight. "This is too marvellous! I have wondered all my life about meeting you, you have no idea – and now here you are! Oh, goodness!"

Then, unable to restrain herself, she kissed him on the cheek and threw her arms about him. Carswell resisted, but only for a moment. He bowed his head and allowed the embrace, and returned it.

Feeling a little like an intruder, Giles went into the room where Laura still sat at the piano. He sat down beside her and kissed her hands.

"I am sorry, I have to go away tonight – but only for a day or two. Will you be able to manage without me?"

Laura looked a little grave for a while and then managed a smile.

"I think so," she said. "I have Sukey and Lady Maria to look after me."

"You have made a good friend there," said Giles.

"I never really had a friend before," she said. "I do like it. And we have all this music to work through! If it is not wrong to play when that poor man died so horribly? Lady Maria was worried that Lady Rothborough might think so."

"He would have liked such music in life, from what I saw of him," said Giles. "And I should not want the world to fall silent if I died. I would be happier to think of it carrying on, even if I did not."

Laura nodded.

"Did I hear Mr Carswell out there?" she said.

"Yes."

"I thought he could not come here," she said, puzzled.

"Circumstances demanded it. But we will be gone soon enough."

"Oh."

"Would you like to see him? I shall fetch him in."

"He will not want to see me," she said.

"What makes you think that?"

"He will be angry with me again."

"No, he will be delighted with you. You have done so well – I have been telling him how well you have done! Let me go and fetch him for you, yes?"

He did not allow her to demur but let go of her hands and went to the door, expecting to find Carswell and Lady Maria still in the great passageway. But they were no longer there.

"You see," Laura said, coming to his side, "he has run away from me. And now you are going."

"Yes, I know, I know," he said, turning to take her in his arms, "but it cannot be prevented. But you have Lady Maria and Sukey. They will take care of you, I know it. Think of that pile of music, yes?"

She leant against him, clinging to him, her cheek pressed against his shirt front. He sensed her struggling to steady herself, not to give way to her demons, and felt in awe of her courage. He dropped a kiss onto her head and wondered if it were possible to take her with him. He was planning that they should go on horseback across the moors. In such fine weather, she might ride too, and benefit from that. But that would have its risks and difficulties, as much as leaving her behind at Holbroke. So he kissed her again and hoped that all would be well.

In the reflection of one of the pier glasses he saw Lady Warde enter the room by the door in the far corner, dressed as usual in her dismal black.

"Oh, forgive me," she said, and left again. Giles turned and looked at her as she departed. She appeared to be in darker, fresher mourning than previously, her crepe renewed, as if she had put it on to honour her dead maid.

Laura detached herself from him, went to the glass and adjusted her ringlets, which he had disarranged in embracing her.

"I will manage. I will show you I can," she said.

~

Felix had followed Holt up to Major Vernon's dressing room, wanting to wash his face and steady his nerves. Lady Maria's effusive outpouring had left him shaking. Her warmth, her hands on his cheeks, her tear-filled eyes had been at once too much for him, and joyously right. She had an ardent frankness about her that impressed him profoundly. If Lady Charlotte had met his gaze and then sent him back to his work, clearly struggling with these strange emotions as he had, Lady Maria had embraced them, and by that, had made him face them too. It had been impossible not to let some tears leak from his own eyes and feel something of the same giddy happiness she professed. It was so strange – she had kept saying that – and he had nodded, and taken her hands and squeezed them, and sat there by her side, feeling as if the air had gone from the room. At the same time he remembered that strange moment with Dona Blanca, when the scent of her perfume had taken his heart to a place that his mind had struggled to believe in.

Upstairs, he found Sukey sitting at the window, doing some sewing. Holt at once busied himself packing the Major's things. Felix excused himself and went out to the passageway. He wanted to speak to her but he could not in front of Holt.

As if reading his mind, she followed him out of the room.

"I was wondering, do you have any orders for me about Mrs Vernon?" she said, with quiet formality.

"No, I leave it all quite in your hands. You are well able to deal with anything that may come up. And Lady Maria will –" He broke off. "I have just met her." He could not keep his voice from breaking.

Sukey reached out, touched his shoulder briefly and nodded.

"It was strange," he burst out. "She was crying, and –"

"Of course it was," she said. "Of course. Your own sister."

Her hand was on his shoulder again, and he grabbed it, and held it in both his and bent and kissed it. She did not flinch or withdraw, and he raised his eyes to meet hers.

"One day," he managed to say. "One day, you and I will sit and talk and we will have time, and it will be –"

"Maybe," she said, touching his cheek. "Maybe not."

"It will be," he said. "I promise. One day." But then she shook her head and pulled her hand away. "Believe me, please Sukey, I am not going to trifle with you. I could never. This is too –"

"That's not what I am afraid of," she said, walking away a little, turning from him. "You don't know me, that is the trouble, you don't really know what I am at all. There are things –" She broke off.

Felix laughed nervously.

"Your past sins must be trivial compared to mine!" he managed to say. "Believe me!" And he went to her and folded his arms about her. "I don't care."

She permitted the embrace. Indeed, he understood that she wanted it. She yielded against him, and her lips met his with a rough eagerness that left him startled and hungry. She was, like him, fiery with desire. Then she broke away, remembering herself. He saw her brush her lips with her fingertips, as if his kisses had left visible marks that needed to be removed.

"Just don't build any castles in Spain," she said, and reached to straighten his cravat. "Now, you have to be on your way."

Then, like a cat, she slipped away and back into the dressing room, leaving him standing there in a state of astonishment.

He walked down the long passageway, unable to comprehend the meaning of this encounter, except that he was left aching for more. He turned into the great staircase hall and saw Major and Mrs Vernon coming upstairs.

The Major turned to his wife and said quietly, "I think, perhaps, you and Mr Carswell should talk a little. Yes?"

205

Mrs Vernon was as reluctant as Felix felt, but the Major insisted. He was correct to do so. She was still his patient and he had to remember his duty towards her. So they were left together in the dazzling light of the great sculpture gallery that spanned the first floor of the house.

A consultation in such a place was hardly ideal. At the centre was the prize of Lord Rothborough's collection: a Canova of two luscious white marble nymphs, dancing barefoot on a plinth of red polished granite, their voluptuous figures wrapped in the slightest, most clinging draperies.

"Perhaps we should sit down?" he suggested, indicating the padded bench which had been placed under the great window at the far end.

She nodded meekly and he sat down with her. He reached for her hand and took her pulse, which was steady and strong.

"Have you been troubled any more by headaches?"

She shook her head. Her complexion certainly looked improved. There was a becoming flush to her cheeks which had been for a long time grey and sallow, like those of a prisoner.

"And what have you eaten today?"

"I have been very good," she said.

"Tell me exactly."

"I had chocolate and toast for breakfast – two pieces – the toast is nice here. And just now I had a little cake and half a glass of wine. Lady Rothborough made me have those."

"That's very good. Bravo Lady Rothborough! And bravo Mrs Vernon."

"So you are not angry with me?" she said.

"I was not angry with you."

"You were. At Stanegate, you were."

"I am sorry, I did not mean that. But I was not angry with you, Mrs Vernon. I am sorry if it seemed so. Will you forgive me?"

"You said I was wrong to pick those flowers."

"Forgive me?" he said again.

She did not answer. Instead she glanced around her, at the stupefying grandeur of the room, and said, "I don't know why you are here. I thought you could never be here. I upset Lady Augusta by talking about you. But Lady Charlotte and Lady Maria were not upset."

"No. They have been very kind – to all of us. And they will take good care of you while Major Vernon and I are away. And if you feel afraid or anxious – if those disturbing thoughts return – remember how we spoke of this before?"

"Yes."

"So, what is it you must do?"

"To take up some work – or play the piano."

"And speak to Sukey as soon as you can," he said. "She will keep you straight."

"Yes," she nodded.

"And I am forgiven?" he said.

She pursed her lips for a moment and nodded. Then she burst out, "But I wish you didn't have to go! I wish it could be how we were before we went to Stanegate, when you came in every day to see me and talk to me. I wish, oh I wish that –"

"But you do not need me so much, now," he said. "You do not need me every day. That is because you are so much improved – it is the best outcome."

"I know, I know," she said. "But, but – sometimes I feel that I will crumble again. You have been so kind to me, so patient, and you have understood everything, in a way that no one has ever understood. How can I do without you? How can I bear it? I need you still," she said, grasping his sleeve with her arm. "I know you don't think so, and I'm sure you're right. But it hurts me to think that I'll never, ever see you like I used to. I know I must get on with this new life, and be brave and strong, and you have told me all that so often, but sometimes, I don't think I can do it. And now you are sitting here, like this." She clutched at his arm even more strongly now. "I wish you did not have to go."

"But I must," he said, gently detaching her hand. But she caught his hand and knotted her fingers about his, locking them fast. He tried to pull them away but with little success.

"I love you so very much," she said in a whisper. "I want you to know that. I love you. Sometimes, in my dreams, I find I am your wife. I dream that... that —"

"No, please, ma'am, please do not let your mind go there. It is not good for you."

He managed to detach his hand and got up from the bench. He had feared this declaration for some time, but the reality of it still hit him hard. He had handled matters badly for it to come to this. He had undone so much good work. He should have acted earlier and more harshly to prevent it, he knew, but he still had no idea how he might have managed it, just as he had no idea how to deal with this now.

"It is very good," she said, gazing up at him, her eyes wide. "And I will not let you deny me that! You cannot stop me from loving you, Mr Carswell. I shall, until the day I die!"

"I think we should find Sukey," was all he could manage to say, and went and held the door open for her.

As he took her back to her room, they walked along the long passageway in the most painful silence. Mercifully Sukey was still there, and Holt, who was taking his master's luggage down.

A moment later Major Vernon came in to take his leave. Just as Felix departed, he saw the Major take his wife in his arms and kiss her on the lips. She tipped back her head and accepted his kiss, her eyes closed tight. Was she imagining kissing him? He hurried back down the stairs, stopping only to look back once, feeling he was observed; and indeed, Sukey was standing on the landing, leaning over the rail, mouthing a silent farewell.

~

Lord Rothborough had proposed accompanying them to Ardenthwaite but Major Vernon had, by some means or other, managed to stall him, much to Felix's relief. It was going to be hard enough to explain to his parents why they were there, without Lord Rothborough complicating matters.

It was an easy few miles to the house, for which Felix was grateful, as he was for the large, well-mannered roan mare that had been loaned to him from the Rothborough stables. She was a creature of perfect temperament, who did not need to be mastered or even much guided, and Felix attempted to put his confused thoughts in some order as they approached Ardenthwaite.

They now turned into the long avenue of ancient oak and chestnut which Felix had never seen in full leaf before. The magnificence of it provoked Holt to say, with an appreciative sigh, "There's no finer sight than that. I remember seeing an avenue like this rooted up when I was a boy, and it broke my heart. You are a lucky gentleman, Mr Carswell, to have this to your name." He touched his brim to Felix, in a rare gesture of respect.

At this moment Felix caught sight of a familiar figure at the end of the avenue. The Rev James Carswell stood, black-cloaked and leaning on his shepherd's staff. He looked like a travelling friar or perhaps an Old Testament prophet. Felix felt a sudden sick dread, as if the old man were waiting to give terrible news, and hastened his horse forward, past Major Vernon and Holt, before quickly and clumsily dismounting in order to go the last few yards on foot.

"Is everything – is she...?" he blurted out.

"Comfortable enough," said his father.

"I want to see her," Felix said, struggling with the bridle of his horse.

"Let me take that, sir," said Holt, riding up and coming to his aid. He trotted off with the horse in his charge.

"She is resting," Mr Carswell said. "The change of place upset her. You might have predicted that."

"Yes, indeed, it was a risk, but I thought she would be better here, and you must concede –"

"You thought? I had the impression this was all Lord Rothborough's doing. After all, he was the one who wrote to me to tell me we were to be dispatched like – oh, I don't know, like clocks to be mended. His Lordship says something and it is done! Of course!"

"I am sorry at the manner in which it was done, yes, but it is for the best. Surely you can see that, Papa?"

"And I am informed by the housekeeper," his father went on, "that this is your house? How can that be?"

"It is only mine in name."

"It is either your house or it is not," said Mr Carswell. "There can be no equivocation. If you have accepted this place from him, then –" He broke off, shaking his head, and began to walk towards the house. "That is the case, is it not?"

"Yes," Felix said after a moment.

"That is what we have always feared. Your mother and I – that his influence would prevail, that his world would seduce you, and exploit the weaknesses in you."

Felix had heard this lecture many times before but it still stung him, and he was no longer in the mood for taking it humbly.

"Oh, you may think what you like! I only know he has acted today for my mother's comfort! You may not like his arrangements, or his way of enacting them – it is a matter of taste, that's all. But you cannot deny the kindness! Yes, he is rich enough to throw orders about as a farmer sows his seed corn, and it is no trouble for him to do so, but I know he has done this out of concern and consideration and great respect for you both. He is not what you think he is!"

His father stopped and formed his craggy features into a sour expression, which did not bode well. However, Major Vernon, who had been tactfully keeping his distance, had now dismounted and came strolling up to them. He swept off his hat and made an extremely respectful bow.

"Mr Carswell, a great honour," he said. "Giles Vernon at your service, sir."

Mr Carswell could not ignore such civility, although Felix felt he was scrutinizing every inch of Major Vernon. But there was little even he could find to criticise in such a plain riding costume.

"Major Vernon, it is good to know you at last," Mr Carswell said, with a nod. "Mrs Carswell and I are in your debt. We trespassed upon your hospitality last night, for which I thank you very much."

"I am glad that you did. My wife and I regret that we were not able to be there to receive you as we would have liked."

"I must go in," Felix said. "We do not have much time as it is."

"No, I am afraid we do not," Major Vernon said. "The pursuit of justice can be relentless. We must be off again within the hour."

His father made an uneasy gesture of dismissal, and Felix ran towards the house.

He found his mother was very comfortable, lying on a cane settee in a pretty, panelled parlour off the great hall. Mrs Taylor, the housekeeper, was in attendance. He found them talking amiably about the best breed of hens for laying.

He pulled up a stool, and when the housekeeper had gone, he insisted on taking her pulse and sounding her heart. She told him it was nonsense that he should do this, but she consented. He was pleased to find she was somewhat less frail than previously. She said she had enjoyed the carriage and thought the house beautiful.

"And it is yours, I understand," she said. Unlike his

father's response, it was not said with reproach.

"Yes, I am sorry, it is."

"It is a fine old place," she said. "And you must have a house, I suppose!" She smiled. "I could imagine that one could be quite happy here."

"I have no notion what to do with it at the moment," he said.

"I think it will all become clear enough in time. Perhaps when the right young woman crosses your path?"

"Perhaps," he managed to say, thinking of Sukey and how well the house would suit her, and at the same time how utterly impossible it would be to bring her there as his wife.

"Mr Bodley brought your things from your room in Stanegate. They are over there. He was not sure where you wanted them, so I told him to leave them here. I want to look over your linen."

"You are to do no such thing. You are to rest. That is an order."

"And lie here with my hands idle?"

"Yes, just that," he said. "You have a pleasant view and Father can read to you. There is a vast library upstairs. I shall tell him to find something to amuse you. Perhaps Guy Mannering?"

"You will tell your Papa to sit and read Guy Mannering to me?" she said, with a slight arch of her eyebrow.

"Yes, and he will do what I tell him. I would read to you myself, but I have to go away now for a night or two – speaking of which..."

He got up and opened his portmanteau. Bodley had packed it immaculately, and it was all soon disarranged as he searched for a spare shirt and some stockings to take with him. As he did so, he found the letter case that he had found on the floor of Don Xavier's room, which Dona Blanca had insisted he take. He hesitated, turning it in his hands, wondering what he should do with it. "Do not show them to anyone without telling me first." She had been insistent, and anxious that Don Luis in particular did not know of their existence.

He did not like to go against what she had asked him, yet the possible connection with Edgar, who was now dead, and Don Luiz, seemed to make it necessary that he at least mention the matter to Major Vernon. He stuffed it into his medical bag along with his spare linen.

Chapter Twenty-three

"Is the bed comfortable, Mr Carswell?" Giles enquired, coming into the bedroom from the parlour. Carswell had pulled off his coat and boots and thrown himself onto the bed. He lay spread-eagled, staring up at the ceiling.

"Any bed would be comfortable after that," he said.

It was about nine at night and they had broken their journey at an inn in a remote village on the moors above Swalecliffe.

"It was only twenty-two miles," Giles said.

"It feels like forty. I must have done nearly that, what with riding from Stanegate this morning. My legs tell me so." He gave a groan. "I need a gallon of beer – no, two gallons."

Giles pulled off his own coat and caught sight of his own, dusty, sunburnt face in the looking glass.

"The joys of being on campaign," he remarked, pouring some water to wash with. "Be glad I am not making you sleep by the roadside."

"I could sleep in a ditch," said Carswell. "Ye gods, what a day!"

There was a knock at the door of the parlour, and the landlord and landlady came in with their supper. Carswell staggered up from the bed, and went hobbling across in stockinged feet to claim his drink. He stood and drained his tankard in almost one gulp, and refilled it. Then even before the landlady had finished setting the table, he was in his place and attacking his plate of ham and eggs.

"A fine appetite you have there, sir," she said, a little astonished.

"Please make sure my man gets whatever he needs to

eat," Giles said to the landlord, before he took his own place at table. "And when he is done, would you send him up?"

They ate in silence. The food was plain, but excellent, and Giles found he had an appetite to match that of Carswell. Between them they emptied the beer jug and left only a cheese rind standing. Carswell pushed back his chair, leant back and chewed at a final crust. Then suddenly, he became conscious of his ill-mannered indolence and set himself straight.

"Excuse me."

"Nothing to excuse," Giles said. "It's been a hard day."

Carswell rubbed his face. "At least I know my parents are well lodged – though my father does not like to be comfortable if he can help it."

"I can imagine," Giles said smiling. "But he will see that it is for the best – for Mrs Carswell's sake."

"She is just as bad in her own way. She is not one for cushions." He gave a laugh and reached for the jug and checked to see if there was any beer left. "I am going to ring for some more."

"Be careful," Giles said. "That is strong stuff."

"Exactly," he said, and got up and tugged the bell rope.

Giles also got up from the table and fetched his notebook from his coat pocket. He wanted to review his notes but he made little headway with the task. The beer certainly was powerful, and he felt languid from it and the exertion of the ride. He stared blankly at them, thinking instead of that last kiss he had exchanged with Laura, the sweetness of her lips, how she had tipped her head back and closed her eyes in pure pleasure. He stretched out in his chair, imagining their reunion in a day or two.

"Do you read Spanish?" Carswell said, breaking into his reverie.

"No," said Giles. "Why do you ask?"

"It is just that there is something – it may be relevant to the case. Since you mentioned you think you saw Don Luiz at the dog fight, talking to Edgar, I have been wondering. The thing is, when Don Xavier was dying, he said something which —" He broke off. "It was all extremely strange. Here, let me show you."

Carswell went to his medical bag and produced a dark red leather dispatch case, with a coat of arms embossed on it. "I found this hidden in Don Xavier's room, and Dona Blanca insisted I take custody of it. And tell no one I had it. So I hesitated to mention it before, but why on earth would she expect me to take charge of it?"

"Dona Blanca?"

"She is Don Xavier's sister-in-law – the widow of the late President Martinez. She is an Irish lady, of all things."

"Ah yes, I know who you mean," said Giles picking up the letter case and examining it. "Lord Rothborough mentioned her."

"He did?" Carswell said.

"Yes, he said he wished to meet her. He told me that she was supposed to be a shrewd tactician, and that the new government made a mistake when they did not execute her alongside her husband. But I suppose they did not want to make a martyr of a woman who apparently has the hearts of the people. Very dangerous. And she asked you to take charge of this?"

"Yes. She was adamant. It was rather strange."

"Just as strange as Don Xavier putting off his habit and coming to Stanegate," said Giles, opening the case. "They are all in Spanish?"

"Yes."

"And what was she like?"

"I can't really say. Well, she was Irish, as I said, and clearly she was most upset at Don Xavier's death. She was already in deep mourning for her husband – they had a sort of altar to him in the drawing room with candles burning. The strangest thing. And her manner —"

216

At this moment Holt came in with a servant. The servant was sent for more beer while Holt went to collect their boots and overcoats in order to remove the dust of the road from them. As he did so, Giles spread out the documents on the table and examined the only aspect he could make sense of – the date on the top of each of them.

"Letters. I think they are letters," Carswell said. "It is a damned pity we cannot understand a word of them. If they were French – but Spanish!"

"Spanish, sir?" said Holt, who was almost on the point of leaving again. "I know that language."

"You do, Mr Holt?" Giles said.

"My mother was a Spaniard," Holt said. "My old man brought her back from the Peninsula. I was born just after he got her home and then he was off again, of course. She only lived till I was eight – the weather never suited her – but she made sure I knew her language."

"Good God," said Carswell.

"Can you make anything of these, then, Mr Holt?" said Giles. "Come and sit down with us. As you see, we have quite a quantity to get through."

Holt sat down and Giles brought some more candles to the table so he could see.

"What are these, then, sir?" Holt said.

"We don't know," said Giles. "That is our difficulty."

Holt picked up a sheet and squinted it at it.

"It's a right crabby hand, I can say that for it – Don something or other – I cannot make out the name... anyway, he gives his greetings to the most holy father and asks for his prayers and blessing on the feast of Santa Anna. I think. Then he talks about the weather and his god-daughter. Something about a wedding being off. That's it. Her father cannot find the money that the bridegroom's family is asking for. She's going to have to be a nun after all. Or something like that." He put down the letter and looked across at Giles. "Is this what you wanted, sir?"

"Gossip!" said Carswell. "Why would she want me to hide gossip?"

"Try another one, Mr Holt," said Giles, scanning the letters again. "Are we certain they are all in the same hand? This one – the slope is not quite so pronounced – it looks a little rounder. To whom is it addressed?"

"To a Father Diego," said Holt, taking it. "You are right, sir, that is a different hand. Much easier to make out. Now, what have we got? I write in a hurry. I have a lot of business but I know you will be wanting an answer. You asked me to find the names of those you felt were involved in the case. There is one name that came to light after my questionings but it is such a name as I don't dare to mention in a letter. I will tell you the full particulars soon enough, if Holy Jesus and his mother permitting, I am granted a safe passage." Holt sighed from the labour of translation.

"I don't dare mention in a letter!" exclaimed Carswell. "It sounds as if they have spies everywhere on that god-forsaken island, opening the mails."

"Maybe, maybe not. Perhaps he was simply afraid of being accused of defamation," said Giles. "Who is the letter from, Mr Holt?"

"He doesn't give a name, only initials," said Holt. "A 'J', a 'T' and a 'C'."

"Well, that must be significant, surely!" said Carswell.

"It might be," said Giles. "We really can't say until we have a full translation of them all, and rather more information about Santa Magdalena. And tempting though it would be to sit up till dawn puzzling over them, we had better staunch our curiosity for now. Mr Holt needs his bed, I think."

"Not until I have done the boots, sir," said Holt, getting up from the table. He was obviously relieved to be back on his ordinary duties. "But yes, it's a welcome thought, I must say."

He left, and shortly afterwards the servant came in with

the second jug of beer. They took their drinks in silence for a few minutes, the papers still spread out on the table.

Then Carswell said, "What do you think Lord Rothborough meant by saying that they should have shot Dona Blanca alongside her husband?"

"He was observing, I suppose, that in these troubled, young countries political expediency can become bloody. Enemies need to be eliminated when power is seized."

"Or driven into exile," Carswell said.

"Which is what has happened in this case. She is with her late husband's political ally. He will wish to keep her close if, as is reported, she has the hearts of the common people. I suppose he will want to go back at some point and take back the Presidency for himself. I don't imagine trailing about provincial spa towns is much in his line, even though he did seem to be enjoying himself at the dog-fight. Talking to our dead man. What an extraordinary coincidence – if it is one. I have just remembered something. Someone I spoke to at the dog fight reckoned that he had bought some stolen pistols for gold pieces – foreign gold. It was all hedged about with hearsay, but one never knows. I am glad you showed me these, Mr Carswell."

"I felt I should. She was so fearful. And if she has enemies, perhaps those enemies have followed her here." He drained his tankard. "And is that why Don Xavier wanted to speak to her so desperately? To warn her of something? She told me he loved her. That would be enough to make him take such a risk, when he knew he was dying, when it might kill him to get there. Which it did." He gave a grimace. "He kept repeating her name to me: 'Tell Dona Blanca.' That is what he said, but he never managed to finish his message."

"You have done the best you could in the circumstances."

Carswell nodded and said, "The oddest thing about it was that when I did see her first – on the night he died – when I went to the hotel, when I mentioned my name, she seemed shocked, as if she knew it very well already. How would she know my name? And then, there was a moment, on the second occasion that I remembered something – well, to tell you the truth, I remembered her. I knew I had met her before somewhere."

"Are you sure?" Giles said.

"Yes, quite. It was a most distinct feeling. I felt I had known her as a child, perhaps in Paris. Before I ever came to Scotland. Her voice, her manner, her scent... but that is impossible."

Giles began to fold up the letters.

"We will go and see them when we are done in Swalecliffe. When we know more about Edgar and his business. But first, let us get some sleep. I cannot function a moment longer."

Chapter Twenty-four

Swalecliffe was set on a headland between two great bays.

"The Brighton of the North," said Major Vernon.

"It looks thrown up in the last five minutes," said Felix.

"In the last five years. Since they got the railway."

"Since that quack published his book on the virtues of sea-bathing," said Felix.

"So you think there is nothing in it?"

"In some cases it can help, but to tout it as a cure-all is ridiculous and thoroughly dishonest."

Dominating one bay was a vast hotel, so new that one could almost smell the fresh paint, and on the other bay, terraces of equally modern houses were jostling for position to claim the vital sea view. Trapped in the middle was the old town and harbour, cowering like an old retainer astonished by the fashionable whims of an employer.

It was here that they found the shadowcutter's shop, in a narrow lane of dusty houses. No gilded signboard advertised that it was a shop, but a solitary silhouette of a girl playing with a hoop hung in the little bay window, between the drawn-down blinds and the glass.

A woman opened the door. She was clad in a gaudy pink and gold silk wrapper, with curling papers still in her hair.

"What do you want?" she said with a scowl.

"Mrs Edgar?"

She eyed Major Vernon with great suspicion.

"Who's asking?"

"I am Major Vernon of the Northminster Constabulary. I need to speak to you about your husband."

"He's not here," she said, and was about to slam the door

in their faces, but Major Vernon stopped it with his foot.

"You will need to hear what I have to say, Mrs Edgar," he said. "Will you please let us in?"

She considered it, and then opened the door.

"All right. If you must."

She let them into the narrow hall, but stood defensively, arms folded, leaning against the closed door which presumably led to the living quarters beyond. To the right of her, the little shop lay hidden in shadow, determined to reveal as little as possible.

"Might we go and sit somewhere? I am afraid I have unpleasant news, Mrs Edgar."

"What? What's happened?"

"Do you have anyone with you? A servant?"

"My aunt is upstairs in the parlour."

"Then let us go up, shall we?" He was gentle but insistent.

"Just tell me here," she said. "Whatever it is, just tell me!"

"Very well. I am sorry to have to tell you that your husband is dead."

"Dead?"

"Yes, ma'am."

She turned away, uttering an obscenity. Then she tore open the door, which revealed a staircase and began to stomp upstairs. They followed and went into the sitting room of the house which was papered with an eye-watering pattern of giant bouquets and ribbons. She went straight to a side table and poured herself a generous measure of gin from the bottle that sat waiting. The old woman in black who sat by the window with her sewing, rose in surprise.

"Gin at this time in the morning, dearie?"

"Johnny is dead!" Mrs Edgar said. "And these are policemen." She took a gulp of gin. "I am taking it he didn't die in his bed, then?"

"No, ma'am, I am afraid not. We think he was murdered."

222

She downed her gin and gave a great groan. She refilled her glass.

"Where?" she said. "In Northminster? That's where you're from, didn't you say?"

"No, he was found dead in the gardens at Holbroke, Lord Rothborough's house. You knew he had gone there, I take it?"

"Did I? I don't know. He never says where or when he is going. Oh God! Murdered! Are you sure?"

"Yes."

"How?"

Major Vernon indicated Felix should speak.

"We think he was violently set upon and died as a result of injuries."

She swore again, shaking her head. Then, glass in hand, she went and flopped in one of the armchairs.

"And have you got the bugger?"

"No, not yet. That is why we are here," said the Major.

"Why?" she said. "Do you think I had something to do with it?"

It was said carelessly enough, but there was a touch of fear in it.

"Did you?" Major Vernon said mildly.

"No," she said. "Not that there haven't been moments when —"

"And yet you haven't been married long, I understand."

She gave a snort of amusement.

"Johnny and I have been together five years. It took my first husband a long time to die. I knew well enough what I was getting when I married him." She gave another great sigh, got up and topped up her glass. "And there you were, Auntie, telling me all the time not to do it, and I would go and do it after all, and here we are!" She toasted her Aunt with her glass.

"Nellie dearie," said the Aunt. "You shouldn't be talking like this in front of the gentlemen."

"I've got nothing to hide!" she said. "I made a bad

bargain, I know that, but how could I resist him? When he took it into his head to be sweet to me, well, it was the sweetest thing in the world, and that was worth all the bother of him. But now there won't be any more bother, will there?" She looked down at her glass and her bravado seemed to crumble. "Oh God!"

"Perhaps you should sit down, Mrs Edgar," said Felix. "You have had a great shock."

She allowed him to help her to her chair, but she would not relinquish her glass. She nursed it.

"Did you know if your husband had any enemies, Mrs Edgar?" Major Vernon said.

"We all have enemies," said Mrs Edgar. "Bet you have quite a few."

"Undoubtedly – a hazard of my profession. May we sit down?"

"Please yourself," said Mrs Edgar.

"I wonder if Mr Edgar was in some profession that made him enemies, other than his silhouette-making business, that is?" Major Vernon said, taking a chair and placing it where she could not escape his gaze. "This room is very elegantly furnished, and your earrings – well, I couldn't help but notice them – they are certainly not paste."

She fingered one of them, a smile passing across her face at the compliment. Then she remembered herself.

"I don't know what you mean. There is plenty of money in the shadowcutting – always surprises me, in fact, how much he could make from it. And of course, I let three rooms in the house which gives quite a tidy sum. High-class lodgers, only, of course," she added.

"Yes, I see, but I don't think that would quite cover it," said Major Vernon, glancing around him. "I am simply wondering if he didn't have another line of business. The sort of business that you would be obliged to mention to me, or be complicit in. Do you get my gist?"

She took a mouthful of gin and leaned back in her chair. She gave a little laugh and then said, "Would you believe it! That's one of the reasons he said I should marry him. He said, if I was his wife I couldn't be asked to speak against him in court."

"Well, you are a widow now, Mrs Edgar. And you are obliged," said Major Vernon.

She frowned.

"All right, he may have bought things from certain types and found homes for them."

"He was a fence?"

She nodded and finished her drink.

"I think I might need one of those," said the aunt, getting up and crossing the room. "Did he really do that, Nellie? Oh, my Lord!"

"Yes, didn't you guess, Auntie?"

"I am glad you didn't, ma'am," said Major Vernon.

"So am I!" exclaimed the aunt. "Oh Lord in Heaven, that piece of lace he gave me when you wed – that wasn't stolen, was it?"

"I couldn't say," said Mrs Edgar with a shrug.

"And you still married him!" the old woman exclaimed. "You silly, silly fool! And all those men coming in – that's what it was about! He was a common fence!"

"Not at all common," said Mrs Edgar. "He only dealt in the valuable stuff." It was said almost with pride. "Taken from people who wouldn't miss it, to tell you the truth."

"It's still thieving!" said the aunt. "And you could hang for knowing it. We all could, I dare say." She threw a wild, frightened glance at Major Vernon. "Or transported. Which is just as bad, if not worse. I think I would rather be hanged." She broke off, and poured herself a steadying glass of gin.

"The more information you give us now," Major Vernon said, "the more favourably you will be looked on, ma'am. When you say 'taken from people who wouldn't miss it' do you recall if your husband mentioned any names in particular? Of houses, perhaps?"

Mrs Edgar frowned, looking down at her ring-bedecked fingers. There was a long silence and then she spoke: "I don't know where the stuff came from. But he said it wouldn't be missed. That I wasn't to worry about it. You see, Auntie, I did worry – of course I did." Her voice broke into a sob. "And I suppose you will be telling me I should be glad that he is dead, which I suppose I ought to be! After all, I knew exactly what he was like, and I knew he was never going to be faithful, and that he was mixed up in some shady stuff, but I loved him, and I can't stop myself from feeling what I feel, even if it does make me look like – like goodness-knows what!"

With which she jumped up from her seat and ran weeping from the room, followed quickly by her aunt.

Major Vernon wandered over to the mantelpiece and picked up a tiny silver-gilt box.

"This is a charming piece of work," he said, turning it in his hands. "I think it is a patch box, from the days when ladies and gentlemen wore velvet beauty spots. My mother inherited one from her grandmother – but not so grand as this one. But it did have its owner's name engraved on it. Now I wonder –" He flicked it open and smiled. "A coat of arms, no less. Very readily identified, I should say. Of course," he went on, "it might have been acquired quite legitimately, as might all these expensive bibelots."

"You think these were all stolen?" said Felix, examining a green and gold enamel egg which lay in a gilt lattice basket. When he flicked it open it contained a tiny golden duck, with jewels for eyes. He could not help giving a little gasp of pleasure at the ingenuity of it and at the absurd, whimsical expression that the maker had given the duck.

"That, I should say, is a rare thing," said Major Vernon. "It would make a fine present for a sweetheart."

Felix imagined pressing such an object into Sukey's hand,

and watching her face as she opened the lid and saw the duck. Her smile would be worth seeing. "Or for a guilty husband to offer a forgiving wife?" Major Vernon went on. "Mrs Edgar did just say she had no expectations of his being faithful. And I saw him with a pair of gay girls at the dog fight the other night. There were probably other women who distracted him. I wonder if Eliza Jones might not be one of them."

"But she was dead before he arrived, I thought."

"Yes."

"And there is no evidence that they knew each other," Felix said.

"Not that I have found yet, that's true. But my instincts tell me she was a thief. She is the best candidate I can find at Holbroke for the theft and concealment of the parure. What if she has been travelling about picking up things like this from the great houses where her mistress is asked to stay out of charity? And passing them onto Edgar in return for cash and kisses? We need to know exactly where Lady Warde has been staying."

The door opened and the aunt came in. She closed the door carefully behind her.

"She's having a lie down. She's a bit upset."

"Of course. We will have to talk to her again. And I should like to look through Mr Edgar's shop, if I may?"

"You may do as you please!" said the aunt. "Anything to keep my poor Nell from trouble. She's a silly girl. I knew she shouldn't have married him, I knew he was a bad'un. I've always known. Too slick by half, and always bringing her expensive presents, even when her first husband was alive. I knew he was no good, I've always had my suspicious!"

"Any suspicions in particular, ma'am?"

"If you want the plain truth, and now he's dead, I can speak my mind, but it is my opinion he did for him!"

"Mr Edgar did for whom?" said Major Vernon.

"Jack Baker, Nellie's first husband, God rest his poor

tortured soul. He wasn't much of a looker but he loved her like a man should love his wife. There wasn't anything he wouldn't do for her. He left her all this and I told her that should be enough for her. It was independence, but she would go and marry that wretch Edgar!"

"You think that Edgar murdered Mr Baker?" said Major Vernon.

"Oh yes. He was ill, of course, and dying. The doctor said there was no hope, but I think Edgar finished him off, just to get his hands on his money by marrying Nellie. They were married a week after we put Jack in the ground." She shook her head. "It was shocking! I couldn't look my neighbours in the face."

"And why do you think this?" Major Vernon asked. "Did you see or hear something?"

"I found a pillowcase," she said. "With a funny stain on it. Blood and the like. It made me think... well, you know..."

"You believe he was suffocated?" Felix said. She nodded. "But you told no one at the time? You did not speak to the doctor?"

"Nobody listens to me," she said, with a shrug.

"Do you still have the pillowcase?" Felix asked.

"No," she said. Felix could not help frowning. "I kept it a while, and then I thought, I should just get rid of it and let it go. Nellie was happy. I didn't want to rake it up. But now he's dead..."

"Perhaps we might look over the shop?" Major Vernon said.

She took them downstairs and left them to their investigations.

"I suppose it is too much to hope that Edgar has left a nice neat ledger with all his dubious transactions in it," Felix said. "What are we looking for?"

"I don't think we will know until we find it," said Major Vernon, opening a box lying on the counter. "You search those shallow drawers over there."

Felix did as he was bid. The drawers contained a great many unframed, unfinished miniatures of very poor quality. All the women looked like spaniels. "This looks like a lot of work for not much money," said Felix.

"Perhaps that is why he turned to crime," said Major Vernon who was on his knees behind the counter, turning out a cupboard. Rows of boxes lined the shelves. Major Vernon took each out in turn but they appeared to contain nothing.

"Aha," said Vernon, "that's more like it." He was holding a small drawstring bag that had been put behind the boxes to be out of sight. "Very interesting. This stuff is exactly the same pattern as the bag the jewels at Holbroke were in. I wonder if we could match the stitching. Do different hands have different styles of stitching, do you think?"

"It's possible," Felix said. "Like handwriting, perhaps. It would bear investigation, certainly."

Standing at the counter like a shopman, Major Vernon opened the bag and took out a string of fine, fat pearls, fastened with a jewelled clasp.

"Very, very nice indeed," he said. "I wonder where these came from?"

"Someone will have noticed those missing, for certain," said Felix.

"Yes, but often these things are not reported. Great families do not like to have people like me poking about in their business. And as Mrs Edgar pointed out, they do not feel the loss as you and I might. But there is the loss of reputation to be reckoned with and that is a far great threat to them. It does not look good. Or, this piece, like the Rothborough parure, simply may not have been missed because no one has wanted to wear it. If the lady of the house has evangelical convictions, for example, or she has jewels of her own that she prefers. They think it is still safely locked away. This is a shrewd operation. Excellent insider knowledge."

"Eliza Jones," said Felix.

"Innocently sewing linen bags to stash her takings in and listening to the gossip about the ladies upstairs," said Major Vernon. "One of the maids at Holbroke may even have seen her making them. Of course, taking a whole parure is a daring enterprise, even to a practised hand. Mrs Connolly observed that it was perhaps out of desperation, given Miss Jones was pregnant. One last, big job before she runs away with her lover."

"Edgar, you mean?"

"Perhaps. And perhaps he killed her. They meet by arrangement – he comes to Holbroke a day or two earlier than he has been asked. She gives him part of the parure – possibly the missing bracelet – and tells him there is more to follow. Perhaps it doesn't go well. He decides he has had enough of her and cuts his losses. That the parure is too risky even for him. Perhaps he never thought she would do it? Maybe he is bored with her and she is too demanding and difficult, even though she has been supplying him so faithfully. He loses his temper with her and smashes her against the cave wall, dumps her in the pool and departs with the bracelet."

"But the bracelet was not in his things. There was nothing on him," Felix pointed out.

"No – unfortunately. Already sold on? But there was no sign of any cash."

"So why is he dead?"

"I have no idea, as yet," said Major Vernon. "Was it simply for the money he had on him? Perhaps he sold it at the dog fight and came back to Holbroke with bulging pockets which tempted someone."

"That attack was extremely violent," Felix said. "It was sustained – it continued after he was unconscious. And it would have been messy. It is hard to know how anyone could have concealed the evidence that the attack would have left on their clothes. I cannot imagine that if it had been one of the servants, for example, that it would not have been noticed."

"That's true," said Major Vernon slipping the pearls back into the bag. "And if you were just after the money, wouldn't you be content with knocking the man unconscious, robbing him and then making off as soon as you could? Such an attack involves taking a great risk, which suggests that the destruction of Edgar was important to this person. That it was necessary rather than incidental."

"Revenge?" Felix said. "If he did kill Eliza Jones then perhaps someone decided to teach him a lesson for it. Another lover? A relation?"

"Perhaps," said Major Vernon. "It's a good line of enquiry, certainly. Come, let's finish our search here and then we will go and find out what Holt has turned up."

The search yielded no more pearls – either in the form of necklaces or paperwork.

"I had hoped for a daybook giving me his movements for the shadowcutting business," said Major Vernon, "but perhaps he was too canny to keep obvious records of where he had been and when. I shall take those little boxes and these pearls with us. If I leave them, I fear that Mrs Edgar, who knows that their origins are dubious, will whisk them away."

When it came to it, Mrs Edgar was a little loath to let them take away her trinkets, but the aunt sensibly intervened.

"And if we discovered they have been lawfully purchased, we will of course return them to you at once," Major Vernon said. "I will give you a receipt in the meantime."

She accepted it with a sigh and poured herself another glass of gin.

"Oh, and one more question, and then we will leave you in peace," said Major Vernon. "Do either of you know a young woman called Eliza Jones? Edgar never brought anyone answering to that name here?"

The women shook their heads and their ignorance seemed genuine enough.

231

"That may not have been her real name, of course," Major Vernon said as they walked away from the house. "It is a cipher of a name. Now I know people do have plain names, but anyone in that trade will be liable to have several identities if they are sensible."

~

Holt's enquiries in the public houses and shops in the old town had turned up little that was new about Edgar. He was known as a local character, and some even reckoned him to be tainted with something dubious, but no one had been a fountain of incriminating information. Edgar remained elusive.

Holt had also found rooms for them in a comfortable lodging house on the West Bay. After a well-cooked dinner with an agreeable bottle of claret, Felix and Major Vernon went to walk on the beach. There was a band playing, and because it was a balmy evening at the height of the season, the promenade was thronged.

"This is a fine beach," said Major Vernon, as they headed down to the water's edge where it was much quieter. "It is not quite as fine as the sands at Bamburgh, of course."

He stood gazing out to sea for a moment and then turned north, and began to stride along as if he meant to walk all the way up the coast to the beach he had just mentioned.

Ahead of them, a smartly dressed man and woman were going along, arm-in-arm, heads bent together. She was leaning in on him, and they stopped to exchange a passionate kiss, thinking they were not observed. Or perhaps they simply did not care, Felix thought.

"Wedding journey?" remarked Major Vernon, stooping to pick up a piece of driftwood that resembled a shepherd's crook. He leant on it and gazed out to the sea.

"Perhaps," Felix said, watching them turn back and head up the beach. No doubt they were eager to be back at their lodgings, he thought, not without a touch of envy. For a moment, in his fancy he saw himself with Sukey, walking on the same beach, arm in arm, with the prospect of various intimate pleasures to follow. It made him dry-throated with desire and he had to stuff the idea away.

"Has your father always carried that staff of his?" Major Vernon said.

"For as long as I can remember. I have been falling over it for as long as that. He leaves it about on the floor."

Vernon smiled at that and began to write in the damp sand. He wrote 'Eliza' and 'Edgar' and then made a dotted a line to join the names.

"This connection is, at the moment, pure supposition," he said, "but we have to start somewhere."

Then he drew a question mark below and added two lines to make a triangle. "Who or what might link Miss Jones to Mr Edgar?"

"Lord Rothborough," said Felix, and expecting a reproof, added, "I am being facetious."

"You are to the point," said Major Vernon. "Lord Rothborough brought them both to Holbroke. Edgar would not have come if Lord Rothborough had not wanted to surprise Lady Maria. And if he were not wealthy and generous, Lady Warde and her maid would not be there. But if my theory is correct, and Edgar knew Eliza from some previous association, then Lord Rothborough summoning him is irrelevant. He would have been there anyway, to collect whatever Eliza had stolen for him. Or part of it."

"We ought to be able to find where he stayed before he came to Holbroke," pointed out Felix.

"Exactly. And once we have his movements, then all will be a little clearer, I hope." Major Vernon looked down at his diagram. "You brought up revenge, Mr Carswell," he went on.

"It is worth considering. What if Eliza Jones was not acting alone? That she had a colleague in her enterprise who was –"

"Someone closely connected with her?" Felix said. "But there was nobody, you said so yourself; the woman kept herself resolutely to herself."

"Not entirely – she managed to seduce Syme. There may be someone else, someone I have overlooked entirely. We must go back and look over everything again. But first we will pay a call on the government-in-exile of Santa Magdalena. I still want to know what Edgar was talking to the ex-Chancellor about."

Chapter Twenty-five

They rode back to Stanegate the following day. It was a long, tiresome journey, with the weather turning unpleasantly humid from noon onwards. The end of the journey brought a little relief as the weather finally broke, and the last few miles were accompanied by a thunderstorm. They arrived, soaking wet, to take their shelter in the house in Park Street. Predictably enough, Mrs Bolland was not pleased to see them.

She lost no time telling Giles that she felt he was thoroughly abusing his position and that she would tell the gentleman who owned the house that he should never let the place again to such inconsiderate people. Giles, who had just pulled off his boots and was standing dripping in the hall, was wondering if her tongue had been unleashed by the storm and was for a long moment quite at a loss to know what to do about her. He was formulating some vague put-down, when Holt came upstairs, having dealt with the horses and said, bluntly, "Stop your ruddy grumbling, woman! You should be glad you have a place at all, the way you carry on! Now, will you go and make up the fire in the kitchen! I have these gentlemen's coats to dry."

This had a salutary effect and she went bustling off. Yielding up his soaking coat to Holt, Giles felt grateful to him for his energy and loyalty. It had been a punishing ride, and as Carswell had pointed out rather too acidly, quite unnecessary given the new railway service.

Ahead of him, Carswell was carefully and cautiously climbing upstairs as if every step hurt him.

Noticing this, Holt said, "I've a liniment, Mr Carswell, that you might find useful." Carswell stopped and turned. He looked somewhat grey-faced.

"Oh?" he said.

"Works a treat, sir," said Holt. "The surgeon of the 33rds swore by it. Lard and oil of cloves."

"Sounds excellent," said Giles.

"I'll try anything," Carswell said. "I don't suppose that gorgon would draw me a bath, not even for fifty guineas, so yes, Holt, I will try your liniment."

"And some brandy and hot water," said Giles.

"Yes," Carswell said, starting up the stairs again, "exactly." But he stopped again. "Oh Holt, those papers —"

"The Spanish ones, sir?"

"Yes, I put them in my pack. Where is it? I am worried they got wet."

"They didn't, sir. I took the liberty of redoing your pack. Well, it was a bit... sloppy, sir. Wouldn't pass inspection. They will have been safe as houses in there."

"Oh, thank you," said Carswell, rather astonished.

"How did I ever manage without you, Holt?" said Giles digging in his pocket. "Here."

"There's no need for that, sir," said Holt. "But thank you."

They made their way upstairs and sat in their stockinged feet and damp shirts, drinking brandy in silence while the storm rattled the sashes. There were letters waiting for Giles from Northminster – nothing to alarm, he was thankful to find. After a while, Carswell hauled himself out of his chair and went hobbling off to his bed, and Giles continued to sit alone, with only a guttering candle for company. He was bone-tired, it was true, but his mind would not let go of the problem of Edgar and Eliza and he sat turning the facts over and over in his mind, weighing the possibilities and probabilities.

Then, finally, he went up to his own bed, and coming into the room, remembered Laura lying there in her embroidered shawl, and felt a stab of longing. It was soon assuaged by the knowledge he would see her again tomorrow evening.

~

"There they are," said Carswell.

They were sitting on a rustic seat, with white roses trained over it. Both of them were wearing black, but one woman wore the sort of mourning that had nothing to do with grief, and everything to do with display. As a result she presented a highly picturesque appearance, in a complex lace bonnet and holding a black lace fan, all set off by her dark Spanish colouring.

"That is Mrs Ramirez, Dona Clara, on the right," murmured Carswell, "and the other lady, with the book, is Dona Blanca, Martinez's widow."

If Dona Clara was the showier of the two women, in her way Dona Blanca was equally striking, and far more to Giles' taste. Her attire was quiet but elegant, and she had a beautiful, clear complexion. She was studying her book with great concentration.

Dona Clara looked straight at them and alerted her companion with a touch on her shoulder and a few words. For a moment Dona Blanca was startled, but then she smiled warmly towards them.

"Oh, Mr Carswell," she said, getting up and walking up to them. She had a soft Irish accent that was pleasant on the ear. "How delightful to see you. You remember Dona Clara, I think?"

"Yes, ma'am," Carswell said, bowing to Dona Clara who had not risen. "This is Major Vernon, my employer."

Giles made his bows and said, "We were hoping to speak to Don Luiz – do you know where he might be?"

"I believe he is doing some business," said Dona Blanca.

"He will be here presently. Will you wait?"

"Yes – if you do not mind?" said Carswell.

"Not at all," said Dona Blanca. "It is so pleasant here. I had forgotten how beautiful English roses are!" She reached out and touched one of the blossoms.

At this moment they were interrupted by a boy of about four, his face red with fury and stained with tears. He pushed past Giles and Carswell and hurled himself at Dona Clara, howling. A moment later, his nurse appeared with three other children. All were in a state of uproar, all expressed in loud, rapid Spanish. Dona Clara threw herself into this fray. As she hugged her little boy, her long loose cuff fell back and revealed, for a moment, a most sumptuous and distinctive bracelet set with rubies and pearls which Giles thought he had seen somewhere else.

"Oh dear," exclaimed Dona Blanca. "You must excuse us! Perhaps we should take a little stroll, yes?" She turned and said something in Spanish to Dona Clara who waved them away.

So they began to walk with Dona Blanca, back along the path they had come. Giles wanted to go back and examine the bracelet but could not think of a way of achieving that.

"They are wild children, I'm afraid," said Dona Blanca. "But I think they are missing their home and friends there. It is hard for them, this exile."

"It cannot be easy for any of you," Giles said.

"Necessity demands great sacrifices of us at times," she said. "Let us sit here. Red roses instead of white."

"Lancastrians instead of Yorkists," Giles said.

So they installed themselves in another rustic, rose-bedecked bower, this time on some scattered basket chairs.

"Yes, quite," said Dona Blanca. "Which are you, sir?"

"In my profession it is best not take sides. But one might say that of life in general."

"Oh yes, exactly, but sometimes one finds oneself in

strange places," she remarked.

"Like your poor brother-in-law," Giles said.

"Yes. That he should have come here is still a mystery. But I must thank Our Lord that he sent you gentlemen to him in his last hours. What you both did was so kind. And now he will always be here, in this place." She gestured about her. "He can have English flowers on his grave. I will have to make sure that he does." She gave a sigh. "May I ask, why did you wish to see Don Luiz? Was it something to do with Xavier?"

"You may be able to supply the information we are after, in fact, ma'am," said Giles. "Did Don Luis to your knowledge go to a dog fight at Byrescough on Wednesday, three nights ago – the night of the full moon?"

"The day of Don Xavier's funeral," Carswell added.

"That is an odd question, Major Vernon," said Dona Blanca. "But he may well have done. I did not see him after dinner, and we dined early because of the funeral. He does often go out in the evening. It is the custom of Santa Magdalena, really – our gentlemen are not particularly domesticated."

"So you would not be shocked to know he was seen at an illegal dog fight?" Carswell said.

"Not really. It is a cruel sport, but it is a great passion among the people of the island – that and cock-fighting. It would not be possible, as it has been here, to suppress it. I remember discussing this with my late husband, when the legislation was passed here. We always had an English newspaper – in fact we wondered at it being passed! It was quite impossible to think of such a thing happening in Santa Magdalena."

"Lord Rothborough was one of the men who pushed it through," Carswell said, and Giles was aware that he was studying Dona Blanca's face. "I think you may know him, ma'am?"

Dona Blanca frowned slightly and said, "Why do you say

that?"

"Because," Carswell went on, "and I hope you do not mind me saying this, and forgive me if I am mistaken, but I think we have met before, when I was a child in Paris. I have a distinct memory of you, ma'am, from somewhere."

"You do?"

"Perhaps my memory is playing tricks. But just sitting here these last minutes – and thinking about it, a great deal, since we last met – it seems to me, that I do know you."

"You remember that you were a child in Paris?" she said.

"I have fragments of memories, that is all. I left just after my second birthday, I believe."

"You were just two and two weeks," she said, and then put her hand over her mouth. She was breathing hard, and looking down. "Oh."

"So we have met!" exclaimed Carswell. "I was sure we had. Then you must know Lord Rothborough. Perhaps you helped him, when my mother abandoned me. I think I remember you telling me the English for squirrel."

She got up and walked away, and stood with her back to them. Her shoulders were rising and falling, as if she were struggling with some great emotion.

"It is rather more than that," she said, in a quiet voice. "It is..." She shook her head. "And she did not abandon you. If he told you that –"

Carswell jumped up from his seat, saying, "She did not? Then what did happen?"

She turned and came over to Carswell, her face now riven with misery, her eyes full of tears. Giles saw her reach out and touch Carswell's cheek with her fingertips, her lips parted as if about to speak, but no words came. The gesture was eloquent in itself and he was moved without quite knowing why. But then, as he looked at them both in profile, he began to read that there were similarities there, and despite Carswell's striking resemblance to Lord Rothborough, there was another

240

face that had added to his physiognomy. Carswell himself was staring at her, as if he too were reading the same signs.

A long moment passed and Giles had reached a strange conclusion, which at the same time seemed completely correct. Then suddenly, throwing her arms in the air, Dona Blanca exclaimed, "I did not abandon you, Felix! I gave you to him!"

She waved her arms a little and brought her hands to rest on his shoulders, but only for a moment. She pulled them away again as from a hot surface.

"Are you saying... are you saying..." Carswell said, catching her hands.

"I should not have said anything!" she said, wresting her hands free of his grip. "It does no good to anyone, least of all you! Forgive me!" she said, and this time she walked a fair distance down the path, followed by Carswell.

Giles glanced to his side and saw that Lord Rothborough was strolling along the path, in the company of the man he had seen at the dog fight, who was presumably Don Luiz. Giles remembered Lord Rothborough's intention to call on the government in exile.

"Ma'am, Carswell," he said. "Lord Rothborough —"

He did not need to say any more, for in the same moment they both saw him.

"Don Luiz knows nothing of any of this," she said, reaching for her handkerchief and wiping her face. "And I do not wish him to know."

She began to walk briskly in the other direction. Carswell was about to follow, but Giles caught his arm.

"Let her compose herself," Giles said.

"Did you hear what she said?" Carswell asked. Giles nodded. "What am I to do?"

"Keep your counsel for the moment, if you can bear it. This is not the time or the place. She is not ready. Consider what she must be feeling."

"Do you think she is my mother?"

"I think so," Giles said. "And you must respect her secrets, hard though that is going to be." Carswell nodded and swallowed hard. "You will get to the truth sooner or later." Carswell nodded again. "In the meantime, distract yourself with this – did you notice Dona Clara's bracelet?"

"What? No."

"That's a pity. I want a second look at it. It looked familiar to me."

Their conversation went no further. Lord Rothborough and Don Luiz had arrived.

Chapter Twenty-six

Felix was not quite sure how he got through the next ten minutes of useless small talk, of the sort he detested at the best of times.

But Major Vernon was right. She was entitled to her secrets. He could not go after her, no matter how many questions he wished to ask.

It began to rain, and mercifully all further conversation was at an end. Don Luiz went in to join his wife and children, while Felix, Major Vernon and Lord Rothborough hurried through the gardens to the entrance of the hotel.

"Let's go to The White Hart," said Lord Rothborough. "We can have a decent lunch and then go back to Holbroke."

The White Hart was only a few yards from The Queen's Hotel, so they did not repeat yesterday's drenching. It was cool and discreet, and had a great deal of old-fashioned grandeur about it. Lord Rothborough was its owner and was greeted with more than the usual deference. They were shown into a blue-painted parlour, and a lunch suitable for princes was swiftly brought in.

Felix did not feel much like eating, appetising though it looked. He toyed with a piece of bread while Major Vernon and Lord Rothborough discussed the morning's business.

"The reason I called on Don Luiz this morning was that I got a letter," Lord Rothborough said, "from a reliable source of mine in Paris. He informs me that it is likely that Don Luiz is planning to return to the island sooner rather than later. The rebel government is crumbling fast. It is full of factions."

"And no doubt, Don Luiz has his agents on the ground whipping up quarrels between them," said Major Vernon.

"No doubt. How cynical you are, sir," said Lord Rothborough, with a smile.

"I think he is probably a ruthless operator."

"Certainly he is. My source did wonder what brought them here, though. Surely not just to take the waters. Apparently Dona Blanca was keen to do so, and he must fall in with his political trump card, I suppose. I am rather disappointed not to have met her. You spoke to her, did you not, Felix?"

"Briefly," he managed to say.

"And what was your impression?"

"She was Irish," he said. It was the best he could manage in the circumstances.

Mercifully Major Vernon, interjected: "My lord, how important is it to the Government that Don Luiz's party is back in power in Santa Magdalena?"

"We have interests there, as I said, but it does not matter much who is in power, so long as they will do business with us. Why?"

"I think I may have to arrest him for buying stolen goods."

"Good grief."

"When you kissed Dona Clara's hand, did you see she was wearing a rather opulent bracelet?"

"Yes, I did notice that. Rather surprising, with her mourning. And now that I think of it, it did seem familiar."

"I think there is a good chance that is the missing bracelet from your parure, my lord," said Major Vernon. "That pattern is quite distinctive. And she is a bird of paradise sort of woman. Even in mourning, she cannot resist wearing the new trinket that her husband has given her."

"That he got from Edgar at the dog fight?" said Felix.

"That is my theory at the moment, yes," said Major Vernon.

"Which he got from Eliza Jones," said Felix.

"And he may well have killed her for it," said Major Vernon. "It is a pity I cannot question a dead man. We shall have to contrive a way to get Dona Clara to surrender her bracelet."

"You will probably have to cut her hand off to do it," said Lord Rothborough. "Some women are impossible about jewels. They seem to fall prey to them. They cannot resist their charms."

"Like men fall prey to whores," Felix could not help saying.

"Maybe so," said Lord Rothborough, picking up the carving knife and slicing another piece of raised pie. "Are you going to eat anything more than that?"

"I seem to have lost my appetite," said Felix, getting up and going to the window.

"I wish you would eat, but at least that will leave you hungry for a good dinner at Ardenthwaite tonight," said Lord Rothborough. "I sent a few more people over there from Holbroke, so you will be comfortable. From there you can join Major Vernon tomorrow and discreetly continue your investigations. Sir Arthur seems to be making a noose for poor Walter so you will have your work cut out, I fear."

"That works in our favour," said Major Vernon. "Though it will not be pleasant for Walter, a scapegoat will perhaps lull the real culprit into a false sense of security. It may lead someone to betray themselves."

"You think it is someone at Holbroke?" said Lord Rothborough with a frown.

"Yes, I fear it might be."

"No institution is perfect, of course — and what is a great household but a sort of institution?" Lord Rothborough said, sighing. "I should not be sentimental on that account, because it is such a dear place to me, and all the people in it are my people."

Major Vernon got up from the table, having glanced at

his watch.

"I am going to speak to the house agent," he said. "Since you have been hospitable in asking my wife and myself to stay, sir, I will give up the house here today." Lord Rothborough inclined his head graciously. "We were only supposed to be there another week, after all. When this business at Holbroke is done, we will go straight back to Northminster and will not impose on you any longer."

"It is no imposition at all. You must take your full furlough with us. Maria will not forgive me if I let you take Mrs Vernon away any earlier than is strictly necessary. The place agrees with her. Last night at dinner – well, you will not mind me saying this, I hope – she was on sparkling form! And her playing – quite beautiful."

Major Vernon took his leave and Felix was left alone with Lord Rothborough.

"I've just remembered something," Felix said, and went running from the room after Major Vernon. He chased him halfway down the stairs.

"I think I should speak to him about Dona Blanca," Felix said. "It seems only fair."

"Yes, perhaps," said Major Vernon.

"Perhaps?" said Felix.

"I don't know quite what I should say to you," Major Vernon said. "I'm sorry. It is an extraordinary situation. But yes, perhaps you should warn him that she is here. It could be a great embarrassment for them both otherwise."

"That is what I thought," Felix said, and went back.

This was not true. Sparing Lord Rothborough humiliation had not crossed his mind. He was overflowing with questions and accusations. The subject was an immense one, like a great, stormy ocean which had to be navigated in a gravy boat.

"What was that about?" said Lord Rothborough when he returned.

Felix sat down at his place.

"Dona Blanca," he said, and reached for the glass of wine which he had not previously touched.

"Ah yes," Lord Rothborough smiled. "I had hoped to hear more on that subject. Major Vernon was tight-lipped. I wonder why."

"Because she is my mother," Felix said, thinking there was nothing to be lost by being anything but blunt. "Or at least, she implied she was. Just before you arrived."

"Good God," he said quietly. "What did she say?"

"I told her I remembered her – which I do. The other day, when I saw her before Don Xavier was buried, we had the strangest passage together, and I thought I knew her," Felix said. "And when I saw her again today, I was sure of it. I knew her in Paris. So I said so. And she was affected by my presence and she knew my name. The first time I saw her, and she heard my name, she reacted to it. It was impossible not to see that. And then today, when I said I was barely two when I left Paris, she said I was exactly two years and two weeks and when I asked if she had cared for me after my mother abandoned me, and she said she had not –"

"What? Slow down, Felix."

"She said: 'I did not abandon you. I gave you to him.' What does that mean?"

"I don't know," said Lord Rothborough.

"You don't know?" said Felix. "Of course you do! You were there. You said that she abandoned me, and she flatly denied it."

Lord Rothborough covered his eyes with his hand and murmured, "Dear God in Heaven." He exhaled. "Irish, you said."

"Yes."

"Her name was Blanche Halloran. I suppose Blanca would be the Spanish form. She may have adopted it when she married Martinez. If this is she, of course."

"Why would she claim it, if she is not?"

"To blackmail me, of course!" said Rothborough. "And, if she is who she says, there is still no end of trouble she could make if she is so inclined. She is very good at trouble, I can tell you that for nothing, Felix, before you allow yourself to be carried away on a tide of sentiment. She has come here to make mischief, there is no doubt of that. How else would she know who you were? She did not know to whom I intended to give you. She has found that out, the little schemer. An excellent tactician, a power behind the throne – well, it makes perfect sense! Blanche, oh God, Blanche!"

He got up from the table and began to pace the room.

"She was young and still utterly beautiful when we parted. There is no reason that she could not still have made a respectable marriage. She had an enterprising nature, after all." He shook his head. "Don Luiz even told me it was her idea that they should come to Stanegate. He had never heard of the place! She arranged the whole thing to see you. We shall have to be careful, Felix, very careful indeed."

"I do not see it like that. She was genuinely upset," Felix said. "She regretted being so unguarded. She apologised to me and ran away the moment Major Vernon said you were coming. She was in tears."

"She can cry to order. I have seen her do that on many occasions."

"You saw it over twenty years ago!" Felix said. "What do you know of her now?"

"I know that she cannot have come here except to cause us trouble," Lord Rothborough said.

"I do not believe that. I think she has trouble all of her own – to do with those Santa Magdaleneans. She gave me some documents to look after and she was insistent that Don Luiz should know nothing about it. She struck me as quite genuine and troubled by her brother-in-law's death, which was odd enough in the first place."

"She has got her hooks into you, then," said Lord

Rothborough, with a sigh.

"And you are as bitter as if it were yesterday!" Felix said.

"Of course. What she did to you was appalling. I cannot see how you do not feel it."

"I know it," Felix said. "But seeing her, I do not feel it. She was adamant that she gave you to me."

"That is a form of words. That is all. It is no defence!" he said. "I know what happened. It was shocking."

"I want to speak to her," Felix said, going to the writing table in the corner of the parlour and sitting down. He took a piece of paper and picked up the pen. "I shall send for her. We will have this out for once and for all. She has a right to defend herself to me. I want to know the truth of it."

"I have always told you the truth, Felix," said Lord Rothborough. "Please, I beg you, do not write to her."

Felix sat with the pen in hand.

"Your truth," he said. "Not hers. I looked her in the eyes, and – it was as if she were in pain. And I felt –" He looked round to where Rothborough was standing, his hands gripping the back rail of a chair, his head bowed. He, too, looked as if he was suffering. "If you really do not want me to, sir," he said, putting down the pen.

There was a long silence and then Lord Rothborough straightened himself and came over to the writing table. He laid his hand on Felix's shoulder.

"Write to her," he said. "Let us get this over with."

~

She came, an awkward hour or so later, during which Felix pretended to read a newspaper. Lord Rothborough astonished him by reading his own newspaper with a great deal more attention, to the extent of making occasional notes in his memorandum book as he scanned the dense columns. Felix admired his self-control. He wished he did not feel awash with sentiment.

"You look well, Blanche," Lord Rothborough said, when she had come in.

"And so do you, Will."

Felix had never heard anyone address Lord Rothborough by his Christian name, let alone this diminutive.

"Won't you sit down?"

"Thank you."

He sat at one end of the table, she at the other, Felix between them. A servant brought in tea and put the tray down in front of Dona Blanca. She drew off her gloves, and the silence thickened as the tea brewed.

"I honestly do not know where to begin," Lord Rothborough said.

"Nor I," she said. "I could pour the tea."

"Yes, why not?"

She began to pour, and after a moment Lord Rothborough said, "I remember how you said that your mother would not let you make the tea after dinner. It was always your older sister who did so. And I got a Wedgwood set for you, in Paris, and had tea sent from London, so you could make it for me. And we would take our tea and pretend, like the children we were. Tea was a symptom of our foolishness."

"Yes," she said, "indeed. I kept that set for many years. I took it to Santa Magdalena."

"You are spinning tales."

"No. A few cups and plates remain. At least they did before I left. I could not bring them with me."

Lord Rothborough was shaking his head.

"That cannot be true."

"It is. I swear to God."

"You lied to me so often," he said. "It was part of who

you were, to deceive me."

"No, no," she said, softly. "Not so very often. But yes, sometimes, yes. I was so young."

"Sixteen."

"Yes, and in a trap. A terrible trap."

"I did not trap you."

"No, but it was a trap for us both. That world. That way of being. We tried to defy it. I thought we had, for a while, but then..." She broke off and took up the sugar tongs, and dropped a chip of sugar into one of the cups. "That is right, isn't it?" she said, and offered the cup to him.

"Yes," he said, but he frowned as he took the cup. He sat down again and stirred in the sugar, and said, "I wonder how it might have been if I had met you in Ireland, when you were still in your mother's drawing room, not being allowed to make the tea."

"You would never have been there."

"Your people were respectable enough."

"Only because they chose to be, and then it was always a struggle. That drawing room was smaller than this room. What would you have been doing there? My father was a Roman Catholic attorney, and not a good one, with too many children and a terrible taste for the whiskey. Our paths could not have crossed. Paris was the only place in the world where we could have met."

"Until now," Lord Rothborough said.

"Well, this is no accident," she said. "That is the truth of it. But," and now she turned to Felix, "I had only meant to see you from a distance. That was all I intended."

"What do you mean?" Felix said.

"I meant only to go and look at you from a distance. I just wanted to see what you looked like. It always haunted me, that idea, and after my husband died and we came back to Europe, it was so much worse, that longing to see you. I knew you were in Northminster. I had made enquiries, and I meant only to go there and see if I could catch sight of you. I thought I might see you at church or some such, and that would be enough. And then I could go back. But then you walked in and told me that Xavier was dead, and ever since – well, I don't know!"

"You made enquiries?" Lord Rothborough said.

"Yes. I have done, over the years. Discreetly. I did not wish my husband to know. He knew nothing of my former life, and I did not want to disillusion him. He had such faith and trust in me."

"And yet you lied to him, as you did to me."

"A different sort of lie. One big one, instead of a lot of silly ones. I treated you better, I suppose, or perhaps you were better at getting the truth out of me. I tried to lie to you, and play the game, but you got it out of me. You read me right every time, Will, and you are reading me now."

"I don't think so," he said. "Your behaviour – I can't begin to comprehend it. You have puzzled me for a very long time. And what is this nonsense about wishing to see him from a distance?"

"Not nonsense," she said, with a shake of her head. "What if one of your girls had been whisked away, Will, and you never saw her again? Would you not be wondering, thinking that you might –"

"Whisked away!" exclaimed Rothborough, getting up and leaning across the table. "Ah, now we are getting to it. Whisked away? How dare you imply such a thing! You left this apparently precious object, that you have been having all these fancies about, playing at the feet of half a dozen of the most expensive whores in Paris, remember! You left him, without a word to tell me what had happened or why, in that appalling place, while you galloped away with that fat German prince who you told me, only three days before, was the most repulsive man alive!"

"I surrendered him because I wanted him to have a

decent life!" she said, jumping up. "I knew that you would do the best for him, that you loved him and with you he stood a chance of something better. I pretended I did not care. I always fancied myself as an actress – I think it was the best performance I ever gave in my life. I nearly convinced myself. And I knew you wouldn't stay with us forever, despite everything you said. You would go back and get married and that would be that. You made promises to me that were not promises, in truth."

"I meant every word!"

"But it would not have been possible. I think you knew that even as you told me you would never leave: that your leaving would one day be inevitable. So I thought I would get it all over with as soon as I could. I would move on, find another protector while I still had my looks and my charm. I had my future to think of. I knew you would do your duty by our son. So I gave him to you. And it was one of the hardest things I have ever done in my life." She turned to Felix. "There hasn't been a day since that I haven't longed to see you, to know what you were doing. And your birthday – that was the hardest day of the year. And not even Juan knew, and of course he was very disappointed that I didn't give him children, although he took care to conceal it. How could I tell him I had a son already? It would have broken his heart to know what I had once been. It's a stain that can't be washed out, no matter what you do. No matter how hard you try."

Lord Rothborough sat down rather heavily.

"Then why on earth did you not leave some hint of this?" he said. "Even those wretched women who leave their children in a foundling hospital try to leave a keepsake. You simply left him, like a piece of spoilt meat on the side of your plate! In a brothel, Blanche! What were you thinking?"

"I wanted him to be free of me. Not to have the burden of knowing he had a whore for a mother! What a fool I was to think that you would honour my silence!"

"What the devil was I supposed to do?" Rothborough said, getting up from his chair and striding over to where she stood. "Construct some senseless narrative about a smiling angel in Heaven? Is that what I was supposed to do? Good God, Blanche! After that, how could I? A man needs to know who he is and where he is from, even when the circumstances are unfortunate ones. I was not going to lie to him about it. What precedent would that have set? Mr and Mrs Carswell were in complete agreement with me. He was always to know. I have read of similar cases where the facts have been concealed and the results have been most unhappy for the individual concerned."

"You might have been a little less harsh," she said, "and still have been honest enough. You might have guessed at what I was about. I suppose that was too much to hope for. But to tell him I abandoned him –"

"I might have guessed?" Rothborough said. "When you had cut my heart from my breast and left me bleeding on the floor? You expected me to decipher your bizarre reasoning and speak kindly of you to him, after what you did to us both? Ma'am, I do not think there is a saint in the entire company of Heaven who could have managed that, and the Lord knows, and you certainly know, I am no saint!"

He shouted the words into her face, and she flinched and turned away. She was on the verge of tears, shaking a little, as if she were about to crumble completely. Lord Rothborough's cheek muscles twitched with fury and he raised his hand. Fearful for them both, Felix pushed himself between them, and forced Lord Rothborough to step aside. For a moment he resisted, but then, to Felix's relief, he found his reason again, strode across the room, and threw himself down on the window seat, his face buried in his hands.

Now Dona Blanca turned to Felix.

"I am so sorry," she managed to say. Her cheeks were wet with tears. "But what else could I do? We would not have been allowed to be... it could not have gone on. But we were so happy, for that little time, we were happy. And that was all we ever could have had. You know that as well as I do, Will, you knew it the first time you ever kissed me!" Her words came out in an anguished howl.

Felix saw Lord Rothborough straighten and look at her.

"Were you happy with your husband?" he said at last, getting up.

"Yes," she said. "After a fashion. But it was not the same." He nodded, and walked back across the room to her, taking his handkerchief from his pocket. He handed it to her. "And you?"

"I have my girls, and Felix," Rothborough said. "That has been all my joy." He glanced at Felix. Then after a moment he sighed and said, "You made a great sacrifice, Blanche. I did not think of it as such before today. My anger has clouded my judgement all these years. Please excuse me."

Felix saw her bite her lip as she struggled to stem her tears.

"Please do not be kind to me, Will," she said. "I can't bear that. I can bear your anger better."

Lord Rothborough reached out and caressed her cheek.

"Please," she said again, but Lord Rothborough had taken a step closer and caught her chin his hand, bent over and kissed her full on the lips. She did not appear to resist. Rather, she fell into the embrace with some eagerness.

Felix stared in horror, then quickly turned away. He could only think of escape, so he seized his hat and fled from the room.

Chapter Twenty-seven

Having settled matters with the house agent and the perpetually irritated Mrs Bolland, Giles dispatched Holt back to Holbroke with the rest of their luggage in a gig. He had just got to The White Hart when he met Carswell coming out at some speed.

"Is Lord Rothborough –" Giles began.

"He is there, yes, and so is she. I insisted he send for her."

"Dona Blanca?"

"Yes, and now they are..." Carswell threw up his hands, lost for words. But his flushed cheeks were testament enough. He was in a state of confused mortification.

Old lovers reunited, Giles thought. It was not unknown for long-buried passions to come boiling up in such circumstances – he would have imagined Lord Rothborough might have been a little more circumspect, but then again Dona Blanca was clearly no ordinary woman. He had seen that for himself.

"Why on earth did I force the issue?" Carswell exclaimed. "I might have known. I should have left well alone. She herself said that I should."

"This is not a subject for the street," said Giles. "Let us go up to Mr Bryce's for a moment." The fencing rooms were only a few steps away on the other side of the street. Carswell consented.

"I am glad to see you, sir!" said Mr Bryce, coming out at the sound of footsteps on the stairs. "Very glad. I was on the pointing of writing to you. I have had a visit from that Don Luiz fellow. Very strange it was. He came with some fellow, and all the time he was talking to me, the other man, his servant or secretary, I am not sure what he was, well, he was poking about in the dressing room, as if he were looking for something. I tried to stop him, but Don Luiz would keep me talking in here, and talking a lot of nonsense, to be frank, as if he didn't want me interfering. What on earth was all that about, sir, do you think?"

"Perhaps they were looking for something that Don Xavier may have left here," Carswell said.

"That did cross my mind, Mr Carswell, but I had already told the gentleman that there was nothing here. I told him at the funeral, that I had already brought all his kit back to The White Horse, when he was taken bad – his foils, and jacket, and so forth. You saw the stuff for yourself, I think."

Giles went to the dressing room door and looked into the room. His own kit was hanging where he had left it.

Bryce went on: "I was thorough when I took away Don Xavier's outfit that day. I looked under the benches as I always do, for things do get dropped and lost, but there was nothing. What he was after, I don't know!"

"How many times did Don Xavier come here?" said Giles.

"Twice," said Bryce. "He booked to come five times, and paid me up front for all of it. Poor gentleman," he added with sigh.

"He hid some documents in his room," Giles said. "He may have hidden something here. He seems to have been a man carrying secrets with him. Where did he stow his kit?"

"Over there, in the corner," said Bryce.

On the wall, high about the row of hooks, there was a large framed engraving showing a fencing bout of a hundred years ago. Giles went and studied it, noticing it had been knocked awry a little, revealing the darker colour of the paint below, which the sun had not bleached. He reached up, pulled one corner away from the wall, and slipped his hand behind.

Just as he had hoped, his fingertips discovered the edge of a folded piece of paper, which he extracted.

"I hope this is not an old bill," he said. The document was tightly folded and rolled around itself, as if wishing to keep its secrets for as long as possible. Giles unfurled it, revealing another sheet covered with dense writing, cross-written to save space. "Spanish again," he said, holding it out for the others to examine.

"Now, how did that get there?" said Bryce.

"I think this may be what Don Luiz was after," said Giles. "We should check the other pictures."

Their search yielded nothing else. Giles stood for some moments trying to see if he could extract anything of interest from the document, hoping a name might spring out, but the handwriting was a struggle. He went back into the fencing room where the light was better and went over to the window where Carswell stood. The window gave a perfect view of the entrance to The White Hart.

"Distract yourself with this," said Giles. "Your eyesight may be better than mine."

But Carswell did not take the letter. He was staring out of the window. Giles glanced out – an open carriage bearing a familiar coat of arms had drawn up outside The White Hart. A lady was seated inside, wearing a broad brimmed hat covered by a light veil. It was Lady Charlotte.

Carswell was already running from the room and down the stairs, clearly determined that she should not go into The White Hart. Giles followed with equal haste and got to the door to the street, only to see Carswell speaking to Lady Charlotte as she climbed down from the carriage.

He evidently persuaded her to come with him, and from the door, Giles watched them cross the road.

As they approached, he met her gaze, and she looked away from him. Even through her veil, he could see she was troubled. Her journey to Stanegate had clearly been provoked by some extraordinary circumstance.

She came inside, and at once folded back her veil, but she still avoided meeting his eyes.

"Lady Charlotte, is there something wrong? What has happened?"

He could see now that her eyes were red from crying.

"Oh, Major Vernon, where do... how do I..." she glanced away, and wiped a tear from her face, but it was a futile gesture. The sight of him seemed to reduce her to tears. She forced back the tears, straightened herself and went on, "I am sorry, I have terrible news. It is... Mrs Vernon, she is... she d... There was an accident, a horrible accident. They said I should have sent a message. But I could not bear that you should hear it from a stranger!"

"What sort of an accident?" said Carswell.

"She fell. On the back stairs in the North Pavilion. She must have tripped – it is steep and worn and she fell and broke her neck. Dr Conway came but there was nothing that could be done, it seems. She was already gone... oh, I am so sorry, so very sorry." Her hand flashed out and touched his arm.

"What?" Carswell was saying. "I cannot believe this... no..."

Giles found he was sitting on the stairs. His legs had lost the power to support him. He stared down at the ground, his hands pressed to his mouth, breathing hard, trying to steady himself, trying to hear what was being said, but nothing made sense.

"Would you mind," he began, "saying that again? I am sorry, but I do not quite understand you."

He looked up into Lady Charlotte's face. She was sobbing uncontrollably and then he did understand, and he felt cold hands clawing at his own heart.

Mr Bryce was speaking now behind him, in his gentle Scottish voice.

"Will you no come upstairs, ma'am? A glass of water?"

"Thank you," Lady Charlotte managed to say, and she slipped past him and went up the stairs, her skirts brushing against him. Carswell went after her, and he was alone, in that small hallway, sitting still at the foot of the stairs. His mind swam and then, from nowhere, conjured up the vision of her lying there, in her striped muslin dress, sprawled playfully, as if she had tripped in a silly, boisterous game, and was waiting for him to help her to her feet and kiss her on the lips.

How could she be gone? How, when she had found the will to live again? When he had seen her build herself again from nothing into something, how could she be gone? Lord Rothborough had said she had sparkled at dinner, and he had so looked forward to telling her that, and more.

How could a staircase have destroyed her? How was it possible?

But it was true. Lady Charlotte's face had told him everything. It was not possible to doubt such testimony, no matter how much he might have wished to.

Chapter Twenty-eight

The weather righted itself, even when everything else was turned on its head.

Felix woke the following morning at Ardenthwaite in a room golden with sunshine filtered into beguiling softness by ancient, threadbare curtains. He looked about him – the room was vast; he had not realised the extent of it when he had been shown there last night by the housekeeper. He had simply wanted to go to bed and had not thought of quarrelling with any domestic arrangements. He had been exhausted.

He realised he was lying in a great bed that must have been hundreds of years old, the grandest bedroom in the house, which the master and mistress would traditionally occupy. By accident, he had taken up that place at Ardenthwaite, the place of master and owner. Lord Rothborough had been wanting him to do this for so long, and he had been resisting. Yet now that resistance seemed utterly irrelevant, foolish perhaps. It was simply a bed in a house: he was alive and the way the dice of fortune fell was cruel beyond measure.

For she was suddenly there. Her ghost stole up on him the moment after he had blinked open his eyes. She filled that huge and beautiful room with her fierce tears, her ardent expression and her dry-throated, merciless admission of her love. He lay there, bracing himself against the pain of it, wondering how he would manage to get through the next few days, indeed how anything was ever to be managed.

An accident. A fall down the stairs. He repeated the bare facts to himself again and again, as he lay there. These things happened. It was part of the unspeakable cruelty of life that chance took as many lives as diseases. There was no rhyme and reason to it. Just wretched ill-luck.

The door opened and a boy of about sixteen came in with a jug of hot water and towels.

"Who are you?" Felix said.

"Jacob, sir. Mr Bodley sent me over from Holbroke to see to you. Said his Lordship wanted you properly looked after."

"When did you get here?"

"Last night, sir. I was supposed to come in the afternoon anyway, but we were all at sixes and sevens after the poor lady was found." He turned away and busied himself arranging towels on the washstand. "Will this be enough water, sir?"

"Yes," Felix said getting out of bed. "Tell me, did you see Mrs Connolly?"

"Mrs Connolly, sir?" the boy said. "Yes, sir."

"How did she seem?"

"I don't know, sir. Mrs Hope was looking after her, I think." That was only the slightest comfort. He wished Bodley had sent her to Ardenthwaite.

"And did you see her – Mrs Vernon, I mean?" Felix asked.

"How do mean, sir?"

"I mean, in the stairwell?"

"Oh no, sir. I saw them carry her out, though."

"And what were they all saying about it, the other servants?" The boy looked puzzled. Felix elaborated. "I mean, had there been accidents there before? Did anyone say that? That those stairs were particularly dangerous?"

"No, sir."

"And you never thought they were too steep or dangerous?"

"No, sir. I go up and down them more times a day than I care to say, so I suppose I would know."

"And who cleans them and when?" said Felix. "Are they just swept or scrubbed down with soap and water?"

"One of the girls brushes them down every day," said Jacob. "And they do wash 'em once a week, because I have to dry them, and Mrs Hope is very particular that they are dry in case of accidents."

"And when does that happen?"

"That would be tomorrow, sir."

"So they were not washed yesterday?"

"No, sir," said Jacob. "They were not."

"Where are my clothes?" said Felix, looking around him. "I must get to Holbroke."

"I'll get them, sir. I brushed your black coat. You won't be wanting the drab linen, sir."

Ten minutes later Mr Carswell chose to pay Felix a visit. Jacob, who was clearly enjoying his promotion to gentleman's servant, was unnecessarily helping Felix into the same black coat and doing it with much solemn fuss. Bodley had obviously given him careful instructions. Mr Carswell looked on in disapproving silence until Jacob had finished and Felix dismissed him.

"You will forget who you are," said Mr Carswell.

"He just gave me some valuable information," said Felix.

"About what?"

"Mrs Vernon's death, which strikes me as more and more curious."

"What are you suggesting?"

"That it was not an accident."

"Of course it was an accident," Mr Carswell said. "A dreadful one, but an accident."

"I need to see the evidence for myself. There is too much awry in that house at present to put labels on such serious matters without any consideration. There is something wrong about this."

He was making for the door, but Mr Carswell blocked his way.

"You are in a state of distress – you feel this strongly, of

263

course, but you must accept the hand of fate, and the will of God, Felix, and not ask such questions. It was an accident."

"I do not think Major Vernon will think so."

"Of course he will not! But you must not aid him in thinking so, or you will be doing a wicked thing! He has just lost his wife – he will be in a state of inconsolable distress, and your duty as his friend is to steer him through this terrible passage of his life. You are to show him the path of Christian resignation. That is your only duty, no matter how much it pains you! This is not a time for questions, but for submission to the love and will of our Lord! He has taken her to Him and that is the only answer, the only comfort that there can be in such times."

Felix shook his head throughout this speech.

"If we do not ask questions, we have nothing!" he exclaimed. "We are nothing. We might as well be vegetables. And I shall help Major Vernon, as I see fit, Papa. He *is* my friend – at least I hope he might regard me as such – and I know that he will feel as I do on this: something is not right here."

~

They had carried Mrs Vernon's body into the great State Bedroom on the ground floor.

"By custom, it is reserved for members of the family," Lord Rothborough said to Felix. "But hang custom. The girls said it must be done and they are right. This is too miserable a business to be bound by habit. Did you manage to sleep?"

"A little. And you, sir?"

"I never sleep much these days, even in the best of circumstances," said Lord Rothborough.

"Have you seen Major Vernon this morning?"

"Only briefly. He is –" Lord Rothborough broke off. "He sat with her last night, and he is still with her now, I think. I will leave you. I will be in my business room if you need me."

"Thank you."

Lord Rothborough turned back along the enfilade. Felix opened the door and found himself not in the State Bedroom but a little ante-chamber, where sitting in a corner, on a low chair with a piece of work in her lap, sat Sukey. She rose at the sight of him, her work falling to the floor.

They met in the centre of the room, and he took both her hands and kissed them. He wanted to pull her into his arms, but he felt if he did that he might never be able force himself to let go.

"Are you all right?" he said. She nodded, and he saw her red-rimmed eyes. "What was she doing there?" he said. "On the back stairs?"

"I don't know. I have been going over and over it, and I cannot think of a reason why." She squeezed his hands.

"And Major Vernon?" he asked.

"He's in there, with her. We sat there with her all night."

"Then you must go and rest. No, better still – go and pack. You are going to Ardenthwaite. I don't want you staying here."

She shook her head.

"I won't leave her yet," she said, letting go of his hands. "And I can't just go like that, can I? The Major –"

"I will arrange it all. I want you away from here, Sukey. I want –"

She shook her head and pressed her finger to his lips.

"This is not the time," she said. "Go in now. I will be here if I am needed."

He nodded and went to the door.

The great bed had been draped in white linen while Mrs Vernon's corpse lay covered completely by a finely embroidered white cloth. Vases of flowers had been brought into the room, as well as a pair of candelabras, the candles of which were now burnt down to smoking stubs. The morning light came in through cracks in the drawn-down blinds.

Major Vernon was sitting by the bed, his hands knotted together and pressed to his mouth. He got to his feet rather stiffly, and greeted Felix with a nod.

"I am glad to see you."

"I should have been here last night."

"No, it was better you went to your people," said Vernon. "And got some rest."

"You should rest yourself, sir."

"In time," he said.

"Did you speak to the surgeon last night?"

"Yes, but it was not very enlightening. He said that it was likely that death was instantaneous but since we do not know when she fell, I do not give that much credence. I think he was trying to comfort me. From what I understand she may have lain there some time before she actually –"

"It is likely that she was unconscious and did not suffer too much," Felix said. "That is usually the way with these cases."

"But there is too much about this that I do not understand. Perhaps my suspicions are foolish, but –"

"No, sir, it is troubling."

Major Vernon exhaled.

"Thank God," he murmured. "You have come to the same conclusion?"

"Given the circumstances, what has happened in this house recently, we ought to eliminate any other possibilities. We must ask all the questions, no matter how unpleasant." He took a deep breath. "Apparently the stairs were not considered dangerous and were quite dry."

"Yes," said Major Vernon, "I have heard that too – and that they are well lit. Bodley told me so. So will you examine her now, and see if there is anything that does not seem

266

consistent with an accident? Of course, you may tell me now that there is no way of clearly distinguishing between malicious intent and accident."

"It is not the most straightforward area," Felix said. "I will not lie to you, sir, but there may be some markers." Major Vernon nodded. "And then there is the matter of circumstance. Mrs Connolly could give no reason for Mrs Vernon being on that staircase."

"That was my first question. What was she doing there? And she was not intemperate, and I have never known her stumble or complain of light-headedness. Nor did she ever wear foolish shoes. Of course, she was delicate – you have said yourself that she was still somewhat undernourished, but that would not be enough to make her fall."

"She may have survived such a fall had she been stronger," Felix felt he must say. "Her general debility cannot have aided her, I am afraid to say."

"Will you make a start?" Major Vernon said, going to the window and pulling up the blind.

"Yes," Felix said. "I can only make a superficial examination at present, of course."

His hand trembled for a moment as he turned back the sheet and revealed her face. "I hope that will be enough, although it may not be."

"Then you will do everything that needs to be done. I want the answer to this, Carswell," said Major Vernon, drawing up the other blind. He returned to the bedside and looked down at her. He reached out to touch her cheeks, and then rapidly withdrew his hand, as he visibly mastered his emotion.

"There seems to be more bruising on her face than there was last night," he said.

"Bruising will develop over the twenty-four hours after death," said Felix. "She was discovered at about eleven in the morning, I think?" Vernon nodded. "Then we will see more later, I'm afraid. But even now it gives a clear indication of how she fell, and perhaps, if we look a little closer at the scalp —"

He leant over and tilted her head gently, looking for a fissure. Her hair was still pinned and fixed in the neat pair of fashionable bundled ringlets that had been a source of such pride for her, another sign of her recovery. In the asylum her hair had been cropped short for the purposes of hygiene, and growing back her long hair was a vast pleasure for her. It was not easy to discern anything at first, but he persisted, knowing that the tiniest marks on the skull could conceal extensive trauma beneath. Presently he found a thin, dark line of blood, running from behind her left ear up to the apex of her crown. He sighed at the sight of it, for it meant that the concussion had been a profound one.

"I think we have it, sir," he said. "You can just see it here," he said, passing Major Vernon his hand lens. "That dark line."

"And it means what precisely?"

"That there has been serious damage to the brain. The force of fall caused a severe subcranial haemorrhage which most likely caused her death. That is the only external sign of it. If one were to do a post-mortem examination then one might be able to say more." He winced slightly; he had no wish to say to Major Vernon that he should do any such thing. "But that might be quite unnecessary."

"It is the force of the fall I need to understand," Major Vernon said. "How she could fall fast and hard enough to kill her. That surely is the other side of this question."

"Yes," Felix concurred.

"I want to look at that staircase," said Major Vernon.

Five minutes later they were standing in the narrow hallway, looking up the steep rise of twenty-five stone steps. High above them a cupola gave excellent light.

"And she was lying how, exactly?" said Major Vernon.

"I can show you, sir, better than I can say it," said John, the footman who had first discovered her. "If you don't think it a liberty?"

"Not at all."

John sat down on the bottom step.

"It was like this – well, sort of – her head was down there, where my foot is, and then she was all twisted up and around, and her feet and her skirts all over and up there. I didn't guess she was dead, I thought she might have passed out, so I put down my tray and went to try and help her. But she was past helping; I realised that soon enough. I am very sorry, sir. God rest her soul, sir – we can trust in that at least."

John got up from the step and for some moments they stood in silence, looking at the empty space that her body had occupied. Felix found himself in a state of agitation. He had no wish to make a picture of it in his mind but he knew he must, for all their sakes, not least that justice should be done for her. So he looked at the steps with care and tried to work out how the fissure might have been caused.

Major Vernon broke the silence.

"And you heard no cry, nor anything like that?"

"No, sir. It was quite a shock, all in all, to find her there, in such a state. I think I cried out, though. And the others came straight through, for we were all going back to our work just after our dinner."

"At about one o'clock, I understand?" said Major Vernon. "You sit down at noon, yes?"

"Yes, always."

"And where were you going? Upstairs?"

"No, sir, just through that door there. I was going to the little drawing room. There was a bell – her Ladyship, I think. I had to go because I'm the youngest, and I didn't have the chance to finish my pudding. She usually rings then because she wants her letters taken to catch the post at one."

"And she was warm to the touch?" Felix asked.

"Yes, sir, I'm afraid so. I am very sorry, sir, that I found her so, very sorry –" He broke off and glanced away in distress. "Poor lady."

"Thank you, John," said Major Vernon, his own voice strained with emotion. He reached out briefly and touched the man's shoulder. "I shall be in your debt, always. You could have done nothing better than you did."

John left them, and after some struggle, the Major said, "So, Sukey says she left her resting in her room after a walk with Lady Maria, at about eleven, and then she is discovered at a little before one – that helps a little, does it not? Some time after noon seems most likely, for if all the staff are eating their mutton, there would be no cause for anyone to be on the staircase and see or hear anything because no one in the family or their guests would ring for them, since they knew they were at dinner and not to be disturbed."

"Except Lady Rothborough," Felix said.

"Who no doubt rings at five to one just to get them all up from the table and about their business again," Major Vernon said. "As my mother always did."

"So, a quiet time on this staircase," said Felix, looking up the stairs to the landing above. "But why was she here at all? Did something distress her and she wanted Mrs Connolly? Perhaps she came down here trying to find her, rather than ring for her, knowing she would be at dinner."

"You think she may have had some sort of attack, after Sukey left her?" Major Vernon said.

"It has happened before – though she was much better at dealing with it. She could have become agitated and in her panic lost her footing. If she was dizzy from distress, that might have been enough to send her toppling over."

Major Vernon was nodding.

"That is plausible," he said, sighing, "given she may have been under more stress than we know, when I left her here. Those attacks of hers were worrying, although I thought we had got the better of them. But she was alone and in an unfamiliar place. She may well have been overwhelmed by those dark feelings again." He sat down wearily at the foot of the stairs, and pressed his hands to his face for a moment. "She went looking for Sukey – yes, that makes a great deal of sense."

"It is only a theory," said Felix.

"But it is the most likely one we have so far, given what we know. I've been trying to make connections and imagine enemies where there may be none. There may be no connection at all between this and Eliza Jones and John Edgar. I want there to be a connection because I want this to mean something. But perhaps it does not. It is simply a wretched turn of the wheel of fortune. And perhaps we will never know." He hauled himself to his feet. "I think I need to be alone for a while, if you will excuse me," he said, turning and going up the stairs.

Felix watched him go without another word.

Chapter Twenty-nine

A brutal headache had come over him and Giles was suddenly exhausted beyond endurance. He took off his boots and coat, stretched out on the bed and lay there, bone-tired but unable to rest. All the information grated and pinched at his already inflamed mind. He felt sick with pain and confusion, unable to keep his eyes open.

He found himself in the topsy-turvy world of half-waking dreams. He was on the beach at Swalecliffe again, as he had been with Carswell the other night, with the band playing in the distance. Once again he was writing the names of the dead in the sand: first Eliza Jones, then John Edgar, and then Laura Vernon. He wrote them and was surprised at how little he felt. He had made a collection of marks in the sand, meaning nothing. But then he had turned towards the sea again to see Laura.

She was far out in the water and he saw that she was in difficulty. She was calling out to him. Yet her cries were quite silent, and he could only see them, not hear them. Her distress was very evident, heartbreakingly so – he felt it like a pain in his chest, and yet he stood there still, leaning on the stick with which he had just written her name in the sand, as if there was nothing to be done.

He woke shortly after that, the sight of her pained face vivid in his mind, and immediately felt violently sick. He also found he was sweating and shaking uncontrollably.

Holt came in later and found him retching into the chamber pot.

"I shall get Mr Carswell," he said.

"No, no, I am not ill. It is only –"

"You have taken ill with the shock, sir," Holt said, steering him to a chair. "As much as from a bullet. I'm fetching Mr Carswell."

Realising this was the only way he would get to be left alone, Giles consented to let him go. Alone again, he rinsed out his mouth and attempted to steady himself with a small glass of brandy. He did not feel physically strong, it was true, and his mind was racing about on a thousand courses. He felt he was trapped in a labyrinth, searching in all directions for both the entrance and the exit at the same time. He was determined to master the situation and himself, if only to push away the creeping dread that he had not done enough, that he had left her to die alone.

If I had not have gone away, it would not have happened. This is on my hands.

If he had worked harder and faster he could have broken the puzzle and she would not have died. Because even if there was no immediate connection between her death and those others, he felt sure it might still be discovered, no matter how irrational it was to believe it. For all the questions remained. Carswell's theory was only a theory. Why was she on the staircase and how had she fallen so violently? How could an assault of some kind not be ruled out?

Laura's embroidered shawl was lying on the chair, and he picked it up and twisted it in his hands, pacing the room and attempting to make some sense of his disordered mind, reasoning furiously with himself that he was not inventing causes and effects. Holt was right, he had taken a bullet and he was in shock, but he was clear enough about that. He threw the shawl onto the bed, went to the writing table and searched for a pencil.

"We must ask all the questions, however unpleasant," Carswell had said.

He searched through the papers which he had put in his document case, looking for the list he had made of all the members of the household shortly after they had begun to investigate the death of Eliza Jones. It was an extensive list, not to say bold, for it began with Lord Rothborough himself, and ended with the pantry boy. It spared not a soul, not even the Marchioness. Pencil in hand, he stood in the window and read through each and every name, and then returned to the first page: Lord Rothborough, Lady Rothborough, Lady Charlotte, Lady Augusta, Lady Maria, Lady Warde. He underlined Lady Warde three times. She struck him as a wrong note played in an otherwise melodious piece. There was something not right about her, but what it was he could not yet determine.

The door opened and Carswell came in.

"Holt tells me —"

"I want to talk to Lady Warde," said Giles.

"Now?"

"Remember when we were in Edgar's shop and we talked about insider information? How Eliza may have picked up useful titbits from other servants? Well, perhaps her mistress was —"

"Holt said you were vomiting," Carswell interrupted. He attempted to press his hand to Giles' forehead but Giles manoeuvred out of his reach. "Sir, I beg you."

"It was nothing."

Carswell peered at him.

"You do not look yourself. You look decidedly flushed."

"How could I be myself, in such circumstances?" he said, attempting to move away from Carswell.

"Of course, but you will let me examine you, sir." Carswell grabbed at his wrist. "And you are squinting at the light."

"I have a headache. It is not surprising," said Giles. "But really —"

"Sit down, sir," said Carswell, his hand still on his wrist.

"We have too much to do."

"You will sit down," said Carswell, with some firmness. "You must yield to my opinion in this, sir, if you have an ounce of sense. And you pride yourself on your good sense, I think."

Giles sat down, realising that Carswell was not going to be easily dismissed. Carswell reached for his watch and took his pulse.

"I cannot be ill," said Giles.

"Hush," said Carswell. "You have all the symptoms of a fever – your pulse is elevated, you are flushed and perspiring, and you are shaking."

"Perhaps, but –" Giles began.

"Aching limbs?" Carswell put in. Giles nodded, in spite of himself. "And headache and vomiting. You are going to bed, Major Vernon, and that is an end to it. The sooner you rest the sooner you will be well again."

"There is some truth in that," Giles was forced to concede, now feeling that he really was in the grip of an affliction. "But one thing first, Carswell, before I take your good advice, which I promise I will –" But he got no further, for he found his gorge rising again and was forced to stagger hastily across the room to the washstand.

"Bed, sir, and that's an end to it!" said Carswell, behind him.

~

"Is he going to be all right?" Sukey asked.

"I think so," Felix said. "He is very strong – it is distressing rather than dangerous for him."

"I don't suppose he is a good invalid at the best of times," she said, managing a brief smile.

"No. But Holt can manage him very well. And with luck

275

he will fight it off soon enough."

They were in the dressing room adjoining the bedroom. It was still scattered with Mrs Vernon's things: her books, sketching kit and music lay piled up on a table. Felix picked up the sketchbook and opened it. She had not been as accomplished at drawing as she was at music but the fact she had taken it up had been a triumph at the time. It had been a useful tool in keeping her calm. He looked at a clumsy pencil sketch of a rustic cottage and then at an imperfect portrait of Sukey, but that was all he could manage. He put it down quickly and turned away, so that Sukey should not see him stifling his tears.

"I had better get all these things packed away," said Sukey. "Out of sight –"

"Will not be out of mind," said Felix.

"Not for a while, no," she said, with a sigh. "But we have to keep busy. Which reminds me. I was going to give this to Major Vernon. It is probably nothing, but then again..."

From her pocket she took a ragged scrap of black stuff, stiff and slightly greasy, and handed it to him.

"What is this?"

"I don't know. I found it when we first brought her into the state room – it was caught in her petticoats. I thought it might be important so I kept it. I meant to mention it earlier, but I didn't know quite how to, not with all those other people there; it was not the moment. It's probably nothing at all, but I can't quite work out why it would be there, caught up in her skirts."

Felix looked at it carefully.

"Is it silk?"

"Yes, good quality too, although it's quite worn. I wonder where it came from."

"Is it something that they might use in the household?" said Felix. "I know nothing about these things. I remember my mother cutting up old clothes for cleaning rags, that is all."

276

"Not silk," said Sukey. "Good silk like this, you'd try to turn it and use it for a lining or shoe bags or something like that, but this looks strange to me, as if it has not been done carefully. Do you know what I mean? Look how badly cut it is, as though it has been torn with a knife, in a hurry."

"As if to destroy it?" Felix said and went to the window with it to examine it in a better light. "There is a stain on it, I think. And it was tangled up in her skirts?"

"Yes."

"These loose threads..." he said, pulling at them. "I wonder if – do you have a minute or two?"

"Of course, if you do not want me to sit with Major Vernon."

"Holt is with him. It will not be for long. But I think we should go back to that wretched staircase, while there is still some light."

"Before someone sweeps up too carefully?" Sukey said.

They went along the broad bedroom passageway and were about to pass through the padded door into the gloomy, Spartan otherworld of the domestics, when Sukey suddenly crouched down.

"Hold the door just like that," she said. "And will you see..." He crouched down beside her and saw she was pointing to another scrap of black silk, this time with half a buttonhole worked in it, lying on the corner of the threshold where the door would have hidden it from sight.

"Same stuff?" he said, as she picked it up.

"Perhaps," she said.

"A look with the microscope will tell us for certain," he said.

"So what do you think it means?" Sukey said, going through onto the landing. "What would Major Vernon say?"

"He would say it meant that someone passed through here with a bag of silk scraps and dropped some of them near to where Mrs Vernon fell. That the scrap got caught in her skirts before she fell. That is as much as we can say."

"But it might mean something," said Sukey. "Please God, it might!" She was looking carefully at every inch of floor, stooping down as she did so.

"I know, but – well, you know as well as I do that all the questions we ask in life do not have simple answers. That sometimes we cannot explain things."

"You are the last person I imagined would say that," she said.

"I must have listened to my father for once," he said with a sigh, going to the banister and looking down the well again, at the dizzying steepness of the steps. "He gave me a fine lecture this morning about the necessity of Christian resignation. That I must simply accept this and tell Major Vernon the same thing. Perhaps he is right. Perhaps there is and will never be an adequate explanation. She fell, and we shall never know why because we were not there to see what happened. We can only truly know what we experience with our own faculties. What I'm doing making you get on your hands and knees and look for bits of black silk I don't know! It won't make this hurt any the less, will it, to know exactly what happened?"

"You didn't make me," she said, "and you are tired and in need of your lunch. That is why you are losing heart."

"And you are not, are you?"

"That person with the bag of silk scraps may have seen or heard something. They will not be hard to find, I am sure. There may be something that will help us – and that will help Major Vernon. And I think I have found another one! Yes!"

"You have the eyes of a hawk," he said, going and crouching beside her. This time it was a tiny triangle of silk. "Major Vernon will be impressed."

"Won't he be?" she said, getting to her feet again. "Where does that door go?"

"Up to a lumber room, I think."

"Better see if there are any more up here," she said, opening the door. It revealed another tight little staircase, which she at once climbed up.

"Why would you put a bag of silk scraps in a lumber room?" Felix said, following her.

"You might if you had a box of your own up here. One of the chamber maids – they are no more than girls and I think they are not allowed to keep a box in their room. Perhaps this is where the servants' boxes are stored. She might have been collecting them to send home to her mother for the mending bag."

"And if she had seen something she would probably be afraid to speak," said Felix.

"Certainly, for she may have been in the wrong place at the wrong time. Mrs Hope is very stern with them and a job here is not to be thrown away lightly."

"But such tiny scraps?"

"Those are the ones that were dropped. There may have been bigger pieces well worth squirrelling away. Of course, I am only making stories here, but don't you think there might be something in it?"

"Yes," he said, peering into the cavernous, gloomy space, full of trunks and hampers. It was lit only by a couple of small skylights.

"I have a candle," Sukey said, reaching into her apron pocket.

"And I have a lucifer," he said. "We are well-matched," he could not resist saying as he struck the match and lit the candle she held out to him.

She frowned at that, and turned away with the candle, plunging him into the shadows. He wished he had not spoken, but the sight of her face illuminated in that brief, bright burst of lucifer light had made him weak with desire.

He watched her walk away, and did not follow. There was only light for one of them to search by and he let her get on with the task, hoping the work would make her forget or at least forgive his clumsiness. Well-matched – yes, she must frown at that. There was not one of their friends or relatives who would see it as anything but an abomination if they were to marry. But it did not stop him wanting it, and he had never wanted it more as he watched her explore the shadows of that lumber room.

"Oh Lord in Heaven," he heard her say. "Oh." She turned back to him. "I think –"

He rushed the few steps to her side. She was standing by a large wicker hamper on top of which was sitting a badly tied and quite substantial bundle made of the same black silk, the edges roughly cut and fraying as on that first piece.

"Hold this," she said, thrusting the candle at him.

He held it up while she untied the bundle. It fell open, revealing a further mass of black silk scraps.

"It's a whole gown," she said. "I swear that's what it is. Look, this is a sleeve, and this is a bit of the bodice. All ripped up. Why would you do that?"

"Because it was ruined, and you wanted to destroy it?" said Felix, taking a piece up and looking at it close to the candle flame. The light revealed a large, suspicious stain. "If it had blood on it, for example?"

Chapter Thirty

Sukey Connolly was sitting on the dressing room floor surrounded by scraps of black satin. She jumped to her feet at the sight of Giles in his dressing gown.

"Dear Lord, what are you doing out of bed, sir?"

"I was looking for Holt. I am rather thirsty. What are you doing?"

"I probably shouldn't tell you," she said. "At least not just now. You should go back to your bed at once. Mr Carswell will be cross."

"You will have to tell me now," he said. "And I am feeling a great deal better – well, a little frail still, but not so frail that you cannot tell me your secret. What is all this?" He reached out and took the rag of black silk she held in her hand.

"It is something we found, Mr Carswell and I. You see, first there was this." She went to the table and took up another scrap, this time with a piece of white paper pinned to it. Then she at once put it down. "Your fever? You look so very red, sir."

"I am still feeling rather warm," he said. "But my headache is much improved, and I do not feel so sick. I can stand a few sweats and shivers. So tell me."

"Only if you sit down," she said, indicating the armchair. He obeyed and was glad of it, for he felt more fragile than he had admitted.

She handed him the labelled scrap.

"I found this in Mrs Vernon's petticoat hem, when we first put her in the state bed. I didn't know what it was, and it didn't seem the right moment to mention it. So I showed it to Mr Carswell and we went looking on the staircase to see if there was any more of it. Just to find out how it got there, really, just in case it meant something."

"And?"

"We found all that, up in a lumber room, just above the staircase. The same stuff, all bundled up. And with stains all over it that Mr Carswell thinks might be blood."

"And you are trying to put the pieces together here?"

"Yes, I think it is all from the same dress that has been chopped up."

"And chopped up in a hurry," Giles said. "Do you know whose dress this might be?"

"Do you?" she said.

"It's a widowish sort of gown," he said. "And expensive, but well worn, by someone who has position but not the means that go with it. There is one woman in this house that fits that description."

"Lady Warde," said Sukey. "But why would we find her dress ripped up in the lumber room, with possible blood stains on it?"

"The mistress of a jewel thief may perhaps have a few secrets of her own," said Giles, feeling a little queasy again. "I think I had better go back to bed." He pulled himself up from the armchair, and staggered a little as he did so.

"Here, let me help you," Sukey said. She took his arm and guided him back into the bedroom and into bed, and then insisted on wiping down his face and neck with a cool, damp cloth, an action which brought blessed relief to his burning skin.

"It pains me that you should be put to work like this –" he managed to say. "And I do not know how I can ever repay you, for all that you have done for us. I should demand you go and rest. You have had as great a shock as any of us."

"I am like you," she said, laying a folded cloth on his forehead. "I like to be kept busy. That is the best thing for me at the moment."

She reached to adjust the cloth and he caught her hand in his.

"I cannot thank you enough," he said. "I must say it. You showed her such love, such kindness – you were the greatest of friends to her, and did more than anyone, without ever being asked."

"I liked the work," she said, laying her other hand over his. "There is a great deal of pleasure in being useful. I think you would say that yourself."

"Yes," he said. "I would."

She smiled and laid his hand down on the sheet, and went away from the bed.

"I shall go and get you some tea," she said. "So hush now, and rest."

~

Felix had just finished giving Lord Rothborough an account of the state of Major Vernon's health, when the door to his office opened and Lady Rothborough entered. Lady Charlotte was in her wake, looking somewhat agitated. Felix guessed that she had attempted to prevent this invasion, knowing that he was there.

The Marchioness was tiny but she did not lack presence as she stood there in her freshly donned mourning, a sumptuous black lace cap pinned on her head, in the manner of a Spanish mantilla. She was strong-featured, not at all beautiful in conventional terms, but she had a face that one could not forget once seen.

She looked Felix over with painful thoroughness, her large eyes making him colour and look away. Then, to his relief, she turned this fierce gaze upon her husband and said, "Introductions have, in this case, never been necessary nor desirable, but extraordinary circumstances have come over us all. I must therefore do my duty and acknowledge this young person." She made a curt gesture of her hand towards Felix. "The late Mrs Vernon spoke warmly of him and all he did for her, with an honesty of spirit by which no Christian could fail to be moved – although it pained me greatly, as you may imagine!"

"Perhaps you would like to sit down, ma'am," Lord Rothborough began, bringing forward a chair. She waved it away.

"And now," Lady Rothborough went on, "she has been taken from us, in these dreadful, dreadful circumstances and I find myself here, forced by the inscrutable hand of Providence to examine my own conscience. Therefore I give him leave to be here as long as is necessary, until these matters are settled."

She turned back to Felix, clearly expecting a show of deference. He managed a graceless, mortified bow, but only just. Her tone made him feel stiff-backed and angry.

"He will not, however," Lady Rothborough went on, with a distinct harshness now entering her voice – no doubt she considered his bow quite inadequate – "dine at our table."

"Mama!" exclaimed Charlotte. "That is too –"

"Be quiet!" said Lady Rothborough.

"No, I shall not," said Lady Charlotte. "You shall not speak to Mr Carswell like that. It is too shocking. Of course he must dine with us!"

"Rothborough, do you hear that?" said Lady Rothborough. "How she undermines me? This is all your tutoring."

"Please, ma'am, please!" said Lord Rothborough, very quietly. "I beg you to think before you speak. And you, Charlotte. Your mother has made a great concession, for which we are all grateful. Let it be at that, yes?" He stretched out and took her hand.

Charlotte hesitated for a long moment, and looked as if

she were swallowing down a torrent of words. Then she nodded.

"Forgive me," she said, quickly and in clipped tones as if she were spitting out a bitter seed.

"Of course," Lady Rothborough said, and swept from the room.

Lady Charlotte did not follow but closed the door behind her, and stood for a moment, her arms wrapped about her, as if mastering herself.

"How is Major Vernon?" she said to Felix. "Is he in any danger?"

Felix shook his head.

"But I ought to go and see to him," he said.

"Might I see him also?" she said. "I could make myself useful."

"And keep out of your mother's way?" said Lord Rothborough. "Perhaps. Perhaps not. You should go and make peace properly."

"I cannot," said Charlotte. "That was outrageous! Papa, I cannot."

"If you show her your gratitude and your approval," Lord Rothborough said, gently coming over and putting his arms about her, "yet more concessions may be made. Grace and diplomacy are always the best weapons."

"Maybe," she said, after a moment. She kissed her father on the cheek and then turned to Felix. "But if there is anything I can do for Major Vernon, you must tell me. And let me know how he does."

"Of course," said Felix.

She left them, and Lord Rothborough gave a great sigh and rubbed his face.

"Charlotte is an excellent nurse," he said. "But I do not think her tendre should be encouraged, given the circumstances."

"Her tendre?" Felix said.

"There is always a danger with confronting a girl like Charlotte with an impressive individual like Major Vernon, and now he is in such a vulnerable condition." He sighed again. "She is like a great body of water, waiting to break through a tide wall. She needs a husband, a lover, a life's work, and we have utterly failed to find anyone suitable! And she sees a man whom she must admire, and who is now wrecked! How can she keep her pity in check? We must keep her away from him. Gusta's poor broken heart has been bad enough to bear, but I think she will mend soon enough. But if Charlotte loves – well, she is like you and me, Felix – deep and dangerous in her passions."

Felix could not help recalling that mortifying scene he had witnessed the day before between Lord Rothborough and Dona Blanca. "Do not be kind to me," she had said, and he had kissed her full on the lips and she had yielded. What had passed between them after he had gone? She had not been there when he had returned with the awful news about Mrs Vernon. Had they parted for ever, or was something again going on between them that required Lord Rothborough to mollify his wife?

Chapter Thirty-one

With Lord Rothborough's little homily on unsuitable objects of affection still ringing in his ears, Felix found his own faithfully tending to Major Vernon, who was tossing and turning in a fitful manner that was not encouraging.

"He was up and asking questions," Sukey said.

"Of course he was," said Felix, pulling off his coat.

"He got the whole business about the dress out of me. But then he had the sense to go back to bed. He fell asleep for a while, but he's getting in a poor way now. I have sent Holt for more ice," she added.

"Good," he said. "Any more vomiting?"

"No," she said. "But I don't like this."

"Don't worry. He's very strong," said Felix. "This will pass."

"God willing," she murmured.

"I have seen it before, in weaker constitutions, and they have survived. If we keep him washed down and cool, it will pass. He will not give up. He has too many questions to answer, for one thing."

"He thinks it is Lady Warde's dress," she said. "He said that a woman who had a thief for a maid may have secrets of her own."

"He did wonder if Eliza Jones was working with someone. Perhaps it was with her: mistress and maid, travelling about, taking their pick of snuff boxes and necklaces and then selling them on to Edgar. Maybe that is it."

At this moment, Holt came in with John the footman and a quantity of ice. They discussed nothing further, while they got on with the business of reducing Major's Vernon's fever to a less alarming state. Another hour or so passed, with some critical moments, but by the time the ormolu clock on the mantel struck five, Felix felt that the worst had passed. The Major fell into a comfortable sleep and they were able to catch their breath. James Bodley and Mr Grainger appeared with a lavish tray of refreshments and messages of support from Lord Rothborough.

Pale with exhaustion, Sukey was sitting on the window seat, only upon Felix's insistence that she should. He handed her a cup of bouillon and sat down beside her, determined she should eat and drink.

"Then you are going to your bed," he said. "You had no sleep last night. I did."

"If you say so."

"I do. And you will always do as I say now, if you know what is good for you," he added.

"You are determined to be my master, aren't you?"

"No, not your master. Your protector. Your friend, your —" he broke off, his confidence deserting him. "Perhaps?"

"No castles in Spain," she said.

"You said that before and I don't care for it."

"It is only good sense."

"I am sick of good sense," said Felix. "Heartily sick. There is so little certainty in life, and there are sinking sands everywhere. I can't bear to think that one moment my back might be turned and you could be gone. And I would not have —"

"I will be gone soon enough," she said after a moment. "And that will be that."

"Do not say that," he said. "Do not."

"I will have to look for another situation."

"That I will not have," he said.

"You want me to starve, then," she said. "I have to make my own way."

He shook his head.

288

"Not if –" he began. He took a breath. "Not if you were to marry me." She sighed and shook her head. "It isn't that you wouldn't like to," he went on. "I know that much. And any objections that other people care to put up – well, they can be disregarded."

"You want to make enemies of all your friends and families," she said. "And mine."

"No, because they will soon understand the rightness of this, and all will come around. I am sure of it. My mother, for example –"

"Would be broken-hearted," Sukey cut in. "I am not having that on my conscience." She put down her cup of bouillon and got up from the window seat. "This is a foolish conversation, at the best of times, and this is not the best of times. If you have any feelings for me, you will not pursue this. Please!"

"So we are always to be cast into misery just because of the accidents of our birth?" he said. "And sacrifice our happiness so that no one else can be alarmed or upset?"

"And how do you know we would be happy? I can't imagine a situation better laid to set us at odds than this! I know about this, trust me! I know. Unlike you, I have been married – try to remember that before you speak!"

They had raised their voices in this last exchange and Major Vernon stirred and woke in the great bed.

Sukey threw him a reproachful glance, as if it was all his doing.

"What time is it?" Major Vernon said, hauling himself up onto his elbows, looking about him.

"After six," said Felix.

"How are you feeling now, sir?" asked Sukey, helping him to sit up. "You look a great deal better, I must say."

"Weak, but that headache is gone, thank God," said the Major.

"You should take some beef tea," she said, and went and

busied herself fetching it.

Felix checked his temperature and pulse.

"The fever has passed for now," he said. "I cannot guarantee it will not return, though, and your best defence against that is absolute rest for the next day or so."

Major Vernon nodded wearily and took a cup of soup in an unsteady hand.

"Lady Warde will have to wait," he said, after taking a drink. "But perhaps that is to our advantage. I have a job for you, Mrs Connolly, and perhaps you too, Mr Carswell, since I don't suppose you will be dining with the family tonight."

"No, Lady Rothborough was clear on that point," said Felix.

"Excellent," said Major Vernon. "I want you both to search her room while they are all at dinner. I want you find out all her secrets – for she is keeping some, I am sure of it, and she may be the key to this whole business. A blood-stained dress ripped up and hidden is too interesting a circumstance by far, don't you think?"

Chapter Thirty-two

"Major Vernon, should you be out of bed?" asked Lady Rothborough.

He had timed his entrance perfectly. Just the ladies were there after dinner. His appearance in dressing gown and slippers was enough to make the Marchioness drop her sewing and rise from her seat. He had caught a glimpse of himself in a pier glass in the adjoining room and he looked sufficiently crazed for this escapade. The young ladies looked equally startled. Yet Lady Warde remained in her corner, her head bent over her work, apparently unperturbed by his invasion.

"That tune, Lady Maria," Giles said. "I have to know what it was."

"I ought not to have played," Lady Maria said, closing the piano. "I have disturbed you."

"I am glad you did. Laura would not like you to have stopped – and in music we have a way to deal with our grief."

"You look very unsteady, sir," said Lady Rothborough. "You ought to sit down."

"I think I ought, ma'am, yes, thank you," said Giles, and allowed Lady Rothborough to guide him to the sofa. "Forgive me for troubling you. I am not entirely myself."

"How can you be, in the circumstances?" she said. "This terrible business – such a loss for you, sir," and she took his hand and patted it. "You have been in all our prayers."

"Thank you, ma'am."

He glanced across again at Lady Warde, and saw how she still did not look at him, from her quiet corner.

Then suddenly she rose and approached the door.

"Would you excuse me, dear Catherine?" she said to Lady

Rothborough. "I have some letters to write."

She was taking flight already. He felt all his instincts were validated in that moment.

"Of course," said Lady Rothborough. "If you are writing to Anne Brackenbury, will you give her my best love, as ever?"

"I can tell her that in person. I shall be there soon enough."

"Oh yes, you are off to Marchsteads, I had forgotten. Won't you stay a little longer, though, my dear Frances? It cannot be wise for you to travel so soon after your poor Jones' burial. Anne would agree with me. Mourning cannot be rushed, and she was a good servant to you."

"I have trespassed too long on your kindness, as ever," said Lady Warde, "and Anne is expecting me. She has her grandsons to amuse, and I will be needed."

"Those boys are horrid savages," said Lady Rothborough. "You would be better here with us. I shall write to Anne and tell her myself that I must keep you here, for your own good, grandsons notwithstanding. Besides, who will look after you at Marchsteads? You cannot go without a maid."

"When is Miss Jones is to be buried?" Giles asked.

"Tomorrow morning," said Lady Rothborough. "My husband has arranged it all. She will be buried in the churchyard of St Saviours in the village, as all our estate people are."

"You are too kind, Catherine," murmured Lady Warde.

"You have been a great friend to us," said Lady Rothborough. "It is the least that we could do. And you will stay. I shall write to Anne at once," she added.

"I cannot really –" began Lady Warde.

"You should," Giles put in. "Lady Rothborough is right. In affliction, we should never spurn our friends, though we might be tempted to."

"One can hardly compare our situations, sir," she said.

"She was a good servant to you," Giles said. "And good

servants deserve all our respect. My family was in mourning for a year when my mother's maid, Nancy, died. She was a great friend to her and a second mother to me and my brother and sisters. She was not of our blood, but she was certainly part of our family. As I think Miss Jones must have been with you."

"I really must go to Marchsteads," said Lady Warde. "I cannot disappoint Anne."

"She will understand," said Lady Rothborough. "Major Vernon is quite right. Jones had been with you so long. I cannot remember a time when she was not there. It is so sad... such a wretched turn of events." She took Lady Warde's hand. "Please do not go, my dear Frances."

At this moment Lord Rothborough came into the drawing room, presumably having finished his solitary port and cigar.

"Mes belles dames!" he said in greeting. "Oh, and Major Vernon! This is unexpected, and welcome. You look –"

"Please excuse my appearance," said Giles.

Lord Rothborough gave a dismissive wave. "I am glad to see you out of bed. That is enough."

"Rothborough, will you speak to Frances?" said Lady Rothborough. "She is determined on going after Jones' burial tomorrow. She says she must be at Marchsteads."

"That would be a shame," said Lord Rothborough. "Won't you reconsider, my lady?"

Lady Warde shook her head, and said, "Excuse me. I would like to retire now, if I might?"

Rothborough bowed his acquiescence and she went towards the door.

Giles hauled himself up from the sofa and as he did so, his mind cleared, and he knew the moment had come to speak. A white flame of pure anger leapt up inside him. He knew the truth.

"Of course you would like to, ma'am," he said. "You

would like to vanish and leave no tracks behind you. But it is too late for that. You must stay and face what has happened."

She spun round and looked at him.

"What do you mean?"

"I am speaking of grief and how one deals with it. How one must find the courage to face great loss, what one does, how one conducts oneself in such circumstances. The challenge of it."

"Your loss has been far greater than mine," she said. "And I shall deal with it in my own way, thank you, sir."

"That I would dispute," he said. Her hand was on that locket again. He wished he could rip it from her and see what it contained. "She was like a daughter to you, I think." He saw how her fingers tightened round the locket. He felt light-headed with excitement at being right, and at the same time the darkest despair.

"No," she said, rather quietly.

"Of course you will deny it," he said. "You have to, because if you do not, the whole house of cards will come tumbling down."

"I have no idea what you are talking about," she said, turning again towards the door. "And, circumstances aside, I do not care for your manner, sir."

"Please do not go," said Giles. "There are some questions that have been bothering me, and you could put my mind at rest if you would only answer them. It would be a kindness."

"Catherine," she said to Lady Rothborough. "I do think the poor gentleman is raving – he must still be delirious. Should we not send for that surgeon fellow?"

"Mr Carswell – an excellent plan," said Giles. "If Lady Rothborough does not object?"

"I cannot," she said. "You look very unwell, sir."

"You ought not to have got out of bed," remarked Rothborough, as he rang for a servant.

"You should sit down again, at least, Major Vernon," said

Lady Charlotte, coming to his side. "Please?" she added.

"Of course," said Giles, who was glad enough to sit and feel Lady Charlotte's cool hand on his forehead for a moment. He was fiery-hot, it was true, with sweat pouring down his back. He felt sure his night shirt was drenched through under his dressing gown. But, weak and assaulted though his body felt, he had an inner strength, born of necessity. If he did not accomplish this now, then he knew it would be too late.

"Oh dear Lord," Lady Charlotte murmured.

"He is out of his wits with fever," said Lady Warde.

"No, no," he said, shaking his head. "My wits have never been sharper. Unfortunately for you, ma'am."

"Is this an interview of some sort?" Lord Rothborough said.

"Yes," said Giles. "And I insist that the lady sit down and answer my questions. I would like a record taken of this conversation. Perhaps your secretary might join us, my lord?"

"Yes, of course," Rothborough said, and went and gave the footman instructions.

"And I need Mr Carswell and Mrs Connolly," Giles added.

"Catherine, I beg you, put a stop to this," Lady Warde said, going to Lady Rothborough. "This is monstrous. I cannot believe you will let this happen. Why must I answer the questions of a madman? Please?"

"Major Vernon knows his business," said Lord Rothborough, putting a chair down opposite the sofa. "And if you have done nothing wrong, you have nothing to fear from any questions he will put to you."

"If I have done anything wrong, Lord Rothborough? What on earth can I have done wrong? How, sir, can you even entertain what this man is suggesting? I would have thought that you would have more consideration of the honour of a poor widow, whom your wife has always protected so faithfully."

"Major Vernon knows his business," Lord Rothborough repeated. "Why do you think I asked him here in the first place? So please, ma'am, sit, and assist him."

Chapter Thirty-three

Felix came into the drawing room with Sukey, just as they had discussed earlier with Major Vernon.

There was then a rather bizarre interlude that could only happen at Holbroke, as fancy ices were served. Felix had no idea if he should take one or not when offered the tray, for fear of offending Lady Rothborough. It was certainly the strangest interrogation scene that he had ever witnessed, but Major Vernon had been insistent.

Major Vernon was reclining on a sofa, his face dangerously flushed, looking gaunt and wild-eyed.

"Have you got everything?" he murmured, while Felix took his pulse. Felix nodded. "Just as we discussed?"

"Are you still sure about this?" Felix said, not much liking the colour of the Major's complexion, nor his hoarse, breathy tone. It was entirely uncharacteristic. "It can wait a day or two."

"I might be dead by then," he said.

"Unlikely," said Felix. "But you are prolonging your recovery by this."

"If that is the price, then so be it," Major Vernon said with a shrug.

"At least take some of your ice," Felix said. Major Vernon obeyed him.

Felix glanced over to Lady Warde, who was sitting a little distance away with Lady Rothborough. All her gestures were a pantomime of wronged womanhood, with one hand on her breast, the other clasping at Lady Rothborough's hand. The latter looked from her and then to Major Vernon, obviously painfully conflicted as to the justice of the case.

"She will probably feign illness," said Major Vernon. "Ah, look, here we go –" Lady Warde was now weeping uncontrollably into Lady Rothborough's lap. Lady Rothborough looked mortified. "Carswell, do you think you could disentangle her from my lady?"

"I will help you," murmured Sukey, and together they gently prised her away, and managed to get her to the chair that Lord Rothborough had placed in front of Major Vernon's sofa. She struggled, though, demonstrating a wiry resistance familiar to Felix from dealing with hardened members of Northminster's criminal society. And just as they inevitably did, she protested loudly.

"Major Vernon," said Lady Rothborough, going over to him. "This is becoming an abomination. She is clearly –"

"I apologise for the apparent brutality, ma'am," said Major Vernon. "But it is necessary. And as your husband has said, if she has nothing to hide, why must she object so strongly to answering a few reasonable questions?"

"I beg you then, sir, do it as quickly as you can, if you really must!" Lady Rothborough said, and went and sat at the far end of the room with her daughters.

"I will do my best," said Vernon.

He moved to the edge of the sofa and leant forward, his gaze fixed on Lady Warde.

"I am giving you a chance to find peace, ma'am," he said, gently and quietly. "That is what this is about."

"Peace?" she said. "How dare you!"

"We were talking of grief earlier, and the challenges it brings. Like you I have just suffered a great blow. I know the pain of a fresh wound. It brings us to strange places. Yes?"

"It has made you mad, certainly, sir."

"Mad with grief, yes. Angry, yes. You know what I am talking about."

"As I said before, our cases are quite different, sir. Eliza was not –"

"But she was," said Major Vernon. "And that is the key to all this. What is that about your neck, ma'am?"

"This?" Her hand touched the locket.

"You always wear it."

"Yes."

"An act of sentiment, not vanity. I cannot accuse you of that, can I?"

"No," she said.

"Might I see it?"

"I would rather not take it off."

"And would you like to explain why?" She shook her head. "As I thought. Oh well, we shall have to go the long route after all. But I know where it is we are going, and what the conclusion of this is, Lady Warde. There is no avoiding it. It is all over."

She shook her head again, and looked pointedly away. Still Major Vernon looked at her.

"Do you remember how we talked the other day?" he said after a moment, "when I had to chase you halfway across the house before you would sit down and talk to me then?"

"You were impertinent."

"Yes, I was intruding on your grief. You were in no state to talk sensibly. You had lost something precious and I compounded it by telling you something shocking, did I not?"

"I really don't remember," she said, with a wave of her hand.

"Oh, I think you do," said Major Vernon, "given how shocked you were. I told you that Eliza was with child. How could you forget that?"

There was a long pause and she said, "That was sad news – the loss of an innocent soul. Though it would have been a wretched business. I had not thought Eliza capable of being so foolish and wicked. But the Lord is her judge now." She sighed.

"You will be pleased to know that I am certain now who

killed her, and why," Major Vernon said.

"Yes, of course," she said.

"You do not look pleased," he said. "And neither am I. I will not have the pleasure of seeing John Edgar tried and then hanged for his crimes. Someone in their grief and anger took the law into their own hands."

"I am sure he had many enemies," said Lady Warde.

"Not least the mother of the woman he smashed against the wall of that cave and drowned," said Major Vernon, getting up from the sofa and staggering a few steps towards her. "The angry grieving mother who discovered that her only child was dead, and her unborn grandchild with it. The mother who had, with her daughter, been quietly pocketing treasures from the houses at which they stayed and using John Edgar to fence them."

"I don't know what you are talking about."

"Let us start with this," said Major Vernon. "Mr Carswell, the letter you found, if you please." Felix took the letter from his pocket and gave it Major Vernon. "A letter for the post, addressed to Mrs Edgar at Swalecliffe. Found in your writing table. In your hand, I think? Perhaps Lady Rothborough would confirm that."

He was about to hand the letter to Sukey to take it over to Lady Rothborough, but Lady Warde rose from her seat, determined to take it from her. Major Vernon held it out of reach.

"That is my private correspondence," she said. "That is outrageous! How dare you!"

"Even more outrageously, I have opened it," said Major Vernon, handing it to Sukey. "I am glad I did, because you have been careless, my lady. You did not think anyone would dare. You thought you could hide behind your widow's weeds and your dead husband's name. But you cannot. Lady Rothborough, would you be so kind as to look at this letter?"

"You cannot – you shall not – Catherine, I beg you,

please –"

"Is that Lady Warde's hand?" Major Vernon asked Lady Rothborough.

"Yes, I think so," said Lady Rothborough. She opened the letter and looked at the contents. "Yes." She handed it to her husband. "Yes?"

Lord Rothborough nodded.

"And what does the letter say, my lord?"

Lord Rothborough read out the letter. "'Dear Mrs Edgar, I am writing to inform you that my daughter and I shall not require the rooms we previously engaged for the week starting the tenth of August. Yours sincerely, Mrs John Abbot.' Now who is Mrs Abbot?"

"Abbot was your maiden name, was it not, Frances?" Lady Rothborough said.

"What name I use when I engage lodgings is neither here nor there," said Lady Warde.

"But rooms for your daughter?" Lady Rothborough said. "Your daughter died in India, with your husband – little Eliza whose grave you could not visit. Such a great sadness for you."

"Eliza Warde is certainly dead," Major Vernon said. "But much more recently. Here at Holbroke, in fact. In St Gertrude's cave."

"Are you suggesting that Eliza Jones was Lady Warde's daughter?" said Lord Rothborough.

"Yes. Not suggesting. It is the truth."

"Good grief," said Lord Rothborough.

"He is talking nonsense! Utter nonsense!" protested Lady Warde.

"I think you should sit down again, ma'am," said Major Vernon, returning to his own seat on the sofa. He gestured towards her empty chair.

She stood there still. "No, I shall go," she said. "I shall not stay and listen a moment longer." She moved towards the door but Felix managed to catch her arm. She struggled to be free of him and then, as if her dignity was mightily wounded, eventually returned to perch on the edge of the chair.

"Thank you," said Major Vernon.

"You made your daughter act as your maid?" Lady Rothborough said. "Is that what you are suggesting, Major Vernon?" Vernon nodded. "But why?"

"A question of economy," said Major Vernon. "How else were you going to manage, the two of you, quite penniless, when your husband died? A grieving widow with her loyal maid would be far more easily accepted as an object of charity by the great ladies with whom you hoped to make a life than a widow with a young unmarried daughter. That daughter would be an encumbrance, an expense, a constant worry to all concerned. How were you to afford to clothe and educate her according to her rank? And your friends, with daughters of their own to marry, and unmarried sons, they would hesitate to ask you stay so long. So you decided to leave Eliza Warde dead in India with your husband, and make Eliza into your maid."

"Nonsense!" Lady Warde said.

"Yes, it does seem preposterous, I know," Major Vernon went on. "And I have hesitated to believe it myself for a while. How did you make her do it, my lady? How did you persuade her, a girl of fifteen or so, that she had to deny herself all the privileges of her birth and pretend to be nobody? I can't imagine that would have been easy."

"This man is sick," said Lady Warde.

"It is no wonder she turned to thieving," said Major Vernon. "She wanted revenge and a chance of a better life than being your unpaid servant. And she was lucky to get some expert instruction when you decided to take lodgings in Swalecliffe, at the house of a Mrs Bennett, where the front room had been let to a miniature painter and shadowcutter, John Edgar. Now, as we all know, Edgar recently married the widow Bennett, but his new wife was under no illusions as to what sort of man he was. Eliza would have been a pleasant diversion for him, and as well as seducing her, he saw that she was an excellent business opportunity. He taught her the thieving trade and then took the goods off her hands."

"I cannot believe that you dare to make these allegations, sir –"

"Mr Carswell, will you show Lord and Lady Rothborough the boxes we found at Swalecliffe? Perhaps they will recognise them."

Felix took them from his medical bag and laid them out on a little table in front of Lady Rothborough. She gasped at the sight of them, and at once snatched up the little jewelled egg.

"Where did you find this?" she said. "This belongs to Lady Anna Deveraux. She was most upset at its loss."

"Did she not accuse her son of taking it to pay a gambling debt?" Lord Rothborough said.

"Yes, and they have not spoken since," said Lady Rothborough. "And here it is! How can that be?"

"We found it on Mrs Edgar's mantelpiece at Swalecliffe," Felix said. "She said it was a gift from her husband."

"And you were there!" said Lady Rothborough, getting up and going across to Lady Warde. "Of course you were! I remember very well. It was just before Christmas."

"I was, but that is nothing to do with me. Whatever Eliza Jones chose to do is not my responsibility. You must believe that, Catherine, I beg you! Do not listen to this madman." She grabbed at Lady Rothborough's skirts and looked desperately at her. "How could you think that I – oh Catherine, please...?" Lady Rothborough stared at her and then turned to Major Vernon.

"Are you sure of this, sir?" she said.

"I think she had nothing to do with it at first," said Major Vernon, "but she soon found out, and saw the advantages of the business for herself. Yes, my lady? All that temptation everywhere you went! And how hard always to have to play the humble, grateful widow, always being asked to wind wool and address invitation cards. How tiresome it must have become, year after year! I believe you came to see that Eliza had found the key to your future liberation. And that was how you and she came to steal the parure."

Lady Rothborough stepped back from Lady Warde.

"No," said Lady Warde. "No, I had nothing to do with that, and you cannot prove otherwise."

"Perhaps you might tell us why you have forty Spanish American gold dollars hidden among your possessions? Some of which are from Santa Magdalena. I find that extremely interesting. Mr Carswell, perhaps we might show everyone the purse?"

Felix tipped out the contents of the little red purse that Sukey had found in Lady Warde's room, again on the table in front of Lady Rothborough. The heap of exotic gold glowed even in the grandeur of the Holbroke drawing room.

"How dare you go through my things?"

"I do apologise, but sometimes these things must be done," said Major Vernon. "Perhaps you could tell us where you got these coins? They are not in common circulation, by any means."

"I've never seen them before."

"They were in your bonnet box," Felix said.

"A gentleman from Santa Magdalena, Don Luiz, was talking to Edgar the evening he died," Major Vernon said. "I believe that Edgar sold a bracelet to Don Luiz, that was part of the Rothborough parure that you and your daughter had plotted together to steal. These are the coins that he was paid with. But strangely there was no money on Edgar's body when we found him. Not a shilling. But here are forty gold dollars, in your bonnet box, my lady. How did you get them? Would you like to tell us that? Tell me honestly how you came by them."

But she sat there still shaking her head, her lips pursed.

"Then I shall have to explain to everyone instead," Major

Vernon said. "Later that night, Edgar met you in the garden, as you had arranged, as he was your fence. I think he told you that he had not been able to sell the bracelet yet, but it was only a matter of time. But you had run out of patience. You knew what he had done to your daughter and grandchild and that he was about to defraud you. He gave you a few gold coins and a few cheap, insincere words of sympathy. It was not enough. You knew what he had done to her and you could no longer bear it. And because he was drunk, you could take your chance. You pushed him to the ground, sat on his chest and battered his head with an ormolu ornament from the mantelpiece in your bedroom. Mr Carswell, perhaps you will show everyone the figure of Atlas."

Felix added the heavy, gilded statuette that had decorated the mantelpiece in Lady Warde's bedroom to the display of objects on the table.

"Mr Carswell has observed blood on the statue. You attempted to wash it, but you were not entirely successful. And you left a piece in the poor fellow's skull."

"This is ridiculous," she said, rising from her chair. "I will not stay and listen to a word more of this."

"It was a great struggle, of course," Major Vernon went on quietly. He got to his feet and walked across the room to where she stood. He took her arm and gently guided her back to the chair. She resisted, of course, but he had her under control. "But it had to be done, didn't it? You were so angry. The pain was unbearable, and you wanted to make him feel it, as you were feeling it. That terrible, terrible loss of your daughter. All that love that you had hidden away under cover of deceit for all those long years. All the miserable sacrifices you had both made were now for nothing — because of him! And he had taken an innocent life, a grandchild, who might have brought comfort and solace in your old age. All gone, because of his disgusting treachery. So you cracked him over the head, again and again, until there was no breath left in him."

"No!"

He crouched down beside her, grabbing the back of the chair.

"I know why you did it," he said. "I know how you feel. You and I are alike. We have lost everything in this business, and I feel that same wretched fury that took you over. I too am confronted with the person who destroyed the person I loved more deeply than I knew until she was gone."

He reached out and took her chin and turned her head so she must look him in the eyes.

"Will I give into temptation?" he said. "That is the question we all face at such moments. What do we do with our grief? Oh, how easy it would be, how easy..."

Then he let go of her chin abruptly and sank back on his heels.

"You cannot prove anything," she spat out at him, pushing him away.

There was a long silence and Major Vernon staggered to his feet, shaking his head.

"I also have a ripped-up black gown covered in blood stains," he said, leaning over her, speaking into her face. "Your gown, the one you were wearing when you smashed Edgar's head to pieces. It was found concealed in the lumber room above the staircase where my dear wife had her fall. There was a scrap of that black silk in her petticoats. Shall I tell you what I think happened?"

"It will only be more wild fantasy," she said.

"Laura met you when you were carrying your bundle of scraps. She met you on that landing above the stairs, below the attic where you concealed them. Perhaps you dropped some of them, and she wanted to help you, so she picked them up. Perhaps she saw the stains on them and wondered what you were about. And you, thinking she might speak to me, took alarm – no, you took advantage of the situation, and having taken one life, you took another."

Then he upturned the chair, throwing Lady Warde sprawling onto the floor. She shrieked.

Major Vernon abruptly left the room, leaving Lady Warde to flounder on the floor in a pool of her black skirts.

"Will you not help me?" she exclaimed to Felix. "Will no one take pity on a poor widow?"

I would rather kick you, Felix thought, and followed Major Vernon out of the room.

It was as well he did. He found the Major collapsed on the floor in a dead faint.

Chapter Thirty-four

Sukey lay sleeping on the chintz-covered couch in the dressing room, her print skirts and petticoats twisted up around her, her stockings on display. She did not look at all comfortable, and Felix was tempted to wake her and send her to her room to rest properly, but he did not like to disturb her. She had worked so hard.

In the next room, Major Vernon was asleep too, in a fitful way. But he was a great deal better than he had been. The fever had returned, just as Felix had feared it would, and this time, it had been fierce enough to be genuinely alarming for the space of a couple of hours. But it had passed, and he had fallen into a more or less settled sleep about two hours ago. That it had persisted this long, Felix counted as a good sign, and an hour ago he had sent Sukey and Holt to rest. Holt was on the sofa at the foot of the bed, while Sukey had gone into the dressing room.

It was now a little past seven and promising to be another, fine settled day.

Felix sat down at the window, and watched Sukey sleeping, rubbing his own face in order to stay awake. As well as tired, he felt hungry, dirty and in need of coffee.

The dressing room door opened softly, and Bodley came in.

"How is he, Master Felix?" he asked gently.

"Stable."

"I have a message for you, sir," Bodley said, handing him a folded piece of paper. Felix opened it, supposing it to be from Lord Rothborough, and was a little surprised to see, in an unfamiliar hand, the words: "Lady Rothborough requests

Mr Carswell to wait on her at his earliest convenience."

"She's feeling very low, his Lordship said," said Bodley.

"I cannot go looking like this," Felix said, catching sight of himself in a pier glass. He was in his shirt sleeves.

"We can see to that, sir," said Bodley. "If you judge it safe to come now, of course."

Felix went to the door of the bedroom and looked in. The Major was still sleeping peacefully, but Holt stirred and sat up.

"Lady Rothborough is unwell," Felix said. "I have to go. Send for me if there is any change."

Holt nodded.

Bodley took him to a large, luxuriously-appointed dressing room, which he guessed, from the objects that lay about the place, must belong to Lord Rothborough.

"I shall find you a shirt, sir," said Bodley, when Felix had discarded his own.

Felix could not say he was ungrateful for the luxurious comforts of Lord Rothborough's dressing room, the warm water, the generous towels. It had been an unsettling, exhausting night.

"Perhaps, Master Felix, a shave might be in order?" said Bodley. Felix rubbed his chin. "Her Ladyship detests a beard," Bodley went on, placing a chair.

Felix sat down and allowed himself to be shaved, wondering if this was the chair Lord Rothborough sat on each morning for the same procedure. It was not at all unpleasant.

"I hope Jacob is behaving himself," Bodley said, as he slapped a little cologne on Felix's cheeks before he had a chance to object. "He's a little young, but he will learn soon enough. Your hair, sir," Bodley added as Felix began to rise.

"Oh, do what you must," Felix said, sitting down again.

"It needs a barber, in truth, sir," Bodley said, attempting to comb it.

"Major Vernon would agree with you," said Felix,

wincing as Bodley pulled at the tangles.

"Mr Coxe comes over from Stanegate once a fortnight to cut his Lordship's hair," said Bodley. "I can tell him to wait on you, sir, if you like. Perhaps before the lady's funeral?"

"Yes, I suppose," Felix said, suddenly dry-mouthed at the thought of it.

"Very sad business," Bodley said, turning away. "Very sad."

At this moment the door opened and Lord Rothborough came in, dressed in a blue silk dressing gown.

"How is he?" he asked.

"Much improved," said Felix. "Lady Rothborough – what is the trouble?"

"She had a wretched night, it seems," he said. "She is frightened of a fever in the house, of course. She was anxious. You had better get dressed."

Bodley was holding out a fresh shirt for Felix, and a black silk cravat, both of which belonged to Lord Rothborough. Felix had no time to object, nor to the waistcoat and coat which followed. It was unnerving how well they fitted. However, whatever it was Bodley had done with his hair was far too suggestive of Lord Rothborough, and he pushed his hands through it quickly as he followed Lord Rothborough from the dressing room.

They entered Lord Rothborough's grand bedroom. Rothborough knocked on the door of his wife's adjoining room, and went in.

Lady Rothborough was sitting up in a large, high bed, hung with complicated frilled muslin curtains, and with covers of the same. Behind her were half a dozen large pillows, also frilled and white, and she herself was wearing a ruffled bed-bonnet, tied under the chin with a huge bow. He wondered how on earth he would get close enough to examine her. He could see she looked somewhat flushed, but no doubt that was from the warmth of the room. There was, he saw with

310

astonishment, a fire burning in the grate.

"How is Major Vernon?"

"He is safe now, I think, my lady," he said.

"My prayers have been with you all," she said. "I was afraid, at one time this night, that the husband would have to be buried alongside his dear wife... but..." she gave a slight sob. "But God has spared one of his servants a while longer."

"Yes, ma'am, I hope so."

"So trying; very, very trying," she said, with a slight flap of the handkerchief she held.

"Yes, my dear," said Lord Rothborough.

"I will see Mr Carswell alone," said Lady Rothborough. "La Roche, you may go." She spoke to her maid who was standing in the shadows. The maid went out without another word.

"Are you sure, ma'am?" Felix said, glancing at Lord Rothborough.

"Yes. Leave us, Rothborough." Her manner to her husband was more peremptory than it had been to her maid.

"As you will, my dear," said Lord Rothborough. "I shall go and dress."

Lord Rothborough left and Felix wondered if she was actually sick, or this was all some ruse to have a private conversation with him. If this was the case, what on earth did she want to say to him? She had made her feelings quite clear on the occasion they had first met.

"So, my lady, how may I help you?" he began. "You are unwell?" He came a little closer to the bed, and stood in what he hoped was a respectful manner. She continued to look him over, and he wished he had not let Bodley give him Lord Rothborough's coat to wear. It made him feel as presumptuous as he was sure she thought he was.

"I think the Lord is testing me by making you so resemble my husband, Mr Carswell," she said at length. "And I shall not fail that test," she added. "Come a little closer."

Felix obeyed.

"I did not sleep at all last night," she said. "That awful business – I cannot make any sense of it. Those accusations, so very wild, and Major Vernon's behaviour –"

"It is most unsettling, ma'am. For all of us."

"It irks me to have to ask a person such as you for assistance," she said. "But circumstances demand it and I have seen that you are competent in your profession. I feel – well, rather warm, and it concerns me. And I am hoarse in the throat – I think you can hear it?"

"Would you like me to examine you, ma'am?" said Felix.

"I fear I must ask you to do so," said Lady Rothborough, as if this were a great martyrdom for her.

He proceeded as delicately as he could, for she flinched at his first touch. He took her pulse, sounded her heart, took her temperature and examined her throat. She was not, in fact, at all unwell. The heat of the room was causing most of her discomfort.

"I suggest we open the windows, put out the fire and ask them to bring you a cup of hot water with lemon juice and honey in it, ma'am," he said.

"Oh," she said, as if he had prescribed some dreadful course of treatment. "If you advise it, then I suppose I must."

She gave a great sigh and Felix realised what she was about. Her decision to send for him on this flimsy pretext was to demonstrate her saintliness and her tolerance to her husband. It was not to win his favour or show him love. Rather, it was a convenient weapon to use against him.

"Very well, you may go now," she added.

He left the room with some relief.

Lord Rothborough was in the dressing room, putting the finishing touches to his dress.

"So?" he said.

"She is quite well," said Felix.

"I thought as much," he said, with a frown that only

confirmed Felix's suspicions. He was surprised to find himself feeling something like pity for Lord Rothborough. "Now are you ready for Sir Arthur?"

"If I can have some breakfast and some coffee first?" Felix said, unable to prevent himself yawning.

Lord Rothborough smiled.

"Yes, there is time for that. After all, one must never do battle on an empty stomach. Let us go downstairs and plan what we will say to him. I want that woman out of my house!"

~

"But these allegations," said Sir Arthur, after Felix had laid out what they had discovered. "Where is the evidence?"

"We have the evidence," Felix said, trying to stay calm and feeling that Sir Arthur was being deliberately obtuse. "Major Vernon would present it to you himself if he were not indisposed."

"But I cannot arrest this lady on such flimsy grounds," said Sir Arthur.

"They are not flimsy," said Felix.

"Then do not arrest her, sir," said Lord Rothborough. "Take her into your protection – that is all we are requesting at present. Until Major Vernon is recovered it is the best way to proceed. If she were to leave here as your guest, the presumption of her innocence is maintained, and you will have time to examine her yourself, and the evidence. It is a complex business. It will attract far less notoriety, and when the moment comes when action must be taken, it can be done discreetly."

"You are convinced of her guilt, sir," said Sir Arthur.

"Major Vernon has convinced me. He does not act without good reason."

Sir Arthur considered a long moment and then said, "Very well, I will take her back with me. I shall speak to her, and take what action I think necessary. But, gentlemen, please be aware, I shall not fall into your way of thinking so easily, no matter what the great Major Vernon has said. If I see an innocent woman, then I shall have no choice but to release her."

"It is a gamble, but we may be lucky," said Lord Rothborough, an hour later, as they stood on the portico and watched the carriage containing Sir Arthur and Lady Warde depart. "She will no doubt tell him about that business with the chair. That was unfortunate." Rothborough exhaled. "Understandable, though." He turned, and caught sight of Walter the footman, who had come out on the portico.

"What is it, Walter?"

"Message from her Ladyship, my lord," said Walter, handing him a folded note on a salver.

"What now?" muttered Lord Rothborough, walking away reading it.

"Any answer, my lord?" said Walter.

"As her Ladyship wishes," said Lord Rothborough after a moment. "As ever." He waved his hand in dismissal.

Walter left and Rothborough crumpled up the note.

"She is taking the girls to Sussex directly after –" He broke and took a deep breath. "After we have buried Mrs Vernon! Oh dear God –" He rubbed his face. "Do you think Major Vernon will be fit to go?"

"I can't say. Possibly not."

"Then you and I will have to see the poor lady to her rest for him, my lad," said Rothborough.

314

Chapter Thirty-five

"I'm afraid there is no good news, sir," said Felix.

He had hesitated a while before going up to Major Vernon's room. His strength was much restored – ten days had passed since the events at Holbroke that had led to his collapse, and almost a week since they had come to Ardenthwaite. However, he was still an invalid, and Felix did not wish to burden him unnecessarily. Yet coming in, and finding him out of bed and on the sofa, his writing slope on his lap, he judged that this was as good a moment for unpleasant news as any. It was better to be out with it.

"I hardly expected there would be," said Major Vernon, putting down his pen. "So it did not go well?"

"No," said Felix with a sigh. "No sign of any charges being brought yet." He wandered over to the window and looked out. A figure in a wide-brimmed hat was crossing the lawn, basket in hand. It was Sukey. He wished he might dash down and catch her in his arms. "Warde has contrived to get herself some heavyweight counsel. I think Sir Arthur must be behind it."

"Undoubtedly. Who is it?"

"Someone called Atherton-Barnes." Major Vernon winced. "That was pretty much Lord Rothborough's reaction," Felix said.

"He is very able and quite ruthless. She has done well. I suppose she proposes to bring a civil action against me for assault."

"Yes, I am afraid so."

"I thought she would break," Major Vernon. "I underestimated her determination to survive. But then again her every action was about survival, was it not? Why I thought I could get her to admit it there and then, I do not know. You told me to wait, and I did not listen. I was a fool, and I have pulled you all into a mire now."

"No, you have not, you have done nothing wrong. She made the mire – she and Sir Arthur, who has such a staggering disregard for the truth even when he has it laid out for him. He simply will not countenance charging her. And she is living in his house like an honoured guest! It is unsupportable."

"I should not have pushed that chair over," Major Vernon said. "If I had not done that, then it might have gone differently. I should have simply handed over the evidence to Sir Arthur and climbed back into my bed."

"And what would he have done with it? Ignored it. Just as he is doing now. Taking her words and tears as proof of her innocence. At least you have made it public by your action. There are witnesses who cannot be easily discredited. It will all have to come out if she does bring her action, if you do have to go to court."

"That is Lord Rothborough's opinion, I think," said Major Vernon.

"Yes, and I agree with him. He says you are to weather the storm, and that it can be weathered. That he will put at your disposal the best men."

"I am going to need them," said Major Vernon. "And this is going to become a great noisy thing, isn't it, with the parties lining up against one another, and columns in the newspapers? It is a marvellous tale for them: a half-crazed chief constable brutally interrogates a widow and then physically assaults her! This is a stain that will take some washing out."

"If she is charged and convicted then nothing of it will be remembered, except her notoriety."

"I am not confident that will happen," Major Vernon said. "Are you?"

"Not at this minute, but Lord Rothborough says we must

play a long game with this."

Vernon rubbed his face and said, "He is right, but I don't have the stomach for it yet."

"No, how could you?"

"I was writing to the Watch Committee," he said, "when you came in. I do not suppose they will want me back."

"They will when you are vindicated. In the meantime, you are on sick leave and there is no dishonour in that. You do not need to write to them just yet." Felix took the slope from the Major and placed it on the side table. "I think a brief turn in the garden would do you more good than writing letters," he went on. "It is not too hot today."

"With pleasure," said Major Vernon. "I am grateful for the privilege."

"You can walk with my father," Felix said. "He will keep your pace sensible."

"Agreed," said Major Vernon with a smile. He got up from the sofa, with more ease than Felix had witnessed previously. "Will you ring for Holt, then?"

Leaving Major Vernon in Holt's capable hands, Felix ran downstairs, pulling off his coat. He retrieved his old wide-awake hat from the cloakroom, and went straight into the gardens by the side door, feeling, in spite of himself, a pleasant sense of being comfortably lodged in the house. If he did not yet dare to call himself the master of the place, he was happy to be an honoured guest, charmed by all the advantages of the picturesque old mansion. In late morning, on a summer's day that had been freshened by a night of soft rain, the gardens and old stone paths had a beauty that he could not resist. He was seduced, and various impractical but compelling dreams filled his mind, as the heady scent of the old damask roses filled his nostrils.

The gate to the kitchen garden was ajar, and he slipped in, feeling he was entering the garden of Eden, such was the ridiculous abundance of fruit and vegetables. There, in the far

317

corner, past the scarlet garlands of beans in their rows and the trees already heavily decorated with swollen green apples, he glimpsed Sukey in her dark dress, lost in a tangle of raspberry canes. She was picking fruit.

He dodged through the little orchard and then stopped, suddenly afraid to approach and disturb her. He had no wish to cause her pain, and that was what often seemed to happen when he talked with her now. Perhaps it was better to stand and watch and start to learn the resignation that she had told him, often enough, was their only option.

But then she turned to reach for a berry on a high branch and saw him. She smiled and held out a basket to him.

"You can make yourself useful. There is a great clump there that I cannot reach."

"It still feels too early for raspberries, to me," said Felix, going over to her side. "It's not even August – where? Oh, I see." He reached for a berry and ate it. It was warm and sweet, like a kiss.

"How was Market Craven?" she said, moving away a little and starting to pick again.

"Just about as I predicted," he said.

"Did you see her?"

"No, thank goodness."

"And is she going to sue the Major?"

"It seems so. Wretched woman." He ate another raspberry. "These are good."

"Yes, Mr Macgillray was impressed. He will be stealing cuttings for Holbroke. Oh, and he wants to know what your thoughts are about the West Wall. He has plans, you see, for better apricots, and it will have to be a foot or two higher, apparently."

Macgillray was the head gardener at Holbroke whom Lord Rothborough had sent over to consider what improvements might be made.

"I would rather he did not touch a thing," Felix said. "It

is perfect as it is."

"That is what your mother said. She thought he was going to be extravagant and asked him for a full list of the costs."

"Thank goodness you and she know what you are doing."

"She does," Sukey said. "It was nothing to do with me. I did not say a word. Why should I?"

He felt the rebuff in her words and frowned.

"Please —" he began, but she put up her hand to silence him.

"And I have another bit of news for you. I had a letter from my brother in Manchester this morning," she said.

"And?" Felix said, not wishing at all to ask what the contents of the letter were.

"He has got sight of a post for me. It sounds like a good one. A country house in Cheshire. A silk manufacturer with a young family. The house not too large, and liberal terms."

"I wish you had not asked him to look for you."

"I told you I would."

"But —"

"There isn't any point going over this again. I have to go, sooner or later."

"No you don't," he said. "And I don't suppose you have raised this with Major Vernon yet, have you?"

"No, but it is not his decision."

"I think he might be a little offended —"

"Major Vernon and I will come to our own terms," she said. "You are just using him to muddy the waters again, which is neither fair nor honourable. You know as well as I do —" She broke off and turned away, putting down the basket and wrapping her arms about herself. He saw that she was trembling. It was as if he had hit her. "You know —" she began again, but the words were choking her.

He put down his own basket and stepped tentatively closer to her, wanting desperately to comfort her, and knowing at the same time his comfort could only add to her torment, as it added to his own. About a foot's length divided them and he could not resist reaching out and laying his hand lightly on her shoulder.

Then she reached up and laid her hand over his and he turned her gently to face him, as if they were executing a figure in a dance. They stood there silently for a moment, hand in hand.

"I want to be weak," she said. "That is the trouble. I want to give in. I am so sick of holding back."

He moved a little closer and pressed his forehead to hers, grabbing her other hand and squeezing it.

"Then give in. Say yes. Say you will marry me."

He felt her fingertips brush his cheek, with such gentleness that he could not prevent himself closing his eyes and shuddering with pleasure at it.

"Yes?" he said again.

And then, so softly he was not sure he had heard right, her answer came.

"Yes."

~

Mr Carswell was perhaps not the ideal walking companion. His pace was steady enough for Giles in his present enfeebled state, but there was a mystical, spiritual tinge to all his conversation, and a sense of moral correctness that made Giles uncomfortable. The pastoral staff was much in evidence, and for all that it was extremely well-intentioned, only done out of loving kindness for a soul in distress, he could only bear to hear so much about God's mysterious plans. It began to stir up the smouldering fire of anger that was inside him. At present, his illness had kept it dampened down, but as his strength returned it was growing. No amount of well-meant words or sincere prayers could extinguish it. He wanted more than justice. He wanted terrible things. Carswell's report from Market Craven that morning began to prey on his mind as the homily continued.

Fortunately they had turned now, and were coming back down the lime walk. It was as much as Giles could manage, both physically and mentally. The sun was now at its highest and he was looking forward to retreating inside into the cool great parlour with its stone flagged floor.

Just as they quit the shade of the trees, they saw a smart little gig, pulled by an elegant grey, coming through the gates to draw up by the front door.

It contained two ladies in broad-brimmed hats, one of whom was driving, and a boy in the Rothborough livery perched behind.

"Lady Charlotte and Lady Maria," Giles said to Mr Carswell.

"We are to leave tomorrow, for Sussex," said Lady Maria, when she had been handed down from the gig. "But we could not go without paying a call."

She said it with a blush. It was possible, Giles thought, that neither of their parents knew about this excursion.

"I am glad to see you up and about, Major Vernon," said Lady Charlotte, who was flushed also. "Very glad indeed."

"Let us go and find Mrs Carswell," said Giles. "She will be pleased to see you."

"I have brought her some flowers," said Lady Maria, who was clutching a bouquet of stupendous blooms, such as could only be found at Holbroke.

They went inside and found Mrs Carswell in the little sitting room off the great parlour. Tea was brought in and the normal civilities exchanged.

"I wonder where Felix is," said Mrs Carswell to her husband.

"I shall go and see if I can find him," Giles said, getting

up.

"I think you had better stay in your chair, sir," said Mrs Carswell. "You have had your exercise for the day. You look a little pale."

"I am quite well, ma'am, I promise you," Giles said and left the room.

He found that Lady Charlotte had followed him into the great parlour.

"I know we should not have interrupted your convalescence," she began, and then walked down the room. "But as my sister said, we felt we could not leave without knowing that you were improving." Then she added, "Which you appear to be."

"Very much so, thank you. As you can see, I am in good hands."

"I'm glad to know it. I only wish I might have helped. I felt so useless, and I would have liked to be useful. You have had such a trial and – and not even to be able to go to her burial! Forgive me, perhaps I should not speak of that."

He did not know how to answer.

"I wanted to go to the graveside," she burst out, "but my mother – well, it is against custom, of course, but it is on my conscience. I ought to have gone, for your sake, Major Vernon. I felt that since you could not be there, that someone should have been there who... who..."

"Lord Rothborough and Mr Carswell were there."

"Yes, yes, of course," she said. "But –" She broke off again and walked down the room, her face turned away from him. "You see, I have felt this thing... this friendship, this connection between us, Major Vernon, I have felt it so deeply, and now I cannot think of anything else."

Giles felt overcome with exhaustion suddenly. He sat down rather heavily on a bench against the wall.

"It is as if I have been wounded," she went on. "Oh God help me, I should not have said any of this! But I felt I could not go away and say nothing."

He could not help sighing. The poor brave creature. Her words cut at him like the slash of a sword blade. She dared to turn and look at him, but only for a moment. His weary demeanour as he sat slouched on the bench must have been eloquent. She covered her face with her hands.

"No, I should not have said anything!" she exclaimed. "Oh, dear Lord!"

She made for the door but he reached out and caught her hand. She struggled for a moment with false resistance and then yielded, all too eagerly.

"Sit down," he said, drawing her down onto the bench beside him. "And listen. I am not going to tell you anything you want to hear at this moment but I want you to listen. Yes?"

"Yes," she said.

"This is a path we all walk along, men and women. We feel things that we can do nothing about, and which torment us like devils, but it will pass. You can make it pass. You talked about being useful – well, make yourself useful and find an occupation! You are an unmarried woman, you will say, and you must observe the proprieties, of course, but you are in a position that other women can only dream of. You have the ear of an influential and powerful man – your father. Make it your business to know what he is doing in Parliament – he has an interest in a hundred worthy subjects, and there I am sure you will find some cause that will engage you."

He stopped, realising he did not like the sermonising tone of his voice. Yes, work was a great cure, but it did not stop the ache of the heart, the pain of being lonely, nor the desire to love and be loved. He dared to glance at her. There was a tear rolling down her cheek and he felt a glass shard being pressed into his hand, her pain as well as his own. He wished he could end it, as he knew she wished he would.

How easy it would be to take this beneficent and noble

comfort that she was so willing to offer him! How pleasant it would be to let himself thaw at her fireside over the coming months, to keep her as a secret salve for his bruised soul, to know that in time, he could have a wife again, and such a wife!

No doubt she had spun out all that in her own fancy: that after eighteen months or so, it would be considered decent to come out of the shadows of mourning and look to their future. She would be four-and-twenty by then, and perhaps her parents would look more kindly on him as a suitor, despite his lack of position, fortune or title. She probably knew which of the family properties would be theirs to set up house in and which seat in the House of Commons he might stand for. He would win it, after an energetic campaign which Lady Charlotte Vernon had quietly and brilliantly organised, although the parliamentary agent would get all the ostensible credit. Yet she would not mind, because her thoughts would have turned to the business of the Vernon nursery.

Children.

Yes, that was the hardest thing of all to renounce, that possibility. All the worldly advantages she represented were nothing to that. That was the weak point in him, and he had to struggle hard to overcome it. She was so close to him on that bench – he could reach out and take her hand if he wished, and press it in both his, and that would have been enough to settle it.

So he forced himself to his feet, feeling the weary ache in his bones that his illness had brought on. She gazed up at him with her watery eyes.

He shook his head.

"You are a great prize," he said. "But not for me. It can't be. You know that, I think." She nodded and looked away. "There will be someone, someone better and younger, and he will give you everything that you deserve and more."

"He will have to be in your pattern," she said, getting up.

"I hope not," he said. "You have no idea how imperfect I

am, how unworthy of you I am."

"I do not care!" she exclaimed, throwing her hands up. "I do not!"

She stretched her fingertips towards him, as if she meant at any moment to throw her arms about him. He wanted to yield, but he stepped away with another shake of his head.

"Go back to Mrs Carswell and your sister," he said. "I am going to look for Mr Carswell."

"I cannot go back yet," she said, with a sob in her voice.

"Then sit there and compose yourself."

She complied and he left her sitting there without another glance. He went upstairs to Carswell's room, and passing over the gallery, looked through the latticed screen. She was still sitting there, her hands pressed to her face, her head bent. It was a wretched sight, and he gave up his search for Carswell and retreated to his room.

Chapter Thirty-six

They feasted on raspberries and kisses, and then lay for a little while in the deep shade of a pear tree.

"I must get back to work – I will be missed. We have to be a little careful," she said, tearing herself from him.

Felix wanted to pull her back down into his arms, but he knew she was right.

"We will be careful," he said, propping himself on his elbows and watching her smooth down her skirts.

"I must look a sight," she said. "Is my hair all...?"

"A little wild, yes," he said. "But much better, in my eyes."

"You should see it first thing in the morning. A haystack it is."

The thought of seeing her red-gold curls flowing down her back was almost too much to bear. He scrabbled to his feet and kissed her again.

"I hope I shan't have to wait too long for that."

"How shall we manage it?" she said, a touch plaintively.

"We will find a way," he said. "Now, you had better go," he said, reaching for her hat that was hanging with his on a branch of the pear tree. He dropped it onto her head and tied the ribbons under her chin, before kissing her again on the lips.

When she had gone, he wandered about the garden and out into the park beyond in an ecstatic daze. He hoped he would not encounter anyone, feeling that if he did he would have to blurt out the astounding truth that Sukey was now his and that he was as good as married. The trees and the birds made better companions for this sudden gift of joy. They asked no searching questions.

He would have it done all properly, he decided, with orange blossoms and bride cake, and Sukey honoured as she should be. He resolved to buy her a betrothal ring, even if she could not wear it publicly for the time being. But in the end it did not matter. What mattered was that she, like him, had been unable to face the future alone. They had found each other and now they were one, indivisible, a rock against disaster.

He was idling through an area of rough pasture, set with clumps of trees, where four sweet-faced, decorative, brown-spotted cows were grazing. They had been sent from Holbroke so that Ardenthwaite should have fresh milk — and he knew this because Sukey had taken notice of it. She had been delighted by them and impressed by the quality of their milk. In his mother's hearing she had said that it would make excellent butter and cheese. His mother had been in agreement and pleased by her knowledge of practical dairying. "Mrs Connolly is such a treasure," she had said. At that moment, Felix had wanted desperately to tell her exactly how much of a treasure she was, how she had transformed his life and become the source of all his happiness.

He stood and gazed at the cows, happy that he understood their good points thanks to her, seeing in them all the comfortable possibilities of domestic life with her. Sweet butter for his bread, made in his own dairy under Sukey's diligent supervision, seemed only one of many engaging prospects. He determined then that it would not be long before they let their momentous news out of its captivity. She must take her rightful place sooner rather than later. He would smooth the way and silence all objections. He would save her from all the pains and arguments she feared. All opposition would crumble when people saw the absolute rightness of the match, he was sure of it.

The sound of a carriage on the drive that crossed the park brought him back to the present moment. He turned and saw

Lord Rothborough's light travelling carriage, bowling along the avenue of great elms. He had only seen his Lordship a few hours ago in Market Craven, and wondered what business could bring him there that afternoon.

He had been noticed, and the carriage stopped. Lord Rothborough got out and began to walk towards him while the carriage continued towards the house.

"I am glad to get you alone," Lord Rothborough said, as he approached. "I've just come from Stanegate. I'm a little... well, I don't quite know what, to be frank." This was an unusual thing for Lord Rothborough to say, and Felix was, for a moment, silenced. Lord Rothborough squinted at the cows. "They look settled here. They will not want to come back."

"I should make you an offer for them, then," Felix said. "Isn't that what I am supposed to say? Though I don't know how much they might be worth. I'm not a proper farmer yet."

Lord Rothborough reached out and squeezed Felix's shoulder, as if grateful for this remark. "You also seem settled here," he said, with some emotion in his voice. "Which is excellent."

"I like it," Felix said, realising with a certain humility that he had Lord Rothborough to thank not just for the title deeds to Ardenthwaite, but Sukey's surrender. The quiet magic of the place had brought them together, he was sure of it.

"Good," said Lord Rothborough. He rubbed his face and replaced his hat. "Let us walk back to the house, shall we?"

They began their walk in silence. Felix knew that Lord Rothborough was disquieted, and he had a fair idea of the reason for it. It was a subject that he had scarcely dared think much about. He had allowed more pressing things – Mrs Vernon's death, the Major's illness and Sukey – to push it to a dusty corner of the mind. Yet, Sukey had gently reminded him of it only the night before, when they had snatched twenty minutes together in the garden after dinner.

"When I was sitting with your mother this afternoon,"

she had said, "she was telling me what a wicked little boy you were and all the time I was thinking of that poor Irish lady, and all she had been through, and how she must be feeling now having caught sight of you. Oh, don't frown, Felix. I didn't mean to sting your conscience. I just thought she might want to write to you."

"Or that I should write to her?" he had said. His conscience was stung, but she had done it so sweetly, he had felt he could bear any amount of such guidance from her.

"It couldn't hurt. Since you didn't take leave of her properly."

"No. And I have Lord Rothborough to thank for that." He gave a slight shudder, recalling how they had fallen into each others arms.

"Don't blame him for that," she said.

Her words now made him tender and careful towards Lord Rothborough. After a few minutes of silence he ventured to say, "I suppose that the Santa Magdalena party are still at Stanegate."

"Yes. They are."

"And did you see Dona Blanca?"

"Yes. It was a little hard to judge. I did not see her alone, and she's not herself in that company. But we had decided that day, the day we heard about Mrs Vernon, when you left us, that we would not see each other alone again. For your sake, as much as anything. A scandal is the last thing you want."

"And there would be one if you were alone with her?" Felix could not help saying.

Lord Rothborough considered for a moment and then said, "An old love is a powerful thing. You know I have always been generous with my heart. She is still compelling, perhaps more so than before. She has gravitas and wisdom now. I can't deny she still has a grip on me. To see her among those people was a torture. But she is devoted to the memory of her late husband and to the welfare of his countrymen, who by all accounts, love her like a queen. Which does not surprise me the least. She had that quality of inspiring loyalty and love, even at seventeen. She is also pious and fears for my soul, as well as her own. She will not stray from her resolve, and so I am to feed only on the crumbs of her society while she remains here. I am not even allowed the luxury of a letter." He sighed.

"Do you think she might let me write?" Felix said after a pause.

"I think so, yes. Or you might visit, discreetly. She asked after you, of course, as much as could be permitted in company without arousing any suspicion. Not that it would have been noticed by Dona Clara whose grasp of English is most imperfect, but Don Luiz has a better command of the language. What a pair!"

"Was she still wearing that bracelet?"

"Yes, indeed, and it is the one from the parure, I am certain of it. How we approach the recovery of that is a difficult matter. I don't want to offend him unduly, as he may be the next President and it would cause a great deal of diplomatic embarrassment to accuse him of buying stolen goods. I have no idea if he does or does not know that it has a dubious provenance. If he does not, he is dangerously naive for a man in high office, and that is a worry for our Government. If, however, he is aware that valuable trinkets acquired at illegal dog fights are likely to have been purloined, and he thinks that is an acceptable way of doing business, that is entirely another sort of worry for the gentlemen in the Foreign Office. Our interests there are of some significance and I don't want them spoiled for the sake of a bracelet, no matter how valuable. A delicate business."

"Perhaps Dona Blanca might persuade them to return it quietly, for the sake of her adopted country's prestige," Felix said.

"Indeed," said Lord Rothborough, smiling. "I think she

of all people might manage that. An excellent suggestion. You are getting shrewd, Felix!"

Felix was quite unused to this level of approbation. Lord Rothborough's entire manner was confusing.

They were within sight of the house now, in the rose garden that garnished the south front. A turn of the path found them facing Mrs Carswell and Lady Maria.

"Maria, are you here alone?" Lord Rothborough said. "Does your mother know where you are?"

"No, Papa, she does not," Lady Maria said, flushing. "I am sorry. I came with Chartie. We thought – we wanted, since we are going away – oh dear, I am so sorry. And now she has vanished. Have you seen her?"

"She will not have gone far," said Mrs Carswell.

"She was with Major Vernon," Lady Maria said quietly.

"Oh," said Lord Rothborough, heavily. "Oh. This is great mischief, Maria. I told you that Chartie was not to –"

"I know, I know, Papa," said Lady Maria. "I am sorry."

"You should not have allowed this!" he exclaimed.

She cringed a little at his vehemence.

"I know, but you know what Chartie is like, Papa," she struggled to say, "when she has set her heart on something!"

Lord Rothborough exhaled loudly and glanced around him as if he might catch sight of the errant Charlotte.

"I am sure she will be found soon enough, Lord Rothborough," said Mrs Carswell. "Meanwhile, perhaps we might yield the search to the gentlemen, Lady Maria, as I must admit the sun is a little strong for me. This weather is delightful, but I am not used to it. I would like to sit down again."

"Yes, mother, you should go in," Felix said, taking her arm and guiding her back into the small parlour. Lady Maria, almost in tears now, followed them and sat down, timidly glancing at her father as he came in.

"It is not your fault," Lord Rothborough said, giving her

a brief caress. "You are right, Chartie knows no law except her own. We will find her soon enough. Come, Felix."

They set out on their search on the ground floor of the house.

"At least we can be certain that Major Vernon will not have indulged her," Lord Rothborough said. "But she has allowed her heart too much licence in that direction and it will be painful for her. I already have poor sweet Gusta howling daily at my feet, and now we shall have to deal with Chartie, who will be far more wounded, because she feels everything so deeply. It has always been the way with her. Ah, if only Vernon were ten years younger and with better quarterings, it might have been possible, in time, to entertain it, though Lady Rothborough would never be content with it." He gave a bitter laugh. "And for once, Felix, you are behaving yourself in these matters. There's a novelty! At least, I trust you are?"

Felix felt his throat go dry. He could not answer, for at the end of the passageway stood Sukey.

"Aha," said Lord Rothborough seeing her, and striding forward. "Mrs Connolly, perhaps you can help us?"

"My lord?" Sukey said, making her curtsey.

"Have you seen Lady Charlotte?"

"Yes, my lord. She is –" She indicated a closed door. Lord Rothborough's hand was at once on the latch, but Sukey went on, "She is very distressed, my lord. I have done all I could, but – I hope you don't think I am speaking out of turn, but she needs kindness now."

Lord Rothborough looked Sukey over carefully.

"She has mentioned the trouble to you?" he said.

"Yes," said Sukey. "I found her crying. She said she wanted to take my place. That she would happily be his servant."

"Oh dear," said Lord Rothborough. "We have quite a case, do we not!" He opened the latch and slipped into the room. He shut the door gently behind him.

"I don't suppose he will be so kind to you," Sukey said. "Nor me."

Felix took her hand to kiss it, but she pulled it away.

"I don't care what he thinks," Felix said, snatching back her hand. "His opinion is irrelevant."

"I might believe that if you didn't care for him. But you do. He's your father, for Heaven's sake, Felix. You can't disregard him. We can't!"

"He will have to live with our decision and he will soon see the rightness of it."

Sukey once again pulled her hand from his.

"If he does not think a great gentleman like Major Vernon is good enough for his daughter, then how can I ever be good enough for you?"

"I'm his bastard! That's all," Felix said. "I am a speck of dirt compared to you, Sukey. You are my superior in everything – character, birth, everything." He tried again to embrace her. "Don't be afraid, please – it will be all right. We decided this morning it would be."

She yielded at last, but she was stiff and awkward in his arms. Her pulse was thudding with fear.

"Perhaps this morning was a silly dream," she said. "And we ought to –"

"It was not," he said.

"Yes, yes, I know, but –"

She broke away quickly from him, alerted by a creak on the floor boards. But it was too late; they had been observed, by none other than Holt, coming along from the servants' hall with a tray.

Sukey half walked, half ran away in the other direction, leaving Holt to give Felix a most contemptuous look. He might as well have spat on the floor in front of him with disgust.

"I'm just taking this up to the Major, sir," Holt said. "He seems a little wan. You might want to take a look at him."

"Yes, of course," said Felix, and followed Holt upstairs, feeling like a man mounting the scaffold.

Chapter Thirty-seven

"Mr Holt, is there something wrong?" Giles asked.

Holt stood fingering Giles' cravat as it lay over his arm with a clean shirt.

"Are you sure you are well enough to dine downstairs, sir?" he said.

"Yes, I've rested all afternoon. It will not be too great a trial. Is that all?"

He watched Holt lay the shirt and cravat on a chair, rather slowly and deliberately. It was not his usual way. He was usually swift and precise.

With his back to Giles, Holt said, "There was another matter, sir, which I don't like to raise with you, but I feel I should. About Mr Carswell."

"Yes?" Giles said.

Now Holt turned and faced him.

"Mr Carswell and Mrs Connolly. I saw him –" He hesitated. "At her."

"By which you mean?"

"You know what I mean, sir! At her. Pawing her. His hands all over her. Lover-like. I thought you should know," he added. "I didn't think you would care for such liberties being taken. And she didn't look very happy about it, I must say."

"When was this?" Giles said.

"This afternoon. Just before he came up with me."

"I see. You were a little short with him then, I did notice that."

"He was lucky he didn't get a bloody nose," said Holt. "But I reckon I should leave that to you, given you are the master."

Giles found himself frowning as he got up from the couch. Suddenly the thought of going down to dinner felt a great deal less attractive.

"I thought of mentioning it to his Lordship when he was here," Holt went on, taking up the clothes brush and attacking Giles' evening coat over-vigorously with it. "But I thought, like father, like son."

"That's quite enough, Holt," said Giles. "Don't worry, I will speak to Mr Carswell about it. And please would you treat my coat with a little more kindness. It is too old to bear your ill-humour!"

Holt stopped brushing and scowled.

"Don't spare him your tongue, sir," he said. "Mrs Connolly deserves better than that sort of mucky behaviour. She's too fine by half for the likes of him!"

Holt left, banging the door rather peevishly behind him. Giles finished dressing and went into the library. There he discovered Carswell pacing the room in his shirt sleeves, not yet dressed for dinner and in a state of some agitation. There was a cheroot stuck in his mouth, and there was a dish of stubs and a half-drunk decanter of claret on the table.

He threw the cheroot into the empty fireplace at the sight of Giles.

"This is your house," Giles said, though the smell of smoke was not pleasant.

Carswell went to the window and pushed it open.

"I ought to give them up. You are right – they are an abomination," he said. "And this is not my house. I am master of nothing here, not even myself!" He pushed his hands through his hair and threw himself into a chair. "And I suppose Holt has said something to you. I can't believe that he would keep that from you for long."

"Yes, he has."

"What did he say?"

"That he saw you – and I am using his word here –

pawing Mrs Connolly. Lover-like, was the other expression he used."

Carswell groaned and dragged the wine tray towards him.

"Will you?" he said as he filled his glass.

"Yes, just a little," Giles said, sitting down opposite Carswell at the table. Carswell passed him a glass of wine. "So, will you explain it?" Giles went on. Carswell sipped his wine and glanced away. "She is my employee, and under my protection. I must ask what is going on." Still Carswell did not answer. "What disturbs me most about this report is that Holt suggested that the attentions were unwelcome to her."

Now Carswell drained his glass and set it down carefully on the table, as he considered what to say.

"I wish I knew. I know she loves me, as I love her, but she is so afraid! It is all suddenly so unwelcome to her. Perhaps it is all poisoned and impossible. She is right about everything, always, and no doubt she is right about this. But I cannot give it up! I cannot give her up."

"How serious are things between you?" Giles said. "You intend to marry?"

"Yes!" Carswell exclaimed. "And this morning we finally agreed on it. I thought I had her – at last! But then Lord Rothborough arrived, and –"

"Does he know of this?"

"No! But she saw Lady Charlotte and all that business, and it made her take fright again. That was what Holt saw. I was attempting to reassure her, but –" He reached for the decanter again. "How can I give her up? How? She is the best thing that has ever happened to me. I have told her a hundred times that I will smooth the way and she will not suffer for it. I will make sure of it. I will take all the blows. I will not have her suffer."

"But she will," Giles said, "if you marry, no matter what you do. Her family, for a start –"

"Yes, yes, I know! Do you think I do not? I have known

all along that it is utterly impossible!"

"Then you ought never to have declared yourself," Giles said, without, he hoped, too much reproach in his manner. Yet still Carswell looked across at him contemptuously. "If you truly cared for her."

"And now, of course, you will accuse me of self-indulgence!" exclaimed Carswell, jumping up from the table.

"Have you not just done that yourself?" Giles said.

"To grab at happiness, at peace, at love?" said Carswell. "Is that self-indulgence? Sukey and I – it is a miracle! The finest thing I have ever known is to be in her company. I am a better man for her – you have seen that yourself – she has improved me in every way. I might walk a thousand miles and then another and not find another woman so perfectly formed to be my wife!"

"Except that none of your family or friends will agree with you."

"Not even you?" said Carswell, leaning across the table towards him.

"I'm sorry, but I cannot approve it. It would offend too many people I care for. Mr and Mrs O'Brien, whom I regard as my friends, did not put her in my care to find her such an unsuitable match."

"And they did such a fine job with her first husband! Who was by all accounts approved by them all – he was a wastrel, a drunkard who left her starving. She will want for nothing with me. This house – can you think of a better mistress for the place? It is everything she deserves." Giles was about to reply, but Carswell went on, "You have seen her with my parents? I think my mother loves her already. Sukey is exactly the daughter that she has always wanted. It is only a matter of overturning these ridiculous prejudices. She is not my equal, she is my superior!"

Giles sighed.

"I have also heard your father lamenting that the Irish will not turn away from the Papacy. Have you given any thought to religion? She may not wish to give that up. Have you spoken to her about that?"

"That is of no consequence to me," said Carswell, airily. "I will turn Papist if that is what it takes. I will do anything necessary."

"That would be a drastic step," Giles said. "Given all this, and from whom it came."

"He cannot take this away from me now," said Carswell. "It is mine."

"True enough. You can take your prize and live your life in blissful solitude. You will have made your point. But to make your wife's position untenable with her neighbours is quite another thing. If Holbroke slams its door in your face – and it will, undoubtedly, if you turn to Rome – then all the other houses, great and small, will follow. Then Ardenthwaite is nothing but a miserable prison for her. No wonder she is afraid of what you suggest. She is no fool. And what of your children? Are you really prepared to have doors closed in their faces as they grow up? Given what you have suffered yourself?"

"I am not intending to father a race of bastards!" Carswell said. "How can you make such a comparison?"

"Because unfortunately many people will see it like that. An unequal marriage is not easily forgiven, nor would you leaving your religion. You will be judged harshly."

"Only by narrow-minded bigots for whom I have no time!" Carswell said, slamming his palm on the table and making the glasses dance. "I don't care about such people, and neither does Sukey. We will make our own society. We do not need such neighbours!"

"I think –" Giles began again, but the argument was making him tired, and it was clear that Carswell was unlikely in this mood to listen to reason. He reached for his wine and drank a mouthful, wishing he could give the approval Carswell so desperately craved. His pain and frustration in love, like that of his half-sister earlier that day, played on Giles' nerves, stirring up his own wretchedness. How impossible human relations were and how cruel life was!

The image of Laura's lifeless form lying in the state bed rose up in his mind and he reached for his glass again, hoping desperately that it might leave him, along with the choking fumes of anger that now clouded his thoughts.

At last he managed to say, "Marriage is a hard enough path without such difficulties. Yes, you are in love, and the object of your love is a worthy one, but she is right to resist your plans. It is better that you part before you damage each other too much. Please spare yourselves the pain of that."

~

Dinner was awkward beyond measure, and it was a relief that his parents and Major Vernon retired almost as soon as they rose from the table. Glad to be left to his own devices, Felix went out into the garden, where a balmy golden-blue dusk of heartbreaking perfection was enveloping the long walks and rose bushes. He lit a cheroot, his earlier resolutions quite thrust aside, and he made a long circuit, remembering those pleasant evenings after dinner where, by accident at first and then by design, he had met with Sukey.

He had no hope of seeing her that night, though, but when he turned a corner he saw her sitting on a bench, just where she had been the night before. She met his gaze with a brief crooked smile that made his heart ache.

"So –" she began.

"Yes?" he said.

"I am guessing from the way Holt was looking at me that he has said something to Major Vernon."

340

"Yes, he did."

"And was he angry? Major Vernon, I mean?"

"Yes, but quietly so."

"Which is worse," Sukey said. "Oh dear."

"He is quite on your side," said Felix, rather bitterly. "I shouldn't worry." He sat down on the far end of the bench and sucked on his cheroot. "He thinks I would be making a wretched prisoner of you if I married you. That I would be punishing our children even before they were born. Quite a fine argument, I must say!" He got up again, and threw the cheroot down onto the path, grinding it out with his foot. "He is no saint," he went on. "He has no right to lecture me!"

"And now you are at loggerheads!" Sukey said. "And saying things about him that you do not mean. This is what I have been telling you along – that it spoils everything good in our lives if we go on with this! Everything!"

"And is it not worth it?" he said.

"I am not sure it is," she said. "Perhaps it is just a silly dream, this thing between us, a silly summer dream!"

"But we love one another," Felix said, throwing himself down beside her. "We want one another. There is a sort of magnificence about us. You can't deny that. You feel it as I feel it."

"Yes," she said, but she was shaking her head. "But –"

"So?"

"It isn't enough just to want and to love. In our position, it isn't. It isn't enough to spoil everything for. And as for wanting – well, women love and want like men do. Perhaps you don't understand that. We women don't say it because we are not supposed to. But I said it to you because I am a fool and you took down my guard." She got up and walked a pace or two away from him. "And I know what it is like to love and want a man. And I know as well that all can change. You can love and then you can hate. Summer can turn to winter, just like that!" She snatched a wilting rose head from the bush and

341

tossed the petals in the air. "At least this way I won't grow to hate you too."

Felix got up.

"I am not James Connolly. I will never treat you as he treated you."

"And how do you know that? He was as sweet-tongued and as handsome as you, and as determined. He brought out the devil in me, just as you do. And I brought out the devil in him, sure enough I did, and then we led each other straight to hell!"

"I am not like him," Felix said.

"Maybe, maybe not," she said. "But I am the same person. I haven't changed. I keep telling you that you don't know me, not really. If we go through with this, I swear that in a year you will be cursing what you have brought on yourself! When all your friends desert you and you are left with a wife you cannot love because she's not what you thought she was. It isn't worth the candle, Felix, I'm not worth it! Let me go, for the Lord's sake. Let it go!"

With which she ran back towards the house, leaving the master of Ardenthwaite kicking at the fallen rose petals.

Chapter Thirty-eight

"You and I, Mr Carswell," said Major Vernon coming into the library, "are in need of purposeful activity. Sooner rather than later. May I?" he added, his hand on a chair rail.

"Of course," Felix said.

"I know you have not been much in the mood for company," Major Vernon said, pulling out the chair and sitting down opposite him at the table. "I have made sure you were not disturbed."

Felix had been left for the last two days to keep his counsel in the library. Not even Mr Carswell had come in to bother him on the pretext of searching for a book.

"You must have said something to my father," Felix said.

"I saw you had made yourself comfortable in here," Vernon said, "and that your father was equally comfortable in that little room downstairs, so I had Holt move some books there for him. Mostly the divinity. We did not think you would miss those."

"No," Felix said, in some amazement, noticing now the dozen empty shelves on the far side of the room. In fact he had scarcely taken a book from the shelves. He had established himself a sort of desk on the large table in the middle of the room, and he had attempted to distract himself with some medical work. All the summer he had been toting about two thick French volumes on respiratory and pulmonary conditions. Now they lay on the table reproaching him. He had not opened them. He had spent his time gazing out of the windows and wondering what Sukey was doing, where she might be in the house and what she might be feeling at any instant of the day. He had begun dozens of letters to her, and then, revolted by the self-pitying tone of them, fearing she would laugh at them, he had burnt them in the grate.

Since he had seen her in the garden, she had become invisible. Like him, he supposed, she had contrived to hide herself away. Ardenthwaite was a large, rambling house full of places to hide. What might have been sweet refuges for lovers now became sanctuaries for those attempting valiantly not to be in love.

"And Holt was also in need of purposeful activity," Major Vernon added. "Not that moving a few books is enough for a man like him."

"You might send him out to shoot rabbits," Felix said. "Or set traps for the moles. Have you seen the state of the lawn?" He had stared at it a great deal in his misery, and had begun to believe that each fresh molehill was proof of the wretched and imperfect nature of the world.

"You could take a gun out yourself," said Major Vernon.

"I am a terrible shot," Felix said. He did not add he would be too tempted to turn it on himself.

"I have another idea," Major Vernon said. "Assuming, of course, that my physician says I am well enough."

"It would depend on what you had in mind," Felix said. He had examined the Major that morning after breakfast and had been heartened by his progress. "But, as I said this morning, you are definitely on a favourable course."

"All I propose is this – that in a day or two, we go back to Stanegate, and try to get back that bracelet. I want to talk to Don Luiz properly. Actually, I want him to admit how he came by it and swear to it, if at all possible, but that may be asking too much. But an admission will help with the weight of evidence against Lady Warde."

"I told Lord Rothborough we should enlist Dona Blanca's help in that. Ask her to return it quietly for the sake of national prestige. But that would not help you, sir, would it?"

"It's possible she does not have that sort of influence over him," Vernon said.

"She is a queen in exile, from what I understand," Felix said. "And he has to listen to her, because of her popularity with the people."

"And Ramirez is what? The king-in-waiting, apparently – and how close are they, in truth? It is quite intriguing. She is a strong woman and if I were him, I would be wary of her and her motivations. He may be pretending to be an ally for the sake of it."

"Keep your enemies close," said Felix.

"Quite," said Major Vernon. "And I think, given the matter of those letters, and her excessive caution and secrecy, that she is not showing her true colours towards him. That it is a mutual case of keeping enemies close. What was it you told me she said about Don Xavier – that he took care not to be found? Interesting, don't you think?" Major Vernon was tracing circles with his forefinger on the table top as he spoke. He went on, "Lord Rothborough's secretary, Mr Woodward, speaks excellent Spanish. I think we should commission a translation of those letters she gave you, post haste."

"We would have to go over to Holbroke, then," Felix said, thinking of the family chapel adjoining the parish church where he had attended Mrs Vernon's internment only a week ago. "Do you think –?" he ventured.

"I am ready for it," Major Vernon said. "I want to see where she is laid – sooner rather than later."

Felix nodded and got up from the table.

"We could go today," he said. "You are right, sir. I have had quite enough of my own company."

The carriage was ordered for after lunch. Felix had the dispatch case tucked inside his coat, and he could not deny that the prospect of learning what the letters contained was a useful distraction.

When they were just about to climb into the carriage, his

mother came out of the house carrying a small but carefully arranged posy of flowers, which she handed to Major Vernon.

"I have found all the things you asked for," she said. "And one or two others, which I hope you do not object to. Myrtle and rosemary, chiefly. And our prayers are with you."

Major Vernon took it, and slightly to Felix's astonishment thanked her with an easy kiss on the forehead, whereupon she wrapped her arms about him for a moment, and returned the kiss. Turning away, he caught sight of Sukey coming out of the shadowy hallway into the sunlight. She was also carrying flowers, this time an armful of colourful blossoms, shining against her dark dress and white apron.

She darted out and thrust the flowers at Major Vernon.

"For Mrs Vernon," she said. She was flushed, he saw, and he longed to press his hand to her cheek and feel the heat of it, as well as to soothe it.

Major Vernon took the flowers with a gracious nod, and she went running back into the house without another word.

"What a dear girl," said Mrs Carswell.

Felix was on the verge of following Sukey, but Major Vernon was already climbing into the carriage.

So they drove to Holbroke with the seat opposite covered in flowers. Felix wanted to gather Sukey's bouquet into his arms and weep into it. There was to be no happiness, no promise, no future. Nothing. Only death remained, the supreme conqueror of all. Major Vernon did not break the silence, but sat fingering a sprig of rosemary from Mrs Carswell's posy.

A previous Marquess of Rothborough – Felix could not recall which – had rebuilt the parish church at Holbroke at the end of the seventeenth century in a chaste baroque style, reminiscent of Wren's City churches. It was elegant and peaceful, with nothing to reprimand or alarm among its white Corinthian columns and handsome altar fittings. A sweet-faced, and – Felix had to admit – extremely beautiful Raphael

Madonna with an equally beautiful Christ-child in her arms, hung above the communion table, against a background of rosy damask.

Major Vernon stood looking at it for a minute.

"Laura would have liked that," he said.

"Lord Rothborough had that put there recently, I think."

Major Vernon nodded.

"And she is...?"

"Through here, in the family chapel."

Lord Rothborough had been insistent that as a guest of the family, Mrs Vernon should be treated as one of them in death, and after the service she had been taken down to the family vault.

They went through to the chapel, guarded by an elaborate gilded gate, and past the many opulent tombs with their elaborate statues and inscriptions. Various lords and ladies with ruffs and stocks and cushions and little pet dogs surrounded them, and Felix felt he was in a drawing room full of dead ancestors. These were his people whether he liked it or not.

The door to the vault was closed but in front of it was another huge heap of fresh flowers, to which Major added his own posy and those from Sukey, and then went back into the main church and sat down, his eyes again fixed on the Madonna and child.

"I'll leave you alone now, sir," Felix said, and went back out into the sunlight.

~

"This is providential!" said Lord Rothborough, when they had stated their business and handed over the dispatch case to Mr Woodward. "Only today I have had another interesting letter from my contact in Paris. Santa Magdalena is a nest of snakes, he says, and this only confirms it. How long do you think it will take you, Woodward?"

"I cannot say at once, my lord. Give me a quarter of an hour and I will come back to you with an estimate. Excuse me please, gentleman."

Woodward left, and Lord Rothborough said to Giles, "It is entirely typical of you, Major Vernon, to discover a talent in one of my men of which I was lamentably unaware. How?"

"I don't know. We were just making conversation," Giles said.

"It is your particular genius to find out all our secrets," Rothborough said. "I think you are wasted in the police business, Major. When we are back in government, you must expect to be asked to act on a broader stage."

Giles shrugged, having no wish to discuss his future at that moment.

"Your correspondent in Paris," he said. "What else does he say?"

"It is really quite sensational, if it is true," said Rothborough. "Now you may know that the island is principally known for coffee and sugar production. A few little seams of gold and silver here and there, but nothing for anyone to get excited about. Until recently. According to my correspondent, Don Luiz has been talking up the mineral rights to his potential political backers in Paris. There is a new geological survey of the island from some Prussian fellow called Valk. Valk has all the right credentials and swears blind that there is a mountain of gold in Santa Magdalena just waiting for the taking."

"And as the future president, Don Luiz will of course control the mineral rights and will look kindly on any political supporters who would like to exploit them in future?" Giles said.

"Naturally," said Lord Rothborough.

"But the existing government, which is falling apart, knows nothing of this?"

"No. I am not convinced this Herr Valk has even been to the island. That was my immediate thought. A few clever maps and talk of limitless gold can make men crazy with thoughts of what might be. It has happened before and it will happen again."

"It ought to be easy enough to find out if Valk is genuine," said Carswell.

"It is already in hand," Rothborough said. "However, there is a chance that my cynicism will be unjustified, and there is a mound of gold on the island, in which case the matter becomes a great deal more serious. It becomes a matter of our national interest – we would need our own chance at that gold, and to be certain that the government is one that we can do business with. As it stands I cannot think that Don Luiz will be sympathetic or useful to our interest if he becomes President. He is clearly a rogue, but of a lesser or larger sort, we do not yet know!"

At this point a servant came in with a tray of refreshments and a message from Woodward that he was hard at work at the letters and it would be two days' work.

Rothborough poured the wine and said, handing a glass to Giles, "I understand you went to the church?"

"Yes, and thank you again for all that you have done for us, for her."

"I wanted to show you this," Lord Rothborough said. "Maria took her profile. It is rather nicely done. She left it here for you – but her suggestion was that it should be sent away and done in marble – bas-relief? Or bronze, perhaps?"

Giles took the paper from Lord Rothborough and went to the window to look at it properly. Lady Maria was no great artist, but in her clumsy way she had got Laura's character, and oddly enough, a flavour of how she had been when he had first known and fallen in love with her.

The sight of it was too much for him. He could not contain his grief any longer. His stoicism gave way, and he was obliged to excuse himself.

He made his way through the great rooms, now all shut up, the rugs covered, the furniture shrouded. He found what he hoped was an inconspicuous corner of an ante-room and gave way to his grief in a way he had not yet done.

He did not know how long he was there, but eventually the spasms subsided and he looked up, with damp and stinging eyes, to see Lady Charlotte standing on the threshold.

"Forgive me," she said. "I could not help but..."

"I thought you had gone to Sussex," he said, getting up.

"No, I am going to Scotland. I begged my father for that indulgence. Besides, there is someone he wishes me to meet. Lord Dunbar. Perhaps you have heard of him?"

"Yes, I think I have read a pamphlet of his on factory legislation."

"Maria has met him. Apparently he is twenty-seven, tall, quite ugly, but very clever and energetic. He is mad for reform. My father thinks highly of him, of course." She spoke brightly but not quite brightly enough to conceal the crack in her voice.

"Oh, I am so sorry," he managed to say.

"For what?" she said. "It is not for you to apologise. You are not at fault. I am the one who let my fancy gallop away with me, and very embarrassing it is. But at least I know that you are discreet and honourable! And now I have seen your great distress for your dear wife – which I should not have intruded upon – please, please forgive me?"

"There is nothing to forgive," Giles said. "I am glad to see you. We ought to be friends, for God knows, that's a precious thing! Life is too short and too fragile. Please?" He put out his hand. "Will you shake on that, Lady Charlotte?"

"With great pleasure," she said. "And will you wish me luck in Scotland?"

"Certainly," he said, as they shook hands. "And he may

not be so ugly."

"Perhaps," she said with a smile. "I have read a speech of his on education for the labouring classes and it was impressive. He was quite interesting on the importance of the education of women. I will go away now. I don't want to distress Papa any more. If he knows I have seen you – he has been so kind, you see, so understanding."

She said no more and left, carefully closing the door behind her.

Giles retraced his steps to Lord Rothborough's office, under the chandeliers in their muslin drapes and past the pier glasses hung with calico veils. If Laura's ghost were to walk anywhere, then those great rooms at Holbroke, where for a brief moment she had shone like a goddess of the moon, were as good as any.

Chapter Thirty-nine

Two days later, Lord Rothborough returned to Ardenthwaite with Woodward's translations of the letters, and the original letters in their crimson dispatch case. He delivered them straight into Giles' hands as he sat in his bedroom.

"You have had your man working through the night on this," Giles said.

"Yes, and I have given him a gratuity for it. He is off on his holiday now – free of me for a whole month, which is probably a great relief to him! But he was glad to do it – he was worried his Spanish was getting a little rusty."

"I feel I should contribute," Giles said.

"Think nothing of it," said Rothborough. "And now I shall take my leave. I am heading to Scotland myself today – by way of your country, in fact, Vernon. I believe your brother's place is not far from Hougham?" Giles nodded. "Charlotte is going with me, and we are going to her godmother's house there for a few days. Lady Clarkfield – doubtless, you know her?"

"Only very distantly," Giles said, remembering how his sisters had spent much time dreaming of being taken up by that family. They were reputed to give the best balls. But it had never been managed, and Sally had even got a long and rather humiliating lecture from their mother on the folly and vulgarity of attempting to over-reach one's divinely ordained social position. He realised his mother would not have approved of his present intimacy with Lord Rothborough.

"Now, where is Mr Carswell? I should like a word with him before I go," Rothborough said.

"He was in the servants' hall. There was an accident

earlier with a scythe in the yard – one of the farm servants, poor fellow."

"Goodness. Well, he is fortunate to have a surgeon as his new master," said Rothborough.

~

Sukey was the best dresser a surgeon could have asked for, and Felix had no doubt that she could have learnt the profession, given the chance.

The wound was a messy one: the farm servant had been astonishingly clumsy and the blade newly honed. The man's life was not in danger, but it had to be seen to with some care to make sure that there were no complications. Felix would not have managed such a neat job single-handed, and was grateful for someone who understood and accepted his directions without demur or question.

It was the first time he had seen her since she had appeared with the flowers before they left for Holbroke. He had sent for her at once on first seeing the man, hardly expecting that she would answer the summons. But she had come straight from the still room, where she had been making jam. Without a word she had followed his every instruction, but she had not met his gaze. She was the quiet, obedient servant, nothing more.

When the man had been got comfortable she left, carrying away the dirty cloths and basins. He followed her into the scullery and they were at last alone together. She cranked the pump handle, and he washed his hands, standing by her. All the feelings he had worked so hard to push aside now came back to him, like the wiry branches of a briar bush, determined to entangle him.

"I hear you are away soon," he said.

"Yes. I am taking the mail on Friday, to Leeds. Then there is a train to Manchester, and Mr Hall will meet me there. It is kind of him."

"I thought you were going to Northminster first to spend a week or two with your sister."

"I can't disappoint Mr and Mrs Hall. They have said they will give me a week at Christmas. I will go then – perhaps."

"Perhaps?"

"If I am sure you will not be there," she said after a moment.

"You are so cruel," he said.

"It is for the best. I am tired of discussing this."

"Given I have not seen you for days, you don't have much to complain about." She did not reply, and went on with washing out the cloths. "And what if you do come to Northminster and I am there, and by some terrible chance we meet – by which I mean if fate determines we do?"

"It's better that we don't meet or even think of it! Don't be such a fool."

"We cannot alter what is unalterable. What must be, must be. I will not give up on this as easily as you, Sukey, and you will come to thank me for it!"

"Stop this! Stop this at once. You say you care for me! Then let it go, Felix, for Heaven's sake – no, for my sake!"

He caught her hand in his and she struggled to free herself. When she did, she cracked her hand across his face, fast and hard. It made him cry out, not so much from pain as from shock. He sat down on the stool, startled, while she stood there nursing her own hand, a horrified expression on her face.

"You're bleeding –" she said. "Oh saints above, I've made you bleed." He touched his lip and found it sticky with blood. He winced.

Suddenly she was crouching down by him, dabbing at his face with towel.

Her nearness and tenderness was unbearable. To feel her soft fingertips on his cheek as she pressed the towel to his lip made him dizzy with desire. He struggled to resist and to remember that the only reason she was showing him this solicitude was because she had hit him. But he did not care. He would let her hit him a hundred times if it meant she would come so close.

"It doesn't matter," he said, wrapping his arms around her and pulling her towards him. To his surprise she did not resist; rather she collapsed against him, and pressed herself to him. In a moment, she was on his lap, her arms garlanding his neck, her head bent and pressed against his chest. She was shaking with sobs, and he held her firm, his head feeling the strangest mixture of misery and ecstasy. He pressed his lips to her linen-capped head, leaving a bloody mark. "It doesn't."

She mastered herself a little and said, "It does. That's the whole trouble."

She did not break from him, though any moment he expected she would, and he was steeling himself against the loss, which he knew would be far more painful than any slap she gave him. But she stayed there, on his lap and in his arms.

"I wish, oh, how I wish that everything you say could be, but –" She dissolved in tears again, and he cradled her head in his hand.

Gently he lifted her chin and pressed his lips to hers. They exchanged a long, bitter-sweet, tear-drowned kiss.

"Forgive me if I am interrupting..."

The sound of Lord Rothborough's voice, gentle but utterly startling, broke into his consciousness.

"You have nothing to worry about, my lord," Sukey said, at once slithering off his lap. Felix rose to stop her, but she was halfway across the room before he had a chance. She turned quickly away to hide her tear-stained face. "There is nothing going on here. At least not any more!" Her voice was taught with distress. "Excuse me –" She was heading for the

355

door, but Lord Rothborough caught her arm and made her face him. He looked her over carefully.

"You should sit down for a moment, ma'am, and compose yourself," he said, and guided her to the stool with a gracious gesture, as if she were a duchess being escorted across a drawing room.

Lord Rothborough then folded his arms and looked at both of them.

"I suppose I should not be entirely surprised," he said after a moment. "The question being how we deal with this."

"As I said, my lord, there is nothing to be done," said Sukey.

"We wish to marry," Felix said, and attempted to take Sukey's hand but she flicked it away from him.

"And that is impossible!" she exclaimed, jumping up again.

"And that is distressing to you," said Lord Rothborough, taking her hand in both his and gazing at her. "Your feelings are engaged, yes?"

Felix wanted to push him away, disliking the liberty of this question, and the way he had taken her hands, but Sukey did not seem to object, although she looked away to avoid his gaze. But she nodded, biting her lip as she did so. Lord Rothborough patted her hand and said, "I understand, my dear; believe me, I do. Very distressing."

He guided her back to the stool and turned his attention to Felix.

"Mrs Connolly is perfectly right, Felix, you cannot marry. It is entirely out of the question. However —"

"However?" Felix said.

"There is another arrangement you might not have considered. A little establishment in Northminster – discreetly placed, but comfortable. And an allowance, yes?" He glanced at Sukey. "Forgive me, ma'am, if that idea offends you. If it does, then we will say no more about it, but I thought I would mention it at least."

There was a silence and then Sukey said, looking up at him, "No, it does not offend me, my lord."

Felix found himself now even more bereft for words than he had been by Lord Rothborough's speech.

Lord Rothborough smiled graciously at her.

"I can see," Sukey went on, "that there might be advantages in it."

"Since you are a widow, no one will think it odd that you live alone," Lord Rothborough said. "You can both enjoy each other's company and preserve your reputations. Now, if Mrs Connolly were to meet a suitable gentleman, she is still free to marry him, and you are free to marry, likewise. You are both very young."

"I can't think that Mr and Mrs O'Brien..." began Felix.

"They need not know, if you are discreet. There are ways these things can be managed. Perhaps some connection of your late husband has decided to give you an allowance, Mrs Connolly?"

"Perhaps," she said.

"I see we understand each other," Lord Rothborough said with a smile. "It is a possibility that we ought to explore. After all, excellent housekeeper though you are, ma'am, I think you would prefer not to be at the beck and call of an employer. An establishment of your own, albeit a small one –"

"And Major Vernon?" Felix said.

"He does not need to know either," said Lord Rothborough.

"As if he will not guess!" exclaimed Felix. "He is a seer! He will take one look at me and know everything, and then he will try and put a stop to it. You know what he is like, Sukey!"

"But he is not my master! Not now!" said Sukey. "No one is. And I will do as I choose. If I choose this, it is because it is my free will – not because you want it or he does not! And yes, my lord, it does tempt me, it tempts me very much indeed. I

357

do not really want to go to Mr and Mrs Hall. I was dreading it, to tell you the truth, absolutely dreading it."

"I shall leave you to discuss it," said Lord Rothborough.

"There is nothing to discuss!" Felix said. "This is a ridiculous idea!"

"Good day, ma'am," said Lord Rothborough, taking her hand and kissing it. "Please do not hesitate to write to me if you are in any difficulty."

He left, and Felix said again, "There is nothing to discuss."

"No, because he is suggesting something you do not want! Forget what I might want, won't you?"

"I cannot allow this!" Felix said. "And what are you thinking, truly?"

"I am thinking that marriage is a prison that two people make for themselves before they have any idea of the other's character. If I had been my husband's mistress – well, who knows what misery might have been prevented! I was never so wretched as when I was married, and if I had known I could end it, just simply walk away, that would have been better. This way, if it does not work, then there is an end to it!"

"Marriage is not a prison."

"It can be! It can be the most wretched state. Believe me. Your father knows that! That is why he suggested this, I am sure of it. And you should be thankful he cares enough about you to make sure you are not locked up. I think he wants you to be happy," she said.

"And so he suggests I ruin you!" Felix said.

"There is nothing to ruin, I have told you that before. I am not the virtuous girl you think I am," she said, with a great sigh. "How is it he can see that and you can't?"

"Because I love you?"

"And that sort of love, your sort of love, is blind."

"Unlike his sort of love, I suppose?"

"He knows the world, and he's had his heart broken a fair

few times, I imagine. And he's married to a woman he doesn't love, from what I have heard. He knows what can happen between a man and a woman, how the milk can go sour!"

"I am beginning to think you would rather be *his* mistress than my wife!" Felix said. "Go on, run after him, why don't you? He would take you just like that! I dare say this is why he has brought up this whole disgusting proposition, so that he can take you for himself! 'Do not hesitate to write to me'! For the Lord's sake!"

"That settles it!" said Sukey. "I am going to Cheshire and you can go to the devil, Felix Carswell! And don't think you can write to me!"

~

Giles finished the last page of Woodward's transcripts with a sigh.

Even with a careful translation, they were not easy to unravel. The documents were, as they had guessed before, a collection of gossipy letters to and from individuals with strange titles and names. They covered the everyday concerns of what appeared to be the planter classes in Santa Magdalena, particularly the Martinez family and their many relations. He now knew about the state of various crops (including a disastrous tea plantation), the smuggling of slaves from the French West Indies, and who was marrying whom and the dowries involved down to the last Santa Magdalenean half gold dollar. He had learnt a little more about Dona Blanca and her charitable activities (she had founded a hospital and two orphanages) and also about President Martinez and his reforms. He had offended the clergy on occasion with his modernising zeal, it appeared, which was a concern for his third cousin – a pious, prosy individual called Don Almerigo

359

who was the author of at least half the letters. The family honour was of great importance to him and little fragments of information about the Martinez family were scattered about the letters, and also that of the Ramirez family, who were an impoverished cadet branch, regarded with great disdain by Don Almerigo. Don Luiz, the Chancellor, was painted as a thorough villain, a jumped-up peasant who was only in favour by grace of the President. *"Why our cousin the President put that man in power will remain one of the great mysteries of this age,"* Don Almerigo wrote to his brother in the monastery. *"We must pray that he does not live to regret it."*

He may well have done, Giles thought, and possibly died for it. For after the assassination and the change of government there was this, written again by Don Almerigo: *"I have spoken to a man, who is prepared to swear that he saw Don Luiz Ramirez in clandestine conversation with the agitator Christobal Rejados four days before the assassination of President Martinez, and that Rejados then instructed one of his men to carry out the assassination."*

Yet, Giles thought, looking through the letter again, *"A man who is prepared to swear that"* was a troubling phrase for anyone looking for hard evidence. Even allowing for formality of language and an element of mistranslation, those words seemed like a deliberate side-step away from the truth. Don Almerigo did not bother to specify who the man was and Giles' supposition was that he was merely transmuting rumour into something that sounded like evidence. He wanted his brother to believe that Don Luiz was intimately associated with the assignation.

The sum of the letters were damaging to Don Luiz's reputation. They would certainly stoke rumours, but there was so much hearsay and bias that they would not represent a real threat to his position. Any adept politician could deflect such accusations. Then why had Dona Blanca been so insistent they remain hidden? Perhaps she imagined the contents to be more explosive and more useful to her than they were, or perhaps he, as an outsider who had no knowledge of all the plots and cliques, could not possibly know of their real value. He even wondered if they might not be some elaborate fabrication by the Martinez family to discredit Ramirez. He began to doubt the very existence of Don Almerigo.

It was a mystery, and he got up from his chair, ruminating over it all. He would need an excellent pretext to talk to both Ramirez and Dona Blanca about this, and that was going to require some contrivance.

Chapter Forty

"What I propose is this," said Major Vernon, as they drove away from Ardenthwaite to Stanegate the following morning. "We speak to Ramirez first – nothing confrontational. I shall say I want his account of Edgar merely for the sake of my enquiries, and no mention of jewellery at this stage – yes?"

Felix was scarcely listening, but he nodded.

"And then there is the matter of that other letter, the one we found at Mr Bryce's. I think he will still have it safe somewhere – at least I hope he does. Perhaps that is the key that unlocks the others. By the way, you had better take these." He took the dispatch case from inside his coat. "Since they were entrusted to your keeping."

Felix took the case from him.

"And," Major Vernon went on, picking up the blue bound folio that lay on the seat between them, "you might want to glance over the translation. It would be useful if you could. I have underlined some of the more relevant passages. It will be a distraction for you."

Felix took up the folio and unfastened the bows. He did not feel like reading, but he supposed he should make a show of it.

"I do not need distraction," he said. "Whatever gave you that impression?"

"Forgive me," said the Major in that mild way of his that never failed to hit at Felix's weakest spots. "Oh, and I forgot to mention, I had a letter from O'Brien yesterday. He has heard a good account of Mr and Mrs Hall. They are apparently excellent people – Quakers. She will not be treated like a servant there. It is a good place for her."

"And that is supposed to comfort me?" he said.

"Yes," said Major Vernon. "I for one am glad to think that she will be in good circumstances. We are all going to miss her – not just you."

Felix heard the reproach and it annoyed him.

"If you don't mind, sir, that is a subject I would rather not pursue just now," he said.

"As you wish," said Vernon.

In fact, he would have liked very much to pursue it. He wanted more than anything to unburden himself about all that had happened the previous day. He had been on the verge of it that night after dinner, but the Major had retired early, and then his father had insisted on a game of chess. This had been an interminable misery, to the extent he had invented a headache and gone to bed early himself, only to lie tossing and turning on the rack of physical longing and pierced through with a thousand swords of anguished love.

In the small hours he had got up and dressed, intending to go to her room and talk to her, only to realise he had neither the courage nor the least idea what to say to her to make it right. Was that the bitter truth of it all now – that there was no future, no getting back to the ecstasy of that moment when she had pressed against him, her arms about his neck?

He longed to speak of it, but he was afraid that Major Vernon would give him no hope. That was the long and the short of it.

He stared down at the first letter and the carriage rolled on towards Stanegate.

~

For once, fate had played him a useful card. Giles could not quite believe it. For there, at Mr Bryce's fencing rooms, where they had first called intending to retrieve the document they had found behind the picture, was Don Luiz Ramirez in person.

He had apparently brought his two sons for a fencing lesson with Mr Bryce. Don Luiz sat perched on one of the benches, watching them intently, occasionally giving some direction in Spanish. He was also dressed for fencing, and clearly actively engaged in the lesson. But the moment he caught sight of Giles and Carswell standing in the doorway, he came to greet them.

"I wonder if he is still after that paper," Giles murmured. "I hope Mr Bryce tucked it away."

"Perhaps, sir, you might care for a bout or two?" Don Luiz said.

"Major Vernon will not be fencing today," said Carswell. "He is a convalescent."

Giles could not deny the sense of this. Don Luiz would have made a formidable opponent in the best of circumstances. Yet he wished he might accept the challenge. There was something about seeing the flash of the foils in the sunshine that made him recall the intense pleasure he had had in the sport when younger. It had grown to be more than pleasure, but a careful and ritualised release from anger and frustration.

Perhaps it might help to control the foul cloud of anger that was brewing inside him, poisoning his sleep. Last night he had jolted into wakefulness from the most vivid and painful nightmare, a repetition of one he had experienced now for several nights running. He had found himself acting as the hangman at the execution of Lady Warde, standing there with the rope in his hands while a clergyman read the prayers. Fortunately he had woken before he had actually put the noose around her neck, but the texture of the hemp against his fingers remained, as did a feeling of desire mingled with horror. He had lain there shivering, his heart pounding so violently that he thought he was about to die of apoplexy. Mercifully it had passed, and morning had come, with a sort of fitful sleep. But the memory lingered on to disgust him.

"Oh, I don't know," said Giles, picking up a foil and enjoying the feel of it in his hand. "It is very moderate exercise – especially if Don Luiz is prepared to indulge me a little? It will not be great sport for you, sir, but perhaps, in memory of your cousin, a most expert fencer?"

Don Luiz bowed.

"It would be an honour," he said.

"My kit is still here, Bryce?"

"Yes, sir," said Bryce.

"I really do not think I can advise this," said Carswell.

"Indulge me, Mr Carswell," said Giles, strolling towards the dressing room.

Carswell followed him.

"Sir, you are not fit enough for this," he said when they were alone.

Giles pulled off his coat.

"It will only be for a few minutes and I don't mean to be anything but a feeble opponent," he said. "I have no intention of attempting to win. I want to put Don Luiz at his ease, and what better way than letting him thrash me in front of his sons?"

"Are you sure you can bear to do that?" said Carswell. "Your instincts may not allow you to hold back."

Giles glanced at him, a little unsettled that Carswell should read him so well.

"Oh, I think I have them well tamped down at present," Giles said.

"It is just as well it is a game," said Carswell, handing him his chamois jacket. "And no more than a quarter hour of it. Yes?"

"That will be more than adequate," said Giles.

He planned to show Don Luiz that he was no threat and

a fellow sportsman so that he would talk comfortably to him about the acquisition of the bracelet. If he allowed himself to be defeated, he would not seem to be an enemy.

But when he took up his position on the piste, he did feel the fierce urge to play to win, and preserve his honour. To make a plan was one thing, but suddenly he felt like throwing it to the wind.

Don Luiz matched him in height, but he had a highly developed physique that the tight fencing jacket displayed to some advantage. Giles was glad he was not engaging him in a bare knuckle fight. However, bulk and muscle were not necessarily to a fencer's advantage: agility and a nimbleness gave a lighter man an edge, a fact which Giles, in his youth, had exploited to some effect. It was not entirely a lost cause to think of winning, even in his present enfeebled state.

But fencing was a mental sport as well as a physical one, a game of chess played with swords, and he was about to face a practised politician. Don Luiz was the possible mastermind behind frauds and assassinations and he could, no doubt, project a dozen causes and effects simultaneously. That gave him a striking advantage.

He made for a fascinating opponent. It excited Giles to be standing there, waiting to begin. He decided to make a good show of resistance. He could not simply roll over like a dog. Don Luiz needed to see both his submission and his strength. That way he would gain the greatest respect.

The little boys were watching them keenly. A handsome pair of children, and no doubt objects of great paternal pride. Edward would have been about the age of the elder one, he thought. Then, quite unbidden, an image of Laura holding Edward in her arms half an hour after his birth came into his mind. It had been when he had come in to see them both together for the first time, and how in the silence of the early morning they had sat together, the three of them, in a sort of delirium of happiness that he had never known before or since. Edward was wide awake and looking at him with the strange wisdom of the newborn child, as if his character was fully formed, and that each tiny gesture, each wide-eyed stare, formed his part of the conversation.

Then his ghosts, Laura and Edward, took possession of him and he longed for them to be alive. But he knew that they were lost to him forever.

This knowledge brought an intense pain with it, as acute as if Don Luiz had advanced on him and stabbed his sword straight into his stomach. With the pain came anger that it should be so, and that drove him now, banishing the uncomfortable languor of the last few weeks and filling him with a violent energy that had him twitching on the piste.

"En garde!"

He engaged and attacked Don Luiz as if his life depended on it, as if the foils were cutlasses and there were no masks or leather jackets to protect him. He wanted to see blood – or rather, he was seeing blood already.

Don Luiz countered well enough, but Giles soon realised, with mounting satisfaction, that he had him on the back foot. He had no doubt expected something more mannerly, more restrained, not such a show of raw aggression, and he had no time to adjust his strategy. Giles scored a hit in moments and demanded they launch at once into the next bout, pressing the advantage he had already established. This time he determined to yield, but only just, giving Don Luiz the illusion that he still had a chance to win. And just as Giles hoped, Don Luiz, having won his bout, at once became a touch cocky. The final bout went just as he had wished: Giles made his hit and claimed his victory.

He could, in fact, have gone so far as to knock the foil from Don Luiz's hand, but decided that would be ungracious, especially in the presence of the children.

He pulled off his mask and bowed.

"Thank you, sir," he said, but it was a struggle to find the breath to speak. He realised that he had pushed himself too hard. He turned and made his retreat to the dressing room.

Carswell, who was lounging by the door, stared at him questioningly.

"I changed my mind," Giles said, with all the nonchalance he could manage.

He staggered through to the dressing room, threw down his gloves and foil, and struggled to get out of his jacket which now was intolerably tight. He stripped off his shirt and sat down on the bench, breathless and sweating, wishing he had a pail of water to tip over himself. The effort had been greater than he thought. He felt weak with exhaustion now, but as the door to the dressing room opened, he reached for another towel and attempted to look a little more composed. It was just as well, for it was Don Luiz.

Don Luiz made a slight bow.

"You fight, sir, like a true warrior." Giles managed a gracious nod. "But I do trust you have not made yourself ill, for the sake of my sport."

"As I said, it was in memory of Don Xavier. We could not disgrace his memory, sir, could we?"

Don Luiz bowed again and began to get out of his own kit.

"I am lucky to have run across you," Giles said, when he had cooled off a little. He reached for his shirt and pulled it over his head. "I wanted to speak to you anyway, sir. You may be able to help me in a little professional business of mine."

"Of course. I am your servant, sir."

"I believe you may have had some dealings with a man who was recently murdered."

"Oh?"

"Nothing to alarm you, sir, I assure you. We have the culprit. No, I am just making my case watertight. Justice must be done."

"Indeed, sir, it must. So how may I assist?"

He was now standing at the looking glass, rearranging his cravat. Giles remained on his bench, still not feeling equal to standing.

"I have been informed – and believe me, I shall use this knowledge with discretion – that you were present at a dog fight at Byrescough on the night of the fifteenth."

"Explain a little further, sir, if you please?" said Don Luiz, glancing at him.

"The thing is, sir, you may not be aware of this, but recent legislation has outlawed such traditional gatherings in this country. If it were to emerge you attended such an event it would perhaps be a little embarrassing for a man in your position, or perhaps, I should say, in your future position?"

Now Don Luiz came and sat down opposite him.

"I had heard something to this effect," he said. "A regrettable piece of legislation, I think, sir, to deny the common countryman his entertainments. Now, might I ask how you heard I was there?"

"I saw you myself," Giles said.

"You did. Ha! How interesting."

"You may be assured of my discretion, as I said."

"Because you wish for mine, perhaps?" said Don Luiz with a laugh. "I see you are a sportsman, Major Vernon. It is a shame I did not know you then – it would have been interesting to hear your opinions, and perhaps lay a wager or two with you."

"Those Irish dogs were impressive," said Giles.

"Yes! How I would like to take such a pair of hounds back with me to Santa Magdalena, and a couple of bitches too. But alas, I will have no leisure."

"That, as I said, I had heard also."

"You are a well-informed man, Major Vernon," Don Luiz said, laying his palms down on his massive thighs and looking at him carefully. "This murdered man?"

"Yes, I saw you in his company. Fellow named John

Edgar. You were drinking together – with two young women as well, I could not help observing."

"Edgar? I am not sure I remember."

"You remember the girls, surely," Giles said. "I do. A dark-haired girl in a pink dress and the other, small and pretty, with nice white teeth. She would have been my choice," he added.

Don Luiz exhaled.

"If I did speak to him, how does it help you?"

"Edgar was a criminal," said Giles, "and I was hoping he might have made a proposition to you, offered you something for sale? Any information you can give me will be of great assistance, sir."

"I do vaguely remember the man," he said. "But that is all. I am sorry, sir, sorry not to be able to help."

~

Felix followed Bryce into his little office where, without saying another word, Bryce handed over the letter.

"I'd better go and see if the Major is all right," said Felix, tucking the letter into his coat. The Major's display of bravado had been impressive but alarming.

"I will make him some tea," said Bryce.

Don Luiz was just leaving the dressing room as Felix went in. He gave a civil bow and said, "Perhaps you gentlemen would honour us by joining us for luncheon? I know that my sister-in-law would like to repay your kindness to my late cousin."

"Yes, we would be honoured," said Major Vernon.

Major Vernon was sitting down, dressed only in his shirt. His colour was high and his skin was glazed with sweat. His gaze, in addition, was a little glassy. Felix sat down beside him, and took his pulse and checked his temperature. He was relieved to find that both were settling to normality.

"I needn't have wasted my breath," Major Vernon said. "He admitted to nothing."

"Oh, I don't know," said Felix. "Hasn't he just invited us into the lion's den?"

"True," said Major Vernon. "We can have another tilt at the lists."

"I have the letter," Felix added.

"Excellent. I only wish I had a clean shirt."

Chapter Forty-one

When they arrived at The Queen's Hotel, they were met in the hall by none other than Dona Blanca.

"I must speak to you both alone," she said. "Come, we do not have much time."

With which she hurried them outside into the gardens again, and led them briskly down a path to one of the secluded bowers in which they had talked the other day.

"This will have to do. When Don Luiz said he had seen you both this morning, and invited you to lunch, I was alarmed. I think Lord Rothborough's visit the other day was most dangerous. He may have guessed that there is an important connection between us," she said glancing at Felix. "If that is known, it will cause me great difficulty."

"You do not trust him to be discreet about it?" Major Vernon said.

She shook her head.

"I have not trusted him for some time. Even before my husband's death, I was wary of him, although Juan trusted him. In fact, Juan trusted him too much."

"And yet you decided to travel with him?" Felix said.

"I was not yet certain. I am still not. I could not afford to break from him until I was. That dispatch case which I gave you may have the evidence I need. I hope you still have it safe?"

"I have it here," said Felix tapping his coat.

"I wish you did not!" she said.

"I should tell you, ma'am," said Major Vernon, "that we have both read those documents."

"I see," she said. "So you know what my suspicions are."

"About the death of your husband?" Major Vernon said. "I understand a little, but it is hard for me to form a clear picture."

"It is a complex business," she said. "I have never believed that the man who murdered him was anything but a hired assassin. I spoke to him on the night before his execution. He was a devil, but he was in the pay of another devil."

"And you think that devil might be Don Luiz?" said Major Vernon.

"Perhaps. So what do you think of them?" she said. "As evidence, I mean?"

"It's a little hard to judge," Major Vernon said. "They paint a clear picture of a conspiracy, and Don Luiz is certainly implicated in it. But a great deal is hearsay – and without first hand accounts from witnesses, it is difficult to pin anything on him."

She nodded and sighed.

"This has been the problem all along. He is cunning. And poor Xavier risked so much to get those to me. I ought never to have confided my fears to him. He should have stayed with his order, and he might still be alive, instead of dying alone, so wretchedly far from his home."

"Mr Carswell was with him," Giles pointed out.

"Yes, of course," she said. "And that strikes me as the strangest thing of all. I had not expected my prayers to be answered in such a fashion. What is the lesson in that for me?"

"There is another letter," Felix said, reaching into his coat. "Don Xavier hid it behind a picture at Mr Bryce's fencing rooms. Perhaps this is the one you need to settle the matter for once and for all."

He took out the document and handed it to her. Her hand touched his as they did, and he wondered at her strength and calmness in the face of such impossible intrigues.

"Perhaps," she said. "Excuse me while I look at this."

She sat down on a rustic bench and began to read the letter.

"You will need some time; I shall go and stall Don Luiz," Giles said. "You stay here, Carswell."

Felix sat at the far end of the bench as she continued to read. She glanced at him for a moment and then went on with her reading. He stared ahead of him, wondering what might happen if Major Vernon failed to keep Don Luiz at bay.

At length she folded the letter and held it out to him.

"It is best you keep it with the others," she said.

"What did it say? Is it of use?"

"It may be," she said.

"So what will you do? Surely you should detach yourself from him now, for your own sake? Lord Rothborough has heard Don Luiz is peddling a fake gold mine to get support for his coup. You can't associate with him any longer, surely, if that's true?"

"That mine is not fake," she said, with a sigh. "That is one of my difficulties. My husband commissioned the survey from Herr Valk. It is an impeccable piece of work. We made sure it was, and dear Lord, we were so happy when we saw it first, to know how much it would help the country! But it was our downfall. I think that was the reason Juan had to die. Luiz could not resist such a prize." She pressed her face to her hands for a moment. "I wish I could walk away, but I can't."

"You can," said Felix. "You must."

She uncovered her face and reached for his hand, and squeezed it for a moment before letting it go. "Oh, how sweet it would be to stay here forever, to turn my back on it all, but it is quite impossible." She gazed at him, long and hard. "I never dared dream that you would have grown so handsome. You were such a beautiful child – but now – and even with this!" Her finger traced the scar on his cheek. "However did you come by that?"

"It's a long story and not a pleasant one," he said, as lightly as he could.

"Oh dear. I hope you do not have too many of those," she said. "I hope life is kind to you." He gave slight shrug, and looked away from her searching eyes.

"I have all I need," he managed to say.

"That's a troubling answer," she said.

"Please don't be troubled on my account," he said.

"I can hardly prevent it," she said. "Can I? I have never stopped loving you, Felix, not for a moment. Every day I have thought of you, and wondered and longed, and now here you are, looking stoop-shouldered and wretched!"

He flushed a little at the warmth of this and found himself speculating what sort of life it would have been for him, for them both, had she not given him over to Lord Rothborough – to have grown up her son in that shifting, ambiguous world, where plenty reigned at one moment and poverty another. Martinez would never have married her with a little bastard in tow, that was certain. His presence would have ruined all her chances of respectability, and his own life would have been equally blighted. That they should now be strangers was the price she had paid to save them from that.

He straightened himself a little and said, "It's nothing, really – please don't worry about me. You have already done so much for me. More than anyone should have to do, in fact."

She smiled briefly at that and got to her feet.

"We should go in," she said. "They'll be wondering where I am."

"There is something else you should know," Felix said. "It might help you. That bracelet that Dona Clara is wearing – the one with the rubies on it." She nodded. "It was stolen from Holbroke and we think Don Luiz bought it from a fence, knowing it was stolen. Major Vernon could arrest Don Luiz for buying stolen goods and make the charge stick, I'm sure of it."

"Oh, is that where it came from?" she said.

"Yes. Will that not help you?"

"It might," she said.

"It would raise a great many questions about his general conduct. It will make a certain amount of noise, and with luck, lose him what support he has garnered. But he needs to be made to admit it."

"That is the great difficulty," she said. "He never admits to anything."

"But something might be contrived," said Felix. "In fact, I have an idea of what might be done to catch him out."

"You must not do anything foolish," she said. "Please."

"It won't be foolish," he said. "And I must do something. Your life might be in danger."

She seemed to reflect on what he had said for a long moment. Then she laid her hands on his shoulders briefly, and said, "If I am not allowed to trouble myself about you, then you must do the same for me."

He did not know how to answer this and she gave him no chance. "Come," she said, and they began to walk back towards the hotel.

A moment later, Major Vernon appeared, coming down the path to find them.

"I've excused ourselves from lunch," he said. "You are right, ma'am, he is interested in Mr Carswell and asking a great many questions. I have deflected him for now, I think, but I judged it better that he does not lay eyes on him just now."

"That is for the best," said Dona Blanca. "I will go straight up. Good day, gentlemen, and thank you," with which she hurried away.

"What was in the letter?" Major Vernon asked.

"Nothing startling, it seems. But that gold mine is real."

"It is?"

"She thinks that is why her husband was murdered. For

the gold."

"That makes perfect sense."

"Don Luiz may murder her yet," Felix said. "If he knows what she knows she does not stand a chance. We must do something. I've had an idea about the bracelet."

"Yes?"

"Obviously he will not admit to it being fenced. He is too wily for that. But the fact is, he has done it once and might be persuaded to do it again. What if we suggest to him that there is another to match it and at a better price? Could we tempt him into a compromising situation?"

"That's a good thought. Dona Clara was there just now, and she was still wearing it. She is clearly infatuated with it. Perhaps she is the one we should be tempting? If she were to hear that there is another? I wonder how we could contrive this. There must be a way, I am sure of it. But first, let's go and get something to eat. I need to sit down."

They went into the coffee room of the hotel and settled themselves in a quiet corner.

Felix was glad of the chance to gather his own thoughts. His conversation with Dona Blanca had unsettled him. He could not understand how he was supposed to feel towards her, or how he could feel anything but confusion. She was familiar and yet so strange to him.

They had just finished their lunch and Felix was wondering if the Major would allow him to light a cheroot, when a man came running into the coffee room and asked, in a very agitated manner, "Is there a doctor here? There has been –" He broke off, seeing Felix rise from his seat.

"I am," he said. "What is the trouble?"

"Thank God!" said the man. "Will you come at once, sir? There has been a terrible accident."

Chapter Forty-two

Giles went with Carswell, presenting his own credentials to the man, who turned out to be the hotel manager.

"This way," he said, leading them out onto the south side of the hotel and the broad terrace opening from it. At the far end were two men, crouching by a body. They had both removed their hats.

Carswell ran the last distance towards them, and throwing himself on his knees, began to check for any signs of life.

"I believe the gentleman is —" began the manager as they drew nearer.

"Don Luiz Ramirez," said Giles. His form was unmistakable, large and muscled, but now lying prone like a giant felled in a nursery tale.

Carswell rested back on his heels, frowning.

"Nothing?" Giles said.

"Nothing," Carswell said. "He's gone." He slid his hand under the dead man's neck. "Fracture of the third vertebra, I'd say, judging by the dislocation. No one survives that. If he had fallen differently, there might have been some chance. But that flower trough is the culprit."

"And that," said Giles, pointing up at the intricate ironwork balcony which was now dangling by a single hinge from the side of the building. "It must have given way under his weight."

Carswell looked up at it and grimaced.

"Damnable things. I attended the post-mortem of a woman who was killed by one of those in Edinburgh. She fell onto the railings below. He's had a mercifully quick death. She was alive for some hours." He shuddered.

"I don't understand it," said the manager. "We are very careful about checking them for rust and decay."

"Possibly not careful enough," said Carswell, getting up. He took off his coat and was about to lay it over the corpse.

"One moment," said Giles, catching sight of something on the man's forehead. He squatted down and peered at it. A red mark in the skin, as if something had been pressed hard against it.

He pointed it out to Carswell and said, "Any idea what might have caused that?"

"Not immediately."

"Cover him up," said Giles, turning over various possibilities in his mind. He got up and turned to the gardeners. "Did any of you see what happened?"

"No, sir, we just heard him hit the ground," the elder of them said. "We were working just down there, clipping the hedge, with our backs to the hotel."

"He gave this great cry," said the other. "Chilled me blood, it did. And by the time we got here, he was wheezing away and then he was gone. Just like that, in no more than a snap of your fingers." He shook his head. "God rest his soul."

"You are acquainted with the gentleman, sir?" said the manager to Giles. "And his family?"

Giles could not help sighing slightly, thinking of the dark-eyed boys at the fencing rooms that morning and how this news would hurt them.

"Yes. And I will go and speak to them. They do not seem to be aware that anything has happened. Will you send for a constable? The coroner will need to be informed. Mr Carswell, are you happy to leave him? I think you may be needed upstairs."

"Natural justice?" said Carswell as they climbed the grand staircase.

"Perhaps," said Giles.

They went straight into the suite, into the reception room

where he had so recently made his excuses to Don Luiz, where the candles to the late President still burned before his portrait, and the curtains were drawn. There was no one there.

"Now which room was it?" he said, going to the right-hand door. It opened onto a passageway, with rooms opening on both sides. Mercifully, there was no sign of the women and children.

"That one, I should say," said Felix, and opened the door.

He was right. The sash was pushed right up and the muslin curtains drawn to one side to allow easy access to the balcony. A chair had been placed by the window, and on a small table nearby was a box of cigars.

"So was he in the habit of sitting there with his cigar?" said Giles. "This looks like his dressing room." There was a writing desk with many papers on it.

"And then wandering out onto the balcony with it?" said Carswell, who was at the window looking down.

"You know more about the habits of smokers than I do," said Giles. "But perhaps the ladies objected to him smoking inside."

"How long have they been staying here?" Carswell said. "If he went out more than once or twice a day, a man of his size – it could have seriously damaged the balcony, particularly if it was already in a parlous state. Perhaps it just gave way today – he leant back too far and went toppling back. Dear God."

"Luiz, Luiz?" A woman's voice at the door – it was Dona Clara.

Giles went to the door and opened it, his heart leaden. To have to break such news...

She was with the children and their nursemaid. They had clearly all been out in the gardens at the front of the hotel for a brief post-luncheon stroll, and had therefore seen and heard nothing.

It proved impossible to keep Dona Clara from the

window and seeing the fallen giant on the terrace below. She rapidly became hysterical from the shock and her screams brought the other servants running in, and increased the horror of the revelation. The handsome boys who had been at the fencing lesson stared at him and then at their howling mother.

"Dona Blanca," Giles said to Carswell, who was attempting to calm Dona Clara. "Where is she?"

"We need her," said Carswell. "Where is Dona Blanca?" he said to one of the servants.

One of the boys went running out of the room and Giles followed him, guessing he had gone to fetch her. They crossed the darkened shrine to the President and into the passageway beyond. The boy was about to knock on the door but Giles put his finger to his lips. His mind was filling with uncomfortable thoughts about why she had not at once appeared when Dona Clara began screaming.

"Go back to your mother," he said to the boy.

He knocked but there was no answer. He gently tried the door. It was not locked. He opened it a chink and saw she was there, sitting in a shadowy corner on a low chair.

"May I come in?" he asked, opening the door a little wider. Now he noticed she was holding something but had concealed it in the folds of her black skirts.

She did not answer. Another glance revealed a box lying open on the dressing table. It looked like a pistol case. Was that a weapon she was holding?

He came in a little further without waiting for her permission, and carefully closed the door behind him. He saw the powder flask now and the capper beside it. There was a loaded gun somewhere in this room. Was it a pistol that had made that mark on Don Luiz's forehead?

He came closer to her. She seemed to stiffen as he approached – she was wary, watching him as carefully as he watched her, her breast rising and falling conspicuously. He thought he saw her hand stir. Was she tightening her grip on the pistol?

"Ma'am?" he said.

"Yes?" she said at last.

"Don Luiz is –"

"Dead. Yes," she said. "I know."

"An accident," he said.

"No."

"It looks very like one."

"It was not," she said, and buried her other hand into the folds of her skirt.

"He fell. That balcony was not sound."

"But he would not have gone out there had I not..."

Now she moved her hands, and the folds of stuff fell aside to reveal the gun. Her right hand was firmly on the pistol butt, while the fingers of the left were curled about the barrel, cradling it, as if it were something very precious to her.

"It's loaded, I think?" he said, stepping a little closer. "You should give that to me, ma'am."

She shook her head and lifted it in both hands towards her breast, and so it lay there, rather in the manner of a saint clutching a crucifix in a religious painting.

"Juan gave me this. He taught me to use it, too. He was always more worried for my safety than his own. In fact, he sent all the way to Texas for it. It is the latest thing. It has a revolving chamber. One can shoot five bullets in succession. Quite an instrument for an execution, wouldn't you say?"

"Ma'am, give that to me, I beg you."

"No, I am not done with it yet," and with shaking hands she aimed the gun towards her temple.

"Please," he said softly, edging towards her. "For the love of God, please give me that. That is a worse crime than anything you think you may have done. Please do not. You are afraid, yes, but there is nothing to fear. Let God judge you. Do not judge yourself."

Steeling himself, he reached towards her hand and laying his own over it, pulled it away. She struggled against him but he had the better of her. She yielded, and the pistol tumbled from her hand. It crashed to the floor.

She stared at him, her eyes filling with tears.

"Oh, dear God," she said.

He bent down and picked up the gun. His own hands were trembling and clumsy as he made it safe again – the mechanism was unfamiliar, and the darkened room did not help him.

"I am going to clean this and put it away," he said. "No one saw you with it. This need go no further."

"You would do that?" Her voice was strangled with tears. "A man in your position –"

"The weapon was not discharged. The death was an accident."

She rose to her feet and crossed herself.

"You are an angel, truly," she said.

"No, far from it. It is just..." He found it a little hard to speak. "I find some satisfaction in helping you. Justice is sometimes elusive."

"Yes," she said. "Oh dear Lord, it is. And I lost my patience. That is what happened today. I grew tired of telling myself that I will go back to Santa Magdalena and plunge myself into the dirty politics and the factions, and fight and fight to get justice for my dead husband!"

"Was it something in that letter?"

She nodded.

"It proved without doubt something that I had long suspected. He had been embezzling government funds, over some years, bleeding the country dry. Juan and I knew there was corruption and I always felt it was close at hand, but never could prove it. And then the proof came today, and I had it in my hand, and I could not bear it any more. I wanted it to be over. I came back here and tried to pray for guidance, but there was nothing. Just this feeling of helplessness."

She broke off and walked across the room, her hands pressed to her face.

"And Ramirez was being despicable!" she went on. "You had him so riled up, Major Vernon. You had beaten him at fencing, and then refusing to come to lunch. He was so suspicious! He started needling me, asking all these questions about you and Felix. Then he said that Felix was the image of Lord Rothborough and wasn't that interesting? I knew then that one of his spies had found out that I had made enquiries about Felix and he was far ahead of me in the game. I knew I had to do something. Something snapped inside me. I couldn't bear it any longer. So I came in here and got out the gun. And I went back to him in his study where he was smoking one those disgusting cigars, and –"

"You did not fire the gun," he said.

"But I meant to. I wanted to. I threatened him. I had it pressed to his forehead. That's why he went back out onto the balcony. I forced him out there."

"And the balcony was unsound and he fell," Giles said. "We all make mistakes. All of us."

"You too?" Her hand was on his arm.

"My wife was killed," Giles said. "Not three weeks ago. It was that day when you were first with Lord Rothborough. I found out who was responsible and I tried to force a confession out of them, but I lost my temper and overplayed my hand. I failed and now I have ruined my case. Because of my actions, Laura's killer will probably never be punished."

He put the last piece of the gun back into the box and shut the lid.

"If you gave me a gun and an opportunity..." he said, and brushed his fingers across the top of the box. There was an engraved plate bearing an inscription in Spanish. "What does that say?" he said.

"It says, 'From Juan to his little dove Blanca.'" She gave a sigh. "So what shall I do now?"

"Go to Dona Clara and the children," he said. "They will need you."

She nodded and went to the glass, where she wiped away the tears and adjusted her lace cap. He opened the door for her and she walked past him, her carriage now that of a queen about to make an entrance. In short, it was a miracle of self-possession.

He followed her the few paces into the central reception room. The little boy who had shown him the way had not gone back to his mother but was standing there, waiting for Dona Blanca. He ran towards her as she came in, and she fell to her knees and took him into her arms, whispering to him in Spanish and letting him cry out his heart.

That, he told himself firmly, was enough to justify his actions.

Chapter Forty-three

"That mark on his forehead," said Felix. "I have an idea what it might have been."

"It was merely a blemish," Major Vernon said, with a suspicious lack of curiosity.

They were driving back to Ardenthwaite at a little past seven. It felt like midnight.

"It is the sort of mark a pistol might make. What if he were forced out onto the balcony and then fell?"

Major Vernon did not answer. Instead he began to massage his temples.

"I noticed a box on Dona Blanca's dressing table," Felix went on. "That looked like a pistol case."

"What on earth would she be doing with a pistol case on her dressing table?" Major Vernon said. "It was, no doubt, just a box."

"Did you not notice it, sir, when you were talking to her in there?"

"Sometimes there are questions that we should not ask aloud. That you certainly should not. Draw what conclusions you like, but keep them to yourself. For the sake of the lady in question, for your own sake." Major Vernon made a gesture that suggested the sweeping away of some debris from a table top. "Please?"

It was not a command. It was a pained request, almost a supplication.

Felix felt uneasy. What exactly had passed between Dona Blanca and Major Vernon? They had been alone together for a strangely long interview.

He, for his part, had been astonished by her composure

on learning the news. She was shaken, it was clear enough, but the needs of the others had been her first priority. She had brought a sort of order to the whirlwind of hysterical chaos that Dona Clara's extreme distress had unleashed into those about her. She knew how to deal with them all – be comforting and calm, give orders and make arrangements. She became the centre of authority. It was easy to see how she had won her reputation as a leader.

He had not exchanged a word with her alone. He had only been able to take a public leave of her with all the usual formality, and that had felt entirely inadequate. He had been tempted to run back to her, afraid for her in some fashion, his heart stirred up in a way he could scarcely deal with.

The Major had leant back into the corner and was massaging his temples again with his hand.

"Your head, sir – is it troubling you again?"

"A little."

"I can give you something for that when we get back."

"Thank you."

He did not raise the subject again on the drive back, and they spoke little more. The Major either slept or feigned sleep, and Felix was left with his own turbulent thoughts as the carriage crawled back to Ardenthwaite. Through the window he saw the country fade into a blackness that matched his own mood. As they finally turned up towards the house and plunged into the shadowy tunnel of elms, he wondered if he could bear to go in. Could the carriage not simple rattle and jolt on for ever into some kind of oblivion where it was not necessary to act or think or, worse still, feel?

For Sukey would be gone the day after next. She would have packed her boxes already. It was too much to hope that she had done it with tears in her eyes. She would have no tears for him, not after what he had said.

How easy it was to break a thing: a neck, a back, a heart. A flower trough and a faulty balcony could kill a man, and a careless show of temper could break a woman's heart in half. How could he have said that to her?

He remembered her misery at hitting him, her horror at herself for what was only a little slap, which he had deserved. But what he had done was far worse.

He followed Major Vernon into the house and went with him upstairs. His condition was a little patchy but nothing to alarm. His duty there discharged, he did not go downstairs as he ought to the little parlour where his parents would be sitting after dinner, but into the library where he intended to smoke many cheroots and drink brandy until he fell asleep in his chair.

And there he found Sukey, sitting in the large tapestry-covered wing chair, where he had himself sat for many hours, nursing his own wounds. She had huddled herself up in it, her knees drawn up under her chin, her skirts wrapped tightly about her and looking wretched and yet so lovely that he was in that moment both miserable and full of impossible hope.

She stumbled up from the chair at the sight of him, and was at once making for the door.

"I thought you would be downstairs," she said, slipping past him.

"I can't face them," he said.

He wanted to catch her arm and stop her from going. But he did not quite dare. Instead he blocked her way and gestured back to the chair.

"Please, let me apologise, at least? Before you go." She stood there knotting her fingers, avoiding his gaze. "Please?"

At length she nodded, and then went back to the chair and sat down with more decorum this time, perching herself on the edge, ready for flight. Felix was minded to kneel down by her, but thought that he ought not alarm her with such a dramatic gesture. So he took a chair and placed it nearby. He found he too was perching, his nerves now making him shake. He had the sense that this was fate giving him an excellent hand and that he must play it right or all was lost.

"What I said to you," he said, "was unforgivable, and I do not expect you to forgive me for it. Please just understand how much I regret every word of it and I am so sorry, so very sorry —"

"I do forgive you," she said, and then sighed. "Of course I do. What you said was perfectly understandable given what I had just said. I deserved it."

"No, no, you didn't, not at all," he said, pulling his chair closer. "How could you have deserved that?"

"Because I shocked you. And you obviously had not even let such an idea cross your head, and I had been... well, thinking of it even before your father mentioned it."

The honesty of this was humbling.

"I have had such ideas before," he said. "In relation to other women. But with you, it just seemed..." He broke off. "I want you as my wife, Sukey, not my mistress."

"Then we had better never see each other again," she said. "Because I can't be your wife and life is not a fairytale, is it?"

"No," he said, thinking of the day's events. "No, it certainly is not." He took a deep breath. "Maybe we must take our happiness where we can find it. Maybe..." He reached out for her hand. "I can't bear the thought of never seeing you again, and if this is the only way, then..." He bent over and kissed her hand. "We will do it."

He straightened and looked her in the face. There were tears in her eyes and she nodded solemnly and pressed her hand to his cheek.

"We shall," she said. "Somehow or other."

Chapter Forty-four

"Are you not supposed to be resting, Major Vernon?" said Sukey Connolly, meeting him in the hall, dressed to go out.

"I have got my taste for freedom again," he said, taking up his hat. It was true that his room had felt like a prison last night. His mind and spirits had been churned up but his trains of thought had been curiously productive. The headache that tormented him for some hours seemed to have made his faculties work harder. "I am only driving into Market Craven to do a little business. Holt will be with me."

"Have you told Mr Carswell?" she said.

"I haven't seen him yet this morning. Therefore he cannot forbid me, can he?"

"No," she said with a smile. "He cannot."

"Do you have everything you need for your journey?" Giles said. "Do you have any commissions for me?" She shook her head. "It is a shame you have to leave so early, but I understand that such good opportunities do not come along often. Your brother-in-law was very to the point about it in his last letter."

"He would be," she said. "It's because my sister gets anxious about me. I've always been something of a bother to her, I suppose. They are glad to know I'll be out of trouble." Then after a moment she added, "You've not mentioned to him the business with Mr Carswell?"

He shook his head. "That was not my business to tattle about."

"Thank you," she said and glanced away, her expression a mixture of pain and embarrassment.

It was a sorry business, but it was to be hoped that

separation would, in time, lessen the attachment. Yet it was a cruel remedy and he wished, for both their sakes, it could be otherwise. He knew he would feel her absence keenly. She was a kindred spirit.

They spoke no further, for Holt came in, announcing that the gig was ready.

Market Craven was a picturesque town in the process of slithering from pleasant obscurity into something quite new and altogether dismal. Four extremely large textile mills had been established there within three years, and the place showed abundant signs of all the human misery and vice that came with a supposed advance in prosperity: old stone houses, falling into disrepair and packed to the rafters with the hands who had swarmed into town to find work. The old town sewers were not equal to this and on a fine day at the end of July, the place stank to high heaven. It was far worse than Northminster, where they had begun to address the problem in at least some districts of the city.

"We are a little well-dressed for this, perhaps," Giles said, as Holt drove the gig along a dreary thoroughfare where a ragged populace filled the pavements.

Holt, who took great pride in his appearance, shrugged.

"Those girls were high class tarts, sir," he said. "They didn't climb out of the gutter. No need for us to get into it."

It was Giles' intention that morning to attempt to locate the two prostitutes he had seen with Edgar and Don Luiz at the dog fight. He hoped they might have witnessed the transaction with the bracelet, and perhaps could give some information about its theft. It was a quest that could easily be perfectly futile, but Giles felt he must attempt it.

They turned into a broad street leading to the Market Place where the post office and the principal inns were to be found. Here it was more orderly and prosperous looking.

They left the gig at The Saracen's Head, which was clearly the best inn in the town, and Holt went to make his enquiry in the tap room, while Giles put his own discreet questions to the waiter in the coffee room. Between them they were able to establish where they should go next. The suggestions had been a house in Water Street, and several alleys in the vicinity of the Corn Exchange. Giles elected to investigate the first.

"Ask for Mrs Honeywell," said Holt, grinning broadly.

"That can't be her real name," Giles said. "I hope to God it is not."

The house was shuttered and drowsy looking. Noontide was not the most auspicious time to call, perhaps, but the maid who opened the door to him took in every detail of his appearance with a practised glance and admitted him without hesitation.

She took him upstairs to a large sitting room, where the midday heat was much in evidence, and the sun came in only through chinks in the shutters, making it hard to see anything much. Here sat four females in their wrappers playing cards. Three of them rose at once and left the room, leaving only one at the card table. From her appearance Giles guessed this was Mrs Honeywell. She was handsome, but hard-looking, and she gave him the same careful appraisal as the maid.

"Interesting time to call, sir," she said, gathering up the cards.

"Forgive me. I was bored," he said, sitting down opposite at her. "And I have heard excellent things about this establishment."

"Have you?" she said. "From whom?"

"Acquaintances," he said.

She shuffled the cards with a deft hand.

"And I think I saw some of your young ladies at Byrescough the other week," he added.

She furrowed her brow.

"Perhaps you did," she said after a moment.

"Will you let me have a look?"

"Show me you are in good faith, sir," she said.

He put a sovereign on the table, and her manner visibly softened.

"You will not be disappointed, sir," she said, getting up. She rang a bell. There would be wine coming soon, he knew, and in the rooms beyond, the girls would be getting ready to reappear, in quite a different guise.

He had been in such places before. Indeed at one time he was shamefully familiar with them. He had been inducted into them as a raw ensign and continued, as his finances permitted, until about the age of four and twenty. But then a fellow officer contracted a particularly nasty case of the clap and almost died from it. That had cured him of the habit.

But here, he found that that old fascination resurrected itself, despite his better efforts. He knew that it was a lamentable stain on his character, but one which he could not erase. Although he had a legitimate reason to be there in that stuffy parlour, waiting for the girls to appear, the sordid excitement of it all held him in its claws.

He felt dangerously weak and desirous, as if he were there to make a transaction, not find a witness. His body suddenly craved the distracting pleasures of congress and the brief, stupefying peace that came after.

His wife was dead, taken from him by malicious fate, just as he had begun to know what it was to love her again, and now what was left but the yawning grave? He was wretched and hungry for oblivion, and now the girls came in, their dull wrappers exchanged for more luxurious silk ones. They smiled at him, offering him a salve for his pain. How easy it would be, and how in that moment he craved it, although at the same time his disgust at himself was considerable.

"Would you mind opening the shutter a little?" he said to Mrs Honeywell. "I can't see properly."

She obliged and they all stood blinking as the bright sun filled a portion of the room, catching their rouged cheeks, carefully tweaked ringlets and the trinkets that they wore.

These girls were pretty scraps, plump and clearly not ill-treated, not like the desperate creatures who found their way into the cells at Northminster having been caught soliciting. One of them was most certainly the girl who had been with Edgar and who then went to sit on Don Luiz's knee.

"That one," he said, pointing her out to Madam Honeywell.

The girl led him down the passageway, up a few steps into a room which was dominated by a large bed in glossy mahogany, hung with fleshy pink silk. All the furnishings were quite new and the linen looked spotless. Mrs Honeywell was clearly doing well.

He wondered how much money this little business was pulling in. He would not have thought there was enough money in Market Craven for such a high class operation, but it was a discreet location, and men might come considerable distances for pleasure under the guise of business, especially with the railway. A man would not raise any suspicions with his wife with a journey to such a town. If she was at all upset, she could be pacified by a gift from the fashionable haberdashery in the square next to The Saracen's Head. A large sign had advertised that it sold 'French silks, Italian gloves and all the fashionable novelties.'

"What's your name?" he asked the girl.

"Janey," she said, sitting down on the bed and patting the space beside him. "What's your fancy? I do most things, but if you want anything French it's extra."

He hardly heard what she said. He had noticed she was wearing heeled slippers in pale-blue damask with striped rosettes. They were the double of a pair that Laura had bought in Stanegate. She had been most unwilling to tell him much they had cost, as if she expected him to be angry at her extravagance. Certainly a fashionable novelty, and they had been shockingly expensive, but he had not cared, because her amusement in getting them had been so delightful to him. And they had suited her well. Now the sight of them, on the feet of this strange creature who was offering indecencies for a handful of shillings, threatened to break him. He felt he could have sat down in the armchair and wept from the pain at the sight of them and the thought of their forlorn companions, hidden swiftly away in her boxes by Sukey so that he should not have to see them.

He took a deep breath, mastered himself and said, "I want a word with you."

"Oh," she said. "One of those. You're not a preacher, are you? Talk away, but just spare me the tract. Well, you don't have to. We use them in the privy."

He had to smile at that.

"I'm not a preacher. I saw you at the dog fight at Byrescough," he said.

"Oh, did you? So what?"

"The men you were with – punters, I suppose? A foreigner and a man who cuts shadow pictures."

"How do you know that?" she said, her eyes narrowing. "Who are you?"

"Not your concern," he said. "So, I want to know what happened that evening. Every little detail."

"You really don't want a fuck, then?" she said, plucking at the ribbon of her chemise, exposing a little more flesh to entice him.

He shook his head.

"Tell me about the night of the dog fight. Did you know who those men were?"

"Johnny Edgar and the other, he was something grand and fancy sounding – foreign like you said. Don Loois?"

"And why were you there?"

"The landlord is a friend of the missus. We were all there – it was a bit of a spree, all in all, and the missus was in a good mood, which makes a change, I can tell you. I did go upstairs later with the foreign gent. He was nice enough and he gave

395

me this funny gold coin – the missus has it. I was a bit worried in case it wasn't the real thing but she was happy enough. And I suppose he did have plenty of tin on him, because he bought that bracelet."

"Tell me more," he said, now sitting down beside her.

"Johnny Edgar had it. And I have never seen the like! Lovely thing it was. Lovely. Gawd only knows where it came from," she added with a giggle. "Not the sort of question you want to ask, is it, when you're being asked to model a bracelet?"

"You modelled it?"

"Oh yes. Didn't want to take it off!" she said, laughing. "Rubies, pearls and gold. Though I suppose the rubies were paste, I mean they couldn't have been real, could they?" She looked at him, rather searchingly. "Could they? Oh my God... Was it knocked off, then? What do you know about it? It wasn't yours, was it?"

"Belongs to a friend of mine," Giles said.

"I knew it was hot!" she exclaimed. "And you were watching us all that time? What's your game?"

"Trying to get it back, that's all."

"I can't help you there."

"No, you've been very helpful."

"Have I?" she said, and she playfully reclined herself on the pillows, a practised, enticing move. "Do I deserve a reward?"

The false flattery of the whore, Giles thought; make the fellow feel she wants him – a counterfeit of love. It was extraordinary what money could buy. She adjusted her position a little further, showing him more of the goods and reaching for his hand.

He got up from the bed.

"You'd know this bracelet if you saw it again?" he said.

"Yes."

"And would you be prepared to say what you just said to

some other gentlemen?" She frowned. "I'd make it right with your missus," he added.

"Who are you?" she said, getting up from the bed. "You're not the police, are you?"

"What if I am?" he said.

"Then you shouldn't be poking your nose around here. We have an arrangement. No one bothers us."

"We?" he said.

"The missus," she said. "With his nibs."

"His nibs being?"

"The boss," she said, and then stared at him as if he was being a fool. "Sir Arthur. Your boss, ain't he, if you're a policeman?"

"Yes," Giles said. "But he hasn't told me about this."

"He bloody should have done. Lord knows he's always going on about it, how grateful we should be and all that."

"You know him?" She nodded. "He comes here?"

"Three times a week, without fail." She sniggered. "We draw lots for him. He's such a fussy bugger, no mistake. And he farts." She looked at him narrowly. "Do you really work for him?"

"We're in the same profession, let's put it like that."

"Shame you're not the boss," she said. "We wouldn't be drawing lots for you, we'd be fighting over you." She reached and tried to caress his cheek, at the same time smiling suggestively at him.

"Ah yes," he said, catching her hand. "Take me for a fool, do you?"

"Can't a girl admire a nice-looking gentleman?" she said, wresting her hand free, and catching hold of his lapels, pressing herself against him. "Come now, sir, since you've taken the trouble to come here, you might as well take what's due. I know that you're inclined. I can see that you are." Now, she attempted to lay her hand on the fall of his breeches, and he was obliged to push her away rather sharply.

"Don't worry, I will tell the missus you were more than obliging," he said.

"Suit yourself," she said, and yawned.

Giles made his way back to The Saracen's Head wondering what could be done with the information Janey had given him.

It would not help him a great deal with undermining Lady Warde's monstrous presumption of innocence, but he now had a powerful weapon with which to discredit Sir Arthur.

In fact it would be enough to get him dismissed from his post. It would be a great scandal, enough to raise the question of reform of the county constabulary at the highest level. If the two forces were to be amalgamated, then this might be the moment. Reform in the wake of corruption. Lord Rothborough would be delighted.

The threat of exposure would perhaps be enough to make Sir Arthur sacrifice Lady Warde for his own skin. Should he use the threat of disgrace to make him drop the cause, and press the charges against her? It was rather a devious strategy, useful in the short term, but it did him no credit in the long term. It was not advisable.

He would have to take the longer route.

Sir Arthur would have to go, and if they all came down with him, then so be it. Lord Rothborough would no doubt advise him to look to his own future and seize the chance to take control of both forces, and a year or two ago, he realised he would have had no hesitation in doing so.

But such ambition was anathema to him now. He stood looking into the haberdasher's window by The Saracen's Head, as he waited for Holt. He stared at the lace collars and cuffs and at the Best Quality Fancy Northminster Ribbons, and could only think how short life was, and how fragile.

Holt's reflection, ghost-like, appeared behind him.

"Any luck?" he said, turning.

Holt shook his head and tugged at his collar. He looked

hot and uncomfortable.

"This town is a right midden, sir," he said. "It's a disgrace."

"Yes," Giles said. "I've had enough for today."

"Very glad to hear it, sir. You look like death, sir, and no mistake. This place would give you a fever just to look at it. I'll go and get the gig."

Chapter Forty-five

Felix stood on the platform at Swalecliffe Station, waiting for the train to arrive from Northminster. He had only been there an hour himself, having just got in from Stanegate. It was really remarkable, the possibilities that the new railways allowed a man. Major Vernon had once said they were a gift to the criminal classes, and Felix, feeling something of a criminal himself in that moment, was inclined to agree.

For Sukey would be on the Northminster train. She had not gone to Leeds and thence to Manchester to take up her new position. Instead they had determined on a tryst in Swalecliffe.

The train came steaming in, and the platform was soon filled with passengers and their baggage. He could not see her at first, and he wondered if she had decided at the last moment not to come. Perhaps her courage had failed her.

But there she was, by the luggage van, retrieving her boxes. He ran down the platform towards her, his heart in his throat.

"So the Major didn't ask too many questions about your coming here alone?" she said, as they drove away from the station towards that pleasant lodging where he had stayed previously at Swalecliffe. "I've been sick with worry that he'd insist on coming with you."

"No, he said he was too tired to travel anywhere. But he was delighted with my idea. He thought it very likely that Lady Warde would have left something here."

"Let's hope she has," Sukey said. She glanced out of the carriage window. "Oh, there's the sea! Goodness, this is quite the spot, isn't it?"

"I thought you'd like it," Felix said. "The band plays on the beach in the evening. When we were here before, I wanted to walk on the beach with you and listen to it, and then..." He broke off. "He is not expecting me back until tomorrow. I lied about the trains back." He reached for her hand, wanting the reassurance of it. "I hope there are rooms." He could not bring himself to say a room, but that was all they would need. "It seems very busy today." The promenade on the West Bay was thronged with people.

The cab drew up at the lodging house where they had stayed before.

"Shall I stay here, while you go and see?" Sukey said.

This struck him as a good plan, but the moment his hand was on the door to the house, he wished she was with him. He felt a species of fear he had never experienced before as he walked up to the owner, who was standing at her desk in the broad hall. She remembered him and greeted him politely.

"A single room, Mr Carswell, as before?"

"No, I am with my wife. We should like it for two weeks." He was astonished he got the words out. He thought his voice must sound strange. "Do you have anything suitable, perhaps with a view of the sea?"

"I have just the thing, sir, with a sitting room next door. On the second floor."

"That sounds excellent."

"Here are the terms," she said, handing him a card. "Is that agreeable?"

"Perfectly," he said, glad he had gone to the bank and cashed the large cheque that Lord Rothborough had left for him before he departed for Scotland. It had infuriated him at the time to find it lying on his desk so recently after that terrible scene with Sukey. He had almost ripped it up.

Having settled with Mrs Peel, he went and got Sukey from the cab, and the porter got their bags. Together they went upstairs, in the guise of a married couple, Mr and Mrs

Carswell, to the large comfortable bedroom and well-furnished adjoining sitting room he had so brazenly engaged for two weeks. They made the correct noises of approbation, he gave a tip to the porter, and suddenly they were alone together, in a bedroom washed with brilliant light from the sea. Sukey went into the bay window and gazed out, taking off her bonnet.

Felix sat down on the chaise at the foot of the bed, now feeling violently sick. He stared down at his boots and then up at the ceiling, anywhere but at Sukey, who stood still in the window, gazing out at the sea. He thought of all the times that he had in his fancy imagined himself alone with her on their wedding night, and all that might proceed from that. But he had never dreamt of this awkward terror which now possessed him.

"I am going to change," she said, suddenly breaking the silence. "This dress is not smart enough for here. I don't want to look all wrong."

He glanced at her. She had come away from the window and was unhooking the front of her bodice. She took it off and laid it carefully on a chair, and then took off her skirt. Dressed now in her underclothes she went and opened her box, using a key she retrieved from the embroidered pocket hanging around her waist on a coral-coloured ribbon. This arrangement of things, presumably common to many women, he had never guessed at before. It struck him as delightful that they should keep their secrets in such a manner, hidden from the eyes of men.

He watched as she knelt down and begun to sort through her clothes, bending over the box so that her shift slipped from her shoulders and the pale skin of her back above her shift and stays shone in the brilliant sea light. The same light caught the red in her hair.

His fear was pushed away by sudden, urgent desire. He went to her, and knelt behind her, pressing his lips to her back, smelling her hair, putting his hands about her waist. He pulled her back towards him, his lips on her bare shoulder now. He felt her fingers on his ear and in his hair. He felt her own hot kisses on his skin as she twisted around to face him.

He staggered to his feet and began to strip off his clothes. At the same time she went and sat on the edge of the bed and loosened her stays, an action that transfixed him. When she had removed them and sat there, in only her shift and stockings, she stretched out her hand to him, and doing so, the linen covering her shoulders slipped away further.

He dropped his shirt onto the floor and took her hand. He bent and kissed her, and he dared to press his other hand to her naked breast: warm, rounded and soft.

Now he felt her hand on him, just on his belly, but close to where his now solid member lay tight up against him. It was exquisite and delightful agony to feel her fingertips brush his skin, and then her finger grazed against his member.

A moment later, he had spent himself. Her touch had been too much for him.

Horrified, he scrabbled to find his shirt to cover himself.

"It's my fault," she said, turning away from him so that her disordered, falling hair screened her face. "I shouldn't have... I should have been more modest." And she covered her face with her hands.

He grabbed the rest of his clothes and his portmanteau and fled into the sitting room. He dried himself off with his shirt and then threw it across the room in disgust. He sat down, breathing hard still, his body quite at war with itself, wanting to acknowledge the pleasure of the release but at the same time feeling sick with shame and mortification. Was this some dreadful punishment for them?

He dressed again, getting a clean shirt from his bag and attempting to make himself look respectable. His appearance in the looking glass above the fireplace was not encouraging – he was flushed and his hair wild.

At length he went to the doorway to the other room and

gently pushed it open. Sukey was still lying on the bed. She had rolled herself up in the coverlet and as he came in, she retreated further into it.

He went quietly across the room to retrieve his hat.

"I'd better go to Edgar's," he said.

"Yes, you'd better," she said.

~

Mrs Edgar was not at home – she had gone to visit friends for a few days – but the old aunt, Mrs Carnbee, was. She was still afraid of reprisals and was more than obliging. He had been worried that his authority to search the house might be questioned, but she was happy to allow him to wander where he would.

Lady Warde and her daughter had always taken the two rooms on the second floor. "Our best rooms," she pointed out with pride. Compared to Mrs Peel's house on the Esplanade, they were small and shabby and a great contrast to all the great houses she must have stayed at.

He conducted what he hoped was a thorough search, checking for loose boards and under the mattresses. There was nothing to catch his attention in the first room, and there seemed to be nothing in the second, until he opened the press that was set so high up in the wall that he was obliged to stand on a chair to look into it properly. It contained a carpet bag, carefully closed with a leather strap, on the buckle of which was a padlock. The bag was not stuffed full, but it clearly contained something – it had some weight to it. He wondered if it had belonged to Lady Warde.

He went downstairs carrying it and found Mrs Carnbee at the front door, taking in the post.

"Nowt for me, today!" she said, coming upstairs to meet

him by the parlour door. She held up the letters. "These are all for Mrs Edgar. Nobody ever writes to a poor old woman," she added with a sigh.

"Is there anything that might be from Mrs Abbot?" Felix said. It had occurred to him she might have ventured a letter from Sir Arthur's house.

"This one? I think that's her hand," she said. "I see you found her bag. I remembered it when you went upstairs. I would have come up and told you, but then the postman came."

He looked at the letter she held out to him. The hand was certainly that of Lady Warde.

"May I take this?"

"Aye, you'd better. She won't like it, I dare say, but I think it's for the best. If Mrs Abbot is as wicked as you say, sir." She shook her head. "Now, will you take a cup of tea? I have just made a pot."

He could not find any adequate excuse to refuse her, finding that a strong, sweet cup of tea with cream in it was exactly what he wanted. She made him eat some bread and butter too, which was equally good.

"Let me read your leaves for you," she said, when he had drained his cup. "My mother taught me, and she was considered quite the seer."

He indulged her, realising he was in no hurry to get back to Sukey, for he had still not the slightest idea what he ought to say and do.

"Aha," said the old woman, swirling round the dregs and smiling. "Trouble in love."

It was, of course, very likely that most men of his age could happily agree with such a diagnosis. It was a platitude, a safe generality and he tried to throw it away with a smile.

"I thought as much," she went on, turning the cup again, "trouble in love and a vale of tears." She looked up at him. "But it will all come right in the end, that's clear enough."

He repressed any ungenerous remarks about superstitious nonsense, thanked her and left.

He dawdled back to the Esplanade by way of the Old Town, wondering how on earth he could begin again with Sukey, and what could be said and done to make it right.

He found himself in a street of enticing shops, and in the window of a jeweller a necklace of coral beads caught his eye. He went in and bought it, and then went into the circulating library and put down her name as a subscriber. While he was there he snared a just-returned copy of the first volume of Ainsworth's 'Rookwood'.

Finally he made his way back to their lodgings.

She was sitting at the round table at the window, knitting. She had put on a high-necked white muslin dress he had never seen before, and arranged her hair in quite a new fashion. It was a scene that demanded to be painted. But a moment's closer glance showed her eyes were still red from crying.

He put his little offerings down in front of her: the library ticket, the book and the parcel in blue paper.

"Did you find anything?" she asked.

"Yes. Her carpet bag – and better than that – a letter asking for it to be sent to her."

"Worth the journey, then," she said, and continued with her knitting.

He sat down by her and rested his elbows on his knees, and his chin on his knotted hands. He watched her knitting for some minutes before he spoke.

"These are for you," he said. "The library looks a good one. I have got Ainsworth's 'Rookwood'. You haven't read it?"

"No," she said, putting down her work and picking up the book. She did not open it, but rather held it up in front of her, and turned it in her hands, as it were something curious.

"It's very good," he said.

"I'm sure," she said, putting it down. Then he pushed the parcel containing the necklace towards her.

"And this," he said. "To mark the day," he managed to say.

She stared across at him.

"To mark the day?" she said.

"To mark the day," he said again.

"To mark the day when I... when I..." She got up and wrapped her arms about her, walking to the other end of the room, turning pointedly away from him.

"It wasn't your fault," he said, getting up. "How can that have been your fault?"

"Because this is all my fault!" she exclaimed. "All this!" She gestured about her. "James always said I was as good as a whore! And here I am, at the seaside, calling myself Mrs Carswell." She marched back to the table and snatched up the parcel and unceremoniously ripped off the paper. She opened the case and saw the coral necklace lying there on the white satin, and then sighed and set it down on the table, without taking it out. "Oh, dear God..."

"They are just a trifle – to say I am sorry," he said.

"Sorry for what?"

"For what happened. I think a man ought always to see to his wife's pleasure first. And women have passions, just as men do, that need expression. You said so yourself."

"I am just..." she said, "so frightened. Frightened of myself. Frightened that I will do something to make you hate me."

He pulled her into his arms.

"How could I ever hate you?" he said. "And I am not like him. You know that."

"I do," she said, pressing herself against him. "I do! But sometimes he creeps about my mind and poisons everything. It's like he is here sometimes, sitting in the corner watching us, mocking us. And sometimes I think he isn't dead at all, and at any moment he will be back and insisting on his rights, and then telling me that I'm a whore for consenting to it."

She broke off and buried her face into his chest, sobbing.

"He is rotting in Hell, Sukey, or worse, if there is any justice," he said. "He can't touch you now."

She cried for some minutes, and then she collected herself and broke from his arms.

"I need to wash my face," she said, and went through to the bedroom.

He followed her and watched her as she went to the washstand and poured out some water. His own cheeks were sticky with tears and he went to her side as she rinsed her face. He plunged his hand into the bowl, next to hers, catching her fingers. This made her smile a little.

"I am going to buy you a new ring," he said, touching her wedding ring under the water. "To replace that one."

She took her hand out of the water and attempted to remove the ring. It proved obstinate even using soap, but at length she succeeded.

"There," she said, tossing it back into the water. Then she laughed. "But I had better wear it for now. I can't go down and eat my dinner here without it, can I?"

He did not much like the thought of that, but she had a point.

"It is just a piece of metal," he said, taking it from the water. He took her hand and slipped it back onto her finger. "He's dead. It doesn't matter now. What matters now is that we are here."

Chapter Forty-six

"A successful trip, then?" asked Major Vernon as they sat in the library after dinner. "And was it a distraction?"

Felix found it difficult to meet Major Vernon's gaze.

"Yes," he said. "And my instincts were correct."

There was no pleasure dissembling to him, but it had to be done.

Throughout dinner he felt his spirits had been low enough to give him the look of a man suffering from a disappointment in love. He felt her absence keenly and could not stop thinking of her standing alone on the breezy esplanade where they had parted that morning. As he had taken one last kiss, the wind had whipped about them as if meant to bind them forever. It had been such an effort to break away and turn his back on her.

Over the soup, Mrs Carswell artlessly remarked that she hoped Mrs Connolly had made a safe journey, and that there would be a letter soon. Major Vernon skilfully turned the conversation away, and before long was asking her about her experiences of running a parish school for girls. Might such a model be extended to industrial areas? It was a worthy subject, calculated to please both his parents, and one which required Felix to say absolutely nothing.

He was grateful, but it was uncomfortable to bear Major Vernon's delicate sympathy at a necessary renunciation, when all he had done was conspire to do exactly the opposite of what he had advised.

Alone with him, it was worse. The taste of duplicity was bitter.

He tried to comfort himself with the memories of the

previous night. After dinner, they had walked on the beach, before going up to bed. The difficulties of earlier that day had slipped away, like the tide pulling out of the bay below their windows. They had been passionate, intimate and yet careful. They had agreed on the last with little difficulty and few words, understanding each other in a way that Felix found as moving as the sight of her in only her shift with her hair loosened. They would not be fools.

"So what did you find?" Major Vernon asked.

It was a relief to turn to business. He was aching with longing.

"A letter," Felix said, handing it to Major Vernon. "From Lady Warde – alias Mrs Abbott – to Mrs Edgar, marked from Market Craven. She asks that her carpet bag be sent care of Bertram's Haberdashers, at Market Craven."

"Really?" said Giles. "Good grief. I was only looking in their window the other day. And that is the bag?"

"Yes," said Felix. "I could not get into it, though. I'll leave that pleasure to you."

"This could not better," said Major Vernon, having finished reading the letter. "A day or two's delay and Mrs Edgar might have sent it away, and we would have lost it. Thank you."

Carswell shrugged.

"I seem to be getting into the way of thinking like a criminal," he said.

Major Vernon smiled. "That comes all too naturally to me," he said. "I wonder what that says about my character." As he spoke he was matching one of his lock-picking keys to the delicate padlock that secured the strap of the carpet bag. "Ah yes, there we have it." He had gently manipulated the lock open. "This is a trick you could learn, Carswell. You would probably master it far more quickly than I did, with your dexterous fingers."

"Some lessons in the autumn, perhaps?" Felix said,

410

wondering if Major Vernon would still be speaking to him then. It would only be a matter of time before he discovered the arrangement he had entered into with Sukey.

They had talked of it for some time that morning on the beach. It had been a conversation that had no satisfactory end.

"We shall cross that bridge when we come to it," Sukey had said. Now he wondered if he ought to come to it now and simply tell him. But he could not think quite how to begin, and he did not like to do it without her consent.

"Yes, certainly," said Major Vernon. "Now, what have we here?"

"Letters, by the look of it," said Felix.

"With interesting addresses – Marchsteads, Limpersleigh, Avonix Park. Coronets aplenty," he said.

"And an account book," said Felix. "The stupid woman!" he added, flipping through it. "She has recorded all their transactions with Edgar. What a fool!"

He handed it to Major Vernon.

"Yes and no," said Major Vernon. "It may seem foolish to us, but to her this was work, survival – a record of all the successes and hope for the future. This is a fight against humiliation from Lady Anne and Lady Rothborough and the Duchess of goodness knows where else. This is what was driving her. No one was ever supposed to see this."

He reached into the bag and began patting the interior.

"There is something sewn into the base," he said. "Have you a knife to hand? I need to rip this seam."

Carswell fetched a scalpel from his medical bag, while Major Vernon lit some more candles. The seam ripped away to reveal several neat packets made up in striped linen, also carefully stitched up. They contained money, two diamond bracelets, and four strings of pearls.

"We have her now, surely," said Felix. "Yes?"

"None of this puts a weapon in her hands," said Major Vernon. "But at least she may be charged for her part in the thefts. This is the same pattern of linen as the bag the parure was found in. That is something."

"But theft is not enough. She is a murderer. She..." He broke off.

Major Vernon pooled the pearls into the open palm of his hand.

"The only way we can prove that is if she admits to it. And that she will never do."

"I am sure you could get her to admit it," said Felix, "if anyone can."

"I doubt I will be allowed to interview her again," Major Vernon said, "unless I play my trump card, but I am wary about doing that."

"What trump card is that?" said Felix.

"I discovered something discreditable about Sir Arthur which could bring him to his knees. I do not like to use it simply to get my way on this. It is too serious a matter for that and I am in no position to be seen threatening Sir Arthur. We shall have to think of something else."

He carefully replaced the pearls in their bag, and took up the letter.

"Did Mrs Edgar reply to this?"

"No, it only arrived yesterday," said Felix.

"Perhaps she does not expect a reply. Just the bag. She will not feel safe until she gets her bag and her secrets, will she?"

"No."

"Then we should let her have it," Major Vernon said.

Chapter Forty-seven

There was no Mr Bertram, they soon discovered, when they enquired of the shop girl.

"It's Mrs Bertram, sir," she said. "Do you want me to fetch her? She's just in the back shop."

"No need," said Giles, flipping up the counter barrier and pulling back the blue velvet curtain that led to the back shop.

The back shop was a large, airy room lined with shelves, and at the centre, sitting at a baize-covered table, sat Mrs Bertram. She was handsome and superbly turned out, in a dress of steel-coloured silk. She had a strong look of Mrs Honeywell about her and Giles wondered whether they were sisters. That was an unholy connection if it were so.

There were piles of artificial flowers of every description on the table in front of her, with which she was making posies, tied with fancy ribbons.

"Excuse me?" she said, rising and clearly annoyed at his intrusion.

"I am Major Vernon, of the Northminster Constabulary. And this is Mr Carswell. We are making enquiries about a woman whom I believe to be a customer of yours: Lady Warde."

"Oh, really, sir?" said Mrs Bertram. "Her Ladyship that is a guest of Sir Arthur Felpsham and his lady at Brook House?"

"The same."

"Well, I don't know what enquiries you might have about her, sir; she is a most respectable lady, and Lady Felpsham is a good customer."

"I understand that she may have been using this establishment as a receiving address," Giles said.

"That is not against any law I know of," said Mrs Bertram.

"No, it is not. But why would it be necessary for a lady with such respectable friends to have her letters sent to a flashy draper's shop?"

She pursed her lips at that, and again Giles saw the resemblance to Mrs Honeywell.

"I think I may have had the pleasure of meeting your sister, Mrs Bertram. Mrs Honeywell?"

"What of it?" she said after a moment.

"That cannot be a comfortable connection for you. A respectable business like this – if it is a respectable business?"

"There ain't no law about taking people's letters," she said. "And this is a respectable business. As I said, Lady Felpsham is one of my best customers."

"And Sir Arthur is one of your sister's best customers," said Giles. "He must always pay his wife's bill on time."

"All right, all right. What do you want?" she said.

"Tell me what your dealings with Lady Warde have been. When did she first come here?"

"She was with Lady Felpsham. It was more than a fortnight ago. I didn't take much notice of her, that time, but she came back alone a day or so later, for some embroidery silk I think. She took her time choosing it, and she would only deal with me, not my girl. Then when she was paying for it she asked me where in town was a good place to have letters sent. So I said she could have anything she liked sent here, for a fee, of course. I have done it before – it isn't against the law – and it's convenient for a lady to come into a shop like this. She can always make an excuse to come in for something or other."

"And how many letters have you had for her?"

"One or two. She has been in regularly asking, though. I think she is waiting for something."

Giles nodded.

"When does she usually come in?"

"A little after eleven. Soon enough. Why?"

"Tell her you have her parcel."

"But I don't."

"Bring her in the back here. I wish to speak to her."

"And why should I do that?" Mrs Bertram said.

"She is a thief and a murderer, Mrs Bertram, and protecting her will get you into no end of trouble. Just send her in here and the matter will be done with. Oh, and tell your girl, when Lady Warde does come in, to run out and find a constable. There was a solid-looking fellow in the vicinity of the post office, I noticed."

"That's George," said Mrs Bertram. "A murderer – are you sure, sir?"

"Quite."

"But staying at Sir Arthur's? How did that come about?"

The bell jangled.

"You have a customer," said Giles. He hoped it was not Lady Warde. He needed Mrs Bertram to settle into a mask of normality. At the moment she was quivering with curiosity.

"Go on," he prompted her.

She left, staring at them as she drew the curtain.

"Who is Mrs Honeywell?" Carswell said.

Giles put his finger to his lips and went to the doorway, hoping to catch what was going on in the shop. But he could not.

Mrs Bertram came back a few moments later and sat down again at the table.

"What were you doing at my sister's?" she said. "Are you going to cause trouble for her?"

"She has caused it for herself," Giles said.

Mrs Bertram sighed. "She won't like any of this. But she has had it easy. Too easy. She was never one for steady work."

She picked up another bundle of flowers and began to bind the stems with ribbons.

"Has she told you about her arrangements with Sir

Arthur?" said Giles.

"Yes," she said with a sigh.

"Then you may help her by being a witness to that. It can be argued that his part was far worse than hers in this. What he has done is a far greater crime, all in all."

"And who would take my word against Sir Arthur?" she said, throwing down the finished posy and beginning to make another. "And if she goes down, so shall I, I dare say. All my hard work for nothing."

The bell rang and she got up again.

"I hope you know what you are about in all this," she said, and went sailing back into the shop, brusquely pulling the curtain shut.

"Oh, my lady, how good to see you," they heard her say. "I have news for you."

"She's a good actress," murmured Carswell.

Giles nodded and summoned his own arts.

~

The expression on Lady Warde's face was interesting, if not gratifying, as she realised what she had walked into.

Major Vernon had taken Mrs Bertram's place at the table and was idly playing with one of the finished posies. He had directed Carswell to stand by the door, and block her way should she turn and attempt to leave, which she did almost at once.

"How dare you!" she said, as Felix jumped into her path. "What is this? How dare you?"

"We have some business to finish," said Major Vernon, getting up and pulling out a chair for her. "Please do sit down."

"Get a constable, Mrs Bertram," said Lady Warde. "This

man is a lunatic. He attacked me! He cannot do this."

"The girl has already gone for one," said Major Vernon. "Why do you not sit down, my lady? We have business and we might as well be civil."

"I shall not speak to you!" she said, still facing towards the doorway.

"Would you not like your parcel, ma'am?" said Major Vernon. "I understand you have been anxious to get this back."

Now she turned a little and stared at him.

He was holding up the carpet bag.

"Is this what you have been waiting for?" he said, putting it down on the table among the artificial flowers.

She dashed forward, snatched it up in her arms and held it against herself like a child she wished to protect. But after a moment, she realised something was amiss with it.

"It is empty," Major Vernon said. "I have removed and examined its contents. All of them. Mr Benson, the magistrate, has them. Including the account book. A meticulous piece of work. He was most intrigued by it. And we identified the clasp on that pretty diamond bracelet as belonging to a member of the Wroxeter family."

"How dare you open my baggage? How dare you? Will you never cease with your outrages, sir? Will you not desist from persecuting me? Wait until I tell my counsel of this, he will –"

"Oh, hold your tongue, you silly woman!" said Major Vernon, calmly but with great firmness. "You have absolutely nowhere to hide now. The magistrate has seen all the evidence, and he will show it to his colleagues. When the constable comes, he will arrest you and take you before them, and they will charge you with theft and that will be an end to all this nonsense."

"No!" she exclaimed.

"And you will eat your dinner in a cell tonight, instead of

at Sir Arthur's table. And you can look forward to a sentence of transportation at least, if not the gallows."

"You will not, you shall not get away with this!" she said.

"It is too late to protest," Major Vernon said. "The cat is out of the bag, so to speak."

And he went to her and with a little struggle wrested the bag from her.

"Sit down," he said, pointing to a chair. "And be quiet. A little composure and contrition will serve you very well."

She was breathing hard, Felix could see, and shaking her head in disbelief.

"I shall not be treated like this," she said. "I shall not! Do you know who I am?"

"A thief and a murderer," said Major Vernon. "And that is how the world will know you henceforth. Your scheming has failed, ma'am. It is done with."

She gulped as if swallowing a torrent of words and, somewhat to Felix's astonishment, she went and sat down as she was bid. He supposed she was planning her next outburst. In the meantime a curious silence fell on the room as they waited for the jangling of the shop bell and the arrival of the constable.

Major Vernon took up one of the posies again.

"These are pretty trifles," he said, breaking the silence and speaking as if nothing at all was amiss. "Are they for bonnets, Mrs Bertram?"

Mrs Bertram looked a little astonished by this. She was standing by the shelves, one hand pressed to her breast, her fingers nervously picking at the pleats of her bodice.

"Er, yes," she said after a moment. "They are the latest thing from Paris. Would you like one for your lady, sir? Or two? They are two for one and six."

Major Vernon nodded and laid down the posy.

"Unfortunately my wife is dead," he said. "I would be a willing customer otherwise. I should have taken great pleasure in taking her home a present like that."

"I am sorry to hear that, sir," said Mrs Bertram. "Not recently, I hope."

"Very recently," said Major Vernon. He sat down at the table again, and picked up a silk rose that had not yet been bound up. "She would have been charmed by these." He laid the rose down on the green baize with great gentleness. "Lady Warde has also lost her daughter recently," he went on.

"Oh my," said Mrs Bertram.

"In shocking circumstances. You may have heard talk about it. She was found in a pool, battered to death and then drowned – and with a child in the womb. It is no wonder her mind is disturbed. Loss leads us into dark places."

"She was... murdered?" Mrs Bertram said, clutching a little harder at her bodice.

"Yes," said Major Vernon, getting up so that his shadow cast itself over Lady Warde who sat, head bent, staring down at her gloved hands. "By a brute who had led her astray. Who had led a mother and daughter astray. A deceitful, manipulative brute. Who promised an escape from a miserable life and then cheated them of it. A piece of filth, yes, ma'am?" His tone was gentle, almost caressing, and there was a hint of the mesmeric about it. Then, as if compelled by him to do so, Lady Warde lifted her eyes and looked up at the Major. "A woman must protect her child. You did exactly that. You loved her so much. No one ever understood how much."

Lady Warde nodded. Felix could see there was a tear glistening in her eye.

"You were a good mother," Major Vernon went on. "The best mother she could have had. And what a fine grandmother you would have been, had that wretch not –"

"I had to," she said in a tiny voice that was half a sob. "I had no choice."

Felix could scarcely believe what he had heard.

Major Vernon now laid his hand on her shoulder. She still

419

gazed up at him for one moment longer before she pressed her hands to her face.

"And after that, it was all fear and confusion, and you did not know what you were about," Major Vernon went on, still quiet, still so gentle. "What happened was an accident. I understand, ma'am. I understand."

She began to weep into her hands, and then, as if collapsing under the weight of his hand, she slithered from the chair and onto her knees, bent over, and howling like an animal in pain. It was an awful sight and a sound worse still.

"Forgive me?" she rasped. "For the love of God, will you forgive me? I did not mean to... I pushed her aside, and she..."

Major Vernon stepped back, his hand on his mouth, breathing hard.

"The stairs," Lady Warde began again, in awful strangulated tones of agony that chilled the heart to hear them. "I did not realise she was so close to the top of the stairs. I did not mean... Dear God, I did not mean... Forgive me, sir, forgive me!"

Epilogue

Northminster, September 1840

"It's certainly a very fine house," Giles said. "Quite an undertaking, though."

"Yes, but nothing I can't manage," Sukey Connolly said. "Now, I must show you the garden. It's the best part of all."

"Of course."

He followed her along the flagged passageway to where a glazed door opened onto a very pleasant, old-fashioned walled garden.

"I had no idea the gardens in Silver Street were so large," he said, as they walked along a lavender-edged path towards a patch of orchard.

"No, it's a bit of a wonder, isn't it?" she said. "My sister couldn't believe it either. And look at these apple trees – well, I don't suppose we will get a crop like this every year – it has been a good year for them – but these are good keeping apples. And there is an apple store. Waste not, want not," she said, stooping to gather up a few windfalls.

"Here, you missed these," he said, picking up a couple for himself and dropping them into her apron, which she had turned into an impromptu container. As he did so, their eyes met, but only for a moment, for she looked away nervously. At the same time, a raft of clouds blew over the sun and a grey chill descended on the garden.

"I suppose," she said, "you will want to know how this all came about. This good fortune of mine."

"Only if you wish to tell me," he said.

At first he had not questioned Sukey's good fortune. Unexpected inheritances did occur, and he knew nothing of the circumstances of her late husband's family. Her plan to put the money into a high-class lodging house, letting rooms to gentleman, struck him as sensible, even though he was surprised she had chosen to do it in Northminster. Yet she had family in the town, which was reason enough. But when he had realised that the handsome house in Silver Street belonged to the Rothborough estates, he had grown a little uneasy.

"You mean you have guessed," she said, with a sigh, turning back towards the house and away from him. "I knew you would sooner or later. And we have been meaning to tell you, sooner rather than later, so –"

She was having difficulty with the door, now that she had her load of apples. He went and opened it for her, and she went straight into the kitchen. He stood at the door and watched as she put the apples into a bowl. She spent a few moments arranging them to her liking and then turned back to him.

"You don't have to say anything," he said.

He had determined that he would not force either of them to say a word, should they not wish to. The moment for heavy-handed moralising seemed long past. Who was to say he would not have done the same thing himself, given the opportunity? It was not exactly immoral, for he knew the scruples of both of them, but rather irregular. Such arrangements were not that uncommon. How could he really object? He did not want to banish either of them from his existence: he had discovered that they were both too important to him for that, and he found in this attempt of theirs, something touching.

"I think I do," she said, turning an apple in her hands, minutely examining it rather than look directly at him. "I can't bear not to. And he…" She glanced across at Giles and went on, "Oh, this isn't the way we wanted it, but in the end, it just seemed that any other way wasn't..."

She turned away again and placed the apple back in the bowl.

"And at least this way," she continued. "I have something to do. Something on my own account."

He nodded.

"You will be your own mistress here," he said.

"Yes," she said. "Yes, quite."

He went and sat down by the fire, and stared into it for a while, considering the situation. She came and sat opposite him. It felt very comfortable to be in her presence again. He had been travelling between Northminster and London for nearly six weeks, attending endless meetings, and he was tired. He had missed her company more than he knew.

"It's a fine house, and I am sure you will do very well with it," he said. "Have you had many enquiries?"

"None as yet," she said. "But I don't want any just yet. I haven't advertised. I wanted to get the place perfectly in order and the servants properly trained."

"Very sensible," he said. "And what will you charge, say for that large sitting room, upstairs, and the bedroom and closet behind?"

"It would depend. With all meals and washing, I should say about a guinea and a half a week."

"And with a manservant – who would obviously need his own room, but who would make himself very useful about the place?"

She stared at him.

"Do you mean a particular manservant?" she said. He nodded. "But, Major Vernon –"

"I am on the verge of losing my quarters," he said. "I thought you might be able to help me – with this fine, empty lodging house of yours."

"Of course," she said. "But are you sure?"

"I owe you a great debt – both of you," he said. "And I

think my presence here might help repay it. Everything will look even more unexceptional if I am here, don't you think?"

"That's very true," she said. "More than true."

"And I shall be very comfortable here," he said. "That I can be sure of."

She smiled again and said, "But why are you losing your quarters at The Unicorn?"

"Because I shall soon no longer be Chief Constable."

"No – ?" she said in astonishment. "Why?"

"I have a new job. Superintendent of the Northern Counties Criminal Intelligence Office."

"Which is?" she asked.

"An experiment that may yet fail," he said with a smile. "But with luck, it will not. It is an idea I had, and Lord Rothborough took it up and ran away with it."

"As he does," she said. "And if it was your idea, then I am sure it will be a good one."

"We shall see," he said. "I have a year to prove the worth of it."

After Sir Arthur's disgrace and resignation, the county magistrates, in consultation with the Home Office (orchestrated by Lord Rothborough) had asked Giles to take over as acting Chief Constable pending the amalgamation of the two forces. Giles had accepted, but on the condition that he could help find his successor. At that point, he had known he did not want to continue indefinitely as he had before, but what else he might do was still not clear in his mind. However, as he began to meet the men who put themselves forward for the job, and talking to them about the problems they had encountered in their own constabularies, a notion had begun to form in his mind. He had not spoken of it until one evening, dining alone with Lord Rothborough; when the cloth had been cleared away and the port was on the table, he had ventured to speculate aloud.

"What is really needed is a criminal intelligence gathering

operation for the northern counties," he had said.

"On the lines of military intelligence?" Rothborough said.

"Yes, but a little more than that," Giles went on. "A cadre of trained men to deal with serious crimes, complex crimes that an individual constabulary may not have the ability to deal with. There are moves to create something similar at Bow Street, I understand. But we have different circumstances in the North – different problems, different terrain. Captain Lazenby, the man I have recommended for Northminster, was extremely interesting on the subject of the lawless gangs in his district, that are causing much local misery. They are complicated in their structure, hard to break up and bring down. That is the sort of problem we need particular skills to deal with."

Rothborough had smiled.

"I can think of a man to put that plan into action, if he were so inclined."

Giles had demurred in the first instance, but the idea, once articulated, had taken hold of him. He had found himself fleshing the idea out in the form of notes, and then a long letter to Lord Rothborough. He had been aware even as he wrote it that he was setting himself on an irrevocable course, because the Marquess would find his proposition irresistible. It had been like giving a child a toy.

~

It had been Felix's first intention to go straight to Silver Street the moment he reached Northminster.

His journey back from Scotland had been tiresome, and over a week with his parents back in Pitfeldry even more so. His only comfort had been Sukey's letters. Conducting a clandestine correspondence in Pitfeldry had been an interesting business. On the one hand, it had been extremely irritating to be forced into such subterfuges, but on the other, it had been oddly exciting. He had never had a correspondence like it. Sukey's letters were so extraordinary that it made being away from her almost desirable.

Crossing the station yard he saw Lord Rothborough's carriage and Lord Rothborough himself strolling across to meet him.

"I thought you were still in London," Felix said, shaking his hand.

"I came back with Major Vernon this morning. Are Mr and Mrs Carswell well?"

"Yes, much better for being safely by their own fire," said Felix.

"Good. Where are you heading? Can I drive you?"

Felix could not really refuse. He was burdened with luggage.

"Silver Street, if that isn't too much trouble?"

"No trouble at all," said Lord Rothborough. "In you get."

The carriage set off and they sat for a few moments in silence.

"That is for Mrs Connolly, by the way," said Lord Rothborough, pointing to a large hamper sitting on the floor. "You may give it to her from me."

"What is it?"

"A surprise for her," he said. "And tell her, if she does not care for it, it can be changed."

"You won't come in?" he knew he must ask, though he was desperate to see her alone.

"No, no, I must get on. I have a few more calls to pay. Take that in to her, and I will have your luggage taken to The Unicorn."

"Thank you," Felix said. "I was going to write to you tonight. I had a letter yesterday from –" He did not quite know how to refer to her, so hesitated before choosing "Dona

Blanca."

"Oh?" said Lord Rothborough.

"She is sailing for the Caribbean."

Lord Rothborough sighed.

"Of course. I hope she knows what she is doing. Well, of course she does, that is self-evident, and one should not underestimate her political instincts, but I would rather she had decided to stay in Europe a little longer. Does she give you any more information than that?"

"You can read it for yourself," said Felix, taking the letter from his coat. The letter had disturbed him. He had written to her, in the first instance with some difficulty, on Sukey's good advice. Yet he had not been satisfied that his letter had said anything that he felt ought to be said. In truth he did not know what he was supposed to say to her, especially as he was attempting to write it in his adopted mother's presence.

Dona Blanca's answer was as unsatisfactory. No doubt it had been equally hard for her to write – there was a sense of her reigning in her natural feelings, of relinquishing again any right to affection. It had ended with the suggestion that further letters would probably not be wise. "I shall always cherish your letter but I am anxious that you should feel no obligation towards me. I have done nothing to earn it."

Now he glanced at Lord Rothborough as he read the letter. He looked pained and laid down the letter with sigh. Then he picked up the letter again. "She sails on Wednesday, from Liverpool," he said. "There might still be time to persuade her otherwise."

"You will go and see her?"

"I should not, but I think –" he broke off. "She will not like it, but I can't quite bring myself to forbear. Even if it is just for half an hour of her company." He shrugged and handed the letter back to Felix.

"Keep it," Felix said.

"I think, I shall, if you don't mind," said Lord

Rothborough. There was silence until the carriage turned up Silver Street.

"Now, just another thing, before you go," Lord Rothborough, "before I forget to mention it."

"Yes?"

"This is, no doubt, superfluous advice to you, as a man of science, but I give it to you anyway, just in case – there are ways that a man and a woman can avoid the natural consequences of –"

"Oh, yes, I am well aware," Felix said, hastily.

"I thought you would be, but one can never be too careful about these things. The glove is a very good method, I have always found –"

"Yes, quite!" said Felix, wishing he would stop.

"There is a shop in Old Compton Street, that makes very reliable items," Lord Rothborough went on, quite unperturbed. "But perhaps you know that already?"

The carriage had barely stopped and Felix already had the door half open, anxious to escape. He leapt out into the street, even before the footman had let down the steps.

"Don't forget Mrs Connolly's parcel," said Lord Rothborough.

Felix picked it up. It was surprising heavy and he staggered a little under the weight.

"Old Compton Street – Brownes," said Lord Rothborough, as a parting shot, and then the carriage bowled off down the street.

He put down the hamper and rang the bell. He had not yet seen over the house and he was surprised by the size of it.

Mercifully it was Sukey who opened the door. He had been worried that she had already filled the house with servants – she had been setting about the business with formidable efficiency.

His first desire was to enfold her in his arms, but the whole street might have been watching them, so he picked up the hamper and went into the house. The moment the door was closed, he put down the hamper and moved to greet her properly, but she put up her hands and shook her head.

"I'm not alone," she whispered. "Major V..."

"Oh God!"

"He knows. He guessed."

"Of course."

"He wants to live here."

"What?"

She reached for his hand and squeezed it.

"It is for the best. It makes it look –" she said.

"Yes, yes of course," Felix said. "It is just that..." He broke away from her and wandered into the hall, looking up the handsome staircase. "It is vast!"

"Yes. And sunny! I don't think I have even been in a house that caught the sun so well. What is this?" she said, indicating the hamper.

"For you. From my lord."

"What is it?"

"I have no idea what it is. It weighs a tonne."

"It's from Wedgwood," she said examining a label.

"Oh, then it may be a tea service," Felix said, after a moment. He got no chance to explain further, for Major Vernon now came downstairs, looking as if he belonged in the house far more than Felix did himself. He could not decide if he felt disconcerted or pleased at this new development.

Sukey had got the hamper open and was standing with a teacup in her hand.

"Oh, this is very pretty," she said. "But why?"

"Mr Carswell," said Major Vernon, shaking his hand.

"Sir," said Felix.

"A good journey, I hope?"

"Rather tiring," said Felix.

"I should think so. Well, you will excuse me just now? I have a few errands to attend to. Perhaps I will see you for dinner?"

"Certainly," Felix said.

"Good day, Sukey, and thank you again."

"With pleasure," she said, showing him to the door.

When the door had shut, she leant against it and burst out laughing.

"And we're alone now?" Felix said, catching her hands and pinning her against the door.

"Yes," she said, when he had finished kissing her.

"Three weeks was too long," he said. "I almost died of longing."

"Me too," she said.

"So, where is your room, in all this magnificence?"

"Just there. By the back door. Is that all you have been thinking about?"

"No, not at all. It never crossed my mind. Not once."

"Liar," she said, and slipped out of his grasp and ran across the hall to her bedroom door.

~

As he was waiting for Carswell to join him for dinner, Giles looked around his office and wondered if he would miss it. It had been a haven and a retreat for so long, with Snow dozing by the fire. But she too had moved on. Laura had not much cared for Snow and Snow had not cared for Laura. She had gone to live with Sergeant Maple and his family, where she had become the pampered idol of all, a state of existence to which she had taken with her usual sense of entitlement. Maple had plans to breed from her, and promised a puppy from the first litter. Giles wondered if Sukey would mind a dog about the house and if he had time for a dog with the new venture.

Carswell came in, a little late, but that was to be forgiven in the circumstances, and they sat down to their meat and wine, as they had done on so many occasions before.

"So," said Carswell. "When will Captain Lazenby be taking over?"

"In a fortnight. But he is moving here next week. He has a wife and five children to settle in. They have taken a house in Martinsmount."

"So if he gets his way about the new Headquarters on the Leeds Road, that will be very convenient for him."

"He will," said Giles. "He is a forceful man."

"You are filling with me with dread."

"Oh, you have nothing to fear from him, Carswell. He was very impressed by your credentials. He was talking about a cottage hospital for the men and their families."

"That would be a sensible step, given the numbers involved now."

"So that will give you a new challenge?"

"If that is what I want," said Carswell. "To lance boils and deliver babies." He pushed his hands through his hair. "It is useful, but it is not exactly what I would call challenging." He refilled his glass. "I realise that you have scant resources, and that there is not enough money for a full time surgeon on your new staff, but the work we have done together – I do not want to give it up, and necessarily I shall have to, if all matters of interest are now to be referred to your office."

Giles nodded.

"For example," Carswell went on, "I have been attempting to formulate a test to identify the nature of blood stains on various textiles – whether it is human or otherwise. I have some interesting preliminary results, nothing conclusive so far, but given time, I am sure that –" He broke off. "If I continue here I am not sure I will have time for such things."

"You would like me to create a post for you?"

"Could it be done? Would it be of use? I think it would, if you do not mind me saying."

"I had been thinking along the same lines myself. I am sorry I have not had a chance to discuss it with you before this. You are right. There will be no time for such work here."

"Then might I join you?"

"I should like nothing better. But the money – there is very little."

"I have my rents," said Carswell. "And since Ardenthwaite is to be let, I shall be well in pocket."

"You have decided on that?"

"What else am I to do with the place?" he said. "And Mr Millar, who is Lord Rothborough's agent, has a tenant for me. A half-pay officer and his family – no less. Colonel something or other."

"Then I am sure it can be done – but you will have to find yourself somewhere to live," said Giles, and could not help smiling.

"There will be no difficulty about that," said Carswell sheepishly.

"Then, I shall see what can be done," said Giles, topping up his own glass. "Shall we drink to that?"

"Yes," said Carswell, raising his glass. "And to the better identification of blood stains!"

"And to the Northern Office!" Giles added, and they both drained their glasses.

~ THE END ~

Dramatis Personae

Stanegate

Major Giles Vernon: Chief Constable of the Northminster Constabulary

Mrs Laura Vernon: Giles' wife, a convalescent

Mrs Susanna 'Sukey' Connolly: maid and nurse to Mrs Vernon

Felix Carswell: Police Surgeon of the Northminster Constabulary and natural son of Lord Rothborough

Holt: Major Vernon's manservant

Dona Blanca Martinez: the widow of President Juan Martinez, who liberated Santa Magdalena from the Spanish, but was then assassinated by a rival faction, after successfully ruling the island for fifteen years; she has fled to England for safety

Don Luiz Ramirez: the recently deposed Chancellor of Santa Magdalena, a tiny island nation in the Caribbean, formerly a Spanish colony, accompanying Dona Blanca into exile, along with his wife and children and a large retinue

Don Xavier Martinez: a gentleman monk from Santa Magdalena

The Rev and Mrs James Carswell: Felix Carswell's parents by adoption

Mr Bryce: a fencing master

Holbroke

Lord Rothborough: local grandee and natural father of Felix Carswell

Lady Rothborough: Lord Rothborough's wife

Lady Charlotte Haraald: eldest daughter of Lord and Lady Rothborough

Lady Augusta Haraald: middle daughter of Lord and Lady Rothborough

Lady Maria Haraald: youngest daughter of Lord and Lady Rothborough

Lady Warde: a poor but well connected widow, an old friend of Lady Rothborough

Mr Syme: an ambitious young clergyman with evangelical tendencies, a guest of Lady Rothborough

Mr Woodward: Lord Rothborough's secretary

Mrs Hope: housekeeper

Mr Bodley: Lord Rothborough's valet

Eliza Jones: Lady Warde's maid

John Edgar: a maker of silhouettes

Market Craven

Mrs Bertram: a haberdasher

Mrs Honeywell: a brothel keeper

Sir Arthur Felpsham: Chief Constable of the
Northminstershire County Constabulary

About the Author

Harriet Smart was born and brought up in Birmingham. She attended the University of St Andrews, where she read History of Art, and married a fellow student. She now lives with her husband in an eighteenth-century house in Northumberland.

Harriet has an M.A. in screenwriting. She has published twenty novels as well as helping to design the creative writing software Writer's Café and the e-book editor software Jutoh.

She has been writing the Northminster Mysteries since 2010.

You can follow Harriet at www.harrietsmart.com and BookBub.

Made in the USA
Monee, IL
12 August 2023

40921160R00256